Time Will Tell

'What would you say if I told you there was another

## Also by Sally Worboyes

## About Sally Worboyes

Sally Worboyes was born and grew up in Stepney with four brothers and a sister, and she brings some of the raw history of her own family background to her East End sagas. She now lives in Norfolk with her husband, with whom she has three grown-up children. She has written several plays for BBC Radio 4 and Anglia Television. She also adapted her own play and novel, *Wild Hops*, as a musical for production at the Mermaid theatre.

# SALLY WORBOYES

# Time Will Tell

**HODDER**

First published in Great Britain in 2004 by Hodder & Stoughton
An Hachette UK company

This edition published in 2016

I

A CIP catalogue record for this title is available from the British Library

Paperback ISBN 978 1 473 65385 6

Typeset in Plantin Light by Palimpsest Book Production Limited,
Falkirk, Stirlingshire
Printed and bound by CPI Group (UK) Ltd, Croydon, CR0 4YY

Hodder & Stoughton policy is to use papers that are natural, renewable
and recyc̶̶̶̶̶̶̶̶̶̶̶̶̶̶̶̶̶̶̶̶̶̶̶̶̶̶̶̶̶̶le
forests. ̶̶̶̶̶̶̶̶̶̶̶̶̶̶̶̶̶̶̶̶̶̶̶̶
conform

For Patricia and Tony Nice,
my new neighbours and friends.

My thanks to Sara Hulse, Ian Paten
and Alex Bonham.


I used several works of non-fiction when researching
this novel and I am indebted to *Call the Midwife* by
Jennifer Worth for information on the period.

# I

*September 1953*

On this quiet Sunday morning, to the hollering of a vagrant under the arches close by, Maggie Birch twisted and turned in her sleep as the echoing voice merged with her dream and turned it into a chilling nightmare. In reality the drunkard was making no sense at all, but to Maggie his haunting message was aimed at her. Within her distorted sleeping world the man was calling to her from the murky shadows under the railway bridge, where rats scavenged by the filthy kerbside in search of food.

Within her dream the tone of his voice shifted from soft and sorry to loud and cross and it became even more confusing because the stranger was now calling her by name as if he had known her all his life. He was telling her that he was her daddy and coaxing her to come to him. Struggling to wake from the dream, Maggie was breaking into a sweat and moaning beneath her bed covers, 'My daddy's dead. You're not my daddy.'

Trapped in this nightmare where she was not a young woman but a small frightened child, she felt her body as a dead weight as the stranger continued to coax her to come to him. Then, as he began to step out of the shadows towards her, she opened her mouth to call for her mother, Edie, but the only sound that escaped was a distorted wail as his echoing footsteps grew louder and he approached. '*I am your daddy . . . be a good girl now. You've been bad, Maggie. Wicked. And Daddy's not pleased. Why did you do it, Maggie? Why did you let this happen? They'll punish you for it. God will punish you. You should have learned from the Bible. Are you listening to Daddy? Maggie? Maggie?* Maggie!'

The dismal warning now merged with her mother's voice, soft and warm, as it broke through the nightmare, saying, 'Come on, sweetheart, up you get.'

Drawing the covers away from her hot, sweaty face, Maggie peered out to see Edie's comforting smile as she stood in the doorway. Thankful to be back in the real world, she sighed and pulled the bedclothes back over her head.

'Your Sunday breakfast is sizzling in the pan, Mags. Can't you smell it?'

'I'm not hungry,' murmured Maggie from her hiding place, curling into a ball.

'Suit yerself. Your Aunt Naomi's coming round this morning. She'll finish yours off.'

The sound of Edie closing the bedroom door behind her brought Maggie up for air. Relaxing into her pillow, she gazed at the shaft of sunlight coming in through the gap in the curtains and felt sad that her dad, whom she had never known, had been drowned at sea. Used to not having a father figure to turn to for advice or comfort, she had learned to live within the feminine realm of her caring mother and her bizarre great-aunt Naomi, and this new sense of longing for a paternal hug was alien to her.

Easing herself out of bed, she pulled on her dressing gown to the sound of church music coming from the wireless in the kitchen before drawing back the curtains to allow September to stream into her room. Peering into the mirror above her small dressing table, she hoped that Edie would not notice that her eyes were swollen and red from crying into the pillow the night before. Her tears had not been for nothing – Maggie was carrying a guilty secret that weighed heavily on her, and she had made a vow that on this Sunday she would disclose it to her mother.

The delicious smell of bacon sizzling in the pan on the stove in the kitchen, which seemed to be filling the flat, was now making her feel hungry – but still the sense of foreboding filled her. Soon she would have to break the news that she was expecting a baby.

Savouring her few moments alone, she looked out of the window and across to the arches, where the drunk whose voice had invaded her dreams was slouched against a sooty wall, his head drooping forward, himself now asleep. Adjusting the belt of her dressing gown so as not to make it appear too tight, she drew a deep breath, thankful that at least the morning sickness had stopped. Then, with a worsening sense of worry which always tended to assail her at the beginning of the day, she told herself that she must be strong and brave in order to say what she had to without breaking into a flood of tears.

Today Maggie was not only going to have to tell Edie that she was pregnant, but also that she was prepared to go with Tony to Gretna Green. So deeply in love was she that the idea that her boyfriend might be against the idea of her giving birth to his child and the two of them going away to Scotland had not crossed her mind.

Since she had missed her first period Maggie had been struggling to find the right time to tell her mother before breaking the news to her boyfriend, but there never seemed to be one. She had toyed with the possibility of using her great-aunt Naomi as a buffer and confiding in her first, but had decided against it. So today Edie, the hard-working and sensitive woman who had had to bring up her only child as a single parent, was about to have the worst fears of any parent confirmed . . . that her one and only precious daughter had conceived out of wedlock and while still considered to be a minor.

Anxiety washed over Maggie once again. All she really wanted right then was to slip back into bed and under the covers. The sound of her bedroom door opening brought her round sharply. Turning to face Edie, a false smile on her face, she swallowed the lump in her throat and then said, 'That bacon smells delicious, Mum.'

'Hurry up, then, love. I'm just gonna put the eggs in the pan.' The door closed between them again and Maggie, placing the flat of her hand on her swollen stomach and gently stroking it, felt a flow of love for her unborn child. Her hopes and fears had soared and plummeted so many times of late, and now there was a warm sense of tranquillity spreading through her. After all, a new life, her very own baby, was growing inside her.

In a more settled mood and properly awake, she left the bedroom, thinking of the few occasions when she and Tony had showed how much they loved each other. Still she could see no shame in it. As she came into the kitchen, a nervous half-smile on her face and with her light blue candlewick dressing gown over her loose winceyette pyjamas, no one could have been blamed for thinking that Maggie was simply a lovely girl between childhood and maturity, without a care in the world. Nevertheless, as she eased herself between the small Formica-topped table and the kitchen chair, she had to nudge the table back an inch to make room for herself.

'You're gonna have to cut down on the jam doughnuts, Mags,' remarked Edie, glancing at Maggie's stomach and fearing the worst. This was not the first time she had noted that her daughter needed a little more space than she once had. 'You're putting it on under the chin as well.'

'Am I? Why do you reckon that is, then?' said Maggie, provocatively. 'I don't eat any more cakes than I used to.'

'You got through half a packet of ginger nuts the other day, though.' Turning back to her cooking, Edie slipped the fish slice under a fried egg in the pan and turned it.

'That's true,' said Maggie, and then quickly changed the subject. 'What was my dad like, Mum? Did he play football or any other sport?'

Flinching, Edie answered with her own question. 'What makes you ask that, Mags? I can't remember you ever wanting to know anything about your dad.'

'That don't mean I've not thought about 'im now and then. I didn't want to make you sad by bringing it up. I dreamt about him last night, that's all.'

'And that was the first time, was it?' Edie asked, forking the bacon from the pan on to a warmed plate.

'I think so. It was all mixed up. He was calling me.'

'Dreams are always mixed up. What did he want? Was he asking about me?'

'No. He was calling out to me, that's all. Saying things. But as soon as I woke up properly the words slipped from my mind. I can't remember now what he said.'

'Could you see him?' Edie was curious to know more. Her own dreams of Harry had stopped years since. 'Did he look like the photos I've showed you?'

'It was too dark to see his face. He was standing in the shadows where the sparrows nest.' Maggie changed tack again without thinking. 'What would you say if I told you there was another reason for me not being as skinny as I was?'

The beginning of her confession flowed effortlessly, as if she had planned it. Momentarily numbed by her lack of self-control, she held her breath and waited. After what seemed like a long silence, Edie replied.

'It depends on what that reason might be. I take it you haven't seen this month either, then?' Turning her face away, Edie poured boiling water into the teapot as a chilling silence filled the room.

Glancing up at her mother's back, her hands beginning to tremble, Maggie spoke in a broken voice. 'I've missed two months and the third's coming up . . . but I don't think I'll get it.'

'I thought as much.' Turning to face her daughter, her face pale, Edie shook her head. 'Don't even think about having it, Mags.'

Shocked by the forceful tone in Edie's voice, Maggie all but whispered, 'I don't want to have an abortion.'

The word abortion struck through Edie's heart. 'You might not have any choice. And it's called termination.'

'But it's the same thing.' Allowing her tears to spill over while desperate to be brave and strong, Maggie stuck to her guns. 'It wouldn't be right and I don't want to do it.'

'Think of it as a missed period that needs bringing on. That way you won't feel so bad.' Edie could hardly believe she was having this conversation. She felt sick inside.

'I've tried that already and it doesn't work. And that's because it's not right. I wouldn't drown my baby once it was born so why do something just as bad now? It's my baby growing in there. Mine and Tony's.'

Slamming the empty frying pan back down on to the gas stove, Edie allowed her true feelings to surface.

'You should 'ave thought about that at the time! You're not even sixteen yet!'

'What difference does that make?' wailed Maggie. 'If I was it would be just as bad. You still wouldn't want me to have it.'

Edie turned slowly to face her daughter. 'Don't start being defensive over this, Maggie.'

'I'm not being defensive!'

'No? Well, from the tone in your voice and the look on your face I'd say that you are!' Then, pointing a finger, Edie spoke in earnest. 'This is one time that you cannot lay the blame elsewhere. Not at my feet and not at that lad's.'

'I'm not blaming Tony,' said Maggie, her voice quieter now. 'He don't even know about it yet. I'm scared to tell him.'

'Ashamed, more like. You know you should 'ave known better than to have—'

'Why are you saying it's all my fault?' wailed Maggie, tears running freely now. 'I never meant it to happen – we just got carried away a few times, that's all. I didn't ask Tony to—'

'You wouldn't 'ave had to!' snapped Edie, not wanting to hear the details. 'It's natural instinct with boys of his age. It's up to the girl to say no. Everyone knows that and so should you 'ave.'

Maggie wiped a tear away with the back of her hand, saying, 'That's not fair. And it *wasn't* like you think! It just *'appened*. We didn't plan it! And I'm not getting rid of it. If it comes to it I'll take a bottle of aspirins and kill us both.'

Edie knew that this was not the time for her to lose her grip. Later and alone she would shed her tears. 'Mags . . . don't say things like that. It's wicked to even think of taking your own life.'

'No it's not. That's all we own at the end of the day. Our own life to do with what we want. I remember Aunt Naomi saying that.'

'Maybe so, but she wouldn't 'ave been referring to suicide.' Drawing breath, Edie pushed back the memory of her own mother taking her life. That was something she never discussed. Something that she had never even told Maggie.

'Anyway . . .' said Maggie. 'I wouldn't do it. I thought about it enough before now, *before* I was in the family way, and I'm still here.'

As she raised her eyes to meet her daughter's, Edie felt herself go icy cold. 'What do you mean, you've thought about it before?'

'Right up until we moved and Aunt Naomi cut my hair and made me look my age.'

'She never made you look your age, she made you look older. In fact it's probably why you've—'

'No!' said Maggie. 'That's not fair. You mustn't saddle Aunt Nao with this. If she 'adn't done something about the way I looked I might just 'ave walked out in front of a car, I was so ugly.'

Pushing a hand through her hair, Edie spoke quietly. 'You were a bit plain, that's all. Because of the brace and glasses. But you've always been pretty underneath. She brought the best out in you, is all I meant to say.'

'No . . . she did more than that. She changed everything. I used to cover the mirror in my bedroom but I don't any more. I always hated my ginger hair—'

'It's not ginger, it's auburn.'

'Now it is. But it wasn't before. It was carrot. I should know. The boys used to ask if they could 'ave a nibble at school. They called me "Carrot" all the time. Told me to jump in the stew pot and boil myself.'

Her throat dry and her heart feeling as if it were slowly being torn out, Edie wondered whether she was going to cope with all this. Guilt, for not having taken more notice of Maggie when she was young and had so little confidence, was beginning to pervade her. All she could find to say to the one person who meant everything in the world to her was, 'I didn't know. You should 'ave said.'

'And if I had of done you would 'ave laughed at me and said I was as pretty as a flower. You saw me as your little girl for too long. I s'pose it was because I never had a dad around and you tried to make up for it.'

'Maybe. All I know is that I loved you too much to share your suffering. I can see now that I pretended that it was just something you were going through. If that's a crime then I'm guilty. But I still think you've always been pretty – Naomi changed your looks and made you attractive instead. That's all. She made you grow up too fast and too soon.'

'She never. Anyway . . . what does it matter now? The main thing is that no matter what 'appens we'll always 'ave each other. You're my mum and I love you.'

Edie smiled. 'Well, that's all right, then.' She held out her arms. 'Give me a hug, then, plain Jane.'

Laughing through her tears, Maggie was happy to oblige. And as she hugged her daughter and patted her back, it dawned on Edie that Maggie really wanted to have her baby and keep it. 'You can't get married yet on account of your age, sweetheart,' she said, pulling back and looking into her face. 'But you could go away to one of the places that are run by nuns. We're not Catholics but I think they take in Protestant girls who've got themselves in trouble . . .'

Maggie was no longer paying attention. She was thinking about the boy she loved. 'I've got to tell Tony. I don't know what his family are gonna think of me.'

'Don't start that now,' said Edie. 'If your dad was alive I'm sure he'd be straight up there, giving the lad what for. He's a year older than you and should 'ave known better than to take advantage. Maybe I should go up there and speak to the family. What do you think?'

'No,' said Maggie in a quiet voice. 'I'll tell 'im myself. This afternoon we're going to Redbridge . . . by train, for a picnic by the river. Maybe I'll break it to him then. But whatever happens, Mum, I want to tell 'im myself. If not today then soon. But you mustn't say anything until he knows. Not to anyone. It wouldn't be fair.'

It dawned on Edie that she was losing her little girl. Momentarily lost for words, she shrugged, saying, 'Well . . . I can't stop you from doing what you think best but don't set your hopes too high. He might not want to know. History shows a string of girls in your state left high and dry.'

'Tony's not like that.'

'Maybe not – but be prepared for the worst.'

'It won't matter if he doesn't want to know. I've got you and Aunt Naomi. I'll have the both of you to help me. And Tony . . . you see if I'm wrong.'

'Let's hope you're not, sweetheart. Let's hope you're not.'

Tired of thinking about it all and trying to work out right from wrong, Maggie yawned before saying, 'Is it all right if I take my cup of tea back to bed with me? I don't fink I could face a cooked breakfast after all.'

'Whatever you feel like.'

'I'm not ducking out of talking about it so don't think that, will you? And I'm sorry to have caused you all this worry. I need to be by myself, though . . . now that I've told you.'

Once she heard Maggie's bedroom door close behind her, Edie sank down into her chair and gazed at her hands, which were trembling as her thoughts drifted back to when she was first pregnant herself, in the late 1930s. A war had been imminent but still life then somehow seemed to have gone at a much slower pace. And now that baby, her own little girl, had turned into a young woman and was struggling to be independent at too early an age.

To Edie, Stepney, where she had played safely in the streets as a child in the 1920s, was very different from what she remembered. There had always been a mix of immigrants coming and going, so the hustle and bustle of life hadn't altered that much, but nowadays there did seem to be more people, more cars and more noise. But then she had heard her Aunt Naomi saying exactly the same thing about her life as a child in the late 1880s.

Now that it was all out in the open, the worry of Maggie having missed two periods would hardly stop Edie from having disturbed nights, but at least she did feel as if a weight, caused mostly by fear and doubt, had been lifted from her. Watching her only child worrying, a look of despair in her eyes, had been very hard to take. Edie was wise enough to know when to keep silent but she was aware that Maggie had been going through hell, and going through it alone until this morning. She felt sure that having left her to herself thus far had been for the best. Waiting for her to finally break the news was over. Now it was real and not just a nagging fear.

Scraping the eggs and bacon into a mixing bowl, with the idea of turning them into a savoury flan for supper, Edie wished that Harry was there by her side, advising her on what to do for the best. She gazed out of the kitchen window as she washed the frying pan, thinking again of the tragedy of him having been killed so young while fighting for his country.

It seemed that history had a habit of repeating itself. Harry had been her first boyfriend too, except that Edie had been married when she fell pregnant. He had been her first love. She hadn't felt close to another man either before him nor afterwards – until she had met Dennis last New Year's Eve and he had smiled in his kind way before asking her to dance. Now she couldn't imagine being lonely again or living her life without him. Her thoughts flying from one thing to another, she pictured the look of shock on the face of Tony's mother, Ida, once she had been told the news. And in her mind's eye she could see the gossips casting black looks at both her and Maggie.

The more she thought about it the more she realised that there really was only one option. Maggie would have to go away until she had had her baby and return without it. One thing she was sure of was that her Aunt Naomi would hit the roof over this. Imagining what she might say, she felt the blood rush to her face. Now in her seventies, her aunt liked people to believe she was open minded, yet she had been furious the previous Christmas Eve when Maggie had been allowed to go alone with Tony to their old house. She could see now that Naomi had been right, but at the same time believed that she had overreacted. Maggie had gone to collect a box from the loft, inside which had been special things from her childhood, in particular a doll that Naomi had given her for her first Christmas, which by tradition sat at the bottom of the tree every year.

Remembering her aunt's words of caution at the time, Edie couldn't help smiling. She could see the expression on her aunt Naomi's face as if it had been yesterday when she had stood in the doorway of the living room, predicting the worst, saying, 'Edie, please do be *sensible*! My great-niece is only fourteen! And you are letting her loose in the East End of London at night with a foreign young man who no doubt is terribly excited, as all men are, at news of this forth-coming contraceptive pill!' And then, 'And you have agreed to let her go into a dark and empty house with this fertile young man on one of the most romantic evenings of the year! Are you mad?'

'Yes,' murmured Edie, smiling, coming back to the present. 'She is going to say, "I told you so."' Naomi, her mother figure since she had been orphaned, was the last person in the world she wanted to upset. Her aunt had always been there for her, and she knew she could trust Naomi to be open and frank as well as caring.

Certain that her aunt would agree with her that Maggie should go to a place of sanctuary until her time had come, Edie poured a glass of her daughter's favourite cold drink, lemon and barley water, and then went to her bedroom, and tapped on the door. There was no sound from within, so she cautiously turned the handle in case Maggie was sobbing into her pillow. Instead she found her sitting up in bed, the pillow propped behind her.

'Why'd you knock on the door, Mum? I'm not a guest in a bed and breakfast.'

'I thought you might have fallen asleep, sweetheart. I've brought you a cold drink. Besides . . . you're not a child any more. You should 'ave more privacy.'

'If you say so.' Maggie took the drink from Edie and then looked shyly at her. 'You've got over the shock, then?'

'No. But I've come to realise that there's only one way round this. Not that we really have much of a choice . . .'

'I knew this would happen,' whispered Maggie. 'Now it's sunk in properly – you hate me for it.'

'Don't be silly. Of course I don't hate you. I'm disappointed, that's all. And frightened.' There was more than a touch of sadness in Edie's voice. 'My feelings are on hold. It's the only way.' Then, sitting on the edge of the bed, she cast her eyes down to the floor, murmuring, 'We've got to be practical, Mags – and not let our hearts rule our heads. By that I mean that we should keep it to ourselves until arrangements 'ave been made. Even then there's no real need to let anyone know.'

'What arrangements?' Maggie looked at her mother with suspicion in her eyes. Then, in a more defiant tone, she said, 'I do mean it, Mum. I'm not gonna get rid of it. So don't ask me to.'

'Stop talking like that, Mags,' said Edie. 'If you're trying to shock me with that kind of talk it's not working. You're not with your friends on a street corner.'

'What friends? I've only got one. Rita. Don't forget I was seen as a drip at school – before Naomi cut my hair and showed me how to use make-up. They soon changed their tune, though . . . once the boys began to give me wolf whistles. Let's see what they think now when they see me pushing a lovely pram with my baby inside it. The girls in my class were dead jealous over Tony. If that's not ironic I don't know what is. I get to be popular during the last two months of my entire school life.'

'I don't think it matters that much what they say or think when they find out, Mags. They're bound to whisper behind their hands for you to see, and there're bound to be girls who call you names to your face. Girls can be cows when they want. You know that from junior school when they teased you over the brace on your teeth—'

'This is different. I think they'll be impressed more than anyfing else. Or jealous.'

'Maybe so, but jealous or not they might well call you a whore.'

'Whore? Mum, how can you *say* such a thing? That's a *horrible* word!'

'I'm just preparing you for the worst, that's all.'

Her eyes filling with tears, Maggie could hardly speak. 'I can't believe you called me that.'

'I *didn't*. I said that one or two most likely will. Face facts, Maggie. It's much better to be ready for it.' Then, stroking her daughter's dark red hair, Edie sighed deeply. 'It's Jack Blunt time, Mags. If you insist on having this baby you're gonna have to go away so you won't get pointed at.'

'Go away to where, though?'

'Well . . . if you won't agree to not telling Tony that this has happened—'

'Of course I wouldn't agree to that!'

'There are places . . .' Edie shrank from the black look she was getting. 'I'll talk to Tony's mother. Mrs Baroncini's a practising Catholic. I've met her priest on the stairs a couple of times. He seems really nice. And then there's a nun who goes in and out from time to time and—'

'I don't know what you're talking about. What 'ave priests and nuns got to do wiv this? And it's not a sin, before you say it is. If you read a bit more you'd know that fifteen going on sixteen's not *that* young to be having a baby.'

'Oh really?' said Edie, trying to contain her anger. 'And which books should I read to find that out? And where might I find such a book? Because I don't see any in this room.'

'In the library – where else. It's where I work, don't forget. In some countries girls are considered ready for a man to bed once they've grown a single hair on their privates.'

'Oh, *very* nice. So much for education and a pittance of a wage while you train to be a librarian. You've obviously been reading the wrong books.'

'No I've not, and I'll have a career once I'm fully trained up so it's not a waste of time, before you say it is.'

Edie's mind was still on the notion of a single pubic hair and into bed with a man you go. She couldn't imagine what her daughter had been reading in her lunch breaks, but by the sound of it she would have been better off employed at Woolworths full time. Staring as if she were looking into another world across the ocean, she shook her head in disbelief. 'What about under the armpits? Do they look there as well?'

Managing to keep a straight face, Maggie turned up her nose and looked away. 'I'll let you know. I've only read a couple of pages.'

'And which country are we talking about, may I ask? The far reaches of Outer Mongolia?'

'I'll borrow it and you can 'ave a read and find out for yourself. So what about Ida, then?'

'Ida?'

'Tony's mum.'

'I know who you mean but I would have thought that she's Mrs Baroncini to you. I hope you've been showing her respect, Maggie.'

'Of course I have. So what *has* a Catholic priest got to do with all this?'

Edie glanced out of the window, her mind still on Tony's mother. Her daughter had always been a touch on the cantankerous side but her manners had always been impeccable where neighbours were concerned. She turned to face her again, saying, 'You don't call her Ida, do you?'

'No,' said Maggie. 'She said I could, though, if I wanted. But I don't because it wouldn't be right.'

'Well, that's something. Maybe it's not such a good idea getting Tony's family involved after all. I know a lovely woman. One who's on early morning shift at the factory. She's a cleaner. She leaves off around ten to go and give a hand round at Nonnatus House before she goes on to her next cleaning job. You can say what you like about the Catholics being hypocrites, but they're good people. Especially those who follow their religion and help others out. And there's something about the nuns that makes you feel humble.'

'You're not saying that because I'm gonna 'ave Tony's baby I should convert . . . are you? I'm not against it but the reasons should be right, shouldn't they? And being in the club's not really a reason . . . is it?'

'I wasn't thinking of you converting,' said Edie. 'Choice of religion's not something I'd interfere with. I was thinking of Nonnatus House in Leyland Street and the midwives of St Raymund Nonnatus. It's a convent of sorts. I could call in and have a chat with the sister-in-charge. The cleaner reckons that Sister Julienne's an angel come down to care for the poor and destitute mothers-to-be.'

'We're not poor and I'm not destitute.' Maggie couldn't help but wonder where all this was leading.

'From what I gather, Mags, there are places in the country where girls who've got themselves in trouble can go. Small, privately organised hospitals cum refuges, run by nuns who find good homes for orphans and—'

'No,' said Maggie, cutting in. 'I'm not giving my baby away.'

Placing a hand under Maggie's chin, Edie looked into her face. 'You can't 'ave an attitude on this, Mags. It's too important. There's no other way that I can think of—'

'I'll move in with Aunt Naomi. She'll take care of me till Baby comes. I'll be sixteen by then and—'

'You can't put this on Naomi's shoulders. She's

turned seventy, and anyway, she might talk as if she's broad minded but she's not. Underneath she's an old-fashioned lady and a bit on the proper side. She'd rather die than 'ave you walking about pregnant at your age for all to see.'

Maggie lowered her voice to a whisper. 'What *am* I s'posed to do, then? I want to have my baby. If you really think that your idea of a convent is the only choice . . .'

'The father being Catholic will help,' said Edie, hating having to have this conversation.

'I s'pose we've got to tell Naomi . . .' said Maggie, now worried about what her aunt's reaction would be.

'Of course we've got to tell 'er. She'll hit the roof and blame me then you then Tony then his parents and then me agen . . . but she must be the first to know.'

'But we could leave it for a while, couldn't we?'

'It's your choice. You either get it over and done with or dwell on it for days.'

The ring of the doorbell pierced through the flat and Edie went to let Naomi in. She was glad now that her aunt had chosen to call in this morning. Normally she refused to be seen before midday when, in her opinion, the wrinkles on her face had smoothed out and her eyes had got their sparkle back. Whatever her faults, and they were in any case few, Naomi had a way of coming up with a sensible answer to most things in a down-to-earth, clear-cut way. She also had an uncanny sixth sense and could tell if there was trouble in the air. Edie knew that should she detect worry surrounding her beloved Maggie she would soon draw the trouble out of them.

'If only one didn't have to sleep in huts . . .' said Naomi, announcing her arrival in a typically unconventional way as she swept in. 'Nor journey on the back of a lorry. I would go if only to see how a family may survive in the twentieth century living as if they were cavemen and only just beginning to stand up straight.'

'Laura's lift hasn't arrived already, has it?' Edie peered at her wristwatch. 'It's a bit early.'

Flopping down on to a kitchen chair, Naomi leaned back as if exhausted and then stretched her neck as she checked the stove for evidence of a fresh pot of tea. 'I do hope that hasn't stewed, Edith.'

'No, but I'll make a fresh pot anyway. So . . . Laura's off to the hop fields of Kent. I wish I was going on that lorry with 'er.'

'Darling, one doesn't have to have a degree to pluck fruit from a bine. And if my memory serves me right, you hated living in a tin hut.'

'I did, and hops are not fruit,' said Edie, filling the kettle. 'They're herbs.'

'If you say so, dear.' Easing a shoe off each foot with the other, Naomi leaned back and sighed contentedly. 'This must be the very best of all early Septembers. It is beautiful out there. Sunny and warm but equally fresh. I've never known such a morning.'

'You're never outside at this time of day, that's why.'

'I keep a window open at all times, as a matter of

fact. Fresh air and I go hand in hand. And why, may I ask, is there no bacon sizzling? I expected a full cooked breakfast at the very least. Have you eaten already? Without me?'

'No . . . I thought we'd have breakfast around half past ten, eleven . . . and put dinner back a bit.'

'Oh? Brunch. How odd. Has that snooty sister-in-law been to visit? The one from Ed*mon*ton.'

'No she hasn't, and I've only got one sister-in-law and you know very well what her name is. Obviously, we're in one of our tormenting moods. Helen's all right. And since she's been gradually dropping the Hel*ene* bit, I think you should too.'

'Oh, darling, please. Don't be snappy with me. The walk here in the sunshine has done me the world of good. Would you have me long faced and miserable? So that we may both sit and stare into our tea leaves hoping for an answer?'

'An answer to what?' said Edie, suspicious. 'What have you heard?'

'I don't have to hear *anything*. I read your face by instinct or habit, I'm not sure which. It is the *eyes* that are the give-away and the deep lines above them. If you *continue* to crease your brow you will age prematurely, Edith. And none of my face creams will save you. No matter *how* expensive.'

'I'm fine. If I get crow's-feet from frowning, then so be it.' She glanced at Naomi and managed a smile – an attempt to appear tranquil.

'Oh, that's *much* better, darling. You see . . . you can be quite *lovely* when you put your mind to it.

Not one wrinkle in sight.' Tilting her head to one side, Naomi held her niece's gaze. 'What is it, my darling? What's the matter?'

'Nothing. Everything's tickety-boo. How's life with the old 'uns?' This was not the time to confide in her aunt. It was too soon after Maggie's confession. She had hardly been able to take it in herself.

'Well, as a matter of fact . . . rather stimulating. We've formed a group and from that came a rather lovely idea. We aim to maintain a dying trend. Keep it alive, so to speak.'

'And what might that be?'

'Tea dances – to be held in the church hall. St Peter's church hall. A stone's throw away. Which is one of the reasons I came this morning. To tell you about it. Plus it is time my great-niece returned a few of the favours I have done her in the past.' With that Naomi, smiling demurely, rummaged around in her faded red shopping bag to withdraw a batch of leaflets.

'You want her to deliver those?' said Edie, doing her best not to laugh. 'I can't imagine her going door to door . . .'

'Of course she will. She's younger than you and far more energetic, otherwise I would have let you take on the responsibility. If she *could* manage to cover Scott House and Malcolm . . . and the cottages in Long Street . . .'

'She'll be through in a minute. You can ask 'er yourself. I don't fancy your chances, though.'

'Perhaps that's because you do not know your daughter as well as I do.'

'Well . . . let's wait and see what the reaction is, shall we? Now then – would you like a bacon sandwich?'

'That would be lovely, Edith . . . especially if you were to fry an egg to go on top and perhaps some grilled tomatoes . . . and a few baked beans?'

'Don't you think that might be a little too much for you to manage? It's roast pork for dinner.'

'Oh, darling, you weren't expecting me for dinner, were you?'

'I was, but if you've got other plans . . .'

'Oh dear. And I suppose Dennis is not coming for dinner today?'

'No. Why should he be? Why do you ask?'

'Well, it being a Sunday one might have thought . . .'

'He don't come for Sunday roast, Nao. You know that. I never see him on Sundays. But if you're feeling guilty because you can't stop – then don't be silly.' Naomi didn't feel guilty at all – she had simply tried to lodge a question in Edie's mind. The question being: Where does Dennis go on Sundays for his dinner?

'The lovely Benjamin is no doubt preparing a roast shoulder of lamb and Yorkshire with crisp roast potatoes, sprouts and peas as we speak. Joey has been invited too.'

'Ben and Joey. What would we do without people like them? I've met some nice neighbours since I've been living here but nothing like those two. I wish they'd moved on to the estate. I miss them.'

'Cotton Street isn't far away, poppet. You can always visit them.'

'That's true. They were like lovely old uncles – the pair of them. Especially when Dad left and Mum died,' said Edie, remembering. 'Why are you having Sunday lunch together?'

'So that we may discuss the programme for the tea dances. Tomorrow I have an appointment with the genius Shereen, who is going to make a new frock for me from a picture in *Vanity Fair*.'

'Oh. You're not gonna get her to remake one of your old ones this time?'

'Indeed not. I took your advice and strolled along the Waste on a Saturday afternoon and found the most wonderful pale blue crêpe de Chine which cost a fraction of what it might had I been born to shop in Harrods.'

'And what did you think of the rest of the market?' Edie grinned. Naomi had always enjoyed a touch of snobbery and had been secretly nettled when Edie's brother Jimmy had married and Helene (christened Helen) had intruded into her world and taken on the role of Lady Muck. Still living in Ed*mon*ton, as she liked to call it, Helene was driving Jimmy mad with her obsession about keeping up with the Joneses.

'I love all of the Waste. A more colourful market I have yet to find. Not quite Portobello Road, it's true, but the advantages outweigh the shortcomings. To see so many down-and-outs is rather depressing. But there . . . we live in an unfair society.'

'Hello, Aunt Naomi,' said Maggie, coming into the kitchen.

'Good morning, Margaret. I am very well, thank you.'

'So am I, so that's all right. Has Mum told you, then?'

'Told me what exactly? That you too are off to the hop fields in Kent to live the life of a Romany with Laura Jackson?'

'No. That I've got a bun in the oven.'

# 2

A few doors farther along the balcony from Edie in Scott House, Laura and Jessie, her friends, were enjoying a cup of tea before Laura embarked on her journey to the hop fields of Kent. Jessie had been telling of her time spent in the countryside, in Norfolk, where she had been evacuated during the war. The story had been provoked by Laura's sudden confession of a budding romance outside her marriage, with the rich owner of the hop farm. Inspired by her honesty, Jessie was now telling of her one and only flirtation with a young man, also from the gentry, who had been taken with her while she was staying in a small village, Elmshill. She was explaining exactly *why* she hadn't felt guilty about his advances and why, had she stayed longer, she might well have become his lover. She was entrusting her secret without guilt or shame. Her husband Tom, who she had once loved so deeply, had had a passionate love affair while convalescing during the war, having had a bullet removed from his leg – an injury received during the evacuation of Dunkirk.

'I found a note in his pocket,' said Jessie sadly. 'Months later. She'd been nursing him and that's when it all started.'

'Sounds more like a fling than an affair, Jess,' said Laura, attempting to console her friend. 'A soldier wounded during the war having a run-in with a nurse while in care? And after he'd seen the horrors of Dunkirk? We could forgive a man for that, couldn't we?'

'Oh, I never bore a grudge. I was racked with jealousy, though. I adored Tom. Worshipped the ground he walked on. So it came as a blow. Imagining him in bed with another woman. It was horrible. I couldn't bear it.'

'And now?'

'I've not thought about it for ages, to be honest. I don't want to either.'

'Would you go back with 'im?' Laura smiled as if she already knew the answer.

'No, of course not! I'm with Max now. Settled down. And the kids love him.'

'So you're not still in love with Tom, then?'

'No! It wasn't the fault of either of us the way things turned out. Not really. The war messed everything up. For lots of families. Max's not to blame either. He didn't come chasing after me. He was just there in the wings during the war, I s'pose.' Jessie shrugged.

'Sounds like your Tom had a bit of a raw deal, though.'

'Maybe he did, Laura. But my life during that time wasn't a bed of roses!'

'I know! I'm not blaming you. Women at home had a rough time of it. Never mind all the stories about going out with the Americans stationed over here. What must our men 'ave thought? Them fighting out there and the Yanks screwing us women.'

'I shouldn't think they were too happy about it.' Jessie leaned back in her chair and looked into Laura's face, a hint of a smile on her face. 'Are you suggesting by any chance that because Tom had a raw deal I should have gone back to him once he deigned to show his face – six years, going on seven, after the war had ended?'

'No, but nor should you feeling sorry for Max be a reason for you to stay with *him*.'

'It's not! I love Max. Not Tom.'

'Of course you do. That's why you're in this state now.'

'What state?'

'Oh, come on. Ever since Tom turned up out of the blue earlier this year you've not stopped talking about 'im.'

'That's *not* true! We only got round to talking about this because you want *me* to tell *you* to have an affair with that landowner. Crafty cow.'

'That is not true. I never said that.'

'Not in so many words, no. You never had to.' Jessie looked away and thought about what Laura had said. 'So . . . you think I'm still in love with Tom. That's interesting. And if I am, what should I do about it?'

'Only you can answer that one, Jessie. Only you.'

'It's too much trouble even to think about all that stuff. You'll be all right, though. Mr Hunk is miles away from where you live. Clever cow.'

'And your Tom's only round the corner. I'm not sure which I would prefer,' said Laura, smiling mischievously.

'I wouldn't do that to Max. I couldn't hurt him. He's lovely. And I do love 'im. 'Course I do.'

'So why don't you divorce Tom and marry Max, then?'

'Why? All that upset for nothing. Divorce papers and courts. No. We're fine as we are – me, Max and the kids.'

'Tom's kids.'

'Yeah . . . and he sees them whenever he wants. Do they look unhappy, Laura?'

'No, they don't . . . and nor do you and Max. Take no notice of me. I'm just trying to justify my own longing to be in that bloody hop field with Richard Wright. He's gorgeous.'

'And rich.'

'Yeah – that too. Although it shouldn't make a difference because he can hardly take me out on the town to posh restaurants, can he? God – what a scandal that would cause in Tonbridge or Maidstone. They all seem to be connected, the country lot. Talk about country cousins.'

'Oh well,' said Jessie, easing herself up from her chair, 'there's nothing else for it, then, is there? It's a roll in the hay for you, my girl! Have a good time whichever way it goes, because me and Edie wanna know all about it when you get back. On the *day* you get back.'

After she had seen Jessie out, Laura went back to

her armchair and her dreams while her husband Jack
and her brother-in-law Bert struggled and cursed as
they carried out a large green-painted trunk, known
as the family 'hopping box', which was crammed full
of everything but the kitchen sink. Her packing finished, Laura was enjoying a much deserved rest and
waiting for Naomi to call in as promised. She had
seen her a little while earlier when she was giving
the flowers in her window box on the balcony a last-
minute soaking. The sight of Naomi swaggering
along in one of her flowing period outfits had, as
ever, been a sight to behold. As far as Laura was
concerned, this majestic, worldly woman had made
it her business to visit her niece on this particular
Sunday morning for a reason. She was here to gently
reinforce all she had said to Laura earlier that year
– that she simply must take advantage of this break
in Kent to enjoy a little romance. Naomi had seemed
set on her new, younger friend taking a seasonal lover
since Laura's confession that Jack was still womanising. Spasmodic though his flirtations were, they
brightened his life while all the time Laura remained
tied to the kitchen sink. She had also let it slip to
Naomi that Richard Wright, the wealthy owner of
the hop farm which she was shortly leaving for, was
not only tall, rugged and handsome, but had given
her a little romantic encouragement during her visits
over the previous two years. From that moment on
Naomi had insisted that she was not to return home
from her working holiday without a tale of illicit love
to report.

While she had been watering her glorious marigolds and the mass of trailing blue lobelia, to the sound of children playing below, Laura had waved to Naomi, hoping that she would pop in once she had been to see Edie. Secretly, she wanted that last-minute pep talk on the benefits of forbidden fruit. She had remembered by heart what Naomi had once said: 'When a man is known to be sowing seeds away from the home, then the woman must seek a tree similar to that from which Eve plucked her fruit.'

Breaking into Laura's fantasies, her eight-year-old daughter Kay came rushing into the room, flushed and excited. 'The sink woman's only standing on 'er balcony! She's watching Dad and Uncle Bert load up the lorry from *outside* 'er flat!'

'Is she now? Well, that's good, Kay. A small step but one in the right direction.'

'But what if she starts coming down the stairs? Billy Smith said that once she starts doin' that there's no telling!'

'No telling what?'

'I don't know!' declared Kay, splaying her hands dramatically. 'She might kidnap one of us!'

'Don't be silly. She's all right. Just shy of people, that's all.'

'She's not!' said Kay, frenziedly shaking her head. 'She still sits in 'er sink and sings! She's bonkers!' Her eyes wide, she stared into Laura's dispassionate face and then calmed down, saying, 'She's got a screw loose, be all accounts.' With that she turned and ran back outside, her long hair flying everywhere.

'And don't go missing!' Laura called after her. 'We'll be off soon!'

'I'm not! I gettin' on the lorry wiv Aunt Liz straight away! To be on the safe side!'

Relaxing back into her armchair, Laura sipped her tea and imagined herself strolling along in the peace and quiet of the country lane in the tiny village of Hunton, which ran from the hop fields to a lovely old church with a stone seat where priests had sat seven hundred years ago. As she recalled the alabaster tomb on which Sir Thomas Fane and his wife lay, as they had from the sixteenth century, she could almost hear her own footsteps echoing around the church and see the ancient stained-glass windows with the sun shining through. This was a place she had gone to time and time again on her hop-picking holiday, not just to collect her thoughts and enjoy the solitude but to be where it felt as if time had stood still.

The sound of Naomi gently calling her name from the open front doorway brought her sharply back to the present. 'I'm in the living room, Nao!' she called back. 'Come on through!'

Sweeping into the room, Naomi showed no sign of her usual broad smile. She lowered herself into an armchair opposite Laura and slowly shook her head, saying, 'I simply cannot take it in. I feel as if the bubble has burst. How fast the young move. It's almost a year since you moved on to this estate . . . is it not?'

'More or less,' said Laura, eyeing her friend warily. 'What's the matter?'

'Well . . . since I have not actually been sworn to secrecy I will tell you, Laura, but I must ask you to keep it to yourself. And if you could appear to be shocked if and when Edith deigns to break the news . . .'

'Edith?'

'Edie.'

Chuckling, Laura said, 'She's obviously been a naughty girl and got herself in your bad books. What's she done?'

'It's not so much what she has done as what she has not done. She has not been as watchful as she might where her daughter is concerned. Margaret – my great-niece of fifteen years – is with child.' Having delivered this news with as few words as possible, Naomi raised her eyes and spoke in a whisper. 'Darling . . . do you think you could possibly pour a cup of tea for me?'

Reeling from the confession, Laura was momentarily lost for words. She could hardly believe that she had heard correctly. Maggie was expecting a baby? At her age? She stared into Naomi's face and eventually found her voice. 'Are you sure, Nao? I mean . . . really sure?'

'It is not *my* body we are talking of, Laura . . . so how can I possibly be sure of anything. But what I do know is that there is an awful atmosphere in that flat and that Maggie has spoken words to me which could not be taken any other way.'

'What exactly did she say?'

'"I have a bun in the oven." Say what you will

about this new breed of teenagers – they are coarsely to the point.'

'God almighty . . .' murmured Laura, pushing a hand through her long wavy hair. 'I can hardly believe it. Poor Edie. What a blow.'

'Indeed. And no doubt she will now become a human sponge and soak in all the grief, pain and blame. As is her wont where her only child is concerned.'

'Oh, stop it, Naomi,' murmured Laura. 'You're no different when it comes to Maggie and you know it. Jesus. Poor cow. What does Edie want to do about the baby?'

'It matters little what she says *now* for minds will be changed back and forth before the inevitable will be arrived at. We shall have to wait and see. My opinion, sadly, was not sought on this occasion, and the reason, I am certain, is that they deemed fit to presume that I would have suggested abortion.'

'You might not 'ave said the words exactly but what might they 'ave read from your expression?'

'Shock. Simply that. I had not been there five seconds before all this was thrown at me. There was hardly time for me to say *anything*. *Had* I have been asked, however, I would have suggested adoption – I *think*.'

'And you're sure you've not got the wrong end of the stick and that it's Edie who's pregnant and not Maggie?'

'Oh, Laura, please . . . pregnant is *such* an ugly word. Maggie's interpretation by comparison is far more acceptable. At least "a bun in the oven" brings a farmhouse kitchen to mind, not to mention the lovely smell of cakes baking.' Then, her eyes smiling, Naomi lifted her chin and gazed at her friend thoughtfully as a new idea came to mind. 'You have sown a seed with skill, Laura. How clever you are. If only I were as down-to-earth as you are. Of course that is the answer. Why on earth had I not seen it for myself?'

'Seen what?'

'The perfect solution to a very awkward situation.' With that Naomi was up from her chair and out of the flat, calling over her shoulder as she went, 'And please do try and come in to say goodbye before you trundle away to see your lover!'

'Jesus,' whispered Laura. 'Let Jack hear that and I won't be goin' anywhere.' Then, with the sun on her face as it streamed through the white net curtains at the balcony window, she allowed the handsome, tanned Richard Wright to drift back into her mind, his searching brown eyes and seductive smile warming every part of her.

Their innocent meeting in the lane in Kent the previous year really could have been passed off as nothing more than the beginning of a casual friendship, but as it all came flooding back she knew that, if she were honest with herself, she would have to admit that his first touch, when he gently brushed a hand across her cheek, could so easily have been the start of a wonderful romance.

'Four or five glorious weeks in Kent,' she murmured, her excitement growing. She fantasised about her dream lover smothering her with passionate kisses, his strong arms holding her tightly, the two of them in a quiet leafy lane with those searching hazel eyes looking deeply into her own as if he were trying to read her thoughts. Five minutes later, with her front door locked and the windows bolted, she was back in the real world and climbing into the rear of her brother-in-law's lorry to join the other hop-pickers, who were eager to be away. Trying as hard as she could not to look incredibly happy, in case any of those aboard began to be suspicious, she sat on a high-back chair next to her sister-in-law, Liz.

'You're looking a bit flushed, Laura,' said Liz, a wry smile on her face. 'And there was me thinking you might be up there shedding a tear 'cos you couldn't bear to be parted from Jack.'

'I won't be parted, Liz, will I,' was Laura's response. 'He'll be stopping over till Sunday night, as well you know.'

'Ah . . .' murmured Liz. She chuckled. 'So it's something else that's putting them roses into your cheeks, eh?' Then lowering her voice and leaning close she said, 'Let's hope he's as good as he looks.'

'I don't know what you're talking about, Liz.'

'Don't you?' said Liz. She slipped her hand into her summer coat pocket and pulled out a blue tin. 'I think you do.' Smiling mischievously, she sprinkled a little snuff on the back of her hand. 'I've seen the way Wright looks at you when he comes on to the hop fields. Just make sure that no one catches you if you do fancy a little roll in the grass. Jack'd go spare if he detected so much as a hint of it.'

'There's nothing for 'im to go spare about, Liz.'

'Not yet, there isn't. But you're gonna 'ave to make a little decision this year. To jump through the hoop of fire or not.' A smile spread across her face as the engine started up. 'Teach that brother of mine a lesson.'

'So I've got your approval, then? If what you're saying is right, that is.'

'So long as you're discreet, Laura. So long as you're discreet.' Then, as the lorry slowly pulled away, Liz, in this mischievous mood, began to sing, knowing that the others would join in. The song she had chosen to see them off on their journey was 'Someone Else's Roses'.

Back in Edie's kitchen, Naomi had an arm around her niece's shoulder and was trying her utmost to make her listen to what she believed to be the answer to their problem. Edie, however, was not in the mood for advice. As much as she loved her aunt's company right then all she wanted was to be alone. But Naomi was beside herself and desperate to pursue her idea. Realising that this was not the time to try to comfort Edie, she drew away from her and sat down, saying, 'Darling, I really do think I may have a solution which might just work.'

'I don't want to talk about it. Not now anyway. Maggie's gone back to bed and she's crying,' said Edie, staring down at the floor. 'I can't think about anything. Listen to her. What am I s'posed to do, Nao? That's all I need to know right now. Am I s'posed to sit here and let her cry like that or go in?'

'No, darling. You mustn't. Leave her alone. She must let it out and crying is the best way. The only way. Screaming and shouting and getting angry or defensive can never be as effective a cure as a good howl.'

'I feel I should go in there and comfort 'er . . . but I don't know what to say.'

'I know, Edie. I know. But won't you just listen to what I have to suggest?'

Raising her eyes, Edie looked into her aunt's face, considering whether to give her free rein or not. She decided on the former, saying, 'Go on, then. But if she comes in, change the subject.'

'Oh, Edie . . . that would make things worse. We are talking of Maggie. Your strong-willed, sometimes petulant, daughter. Now what I suggest is that you bring forward your marriage to, say . . . within a fortnight. At this time of the year they're bound to fit you in. People usually choose Christmas, Easter, Valentine's Day—'

'Bring it forward?' said Edie, cutting in. 'Why?'

'So that you and Maggie may move in with Dennis – into his house in Bow, which by all accounts has a lovely back garden. You could live there for six months and when you come back everyone may be led to believe that it is *your* baby and not Maggie's. That way the child may be brought up as yours and cause no scandal to Maggie whatsoever.'

Slowly shaking her head, finding it almost impossible not to laugh, Edie said, 'That is the crankiest thing you've *ever* come up with. And I don't find it in the least bit amusing. And what do you mean . . . "by all accounts"? Dennis is a keen gardener, so why wouldn't he be telling the truth?'

'Darling, I didn't say that. And actually, none of what I conveyed was meant to be cranky or funny. It could work. It could actually work.'

'Of course it wouldn't work! Do you really think I would leave my flat empty for six months? And what about Den? How do you think he'd feel about it?'

'Well, I can't possibly know that without knowing what he plans to do with his own home. Is he to give it up and live here?'

'We haven't decided yet,' said Edie, wishing that Maggie had not told her aunt yet. She really wasn't in the mood for these kinds of questions.

'Oh,' said Naomi, 'how odd. I would have thought that would have been one of the first things you'd have talked about.'

'Besides,' said Edie, no longer listening, 'if we were to bring our wedding forward and stuff a cushion up my jumper, what's Maggie supposed to do all the while? Hide in a cupboard?'

'No . . . but she might not mind staying indoors until the bump goes down.'

'Don't be ridiculous. And what about Dennis? You think he'll jump for joy when I say we're to be married in a fortnight and I'll soon be walking around in a maternity frock?' Despite her bemusement Edie found herself smiling. 'No . . . I don't think that's one of your best ideas, Nao. I know you're trying your best but you might be trying a bit too hard. Just leave it be for a while.'

Naomi stared into the dregs of tea in her cup, pleased that the sound of Maggie crying in her bedroom had ceased. 'Actually, the idea came from a chance remark made by Laura on my brief visit this morning. It's hardly a new concept. It has taken place *many* times before and in *all* walks of life, from the working class to royalty. Many a child has been brought up believing their mother to be their sister, and many outsiders have been taken in by the trickery. If trickery it be. Of course, it does take courage and meticulous planning to achieve the right end.'

'So you told Laura about it.'

'Well, you didn't say I was to keep it a secret from her. Did I do wrong?'

'It doesn't matter now. But leave it be. Drop it.'

'As you wish,' said Naomi, straightening her back. 'I shall not say another word about it.' After a short pause she went on, 'It's a very strange thing, the mind and memory. I sometimes forget the reason I've gone into a room and what it is I'm looking for, and there are times when I recall things that happened sixty years ago as if it were yesterday.'

'I know,' said Edie, trying to bring an end to the conversation. 'Long-term memory grows stronger and short-term deteriorates. It's quite common among your generation.'

'Is it? I didn't know.'

'Don't tell lies. I know you're leading up to something.'

'Oh. I hadn't realised. But you could be right, my darling.'

'Well, go on, then. What 'ave you remembered?'

'As a matter of fact I was thinking about Mrs Goldberg, a widow who lived with her grown-up daughter and small son. I was a girl of no more than ten at the time so obviously I couldn't possibly have realised or questioned why there was such a huge gap between the age of her daughter, who was still living at home, and the little boy who ran about for most of the time in rags and with no shoes on his feet.'

'You lived in the backstreets of Bethnal Green. Everyone was poor.'

'Not everyone, Edith. There will *always* be a tier system where poverty and wealth are concerned. We had shops, don't forget. And shops, whatever they sold, made some profit. Then there were the market traders who were blessed with a sharp brain and made the most of fortuity. Not to mention those who secured work in the offices above the numerous factories. Some of which are still standing, having defied two world wars.'

'I think I know where this is leading, Nao, but get to the point. Maggie'll be back in this kitchen any second with questions flying. Questions which I don't 'ave the answers to.'

'Well, I can't profess to have the *perfect* answer but

it is a sensible one. The daughter living with her mother was—'

'The mother of the small boy,' interrupted Edie. 'Not his sister. I think I've gleaned that much. So go on, then. How did she manage to fool the neighbours?'

'She didn't, as a matter of fact. Mother and daughter simply brazened it out, and those who knew didn't give a toss and others who were none the wiser, of course, made nothing of it.'

'That's because people then didn't care as much as they do now. You might think pride is best left in the pocket but it helps if you can hold your head up.'

'I don't think you are fully listening to me, Edith. I sometimes wonder who you take full notice of, if *anyone*. You might at least *think* about my idea. It could actually be fun. If one were not to get too heavy over it.'

'For you, maybe, but not for me . . . nor Maggie. I'm not sacrificing my good name, nor am I leaving my flat to hide away for half a year. She can go away to have the baby and it can be adopted. That's the sensible answer and you know it.'

'Well, of course, you must do as you think *fit*. The choice is *yours* and not your daughter's.'

'And yours. You mentioned adoption before I did.'

'I did? Well, then, if that is the case – and I think not – I am sorry for it. As *you* will be later on if you push Maggie into giving up her baby. She will always resent you for it and will forever be wondering what her child looks like and where it might be. Call me old-fashioned, but I think we should do *all* we can to keep one of our own. Too many have gone already.' With that, Naomi picked up her red shopping bag, ready to leave.

Turning to face her aunt, Edie said, 'If you leave us now while we're on the floor like this you're not the aunt I thought you were.' Then, unable to stay her emotions any longer, she began to cry into the palms of her hands. 'Maggie asked about her dad and she's never done that before. I asked her why and she said it was because she didn't want to upset me.'

'Here,' said Naomi, passing her lace-edged handkerchief over. 'Thank goodness the tears have come at last. I was beginning to think dispassion had set in.'

'I wish.' Edie sniffed. 'I wish. It really upset me when she mentioned her dad right out of the blue like that. She must 'ave been bottling up her feelings all these years.' Then, having blown her nose and taken a deep breath, she murmured, 'If he was alive it would all be so different.'

'Do you really think so, my darling?' There was an expression of doubt on Naomi's face.

'I know so. Harry talked of a little cottage in the country with red and pink roses growing up the walls. We might well 'ave been living in one now . . . if he hadn't been killed.'

'And equally you might well have separated by now and still be in the situation you are in. No one can second-guess what might or might not have been if something or the other hadn't happened. If he were to come back out of the blue, would you give up Dennis for him, do you think?'

Edie peered at her aunt. 'That's a strange thing to ask. You're talking about the man I loved and lost.'

'But if you were to find out that he had in fact survived would you have him back, do you think?'

'Of course I would. You shouldn't need to ask that. I don't understand.'

'Well . . . after so much time has passed . . . and as we know, people do change . . . I just wondered, that's all. Time and circumstance do shape what we become and—'

'Nao? Why are you talking like this? It's not like you. Harry can't come back to me and Maggie. I wish he could. Of course I do. It would be the best thing that could ever happen.'

Numbed by the look of grief on her niece's face, Naomi wondered for the first time whether she had done the right thing by her. She had covered up something vitally important to protect Edie from heartache and pain, and was now feeling as if she should have brought the truth out into the open earlier – the truth that Maggie's husband, Harry, had not in fact been killed during the war on the shores of Turkey but had been lying low there, with a beautiful young woman.

Clearing her throat and fiercely suppressing her emotions, she forced herself to say: 'What if he were *not* dead? What if Harry were still alive?'

'But he is dead. And there's *nothing* we can do

about it. I love Dennis, of course I do, but there's nothing like first love. You know that. You've said so before.'

'So if he were to turn up out of the blue . . . you would give up Dennis for him. Is that what you're saying?'

'Of course I would.'

'Oh, my darling Edie . . .' Naomi sighed. 'What have I done? If I thought it would make a difference . . . if it would make you happy . . .'

'What are you saying, Nao? I don't understand.'

'Sometimes it's so hard to know what to do for the best.'

Bewildered by her aunt's behaviour, Edie could do little more than stare at her. Naomi rarely shed a tear, and here she was with her face distorted with sorrow. Finding her voice, albeit a whisper, Edie spoke without a hint of emotion. 'Are you trying to suggest that Harry's alive?'

Rising from her chair, Naomi listened at the doorway for any sound coming from Maggie and then quietly closed it. 'I think that she may have fallen asleep . . . and I also think that you might need a stiff drink, Edith.'

'No I don't. It's too early in the day. Sit down and say what you've got to say. I won't interrupt, but stop if Maggie comes in.'

'Darling, try not to be too hard on me,' said Naomi, back in her chair. 'This moment is something I've been dreading. I knew it would come one day but I didn't know when, obviously.' Then, taking a deep breath, she looked into Edie's distraught face and said, 'Yes . . . Harry is alive.'

'Say it again.'

'Edie . . .'

'Please, Aunt Naomi. Say it again . . . and then explain, and I promise not to ask questions or interrupt. I've got to know what this is all about – and before Maggie comes back into this room, which she could do any minute.'

Avoiding Edie's eyes, Naomi spoke in a quiet voice. 'Harry is alive.'

A chill swept through the very core of Edie as she waited in silence for her aunt to continue. But Naomi was no fool. This was, to her mind, the worst shock any widow could receive. After a few seconds had ticked by she reached out and placed a hand on Edie's. 'Please, don't try and be *too* brave, my darling.'

'It's all right,' said Edie. 'Just give me a minute. I'll be all right in a minute. I'm more scared of Maggie seeing me like this.'

'Darling, she's probably cried herself to sleep, which is no bad thing. Would you like a glass of water?'

'Yes, please . . . but run it first so it's properly cold.'

'Of course I will.' Feeling quite sick, Naomi crossed the kitchen, leaving Edie to stare into space while she turned on the tap and waited.

'I knew he wasn't dead,' whispered Edie, more to herself than to her aunt. 'Deep down I knew. I just knew he was alive . . . somewhere. But God help me if I had ever said so. You would all have thought I was going round the bend.

'But what I don't understand is . . . if you've known all along, why didn't you tell me? Or is it all too horrible to tell? Was he so badly injured as not to know who he is or who I am? Or is he in some god-forsaken Japanese war prison wasting away?'

'Of course not, darling,' said Naomi, placing the glass of water in Edie's trembling hand. 'In fact, Harry is all right. I just couldn't bear for you to know the truth. And I would have kept it a secret and taken it with me to my grave. But I realise now that I was wrong. We can't protect each other from everything, can we? Try though we do.'

'And what is the truth?' said Edie, frightened of what she was about to hear.

Feeling as if she were about to make a guilty confession about something terrible she had done, Naomi knew she was going to have to keep this short and to the point, for both their sakes. Drawing breath, she spoke quietly. 'Harry returned to England in the early autumn of last year. He wasn't killed in Turkey during the war, as we were led to believe. He survived the boat crash.'

Waiting for the expected fierce reaction, Naomi fell silent. But there was none, and she could see from the expression on Edie's face that she wanted to be told the whole story with no interruptions, so she continued. 'He was in fact nursed back to health . . . and once recovered decided to lie low. Not to come home. In short he duped the British authorities and became a deserter.'

'Why?' murmured Edie. 'Why did he do that? If

he was shocked and too frightened to fight again why didn't he come home in '45 when the war was over? And what, after all this time, would make him decide to come back?'

Naomi drew strength from the fact that her niece was not struck dumb. 'He came home for more reasons than one. But mostly to escape the young Turkish woman he had been living with, as man and wife.'

'No, I'm sorry, that won't do. Not Harry. He's not like that. He loved me and he couldn't wait to see his daughter. He would never 'ave stayed away all those years because of another woman. You've got it wrong.'

'Of course Harry loved you, my darling, but that was a very long time ago. And, as many soldiers were, during that dreadful time, he was tempted by the beautiful and kind young woman who had nursed him caringly. It's no reflection on what he once felt towards you.'

'All right,' said Edie, quietly and calmly, 'let's presume that all you're saying is right. Why did he come back at all? And why 'asn't he been arrested for desertion? Or has he been and you're keeping that a secret as well?'

'He came home because he wanted to feel English soil beneath his feet again, apparently. And as for being arrested – he had obtained a false passport and papers. Once here, he made his way to Cotton Street and saw that you had moved out. Ben caught sight of him lurking in the shadows and took him in. Then

Joey, who is the real reason why Harry was in the street, gave him shelter. In certain quarters it was known that Joey had taken in pacifists and those too petrified to go to war in those years. Harry was after a bed and a hiding place until he had got used to being back. But he didn't find it quite so easy to move around the streets where he once lived. Had anyone recognised him he could have been in serious trouble.'

'So Joey, and no doubt your good friend Ben, had taken him in, given him a bed and a hiding place and kept it from me. Have I been made out to be some kind of a monster or something?'

'Of course not. Harry, at first, had hoodwinked them into believing he had lost his memory out there after the boat crash.'

'Oh, come on, Nao. He suddenly gets his memory back after fifteen years? Do me a favour. And Joey's no fool. He would have known that was a load of toffee.'

'I did say *at first*, Edie. It didn't take them many days to realise that he had been telling lies. They let him believe he had pulled the wool over their eyes to keep a check on him. Obviously they were not best pleased when they found out that during this time he had been shadowing you, like a cheap detective.'

'Shadowing me? But why? Why didn't he just come up and hold out his arms? God, Nao . . . I hope you're not making this up to take my mind off Maggie and—'

'He wanted to see how the land lay first!' said Naomi, interrupting. 'Let's not forget that he had let you believe him to be dead when all the time he was very much alive and, by all accounts, enjoying an idyllic lifestyle. He knows you well and would have reached the conclusion that, being an intelligent woman and one who asks questions, you would have seen through his veil of lies. No doubt he would have had a cock-and-bull story to tell you.'

'Where is he now? I need to see him,' said Edie, the anger beginning to show in her face.

'Darling, please . . . don't be so cold towards me. I had my reasons for not telling you he was back . . . and you had at last found love with Dennis and—'

'I just want to know where he is! That's all. I need to know. Surely you can see that?'

'Yes.' Naomi sighed. 'Of course you would want to know.' Collecting herself, she spoke in a voice tinged with sorrow. 'He left England in the spring for the Canary Islands.'

An awesome silence filled the kitchen until Edie managed to say, 'He's gone abroad *again* without coming to see his own daughter?'

'Yes. I had hoped to spare you all this. Had you not touched a chord this morning I would have kept my silence. I'm so sorry, my darling.'

Leaning back in her chair, Edie muttered, 'The bastard. Fifteen long years of waiting and hoping and praying and crying. And I'm not even given the chance to smack 'im in the face.'

'You mean you would, had you the chance?'

'Of course I would! He left me to grieve for years while he was living happily with another woman!'

'Exactly.' Wishing to make the most of Edie's anger, Naomi asked whether she would like to hear more of the story. Her answer was short and to the point. She wanted to know everything. Relieved that she could now pour it all out, Naomi offered a word of caution first. 'You must not under any circumstance blame Ben or Joey for any of this.'

'Why not?' Edie retorted. 'They were *hiding* him! Treating him like a victim. Sheltering him. Feeding him. Why wouldn't I think the worst of 'em?'

'Because you have much to thank them for. They kept his return from me too . . . while they were planning the best way to rid us all of him. They realised that Harry had changed. That he had become self-centred, opinionated and a touch menacing.'

'I don't know about menacing but Harry was always a bit selfish. Not that that stopped me from loving 'im. He had his good side. He was generous, for one thing. If I needed new shoes or a new blouse he would give me the money. He wasn't a bad husband.'

How very noble, thought Naomi, as she recalled how Edie made do until her shoes could no longer be repaired. 'Of course he wasn't a bad husband, sweetheart. I know that.'

'And why did Ben and Joey decide to tell you in the end? Why didn't they just see 'im off, if he was that bad? Why did they involve you? Were they enjoying the drama? Haven't they got anything better to do with their time?'

'They kept it from me at first, Edie . . . until Harry

came here one evening when I was house-sitting. Enjoying my own company and watching the television.' A glazed look came into her eyes as she remembered the night, and she shuddered. 'He frightened me. I asked him to leave before you got back. I thought the shock of seeing him would destroy you. Then there was Dennis – you seemed at last to have found love and happiness . . .'

'He came *here*? To my home?'

'Yes. He'd been watching the flats. He knew I was alone and that you'd gone out with Dennis. He was after sheltering under *my* roof in my tiny apartment and feed from my purse. When I said no, he threatened to wait until you got back – with Dennis. I pleaded with him to leave but he just sat on the settee, grinning at me. Then something worse happened.

'There was a knock on the door and when I opened it I found a young Turkish man standing there. The very gentleman who was at Jessie's party on Christmas Eve and who kept staring at you. Shereen's cousin. Here to take Harry back to face up to his responsibilities.'

'Shereen's cousin?'

'Yes.'

'So Shereen knows about Harry too?'

'The whole Turkish family knows about Harry. His every move was being watched. I arranged with the cousin to go the following afternoon to Shereen's house. For a meeting. They wanted either to force Harry to go back to Turkey to his lover of many years, or have Cicek come over here and live with

Harry as man and wife. I told them in no uncertain terms that unless they arranged for the couple to live in the far reaches of Scotland I would not go along with their plan.'

'Jesus,' murmured Edie. 'All this was going on behind my back. I can hardly believe it. I wonder why Harry even bothered to come to England. Why didn't he just go directly to the Canary Islands?'

'It's all rather complicated. Harry had no choice other than to come to England first. His forged passport and so on,' Naomi said, waving a hand dismissively. 'His main reason for stealing away from Turkey was to get away from his woman, Cicek, who, you would be quite right to presume, he had been living with a long time.' Then, taking a long, slow breath, she added, 'She was carrying his child.'

Stunned by this next bombshell, Edie could do no more than stare open-mouthed at her aunt before eventually saying, 'Tell me that's not true, Naomi. Please tell me that the woman made it up.'

'I can't, Edie, because it is true. This was the reason the cousin came over . . . to make him stand up to his responsibilities.'

'The woman had my husband's baby?' murmured Edie, unable to take this in. 'A baby who is Maggie's sister . . . or brother?'

'Yes . . . and you've got to stop thinking of Harry as your husband. Try to think of it as you having gone through divorce proceedings all those years ago.' Pausing for a moment, she made a snap decision to tell more. 'Apparently . . . from what I heard . . . Cicek is not the first to have been left with a child. Harry, it would seem, has been sowing his oats far and wide.'

'Oh, come on now . . . that's goin' too far. And how could you know?'

'Well, actually, from Harry himself. He boasted of it to me.'

'Did he now,' said Edie, leaning back in her chair. 'The bastard. But then again . . . daft though it may seem, somehow that makes it easier to accept.'

'I see *exactly* what you mean.'

'At least we won't see any of his women wheeling Maggie's brother or sister around Stepney in a pram. I s'pose that's something to be grateful for. I take it no one else knows about all this?'

'Laura,' said Naomi without hesitation. 'And only because she also came in on that dreadful night, while Harry was here, to collect her cigarettes, which she'd left behind earlier on when we were having a small drink together. I kept her on the doorstep, making a pathetic excuse, but you know Laura . . . she came back later to see if I was all right. My self-restraint having been tested to the limit for one day, I broke down and told her what had happened. She came with me to the meeting the next day. The family respect her. They've all known each other for a very long time.'

'And that's it? Ben, Joey, you and Laura?'

'Apart from the Turks, yes. As far as I know.'

'And there's no more that I should know?'

'Well, I'm not sure whether you *should* know but I think you might want to. On the very evening after I had left Shereen's house, after the meeting, I made my way home only to discover, once I was inside, that I had an intruder under my roof. Not that there were any signs whatsoever apart from the fact that there was hot water in my kettle. Harry had forced a window with his penknife and let himself in. Once I had got over the shock I asked him to leave but in the end agreed to him staying for a week until the rented rooms he said he would be going to had been vacated.'

'He *broke* into your home? Harry did *that*?' Edie could hardly believe it.

'Yes, I'm sorry to say that he did. I could easily have had a heart attack when he appeared in my kitchen doorway. I kept out of his way and yours for most of the week and we spent little time together. After he left I didn't see him again until the night of Maggie's fifteenth birthday party. When Ben and a friend of his took Harry to Wapping and saw him on to a cargo ship bound for Gran Canaria.'

'But why, Nao? Why did they help him escape to an island in the sun? I thought they were our friends?'

'They weren't helping him, sweetheart. They were banishing him from your world. He could have caused so much trouble. He would certainly have gone to prison for a very long time had he been caught, or if he had turned up on your doorstep and you hadn't informed the authorities. You too might well have been up in court for fraud and deception. You've been receiving a widow's pension for a very long time, my darling.'

'That's true,' said Edie, trying to make sense of it all. 'And you say he was *here*? At Maggie's party?'

'No, my darling. Not *at* the party – although if Ben and Joey had arrived on the scene a few minutes later than they did, he might well have sneaked in for devilment. They had arranged to take him to the ship but he had slipped their net earlier that evening and made his way here. Ben felt sure this would be where he was heading and he was right. He and Alf—'

'Alf?'

'Alf the Overcoat is Laura's full name for him. You remember . . . he was at her Christmas party, flirting with me. We got on like a house on fire. I hadn't realised then, of course, that this wonderful man who was full of fun was also a member of the local criminal fraternity. Which of course makes him even more of a star. Without his help I can't imagine what the consequences might have been.'

'And they found Harry—'

'Yes. They found him lingering down below, smoking a cigarette, watching the comings and goings, and according to Alf he had every intention of gatecrashing before he left to catch the boat.'

'Well,' said Edie, breathing out heavily, 'he *has* changed. You're right – that was a wicked thing to do. Turn up as if from 'is grave and on Maggie's birthday. Perhaps he did get a knock on the head out there when that boat crashed?'

Preoccupied with her own thoughts, Naomi spoke as if talking to herself. 'Shereen has washed her hands of the whole thing . . . I told her he had disappeared and we have not spoken a word of it since. I've only seen her three or four times, in any case. While out shopping and once when arranging for my new frock to be made.'

'And they're not angry with any of us?'

'They never were . . . they remain as friendly as ever. If anything they feel sorry for all three of us. Especially you.'

'I can understand that,' said Edie, leaning back in her chair. 'They must 'ave been embarrassed once they found out that I was the deserted wife. You really 'ave been fighting my corner, haven't you. It couldn't 'ave been easy. I'm sorry for snapping at you like that.'

'Oh, Edie, darling, *please* don't apologise to me. I would risk life and limb for you and for Maggie. You're all I've got. And I love you both dearly.'

'I know you do. And we love you. Poor Maggie. The only time she had any contact with her dad was when she was a newborn baby, during his two-day compassionate leave from the army. And even then, if truth be told, his paternal instincts were a bit wooden.'

'Yes, but now she has Dennis.' Naomi smiled.

'Now she has Dennis. I feel even closer to him after all this. It's made me realise how lucky I am to 'ave found him.'

'And how lucky he is to have found *you*.'

'I know.' She lifted her eyes to look into Naomi's. 'And you do like 'im, don't you?'

'Of course I do,' said Naomi, keeping her true feelings to herself. She had never entirely trusted Dennis but hadn't yet come to any conclusion as to why not. He just seemed a little too shifty for her liking. The word 'fugitive' had crossed her mind more than once. There was something about him that didn't feel right. Something she could not put her finger on.

'He is unobtrusive in his own quiet way and my only gripe about him was when he proposed on Valentine's Day, after having known you only two months. I didn't think I could trust such a person to marry my niece. But he *has* proved himself. He is steady, sensible and not *overly* demonstrative. What more could I ask for you?'

'You couldn't, Nao, honest to God, you couldn't. He is a lovely man. Gentle and kind. It's not been a whirlwind of passion, but I love him. Not in the way I loved Harry, but I just feel that we're right for each other.'

'Which at *your* age is how it should be. And all I want is for you to be happy again. You've been through too much heartache for one person already.'

When the news that Harry was missing, presumed dead, had first reached Edie, she had been in shock for some time. She had rejected outright any suggestion that one day she would find someone else to take his place, and until recently all thoughts of romance or marriage had been pushed to the farthest depths of her mind. Now, having given in to the warmth of a man's love, she was determined not to let anything spoil what she and Dennis had.

Harry, the man she had vowed to be faithful to, had, after all was said and done, deliberately led everyone to believe that he had been drowned at sea during the Second World War with no conscience whatsoever. By playing dead for just over fourteen years, however, while enjoying himself in the coastal village of Oludeniz in southern Turkey, he had in a way sentenced himself to a very long term in prison. On his return to Britain, it had soon become apparent to him that his only option, other than to be perpetually on the run from the authorities, was to accept life as an expatriate in some other part of the world.

The threat of a heavy prison sentence for desertion and procuring false papers and a passport was the chief reason why Harry, with his possessions in a holdall, had finally boarded a freight ship at Wapping bound for Gran Canaria, arrangements having been made by Naomi's chums for a fifty-year-old cockney, who divided his time between England and Gran Canaria, to meet him there.

After a long and uncomfortable journey, his Aran-knit sweater stuffed into his travelling bag, wearing only a string vest and grey flannels, Harry had strolled off the filthy cargo boat at Gran Canaria eager to begin a new life miles away from Turkey and England – living where he believed he would be a prince among peasants. Peering around the bustling, noisy port of

Gran Canaria in search of his contact, he had sneered at the locals on the dockside and shuddered at the pervasive stink of raw fish and foul-smelling drains.

The sound of a cockney voice had been music to his ears. Turning on his heels, Harry had been over-joyed to see someone of his own nationality who, from his accent, was clearly from his own neck of the woods. His smile had dissolved, however, once he had learned that his journey was not at an end. The cockney, wearing a white shortsleeved shirt to show off his tan, had artfully cajoled Harry's passport from him and then, his gold watch glinting in the sunshine, pointed to a ferry. Walking beside him at an easy pace and with a carefree manner he had chatted non-stop about the lovely island of Fuerteventura for which Harry was bound.

Having seen his ward safely aboard, the man had left him with a snack and something to drink, prom-ising to return once he had jumped formalities and had his passport stamped. Fifteen minutes later, when the engine of the ferry had started up, Harry had been fidgety, craning his neck as he peered along the dockside to catch a sign of the man. He had consid-ered him to be a flash bastard who had overly talked up the island of Fuerteventura. Throughout his patter the cockney had said more than once that the island he was bound for was on the brink of an economic boom and that there would be plenty of work and decent accommodation.

Opening a bottle of beer with his teeth, Harry had stretched his legs and quietly chuckled to himself. As far as he was concerned, even if Naomi's cronies had double-crossed him and the island he was going to was a let-down, it would surely be a far better place than the war-damaged and filthy East End of London. He had also comforted himself with the thought that should the island not be to his taste, he could always slip down into the lower deck of a boat to catch a ride to somewhere else. To Harry's way of thinking, anyone, anywhere, could be bribed. He had discovered this not only in the East End of London but in Turkey too.

Once he had settled down on the ferry his imagination of better things to come had taken over as he pictured sexy, sun-kissed Hispanic whores at his feet, whores who he had felt sure would charge no more than a few pesetas for their services, if they charged a good-looking Englishman like himself at all. With three hundred pounds in his pocket (a pay-off from Naomi for him to get out of Edie's life and out of the country) he had considered himself a gentleman of means who could afford to stay in the best hotel until he had found himself a woman to wait on him hand and foot. With his eyes closed, and ignoring the Spanish peasants around him on the ferry, Harry had cheerfully imagined the good life to come – a big comfortable bed, crisp white sheets, marble floors, Spanish bars, restaurants and live music.

The only accommodation that Harry had seen on arrival, however, apart from the one and only lodging house masquerading as a hotel, had been seedy

seamen's hostels. Plans for super hotels in Fuerteventura, like those on other islands in the Canaries,
had not even reached the drawing-board stage. His
expectations of the place had been shattered from
the moment the ferry docked in the port. No one
had spoken a word of English and everyone had eyed
him with suspicion. Now, having been on the island
for a few months and got over the initial shock of
the islanders not understanding one word of his
native tongue, he was settling into a certain way of
life in a world where the sun shone every day and
which suited him very nicely.

On arrival, Harry had trudged uphill through the
oldest part of the town, past the market and through
narrow alleys and between dilapidated houses, until
he had found the quiet side streets which had been
far more to his liking. But this area, where lovely flower-
ing shrubs and the tops of trees were partly hidden
behind old brick walls, had been purpose-built some
years earlier to house select residential properties in
which the more prosperous islanders could and did
live. Gazing at the whitewashed houses, Harry had
thought of himself one day settling in such a place,
where he would not be a prince among peasants but
a king amidst kings.

It hadn't taken him long to reach the conclusion
that on this island money spoke volumes, and that it
was no different in this respect to England. Compared
to the majority of the locals he was a rich man, and
he had every intention of remaining so. Soon after
he had arrived he had decided that he would not

waste a penny of his remuneration from Naomi. That he would start by living in a simple room in order to blend in with the natives and find out who was who, until he had been accepted as the quiet, mysterious English gentleman who strode around with a certain aura of importance and who was to be held in high esteem.

On one of his walks uphill from the port-side where he was presently lodging, Harry had passed a church surrounded by relatively grand buildings which housed the island's administration, the courthouse and the parliament. As he stopped to soak in the historic atmosphere, another idea had come to him. If he was to be accepted into this community he should be seen at the church services – a humble Christian from England who had found solace in a Catholic church; a lonely spirit who, it would appear, was interested to know more about this sacred place which had apparently touched his soul.

Believing himself to be the only Englishman to have settled in this ancient part of the world, Harry had no idea that others had been there before him. In 1924 the notorious Don Miguel de Unamuno, a university lecturer and writer who had been exiled to the island for criticising the Spanish establishment, had had an English friend to stay, a writer and translator, Mr Crawford-Flitch. This gentle man had stayed with Don Miguel for six weeks at the fine seventeenth-century lodging house known as the Hotel Fuerteventura, in which time both writers had enjoyed not only the local food but walking together and private readings of their prose. During the years that followed more writers and painters had found their way to what they liked to think of as their secret place in the sun.

During his travels around the island Harry had been impressed by the talented local people whom he had every intention of befriending, if for no other reason than to profit from their skills. Within the first few months he had watched with interest the poverty-stricken women and girls sitting outside their simple homes in the poorer areas, weaving rugs, donkey blankets or wall hangings by hand or on small home-made looms. He had also watched men and boys carving pieces of timber to create decorative items for the home, and he had been particularly impressed by the older generation, who were adept at basket-weaving and making rag rugs.

The place which had finally convinced him that he would become a businessman was a small pottery in a remote location where simple jars, dishes and plates were turned and baked in a basic kiln within a time-worn one-storey stone building. The idea of exporting the local arts and crafts made and decorated by the peasants to Gran Canaria, where they could be sold to the middle-class tourists, had started as a possibility and grown into a grand vision. With this thought forever in his mind he continued to travel around the island in search of more talent, on foot or hitching a lift on donkey-drawn carts but refusing rides on the back of camels, which Harry considered to be smelly and repulsive.

Having journeyed as far afield as Corralejo, a small town with a harbour which still had the feel of a fishing village, he believed himself to be in seventh heaven. Bathing in the midday sun in one of the local sandy bays he considered that this might well be the place for him to hang his hat. A ten-minute walk from here would take him to white sandy beaches and wandering dunes. His imagination in full flow, he had fancied himself living in one of the town's simple houses, from where he would conduct his arts and craft trade.

The quizzical, wry looks that had at first been bestowed on Harry by the islanders had slowly been replaced by vague smiles of mutual respect. This change had come about not simply through familiarity but also through the way he now presented himself as a true English gentleman. Having purchased several white shortsleeved cotton shirts, lightweight slacks and tan leather sandals in the market, he could afford to wear a clean set of clothes every day. His laundry, taken care of by a local woman, cost next to nothing.

Now, at siesta time, on his bed in his simple rented rooms above a bakery opposite the entrance to Rosario port, Harry was drifting into a light doze, an image of Edie wandering through his mind. With no sense of guilt whatsoever at having betrayed her, he imagined his wife and their lovely daughter Maggie living in one of the houses either here in Rosario or in Corralejo. To his mind, the fact that Edie had waited so long before courting another man meant only one thing. That her love for him was by no means dead.

'Soon, Edie, darling,' he murmured, before going asleep, 'soon.'

# 3

On her way to work, with the early morning sun on her face, Maggie enjoyed a sudden surge of warmth as she walked in the footsteps of two young mothers, who were pushing their prams and chatting happily as they strolled through the Bethnal Green gardens. She resisted the desire to catch up with them and take a peep at their babies. Up until this moment she had been thinking about the weekend and how right it had been to have laid her cards on the table where her mother and her Aunt Naomi were concerned. She knew them well enough to realise that they would go on discussing alternative solutions, and felt sure that they would both eventually agree that her baby must be kept and loved by all three of them.

Pushing open the heavy oak-and-glass door of the Bethnal Green library, she promised herself that she would, at the end of this week, break it to Tony that he was to be a father. She had intended to tell him on their picnic over the weekend but had simply not had the courage. She was nervous that he would reject her outright. Adjusting the white button-up cardigan she was wearing over her straight skirt, Maggie checked her stomach and pulled it in a little as she

walked into the staffroom. Looking up from the newspaper she was reading, her friend Rita raised an
eyebrow. 'You're five minutes early for a change.
What're you after? A rise?'

'Too right,' said Maggie, giving her friend a wink.
'I'm taking a leaf out of your book. You're always here
when I get in. I want a gold star as well.'

'Some chance of that,' returned Rita, a touch
despondent. 'I come in early because it's better to sit
in the quiet than having to listen to them two goin'
on.'

'Your mum and dad don't row first thing, surely?'
said Maggie, peering at her reflection in a small mirror
on the wall and pushing her hair into place.

'They hardly ever row – that's the trouble.
Sometimes I wish they would. They just dig at each
other all the time . . . till he threatens her with a fist
raised.' Leaning back in her chair, Rita lowered her
voice almost to a whisper. 'If he ever does lay a punch
on 'er face I'll go down for murder. He goads and
goads till she loses 'er temper. All he's waiting for is
an excuse to give 'er a good hiding and say it was in
self-defence.'

Taken a back by her friend's uncharacteristic confession, Maggie was, for a moment, lost for words.
Then, seeing the expression of despair on Rita's face,
she said, 'He wouldn't get away with that, Reet. She's
a woman after all and hardly the robust type. You're
letting your imagination get the better of your
common sense.'

'You wouldn't say that if you lived there. I've seen

the way she looks at him at times. She hates 'im – and I don't blame 'er for it. What if she picks up a -kitchen knife and threatens him in the face with it? Plenty of women in 'er position would do.'

'Well, then you should try and get her to leave him and be done with it.' Maggie tested the brown teapot with the tip of her finger. 'Good. The tea's still hot. I'm gasping.'

'I've only just made it.' Rita's light blue eyes bored into Maggie's face. 'How can she leave 'im? Where's she s'posed to go? And why *should* she leave 'er own home? That miserable old sod should go, not her. His woman from two streets away won't 'ave 'im under 'er roof so that tells you something. He knows where 'is bread's buttered all right. That's the trouble. Uses our house as if it's his board and lodging and no more.'

Maggie gave her friend a sympathetic smile and decided to keep her thoughts to herself. To her mind, even though Rita's mother was perhaps lonely at times, she was much better off not having a sponger always in her shadow. 'Never mind, Reet,' she said finally as she poured her tea. 'Your mum's a lovely woman. And attractive. Maybe she'll find someone else to love and care for 'er.'

'Chance'd be a fine fing. She does three cleaning jobs a day. She's not gonna find a bloke while she's scrubbing floors in offices, is she?'

'She must go out sometimes for a bit of social life, surely? Or hasn't she got any friends?' Sitting down opposite Rita at the small staffroom table, Maggie could see from her friend's expression that her mother was indeed very much alone in this world. 'What about the cleaning jobs? Hasn't she made any friends there? Workmates . . . that sort of thing?'

'No, as it happens. No one ever comes to our house, except her sister now and then. And anyway, Mum's so tired after a day's work it's as much as she can do to eat the dinner she's cooked for us. She listens to a bit of wireless and then goes abed. And *he* sneaks off to 'is bit on the side.'

'And stays out all night?'

'Oh no . . . his tart wouldn't let him get his shoes under her bed. No. She's got it all worked out. He eats and sleeps at home so she only gets 'im for amusement. They go to a little pub over Mile End. He's bin seen there with 'er. He knows which side is bread's buttered.' Having paused for breath, Rita went on, 'I need to find a way of earning more money so we can lock 'im out of a night. He don't give 'er much but what he does give pays the rent.'

'Go on the game, then,' joked Maggie, trying to lift her friend's spirits. 'A couple of girls from our school 'ave done that, you know. Soon as they left they was up Aldgate flashing a stocking top. Do all right as well from what I've seen of 'em parading along the Waste in their nice clothes.'

'I wouldn't give men the satisfaction! All they think about is what's between their legs from what I can make out. Fancy saying a thing like that!'

'Oh, come on, Reet. I was kidding.'

Anyway . . . we can manage. At least I'm earning

a few bob now – so Mum should be able to give up one of 'er cleaning jobs soon. My sister's 'usband's doing all right now. He's got plenty of work and he's not tight like *him*. Them with the money are wanting to 'ave their 'ouses painted inside and out. Soon she won't 'ave to rely on a new apron to cover 'er old baggy frocks. Me and my older sister'll see to that.'

'I'm sorry, Reet,' said Maggie as she sipped her tea. 'I didn't realise things were this bad.'

'It's all right. I'm not so worried now. Things'll change soon.' Rita closed the morning newspaper borrowed from the reading room and folded it neatly. 'If he don't move out we will. Mum can put in for an exchange and be nearer to 'er sister. My aunt and uncle live in Leyton.' A faint smile spread across Rita's face. 'I love my aunt and uncle – they've never got on with Dad. Never liked 'im neither.' She looked into Maggie's face and continued in a more earnest voice, 'I've never been able to work my dad out. I was about to go into our little front room the other day. Can't remember why, mind you . . . we hardly use it. S'posed to be for when visitors come. Some chance of that. He was standing in the half-dark with the framed picture of their wedding day in 'is 'ands – gazing at it. Then he tossed it on to the old settee. When he turned round and saw me in the doorway, he looked straight through me, as if I wasn't there. Then he went out and slammed the street door shut. I felt as if I'd read his mind. I'm sure he wishes I'd never been born. I'm probably the excuse he uses to himself for not having left her.'

'Oh, Reet, don't say that.'

'Why not? It's the truth. She's only just turned forty and she's still lovely looking. Nice clothes is all she needs. Nice clothes and freedom to marry someone who loves her.'

The staffroom door suddenly flew open and brought a brief silence to the room. The forty-three-year-old chief librarian, Mathew Browning, tall and lean, stood in the doorway. Looking sternly from Maggie to Rita, he cleared his throat and then pulled his silver fob from his pocket and watched as the second hand ticked round.

Glancing slyly at each other, the girls stood up and together said, 'Good morning, Mr Browning.'

'Good morning. One minute more and about your duties, if you please.'

'Yes, Mr Browning.'

'And let us remember as we do each day why we are here. That it is our charge to make available for enjoyment and learning the work of our authors, poets and playwrights, who have toiled through the long night with pen in hand in order to give the people of this country their work of fiction. Let us always respect the books in this library and help others to do the same.'

'Yes, Mr Browning,' said Maggie.

Rita, touched by his gullibility, smiled at him, saying, 'You could be a poet, Mr Browning . . . the way you say things sometimes.'

'Who knows what we may or may not be,' was his modest response. 'Good girls. Excellent.' With that he turned, pulled open the door and strode out – his regular footsteps echoing as the steel-capped heels of his shoes struck the old tiled floor of the entrance hall.

'He's like somefing out of the Ark,' said Rita, shaking her head and smiling.

'I know. What I can't make out is the smell that's on 'is clothes. It's a strange mix of . . . I'm not sure what.'

'Old books and mothballs,' said Rita. 'His 'ouse is probably just like this place. Shelves and shelves of books. Right. Let's get out there before he comes back in with 'is cane.'

'Or makes us put a copper in the penalty box for slackness. I've got something to tell you, by the way. About me.'

'Save it for lunch break. I can go to the café. I've just about got enough to buy a cheese sandwich and a cup of tea.'

'Me as well. Come on, let's move ourselves.'

As they walked out of the staffroom they came face to face with Mr Browning again. He was stretched to full height, his hands clasped in front of him, an expression of warning on his face. Smiling graciously at him, the girls went quietly about their duties while he walked slowly through and around his beloved library, checking that his staff were in place and everything was in perfect order. It was important to this gentleman that every book on every shelf should be level with the one beside it. The chief librarian was proud of his position and took his responsibilities seriously.

As a child living in a nearby street, he had personally been involved in the comings and goings of this place – and as a young man had watched while this Georgian building had been converted from a lunatic asylum into what he considered to be one of the finest libraries in England. Set within Bethnal Green park, the grounds, enclosed by tall hedges and trees, had been and still were known within the East End as Barmy Park, a place visited by poor people from Whitechapel, Ratcliffe, St George's, Wapping and other parishes; people who had been coming to Cambridgeheath Road for decades simply to stroll along the tree-lined avenue and take in the sweet air and the scent of cut grass – a marked contrast to the filth and degradation of the backstreets and noisy, smelly markets and factories.

To Mathew Browning, the stained-glass window on the main staircase of the library was the jewel in this crown. To this he privately paid homage each morning on arrival – by way of the Lord's Prayer. While making fun of him and his ministerial ways, what Maggie and Rita could not know was that Mathew Browning had every reason to be proud of his position in this particular building. Prior to its conversion, his mother had been confined in the asylum, where she eventually died. During his regular visits the chief librarian, aged around ten years old, was known locally as Young Mattie. After his mother had passed away he had continued to visit those inmates he had come to know.

The experience for himself, his younger sister and

his mother during her time here had been a pleasant enough one, all things considered. The patients' diet had been healthy enough, and the sitting rooms and dormitories for the pauper inmates clean, warm and well ventilated. Just three years after his mother's death, the patients had been removed to Salisbury, and the following year the site had been purchased and turned into this library. All that Mr Browning and his sister had to remind them of their poor doting mother's last years was this building and the adjoining two-storeyed house, known as the Cottage, also used by the mentally ill. And all that Mattie Browning had dreamt of all those years ago when the changes were being made was of becoming the chief librarian in this building, which he considered to be a monument to his mother and those with mental illness who came before and after her.

That lunchtime, as the girls walked arm in arm to a nearby café in Bethnal Green Road, their casual conversation was mostly to do with Mr Browning and his assistant, the spinster Miss Lightfoot. They had been seen holding hands in the basement room by Maggie while she was on a mission in search of old local maps. Had Mr Browning not been brusque with her, out of embarrassment, she probably wouldn't have taken too much notice, but after he had drawn her attention in this way she had glanced at Miss Lightfoot to see her blushing at having been seen holding his hand.

Having related this story, Maggie, settled in the café with Rita at a table for two by a steamed-up window, with their tea and cheese sandwiches, felt guilty for telling tales. But Rita would have none of it. 'I always did fink he was a bit of a dark 'orse,' she said, in between puffs on a Woodbine cigarette.

'He might just be really shy,' said Maggie, taking the cigarette from her friend for a drag. 'I don't think he's as old as you reckon. Can't blame 'im for enjoying a little bit of romance. He's not made of stone.'

Rita took back her cigarette and sucked on it. 'The fing is,' she said, puffing smoke upwards, 'Miss Lightfoot's really nice once she opens up. Just very shy, that's all. She reminds me of my mum in that way.'

'Oh well, it takes all kinds,' said Maggie. 'Anyway . . . what about you? What's 'appened to your 'andsome Mr Wonderful? Blond Patrick with the bluer-than-blue eyes.'

'I chucked 'im. Too much of a flirt. So what was you gonna tell me, then?'

'Dunno. What was I gonna tell yer?'

'Oh, don't muck about. If you've got nothing to say, say so.'

'I'm pregnant. Will that do? Is that straightforward enough for yer?' Maggie held her friend's gaze and enjoyed her moment of glory. She had rocked the unshakeable.

'That'd better be a joke,' said Rita.

'No,' said Maggie, leaning back and biting into her sandwich. 'I'm coming up three months.'

'You say fings like that,' warned Rita, pointing a finger, 'and it might come true.'

Maggie smiled and then sipped her tea. 'It is true.'

'So why are you grinning, then? You're fifteen, for God's sake. That's too young to be having a baby! And anyway – just because you might 'ave missed a period or two it don't mean a thing. I know lots of girls who that's 'appened to. You only started when you was fourteen and a half. It's your body sorting itself out.'

'I've 'ad morning sickness. And I'm putting it on around the belly. Mum's all right about it. I've already told 'er. And my Aunt Naomi. They're deciding what's for the best, but I already know what I'm gonna do.'

'Stop telling lies. It's not funny and it don't suit you.'

'I'm not telling lies.' Maggie placed one hand on her heart, saying, 'Honest to God. I'm in the club. On my mother's life . . . I really am pregnant.'

'You *think* you are, more like.'

'No. I am. I was gonna kill myself but the trouble with that is that I wouldn't want Mum or Aunt Naomi to find me in bed after taking an overdose or in the bath dead from drowning. And if I walked out in front of a bus they'd 'ave to identify the body and that would devastate 'em. And I couldn't slit my wrists neither. I mean . . . how horrible would that be for Mum?'

'Maggie, you silly cow. You really *are* being serious. You are up the spout.'

'I might just go away where nobody knows me and walk into the sea,' Maggie continued, gazing at nothing, in a world of her own. 'It's the only thing I can think of if things don't work out as I want them to. I'll cut labels out of me clothes and make sure there's nuffin' in me lodgin' room to identify me. That way no one'll know I'm dead.'

'Well,' said Rita, 'I think that's really thoughtful of yer. I should go for that option, if I was you. What d'yer want . . . if you don't top yerself? A boy or a girl?'

'I don't mind as long as it's all right.'

'Mmm. That's what they all seem to say, so I s'pose there's somefing in it. Bloody hell . . . fifteen and with a bun in the oven. I wouldn't want to be in your shoes.'

'I'll be *sixteen* by the time it's born.'

'You're gonna make the gossip column . . . unless you act quick and get rid of it.'

'I would never do a thing like that. And nor would you.'

'Oh, right,' said Rita, sipping her drink. 'You fancy living with a screaming baby stinking of sick and you know what, do yer? And then running round after a snotty-nosed kid once it can crawl and then walk. Yeah, I can just picture it . . . the poky kitchen wiv a line across it and a row of wet nappies drying. Never mind all the breast feeding.'

'Tony'll be there with me. He'll help.'

Rita slowly shook her head. 'You're mad to even fink about having it. You can't even get married till you're sixteen if you wed in Scotland, and eighteen in England. If you want to get married, that is. I wouldn't, but then you're not me.'

'Light another cigarette,' said Maggie, 'and stop preaching. Try to be nice to me. I'm suicidal, don't forget.'

Rita peered into her packet of five and said, 'I've only got two left.'

'I'll buy a packet of five Weights tomorrer and we'll share 'em.'

'Woodbines. Weights are like puffing sawdust.'

'And Woodbines are a man's smoke. Or certain women who like to draw on a pipe.'

'Woodbines or I won't light up.'

'Oh, all right, then.'

'So . . . what are you gonna do, then, little Miss Sexpot?' Rita grinned. 'You know you could be taken into care for this. Not prison exactly, but it'll be just as bad. You're under age, Miss Birchfield.'

'Oh, am I? I never knew that! Thank you so much for telling me!' Leaning forward, Maggie lowered her voice. 'You see . . . my Italian lover didn't tell me anyfing about how old you're supposed to be . . . and at the time I never thought to ask. Don't know why.'

Rita lit another cigarette and then held up the burning match. 'Stop trying to be funny. And if you don't 'ave an abortion and soon, your "Italian lover" will blow you out as simply as this.' She gave out a tiny puff of air but the match flame simply danced a little in the breeze and continued to burn – and to burn her finger. The singed tip was now in her mouth.

'So,' said Maggie, 'I've got three options. Abortion, adoption or living with my Italian lover and our baby in a little love nest tucked away from the rest of the world. What would you choose?'

'I know exactly what I'd do. But I'm not you, am I? And you're not me. This library job's just the beginning as far as I'm concerned.'

'Beginning of what?' Maggie took the cigarette from Rita's fingers, had a puff and then gave it back. 'Well, go on, then. What does *your* future hold in store?'

'A lot more than yours, by the sound of things. I go to evening classes at Morpeth School, if you want to know. Commerce. Shorthand and typing. I'm aiming to be a personal secretary to someone famous – for the money. 'Cos that's what I want. Money to buy me and Mum out of Poverty Place and into somewhere really nice. And by the time I'm eighteen, I'll be driving a little car.'

'So . . . you're a secret learner,' said Maggie, impressed. 'Creeping off to evening classes and not saying a word about it.'

'The term's only just started and I love it. Learning the keyboard is easier than learning the alphabet. And the shorthand is gonna be brilliant. Just like learning another language. I can already write "Abe paid the debt" with just a few lines and squiggles.'

'I should 'ave known you'd want a career. I don't blame you.'

'Well, there's nothing to stop you doing the same thing. If it's what you want. Learning's free.'

'So's love. Finish your tea before it's stone cold. We've got to get back.'

The girls left the café to the sound of quiet asides and soft laughter from a group of older women who had been listening to their conversation. With their arms linked, they walked back to the library and chatted about Rita's evening class and a world outside the only one they had ever known within the East End of London. A world where celebrities and wealthy businessmen reigned supreme. A world of which Rita hoped to be part one day, and a marked contrast to the life that Maggie was now faced with. Whether Rita had meant to sow a seed of doubt or not, Maggie had absorbed all that she had said. This was a turning point, and depending on which choice she made her future would be decided. As she pushed open the main door of the library, another of her Aunt Naomi's sayings drifted through her mind – 'You are a long time dead, my darling. A long time dead.'

By mid-afternoon, after a busy spell and with nothing else on her mind other than the job in hand, Maggie stood beside Miss Lightfoot as she stamped those books which were being taken out. She felt that her senior was being more friendly than usual. When she had returned from the café with Rita she had received a gentle smile from the woman instead of her usual studious look, which tended to make her appear as if she was always deep in thought. Taking her by surprise, Miss Lightfoot opened up a little more than usual. In a quiet voice, she said, 'I wonder if you could give me a little advice, Margaret. I've written out a card to be pinned on the library notice-board and I'm not sure if I've worded it right.'

'A card?' asked Maggie, intrigued. 'What sort of a card?'

'Oh, just a plain white one. We need someone to come in for a few hours each week to polish the brass and so on. Light duties, nothing heavy. Mrs Flinch never seems to find time and it would make such a difference.'

'But surely if you paid 'er for extra time she'd manage. Wouldn't she?'

A soft smile broke out on her senior's face. 'Well, yes . . . but I don't think she would be very good at polishing brass. I'm afraid she thinks it rather a waste of time.'

The image of the robust, short woman who always poured too much bleach down the lavatory pan taking her time with delicate and intricate brass finger-plates on doors amused Maggie. 'I can see that she might not 'ave the patience for it. Let's have a look at it, then.'

'It's rather straight and to the point, but I couldn't think of any other way to word it,' said Miss Lightfoot as she pulled the small white card from under a piece of blotting paper. 'I'll read it to you, shall I?'

'If you like.'

Looking at the card, the woman recited its contents as if she were on a small platform. 'Someone needed to polish brass and wood. Four hours per week. Enquire at desk.'

'Sounds all right to me,' said Maggie, shrugging. 'Short and to the point is good.'

'Oh, well; thank you.' Miss Lightfoot bore an expression of relief and pride. 'I'll pin it up straight away.'

'Actually . . . now you come to mention it. The noticeboard . . . do you think it would be all right if I put a small leaflet up? It's got nothing to do with books or anything, mind.'

'Well, I should think it would be all right, Margaret, depending on *exactly* what it's to do with, of course.' The spinster looked and sounded a touch worried.

'Tea dances to be held at St Peter's church hall. My great-aunt and a couple of 'er friends are organising them.'

With raised eyebrows and an expression of pleasant surprise, Miss Lightfoot revealed another side of herself. In her eyes Maggie could see childish fascination. 'Goodness me,' she whispered, 'how very enterprising.'

'That's exactly what I thought and why I'm helping out. Do you think that people would be interested?'

'Oh, I'm sure lots of our readers would be thrilled. One doesn't want to try to turn back the clock, but to attempt the revival of something that was once very popular is such a lovely thought. Of course you must display it in the library, Margaret.'

'Oh, right,' said Maggie, a touch bemused by her senior's enthusiasm. 'My aunt will be pleased. I've got one in my handbag that I was gonna ask our local greengrocer's to put up. I'll display it here instead.'

'Why not? Excellent.' Miss Lightfoot was positively glowing at the thought of it. 'It does get a little stuffy in the library,' she added, confidentially. 'A bit of light relief goes a long way.'

'I couldn't agree more. Variety being the spice of

life and all that.' Another thought crossed her mind. Maggie considered whether this was the right time to put something else to her colleague and strike while the iron was hot. Not being one to put things off until the morrow, she said, 'Actually, I think I might know just the person to come in and polish the brass. Rita's mum. She's an office cleaner, but apart from that I've seen the way she brings her letter box and that up like gold and in no time at all. I'll tell Rita to mention it, shall I? And she can pop in to see you.'

'Well, that would be rather convenient, I must say. Yes, please do mention it to Rita.' Then after a little pause during which she studied Maggie's face, Miss Lightfoot said, 'Margaret, I do hope you didn't get the wrong impression earlier on.'

Maggie knew exactly what she was referring to and did her best to sound casual as she said, 'You holding Mr Browning's hand, you mean?'

'Well, I wasn't actually holding it, just—'

'It doesn't matter. Holding hands is a nice, friendly thing to do.'

'Well, no, of course it doesn't matter, no. You're quite right, it's just that—'

'You don't 'ave to explain anything to me, Miss Lightfoot. It's none of my business. We're bound to cross shadows now and then . . . working close together the way we do.'

'Well, exactly,' replied the woman, thoughtfully. 'We are all part of a team.'

'You was comforting Mr Browning, that's all. You might find yourself comforting me one day.'

'Oh, I doubt that would ever happen. It would be nice, mind you. For me, I mean.'

'Has Mr Browning had some bad news, then? Is that why you were giving him friendly support?'

'No . . . nothing like that,' was the touching reply. Miss Lightfoot glanced at Maggie cautiously, as if wondering whether she could trust her. 'It's this building, really . . . and the grounds. Some recollections grow stronger with time, whereas others simply fade away.' Then, without thinking, she patted Maggie's hand, saying, 'Take no notice of a foolish old maid. I tend to ramble now and then.'

'You're not a fool, Miss Lightfoot, and not old either.'

'Well . . . perhaps not, but I am a spinster, so people do tend to—'

'Blow what people think. You don't walk around *looking* like an old maid like some do. And anyway, you should be proud of being independent.'

Adjusting a neat pile of books, a coy expression on her face, the woman broke into a smile. 'Actually, you're not the first to have said that, so I suppose I should take more notice of it. My brother has said it to me several times and in different ways.'

'Your brother?'

'My only brother. There are just the two of us. We see each other on a daily basis and most weekends . . . so really it's only the evenings when I sometimes wish I had more than my own silence for company. My brother has a flat in Stratford and I live in Forest Gate.' The woman blushed slightly and turned her face away. 'We hadn't set out to work within the same building, you understand . . . it just happened that way.'

'I don't understand . . .' said Maggie, puzzled. 'Are you talking about *this* library?'

'Yes, I am as a matter of fact. You see, Mr Browning is my brother. Lightfoot is my pen name. I first used it when I wrote a book . . . my first and last book. It was a bit of a flop, I'm afraid. When I came here to work we – my brother and myself – decided it best not to let it be known to the staff or our library members that we were related. It might have seemed, to some, to be a touch unprofessional. One can never tell.'

'And that was why you was holding Mr Browning's hand.' Maggie smiled. 'I think that's really nice. A down-to-earth sisterly gesture. You shouldn't be embarrassed over it.'

'Well, no, but there we are. But really . . . it was a little unprofessional. It's just that Mattie was a touch maudlin over things that had happened in our past. Today is the day, many years ago, of course, on which our mother died.'

'Oh God . . .' Maggie sighed, her eyes closed momentarily. 'And I barged in at a time like that—'

'Oh, goodness me, no,' said Miss Lightfoot. 'Not at all. You had every right to be there. And I'm rather glad you did come in now, to be perfectly honest. It's given me a reason to bring it out into the open. I know my brother would prefer it if you would keep it to yourself for the time being, but you needn't feel—'

'Of course I will. If you don't want people to know,

that's your business. I won't say a word. And that's a promise. Not one word.'

'Thank you, Margaret. You're a very kind and thoughtful girl.'

'I do my best,' Maggie said shyly. Then, raising her eyes, she nodded at a sign which hung on the panelled wall and whispered to her senior, 'Speech is silver but silence is golden.'

# 4

In her kitchen, preoccupied with the dilemma of what to do about Maggie, Edie had been going through her own private turmoil, and had no idea that her neighbour and soulmate, Jessie Smith from the fourth floor, was anything other than content with life when she knocked on her door seeking a little creature comfort. The two women, who had so much in common where their husbands were concerned, had become close friends, and tea for two, in either of their kitchens, was something they both valued.

Now settled in her new home with Max and her two children, Jessie was having to deal with the problem of her husband Tom, from whom she was separated. On Sunday evening, when she called to pick up her children from her in-laws, Emmie and Charlie, Jessie had come face to face with Tom, who clearly could not wait to tell her his good news. He and his brother Stanley were about to purchase a pair of dilapidated cottages in the village of Elmshill, Norfolk. Their children, Billy and Emma-Rose, had been beside themselves with excitement and had not stopped talking about it since – unaware of the heartache it was causing Jessie. Had Tom, the husband she once loved so deeply, not seduced her away with false hopes from that Norfolk village to which she had been evacuated during the war all those years ago, she herself might now be living there, settled and enjoying a completely different way of life. Living in the very cottages that Stanley and Tom were about to purchase for themselves.

Her afternoon shift at the Public Health Office in Whitehorse Road where she worked part time as a copy typist had been busier than usual, and so Jessie was more than ready for a cup of tea and a friendly chat with Edie. When Edie opened the door to her, however, she saw an expression of worry in her friend's eyes. Welcoming though Edie's smile was, anyone who knew her would have realised that she was far from happy, and hardly her usual relaxed self.

Once inside and in the kitchen, Jessie feared that she had intruded on a private moment and was at a loss as to how to deal with the situation. She didn't feel she could tell a white lie to her soulmate and pretend that she had only called in to borrow a cup of sugar because Edie would see right through the fabrication. Instead she decided to be honest, saying, 'Look . . . if this is a bad time to call, Ed, I'll go. It's not a problem.'

'Don't be silly,' said Edie, pulling up a chair for her. 'I was just gonna brew up, as it happens.'

'Honestly?'

'Yes. Honestly.'

'Good. So that's all right, then. Everything's rosy.' Jessie sat down knowing full well that everything was not all right. Edie, with her back to her, was quiet as she filled the kettle, so Jessie took the lead. 'Who's first to have a moan, then – you or me?'

'You,' said Edie, placing the kettle on the stove and lighting the gas ring under it. 'Let's leave the worst to last.'

'Well . . . mine's only a bit of a grumble, really. Tom and 'is brother Stanley are gonna buy a pair of old semi-detached cottages which I always dreamed of living in.'

'The ones you told me about in Norfolk?'

'They're the ones. In a worse state now, so just as cheap as they were during the war when I first found out about 'em. They've all been up to have a second look at them. Tom, Stanley, Dolly . . . and their kids. Then they popped in to see Alice and her brother Jack . . . who made them welcome but never asked about me.'

'The people you stayed with when you were evacuated?' said Edie, already beginning to feel for her friend.

'That's right. They were so good to me and Billy. Everyone made a fuss of 'im and he adored it. It's brought it all back. The look on Alice's face at the breakfast table when I told 'er that we were going back to London. I think she might have thought she'd done something to offend us or that her cottage 'adn't lived up to Tom's expectations. As if.' Jessie shrugged. 'Now it seems as if she's forgot about me. It was a good few years ago so—'

'She hasn't forgotten you! Don't be daft. People

don't just forget people. Not when they've been living under the same roof. This isn't like you, Jess. Alice and Jack understood why you came back to London. You told me so yourself earlier this year when we were getting to know each other properly. Laura was here as well. She's my witness.'

'Did I tell you all that stuff? Honestly?'

'Yes, you did. Ask Laura when she gets home from Kent.'

'Just shows you. We think we're all right and on top of it all and I can't even remember telling you that. Must of been the night we got plastered.'

'It was.'

'That explains it, then. The thing is, I told Alice on the morning I left that being there with her and her brother Jack had been the best days of my life. I loved living in that rustic old village where everything went at a slower pace. Everyone seemed not only content with their lot but so proud of whatever they achieved – a good crop of carrots in the vegetable bed or a decent brew of cider made from apples off their own tree or a neighbour's.'

'An idyllic lifestyle if you're born to it, Jess. But would us townies cope?'

''Course we would. Like ducks to water.'

'Well, you shouldn't have left, then, should you. You were a bit on the pathetic side there, Jess. You should 'ave stuck to your guns and stayed put. It was much safer there for Billy, never mind you.'

'I know. But all Tom kept going on about was having us back in the East End near to 'is mum and dad so that when he jumped ship again he'd know where to find us. It was my own fault. I should 'ave stuck to my guns. My instincts were telling me to stay.'

'Missed opportunities,' said Edie. 'We'll all be regretting something by the time it's too late to do anything about it. I wonder if he's married. The handsome Rupert, son of the rich landowner who fell for you.'

'Trust you to remember that bit.' Jessie smiled. The recollection of someone from an altogether different class paying her attention lightened her mood. 'I s'pose you're right. We can *all* look back and wonder what might 'ave been if we'd have gone left at the crossroads instead of right. No point on dwelling on it.'

'I couldn't agree more,' said Edie. 'So you're upset because you felt as if one of them little cottages had your name on it. Is that it?'

'I think so. We were seriously thinking of selling up and buying them with Stanley. Just after the war was over and before Tom left me.'

'Well . . . why don't you and Max drive up to Norfolk and bid for one yourselves? All's fair in love and war.'

'I wish. We don't 'ave *any* spare cash, Edie – never mind the few hundred pounds we'd need . . . if not more by the time it's finished being fixed up. Me and Max only get from one Friday to the next with a bit put by for a trip to Southend or Margate. Same as most people on this estate. Some can't even afford a day's outing.' She glanced up at Edie and shrugged her shoulders. 'There you go. That's life.'

'True.'

'Things change all the time whether we like it or not. Once Max lost his clients after the war the business went down the drain. That's why I sold my two-up, two-down next door to my mother-in-law. The money from that set us up for a while . . . bought our little car, and new furniture for our flat. That's a lot more than some 'ave got.'

'It is, Jess, you're right, but that won't stop you from longing for what you once had and being resentful over what you can't 'ave now – that cottage in the country, for instance.'

Whether she realised or not, Edie had hit a raw nerve. All she was saying was perfectly true, but to hear it coming from someone else was a little too close to the bone for Jessie. It made it more real. Up until this moment she had considered that she was thinking like a spoilt brat, sulking because she couldn't have what she wanted. And if she was really honest she would have to admit that it wasn't just the cottage that she pined for but also her two-up, two-down next door to Emmie, her mother-in-law, who had been more like a mother to her than her own had.

The vision of Grant Street with its cobbled surface was one of Jessie's most treasured memories. She relished her visits to her in-laws, Emmie and Charlie, who were living as happily as ever in the small terraced house which they owned lock, stock and barrel. It was only a five-minute walk away from the rented house in which they had previously lived and where Tom and his brothers had been born. The family had been content and comfortable there, but when Emmie had heard about the four terraced houses next to each other in nearby Grant Street, available at a low price, she had not been able to resist urging her sons and her husband to purchase them all. This had been in the 1930s, before the war had begun.

The houses had been in a state of disrepair, no one having lived in them for some time. The landlord, engaged in property investment, had needed to sell in order to purchase land in Dagenham which had then been rumoured to be up and coming as a new small community town. The fact that the houses in Grant Street had not been wired for electricity and had been damp and in need of repair had helped to push down the price. With Tom, his dad, Charlie, his brother Stanley and his late brother Johnnie (who had been in the building trade) all working on them every evening and at weekends, it hadn't been many months before they had been able to move in.

Stanley, now a family man, had since sold his and moved on. After Johnnie's death at Dunkirk his had automatically been willed to his next of kin, Emmie and Charlie, and of course Jessie's had had to be sold owing to their financial troubles. She and Tom had been able to buy it in the first place because her family had received compensation from a fund set up by the Dock Labour Board after the tragic accident suffered by her father. Through the negligence of a large shipping company, a faulty crane that he had been driving had tumbled into the Thames with him trapped inside.

'The strange thing is,' said Jessie, as she stared out at nothing, 'it's like a pain or an invisible bruise that throbs and won't go away. Something you feel but can't see.'

'I can understand that,' responded Edie. She smiled and kept a tight hold on her own emotions. She knew that should she be drawn into looking back she would soon be in floods of tears. Tears which had been suppressed for too long.

Jessie sipped her tea and smiled gently at her friend. 'I can remember it as if I'm watching a movie. Linking arms with Tom when we came out of the house in Grant Street, thinking it was wonderful when it was small, damp and filthy. But we didn't care. We knew what it would look like once it was done up. We loved it. Both of us. Loved the idea of it being really ours, I s'pose.

'I was just pregnant then with our Billy. And do you know what Tom said when I broke the news to 'im? I think you'll make the best mum in the world, Jessie Warner. The best mum and the best wife. I'm the luckiest man alive. We'd only known each other a few months. Just like your Maggie and Tony – it was love at first sight.'

'Just what I was thinking,' said Edie. 'But Maggie's far too immature to be this serious about a young man. A first boyfriend at that . . . But whatever happens I can't deny that they're as happy as sandboys.'

'Love's young dream.' Jessie chuckled.

'I wonder where you got that expression from?'

'Naomi – as well you know. It fits, though. Three little words say it all. I think they're right for each other, you know. Your Maggie and Tony. My gut feeling is that when you look back on her falling in love while so young it will seem romantic. The worry'll pass. It always does. In time.'

'I can only hope so,' said Edie, not ready yet to tell her friend that romance was not the biggest worry. 'But what about you? And the cottage?'

'I don't know. Maybe that'll all come right as well. Tom and Max might end up as good friends for all we know. Tom might even let us go up there with the kids once it's been renovated. I never wanted to leave Elmshill. It was perfect . . . and what did I return to? London with all the air raids and the constant threat of being blown to smithereens. I should 'ave put baby Billy before Tom. That's what it amounts to. I put my husband before my son.'

'But it wasn't *just* your decision, don't forget. By the sound of it Tom had no intention of letting you stop there. Anyway . . . no use crying over spilt milk.'

'I had to come back. Tom would 'ave been gutted walking away from me and Billy. He'd suffered enough as it was. Not only did he lose one brother at Dunkirk but his younger one, Stanley, was on the missing-presumed-dead list.'

'Well then, don't be jealous of them making a go of it now.'

'I know, I know,' said Jessie, staring down at her feet. 'In any case . . . my kids will get a chance to be in the country air. He's bound to take them down there at weekends and for school holidays.'

''Course he will. Keep on the right side of 'im and maybe he'll let you and Max spend a weekend there with Billy and Emma. It's hardly the end of the world, is it?'

'No . . . and yet it feels like it if you want the truth. Deep down inside.' She laid the flat of her hand against her breast. 'It hurts in here even though it's not the end of the world.'

'I take it that another woman's not slipped into Tom's life?'

'No,' said Jessie, thoughtfully. Then, shaking her head, she added more forcefully, 'Definitely not. I would know if there was. That's half the trouble. Tom, without actually saying it, has made it clear that he still wants me.' She looked up at her friend and smiled bravely. 'Oh, take no notice of me. It's that time of month.'

'I wish I could say the same for Maggie,' said Edie without thinking.

The room was suddenly quiet. Jessie knew by the expression on her friend's face what she meant. 'Oh no, Ed, surely not?'

'Surely yes, I'm afraid. I wasn't gonna say anything yet. Naomi knows. I think she might have told Laura just before she got on the lorry to go hop-picking. I don't know. Fifteen and expecting a baby. I don't think it's fully sunk in. Not really.'

After a moment of silence Edie went on, in a broken voice, 'I don't know what to do, Jess. How to feel. As if that wasn't enough Naomi told me about my husband. Harry. He's not dead . . . can you believe that? All these years . . . and I never knew for certain one way or the other. And now . . . my only child, my Maggie, is pregnant at fifteen.' Edie pulled her handkerchief from inside the sleeve of her cardigan and dried her eyes.

Jessie leaned back in her chair and slowly shook her head. 'It doesn't rain but it pours, eh? You poor darling. What can I say? Nothing's gonna make you feel any better, is it? Not with all this at your feet. You're a strong woman, Ed, but this is more than enough for anyone. And as for Harry . . . I'm really sorry Jessie but Laura told me earlier on in the year. It was a slip of the tongue, though . . . I promised not to tell anyone.'

'It's all right. It doesn't matter now who knew and who didn't. By the sound of things I think I'm better off with Dennis. He thinks a lot of Maggie and that's important, isn't it.'

'Of course it is. But I do feel like a bit of a Judas. I should 'ave told you. I should 'ave—'

'Leave it, Jess,' said Edie, cutting in. 'It doesn't matter now. I just hope my dirty laundry's not been aired all over the place, that's all. I don't mind you knowing . . . but I don't want to talk about it. Not yet anyway. I've got too much else to think about.'

'You're telling me you 'ave. God, I wouldn't want to be in your shoes for all the tea in China. And there was I wallowing in self-pity and envy over a tiny cottage I couldn't have when all the time—'

'Stop apologising, Jess. I don't want to hear stuff like that right now. And if you want the truth I would rather be in *my* shoes than in *yours*. I'm not daft. You're still in love with your husband and having to make do with second best with Max, and now the little place in the country which you should both be sharing . . . you won't even be allowed a key to it but your children will. It's *you* I feel sorry for.'

'Well, that's giving it to me straight,' said Jessie. 'Anything else you'd like to get off your chest while we're at it?'

'No, there isn't. Apart from all I've just told you, my life's a dream.'

'Good. So how about a little drop of Naomi's hidden brandy? I think we both deserve it, don't you?'

'If you like,' said Edie, blowing her nose. 'That's it, I think. The tap's stopped. No more crying. No more anger.'

'Oh, that's a shame. I thought you were up for a good quarrel. Nothing like it really. A bloody good washerwomen's row.'

'No thanks. If that's what you're in the mood for you'd best go and knock on that vicious cow's door below. Tell 'er you think my water pipe might be leaking into 'er flat. She'll threaten to take you to court as well as me – the same as she's threatened that poor widow who lives next door to 'er. She's like a bloody crow sitting on 'er perch, waiting to peck.'

'I know . . . but we live nose to toes in these flats so there's bound to be one or two mischievous neighbours.'

'Evil is the word. Mischievous doesn't cover it. She picks on people when they're low and could easily be that last little nudge that's all it takes to tip someone over the edge and into a complete breakdown. Not me, though. Not yet. And she'd best not try either. And if she slanders my Maggie's good name I will personally go down there and smack the cow in the face. If anyone needs to be locked away that woman does. Behind bloody bars where she can do no ill.'

Quietly laughing, Jessie reached out and opened the door to the small corner cupboard where she knew Naomi kept her medicinal brandy for when she visited. 'I can't imagine that. But if she does get under your skin, imagine 'er to be where she belongs, in a Dennis Wheatley novel – *To the Devil a Daughter.*'

Distracted now from her reason for calling in – to get a bit of sympathy over the cottage – Jessie poured each of them a small glass of the golden liquid. 'This should warm the cockles of our hearts. I'll treat Nao to a half-bottle at Christmas to make up for it.'

'Well, you've lifted my spirits, Jessie, even though it might not look like it. You've brought me out of my gloom. Thanks. I do feel better for it. A lot better.'

'That's what friends and neighbours are for, Ed. If we all turn to each other for a bit of moral support now and then we'd—'

'At least Maggie didn't know her dad,' said Edie, back on her previous track and not listening to Jessie. 'What you don't 'ave you can't miss. That's what they say, isn't it? And it's true. I remember when my dad stood in the doorway of our house in Cotton Street for the last time. I didn't think I would ever get over him going away. I missed him badly at first, but had to cover my feelings for the sake of my younger brother, our Jimmy – and my broken-hearted mother.' Shaking her head, she continued, 'But after a few years we just got used to him not being there. Especially when Mum took her own life. We had other things to be sad about.' She raised her eyes to meet Jessie's. 'Why does so much have to happen to one family? It's not fair. I know we're not s'posed to blame God when things go wrong but I think He's dished out to us, and still is, more than our fair share of heartache. Am I supposed to be made of stone or what?'

'Of course not. And you have had more than your fair share. No doubt about that. But I'm not so sure it doesn't 'appen to most families. If the curtain was drawn on others we might find that many have been suffering in silence for years on end. But that won't make you feel any better. Nothing will. Except everything going well from now on.'

'You're right. There must be thousands like me bottling it all up. But I'm not now, am I? I'm telling you about it. Pouring out all my grumbles in one go.'

'And there's nothing wrong with that. Do you wanna talk about Maggie or leave it?'

'Leave it. She might come back and I don't know what mood she'll be in.'

'Back from where?'

'Mrs Baroncini's. She told Tony last night after putting it off time and time again. He insisted they tell his parents straight away. I admire him for that. Not many young lads would do the same in his shoes.'

Jessie leaned forward and placed a hand on Edie's, saying, 'Ida won't be horrible to 'er, Edie. She won't be pleased but she'll sort something out. They're a lovely family. Really close.'

'I know. And that one blessing makes up for a lot. Believe me.' Wishing to change the subject, she added, 'I've got some Camp coffee if you'd rather that than tea. We can pour our drop of brandy in it.'

'Suits me,' said Jessie.

'So,' said Edie, rising from her chair, 'you don't think that Mrs Baroncini'll be disgusted and angry with Mags? That's good. Another load off my mind.'

'She'll be fine once Maggie's left their flat, then she'll beat Tony with a stick.'

Edie turned, her eyes wide. 'She wouldn't do that. Would she?'

'No, of course not. It was a silly joke. She'll give 'im a clip round the head, though, and an ear-bashing that'll go on for hours. I s'pose that's why he wanted Maggie to tell 'er straight away. To get it over and done with. Once it's sunk in, and after a few days of shouting the odds, she'll fall into the grandmother-to-be role and come up with an arrangement to suit everyone.'

Edie wasn't so sure. Pouring hot water onto the liquid coffee in the cups, she said, 'There's only one arrangement as far as my strong-headed daughter is concerned, Jess. Maggie wants to keep this baby. And

I know what she's like. Once she digs her heels in that's it. It's set in stone.'

'Well then, she'll find an ally in Ida. I'm not gonna say anything now but I bet what I'm thinking is what will happen.' Jessie smiled at the thought of it.

'Send them both to Italy?'

'Don't be daft. 'Course not. No . . . Tony's her youngest and she adores him. She won't want him to go too far away, and she'll never let one of 'er own be cast from the family. Newborn baby or not.'

'But what about the time leading up until it's arrived into the world? It won't be her daughter of fifteen walking about with a big belly, will it? I can't see any way out other than Maggie going away. I think she should go to one of them retreats for un-married mothers till her time comes.'

'And what does Maggie think about that?'

'That it's the best of the options put forward so far.' Handing Jessie her cup of coffee, Edie slumped back into her chair and pushed her hands through her hair. 'I can't believe this is happening. Where did I go wrong, Jess?'

'Don't even consider going down that road, Ed. It's pointless. Things will work out, you'll see. They always do. It's the period of going through the agony and worry beforehand that's always the worst.'

Once she had drunk her coffee, and after Edie had exhausted the options as to what she and Maggie should or should not do, Jessie, with as much tact as possible, left her to mull things over in private. In her heart she knew that somehow the family would pull through this and within the year would be rejoicing about the addition to their bloodline. Having come to know her friend well, Jessie had every reason to believe that Edie, with the help of her Aunt Naomi, would be strong enough to cope once this initial shock had subsided. And the pleasure that Naomi would get from being a great-great-aunt would be worth all the agonising that Edie was clearly going through.

Inside her own flat Jessie was relieved to find that her offspring, Billy and Emma-Rose, having finished their milk and buttered fruit bread, were quietly reading comics in their bedrooms. She valued her time alone, especially now. Stretching out on the settee in her living room, Jessie asked herself what her worst fear was. The answer came with no thought at all – the fear of losing one of her children through accident or illness. The death of a beloved child to her seemed an impossible thing to have to cope with. The fact that Billy, as a baby during the war, had twice had a narrow escape during air raids had perhaps left its mark.

With the late afternoon sun coming in through the window she ignored the need to prepare the family supper for when Max came home from work. All she wanted right then was to think about Tom and the way things were. This was nothing unusual. Since his return into her world she had found him persistently invading her mind and had often sat alone, mentally reliving all they had done together. Now, for no particular reason, she was recalling the time she had first seen him, brief though it was. She had brushed up against Tom while escaping with her two young brothers, Stephen and Alfie, from the frightening Battle of Cable Street. It had been a similarly clear October day, the sun shining through the trees in the parks and lighting up the rusty autumn leaves before they fell and covered the ground like a glorious carpet.

Clusters of people from around the East End had gathered that day with only one thought on their minds – to stop the fascist blackshirts from marching through their part of London. Many of the people, both adults and children, had filled their pockets with stones from piles prepared throughout the night. Others had armed themselves with pieces of splintered wood and bottles. The mood had been quiet and solemn, similar to when a family gathers before a funeral. But when a local boy had arrived, excited and out of breath, to announce that the march had begun and that the Jewish Party and the communists were making sure that the fascists did not get through without a tough battle, the mood had changed to one of camaraderie. At the time Oswald Mosley had been seen in some quarters as Hitler's errand boy. Tom Smith, the father of Jessie's children, while not a follower of the blackshirt movement, had been interested to see what all the fuss was about and why one man could attract such a following from all over London, and especially in the East End, and equally arouse the anger of thousands who wanted to bring the man down.

Having planned to march along Commercial Road to Limehouse, where a huge outdoor meeting was to be held, Mosley and his army, all wearing black, had changed route at the last moment and marched along the Highway by the docks towards Cable Street.

The police, out in force, had been there to see the procession through without trouble, but they had soon realised that people were ready to fight ferociously with the blackshirts – come what may. Local people had come out en masse to make their voices heard and to show their outrage. The Jewish Party, with a rightful grudge to bear, had set up a first-aid post in Aldgate and a team of cyclist messengers had been deployed between strategic points and headquarters. The sound of a band starting up, playing 'Rule Britannia', had incited even more patriotism.

Jessie had been caught up in the pandemonium simply because she had taken that particular route home with her two younger brothers on their way back from a trip to the Tower of London. Stephen, seven years old at the time, had been terrified, while Alfie, the elder of the two boys, had been excited and wanted to be part of the action. His words, screeched into Jessie's ear at the time, came flooding back. 'The police are on horseback and they've got batons and guns!' She recalled the frightening sound of breaking glass as those who were there to protest showed their anger. Tom had been standing apart from the mob, observing. In her panic to get away she had knocked against him and apologised, not knowing that fate was soon to bring the two of them together in a different situation. Her future had been the last thing on her mind at the time. Later that year she had been introduced to him properly during a workers' strike in the docks. Tom, just like her father, had been a docker at the time, also working mostly in Canary Wharf.

With no thoughts of the stranger who had smiled at her mischievously while she had made her escape, Jessie had arrived at her grandfather's house in Broom Court out of breath and frightened about what was happening in Cable Street. She had explained what she had witnessed to her grandfather, her brothers interrupting excitedly. Her grandfather had quietly laughed at them, saying, 'Blackshirts and communists. Nothing more than gang warfare. Don't worry – give it a month and it'll all be forgotten.'

Sadly, that was the last time Jessie had seen her beloved grandfather. A few weeks later he had returned from a day's work in his cobbler shop, sat down by the fire and lapsed into his last sleep. He had told no one about the severe pains in his chest that had been troubling him. Jessie had taken his sudden death badly, crying into her pillow nightly and asking the same question over and over. Why him? Why my grandfather?

The sound of her son Billy in the adjoining kitchen brought Jessie out of her dreamlike state. Hauling herself up from her comfortable settee, she slid open the hatch door and peered into the kitchen to see her fourteen-year-old son trying to light a cigarette by the gas stove. Startled by the sudden intrusion, he blushed madly and hid both hands behind his back, saying, 'I thought you was asleep in there. You usually 'ave a doze when you come in from work.'

'I haven't just come in from work, Billy,' she said, just managing to keep a straight face. 'I went down to see Edie for a cup of tea. Or had you forgotten?'

'Yeah, I did forget. All right, is she?' he said, his face all innocence, his voice clearly trying to cover his guilt.

Overcome with love for this lad, at that age when the child was trying desperately to be a youth, she wondered why he was asking about Edie. Either it was because he couldn't think of anything else to say while he hid the cigarette behind his back or he had heard a snippet of gossip. 'Any reason why she shouldn't be all right?'

'No. I was just asking, that's all.'

Relieved that the news about Maggie had not leaked out, Jessie spoke more firmly. 'No pocket money for a year, Billy, if I ever catch you smoking again. Is that clear?'

'I wasn't smoking! You can smell my breath if you like!'

'You was trying to light a cigarette by the gas stove. I'm not daft.'

'Well, I never got it lit, did I. I was trying it out, that's all. Horrible,' he said, grimacing and shaking his head. 'I'm never gonna smoke if it tastes like that.'

'How do you know what the taste is like if you never lit it? Or perhaps you've tried it out before?' She held up her hand in protest. 'Don't bother to fib. You must 'ave tried it before to know. Now then, whether you decide to smoke or not once you're older and you've started work I can't control, but until then . . . and that won't be for a couple of years at least, because I'm gonna insist you stay on—'

'You 'ave to stay on till you're sixteen at Reins School, Mum. It's not like the one you went to. Chuck 'em out at fourteen and see if they sink or swim.'

'I know, I know. It's a grammar school, and I'm still as proud as punch that you passed your eleven-plus. And I'll be even prouder if you go on to college. But don't ever let me catch you smoking again. Right?'

'I said I wouldn't.'

'Now say it again.'

'What for?'

'Billy . . .' warned Jessie. 'Don't push yer luck.'

'All right! I won't light up again!'

'Good. Now go back to your room and read a book instead of comics. You might learn something more than you know already.'

Muttering under his breath, Billy slumped off, leaving Jessie to herself. The expression on his face when he had been caught red-handed reminded her of his father. Before she had time to even think about becoming nostalgic again, Billy was back in the kitchen, saying, 'Dad's gonna take me and Emma back to that village we stayed in when I was evacu-ated during the war.'

'Where *we* were evacuated to, don't you mean? I was there as well. Pushing you in a pram.'

'Slip of the tongue,' he said, mimicking Tom. 'Anyway . . . I can't remember anyfing about it but Dad wants me to go. He's finking of buying the cottages with Uncle Stanley for us all to live in one day. Will you mind if I go? I won't if you don't want.'

'I told your dad it was all right. Why should I mind?' said Jessie, touched by his concern for her feelings.

''Cos he's not asked you and Max if you wanted 'em. And you found out about 'em first, when we was evacuated. That's wot Granddad said, anyway. He said you'd be none too pleased about it. Max could take you up there, though, couldn't he? We could all go an' 'ave a look. Go in two cars.'

'We'll see,' said Jessie, tousling her son's hair. 'But right now I'm gonna 'ave to start cooking or there'll be no supper.'

'Max wants to live in the country one day. He's fed up with London. He reckons all the smog gets in yer chest. I s'pose that's what gives 'im heartburn, eh?'

'No, Billy. Worry over work does that. Has he been complaining, then?'

'No. I caught 'im the other day, leaning back in the chair with a hand on 'is breast bone. He said he wasn't in pain when I asked. What's for tea, then? I'm starving.'

'Shepherd's pie.'

'Lovely grub,' he said, disappearing through the doorway and going back to his bedroom.

Well, thought Jessie, it just goes to show what goes on in their minds. Even Billy knows that I'm upset over it. It seemed to her that the cottages in Elmshill were now the focus of attention. Pushing that from her mind, she began to peel the potatoes she had placed in the sink earlier. With young Maggie from below coming back into her thoughts, she was reminded of the time when she herself was pregnant with Billy, two months before she married Tom.

Searching for the right words to say to her mother, Jessie had sat on the low window sill in the back yard of their old house, wishing that her dad were alive to give her moral support. He had been the forgiving type, gentle and understanding. Her mother, on the other hand, had been and still was very proper and churchgoing. Jessie had tried her best to break it as gently as she could but still the sparks had flown. She recalled it as if it were yesterday – allowing it all to come flooding back as if she were watching herself in a film. She could see herself standing in front of her mother, her insides trembling, her mother's face pale, her expression one of suppressed fury.

'Mum, I've got something to tell you,' she had said. 'Something that you're not going to be pleased about.'

Rose, her mother, had answered in a tone so chilly that even now, after all this time, it made her shudder. Clearly she had been expecting this confession from her daughter. 'Go on, then,' she had said after an intimidating silence. 'Your sister hasn't mentioned anything but I could tell from her face that something sinful has come about. You obviously saw fit to confide in her before telling me. So I should think it must something you're deeply ashamed of.'

'Yes, I did tell Dolly,' had been Jessie's sorry reply, and then she added, 'I'm going to get married.'

It was plain to any fool from the silence that

followed that her mother knew exactly what she had meant by this. 'You're pregnant,' had been her cold reply. Then, glaring into Jessie's eyes, she said, 'Does Max know yet?'

Jessie had realised straight away that her mother had got the wrong end of the stick. 'Max isn't the father,' she said. Closing her eyes and fearing the worst, she added, 'I'm carrying *Tom's* baby.'

Without a shadow of doubt her mother had been shocked by this. When she finally did say something it was with loathing in her voice. 'Disgusting. You've not known him for five minutes.' In her defence, Jessie had tried to explain that she was not in love with Max but with Tom. It had cut no ice. Her mother wanted nothing to do with Tom or what she saw as his low, rough family.

'And you think that fly-by-night will make you happy?' had been her bitter response. 'You know nothing about love! You've a lot to learn, my girl! A great deal!' Then, after a few moments' silence, without any feeling in her voice, she said, 'An abortion is the order of the day as far as I'm concerned. Luckily I know a decent midwife who'll do it and who keeps such things under wraps. I'll shame myself by going to her over this, but it'll be less of a disgrace than letting everyone watch your stomach grow, and you only knowing the father for a while. We'll be the mainstay of gossip for months to come.'

Jessie's mother could have no idea just how deeply her impersonal, cold tone had cut through her at a time when she so badly needed a comforting hug.

A fierce argument had broken out. She had pleaded with her mother to let her have Tom's baby but Rose had been adamant, saying it was out of the question. And just like Edie's Maggie now, Jessie made it clear that she was not prepared to kill her own flesh and blood. Her tears had made no difference to her mother, who was not one for allowing emotions to rule the day. Her final harsh words had been the worst of all: 'Either you get rid of it or you leave this house for good. You'll have made your own bed and on that you can lie. I wash my hands of you.' From a middle-class East End background, her mother wanted Jessie to marry the more respectable Max.

As a last-ditch attempt to win Rose over, Jessie suggested that perhaps she should go away until the baby had arrived and then give it up for adoption. Rose had simply shuddered before turning away, leaving Jessie alone in a silent room. Her mother was making it clear that she wished to hear no more – indeed, that she had washed her hands of the whole thing.

Placing the peeled potatoes in a saucepan, Jessie felt for Edie and Maggie and what they had now to face. She wondered whether she should go back to her friend and tell her not to stop her daughter from doing what she truly wanted and not to disapprove of her decision, whatever it might be. But Jessie was no fool, and knew that the last thing Edie wanted was well-meant advice.

Breaking into her thoughts, Billy came back into the kitchen, his forehead creased in a frown. Speaking

in a quiet and serious voice he said, 'You won't mind,
then, if me and Emma go to the cottage?'

'No, darling.' Jessie smiled. 'I won't mind. In fact
I think it'd be lovely for the pair of you.'

'We can go wiv you and Max as well. Dad said so.
Later on when it's all done up like a picture on a
chocolate box.'

'Well, that's good, then. Everyone's happy that way.'

''Cos I like Max and I'd want 'im to see it. Dad
likes 'im as well.'

'Does he now. And how would you know that?'

'He said so.' Billy shrugged, matter-of-fact. 'Well . . .
he said he was a decent sort of bloke when I asked
'im. Bit of a wally but decent enough. And he said
he appreciates that Max looked after me and Emma
while he was away all that time on business.'

'Good,' said Jessie, smiling. 'That makes your dad
an all-right sort of bloke as well, then, don't it?'

'Oh, yeah. He's come round now. Nan said so.
Granddad said that he's burned his bloody bridges.
What d'yer reckon he meant by it?'

'Never you mind,' said Jessie. 'Never you mind.'

'Dinner nearly ready, then, is it? I'm starving
'ungry.' With that Billy turned on his heels and went
back to his room. Filled with a surge of love for her
son, Jessie thanked God she had gone against her
mother's wishes all those years ago and hoped that
Maggie would stick to her guns and have her baby,
come what may. And that Tony Baroncini and his
family would stick by her.

*     *     *

Sitting on the concrete stairs between balconies, arms around each other, sharing a private and special time together, Maggie and Tony could have no idea that Jessie had been comparing her first mistake to theirs. Tony's mother, having listened earlier to her son's confession while Maggie sat beside him on the sofa in their living room, had said nothing. Not one word. Just sat very still with her rosary in her hands, turning it between her fingers. Tony's father had taken a back seat in order to watch all three of them and bring down the hammer of decision at the end of the long debate, had there been one. This man was no fool – he had guessed why his son had summoned them to the sitting room with the look of a grown man but the worries of a lad on his young shoulders. When Ida Baroncini did finally break her silence it was to simply say, 'Leave us now, both of you: tomorrow I will say what is to be done.' The expression on her face had been incontrovertible. She had clearly wanted no discussion or debate.

Now, the two of them alone, Maggie spoke in a concerned voice, saying, 'If you want me to do something, Tony, you've got to say it soon before it's too late.'

'Too late for what?' he said, gazing at her with love in his eyes.

'You know what I mean.'

'I want you to say it out loud. Too late to do what?'

'See someone.'

'Who? See who?'

'An abortionist!' whispered Maggie. 'A decent one and not a backstreet profiteer.'

'Out of the question.' Tony shook his head defiantly. 'If you don't want the baby my family will take it. One of my aunts will bring it up for me. But I'll make sure it knows I'm his dad.'

'It might be a girl.' She smiled.

'Better still.'

'Are you saying you definitely do want me to have it, then?'

'Of course I want you to have it. What else would you expect?'

'But I'm not sixteen yet. We've broken the law.'

'People have been hanged for worse things. We'll live together, and if it doesn't work out we'll go our separate ways.'

'Oh. Right. Well, you seem to have got it all worked out.' Maggie was pleased and proud of her sweetheart.

'My favourite uncle's come up with a plan,' he said, clearly overjoyed but trying to keep an impassive face. 'Do you want to hear it?'

'Go on, then,' said Maggie, not caring any more about plans. She had given herself a headache more than once trying to work out what was for the best.

He kissed her tenderly on the cheek and then said, 'There's a little love nest for two on offer. An attic flat. It's a spacious bedroom by all accounts but the sitting room's small and there's a kitchen-cum-landing where the gas cooker and sink are. And there's a bathroom of sorts with a bath and running hot water but no sink. Just a big jug and bowl on a small wooden table. A pretty jug and bowl, but not as pretty as you. Blue flowers on white china. It can be our little bit of heaven, up in the sky away from the world.'

'You can't 'ave found somewhere already,' said Maggie, thrilled. 'You're making it up.'

'You think so? Well, if you must know, and of course you must . . . I went straight round to my uncle after you told me. He's sworn to secrecy so it won't go any farther than that.' Giving her a gentle kiss on the lips, he looked into her soft green eyes and smiled. 'My uncle will sway my parents towards it . . . and your mother and Aunt Naomi. And that's something else I've settled my mind to. When we're old enough to get married I'm going to wear your great-uncle's army uniform from the First World War.'

'That'll be lovely. So long as you don't ask me to wear Aunt Naomi's wedding frock.' Taking his hand in hers, she rubbed it with the tips of her fingers. 'So where is this attic flat?'

'Our "little bit of heaven" is above a fish-and-chip shop that my uncle has just taken over. He wants us to run it. He offered us rooms above his café in Islington but I don't fancy that. Too hectic.'

'Tony . . . I'm a librarian . . .'

'No, you're not a librarian,' he said, touched by the look of pride in her eyes. 'You're a junior training to be one.'

'Same thing. I don't wanna cook fish and chips for the rest of my life. I'll smell of boiling fat day and night.'

'That's what my uncle said you'd say. So I asked if it would be all right to get a woman in to prepare the chips and help serve, so you could carry on going in to the library, if that's what you want. Think you can manage to do that, though . . . with people coming and going and giving you black looks as you put on more weight?'

'For a while it'll be all right. Until I do begin to show more.'

'And you won't mind people who know you seeing you in the library like that? You expecting a baby while under age.'

Maggie considered her answer. Of course she didn't want everyone to be looking sideways at her, their expressions scornful. 'I think I'd rather help out in an Italian restaurant than a fish-and-chip shop. Even if it does mean moving to Islington. What about the living accommodation?'

'More spacious. A proper kitchen as well – even though the room is small.'

'And 'ave we got time to mull it over or are we supposed to give an answer now?'

'Mull it over.'

'And what do *you* want?' said Maggie, suddenly aware of echoing footsteps on the stone stairs.

'To be with you, Maggie Birch . . . for the rest of my life.'

Their attention was drawn to a gentleman in his mid-fifties who looked a touch on the bohemian side, and another, younger man wearing spectacles and a neat-looking shirt, who were lingering near by as if waiting for something to happen. They were both looking at Maggie. Standing aside to give them room to pass should they need to climb another flight, she and Tony offered a polite smile and waited for them to go up the stairs. The elder of the two, who Maggie thought looked familiar, spoke in a quiet voice, addressing Tony. 'Did I hear you say Maggie Birch, sir?'

'That's right.' Tony smiled, flattered to be called 'sir' by this gentleman who, judging by his accent, was possibly Canadian. 'This is Maggie and I'm Tony. I live on the third floor.'

Looking from Tony to Maggie the gentleman smiled, his hazel eyes warm and friendly. 'Maggie . . . would your mother be at home by any chance?'

'She would,' said Maggie, glancing sideways at Tony and wondering what was going on. 'Did you want to see her, then?'

'I've wanted to see her for a very long time, as a matter of fact. She may not wish to see me, however.'

Her eyes narrowed, Maggie looked at this man, whom she felt she should know, and then she shrank back, an icy-cold sensation shooting down her spine. After a few moments she collected herself and glanced at Tony. She knew that she was blushing as she said, 'I can't really believe it but I think I know who this is.'

A puzzled expression on his face, Tony placed an arm around her shoulders and looked into her face, saying, 'It's all right. Whoever these men are I'm sure they wish you no harm.' He shifted his gaze from her to the elder of the men. 'I didn't catch your name, sir.'

'I didn't give it.' The man smiled and then offered his hand. 'The name's Drake. Alex Drake. I'm Maggie's grandfather.'

Feeling numb, Maggie said quietly, 'So you've come back at last. A bit late, if you don't mind my saying so.' She looked from him to the younger man, who was watching cautiously, pushing his spectacles up on the bridge of his nose. After a few moments she nudged Tony, meaning to suggest it might be better if he left them to it.

Alex Drake cleared his throat. 'Did you know about the advert in *The Times*, Maggie?'

'Yes,' she whispered, her stomach churning. 'I knew about it.' She looked from him to her boyfriend, more for support than anything else. 'Aunt Naomi arranged it, Tony, after Mum got engaged.'

'I know. You told me.' The expression on his face showed his concern for Maggie. To him, a grandfather turning up out of the blue – one she had never set eyes on before – had to be the strangest thing ever. He didn't like it.

Seeing the effect this was having on him, she turned back to the stranger – her mother's father. 'Aunt Nao deliberately put our address in so that should you 'ave read the paper in Canada you'd know where we were. But I never thought in a million years that you'd actually see it.'

'As a matter of fact I do get *The Times* . . . but we could put what happened down to fate.' He smiled. 'I've been in the country for five months. I caught the announcement of your mother's marriage and saw the other piece giving this address. It's taken a while for me to pluck up the courage to call but . . . here I am.' Momentarily overcome by his emotions, he turned to his son. 'Say hello to your niece, Ken.'

'Niece?' said Maggie, irritated by the man's casual manner.

'Sure. Ken is your mother's half-brother.'

'Oh, right . . . of course. The child you kept secret from your family. From Mum, Uncle Jimmy . . . and the grandmother I never knew. She committed suicide after you'd left her for your other woman and gone to Canada. Did you know that?'

'I did, sweetheart,' he said, his voice soft and full of regret. 'I have a lot of making up to do. Not only to you but to Ken.'

'I wanted to meet my half-sister,' said the younger man with a brief nervous smile. 'I guess this is a bit of a shock for you.'

'You could say that,' said Maggie. 'Well . . . do we give Mum a surprise or shall I tell her you're here an' give 'er time to take it in?'

'You know your mother best,' said her grandfather.

'That's true,' Maggie murmured. 'Which is no fault of mine.' Then, thinking briefly about all her mother had told her of the past, she scorned herself for being sarcastic. Her own feelings were going to have to go on the back burner.

'I think I'd best go in first,' she said. Then, leaning forward, she gave Tony a peck on the cheek. 'I'll see you tomorrow.'

Cupping her face, he mouthed 'I love you' and

then whispered in her ear that her mother might not be comfortable with what was coming. Turning to the grandfather, he said, 'It was good to meet you, sir. I hope the reunion turns out well.'

'Oh, come on, son . . . don't be a damp squib,' was the congenial response. 'We need all the support we can get. Wouldn't you rather your friend came along too, Maggie? It might help break the ice.'

'And it might also be embarrassing for 'im.' She nudged Tony again and told him to scarper before he got drawn in.

Giving her arm a squeeze, he turned away. Taking the stairs two at a time, he said, 'Come up and let me know how it goes!'

'No, I'll see you tomorrow. I think your parents 'ave got enough to think about. Don't tell 'em this bit! Tony! Did you hear me?'

'Yes,' he called back, 'I heard you. *Ciao!*'

'Oh dear . . .' said Edie's father, frowning deeply. 'I hadn't really considered the idea that your mother might not want to see me. You think maybe I should have written first? That this might not be such a good idea?'

'Who knows?' said Maggie. 'But you're here now and there's no turning back. I'm hardly gonna keep it a secret from her, am I?'

'No, I guess not,' was the quiet reply.

'I can hardly believe it myself,' she said. 'My long-lost grandfather who I've never seen turns up out of the blue with my mum's brother in tow. Wait here and I'll go in and see what she wants to do.'

Leaving the two men to themselves, Maggie walked slowly into the flat. In the living room Edie was gazing into the small fire in the grate. She had been thinking about Harry, her husband. She had already asked herself over and over what might have been if he had not stayed in Turkey but had come home once the war was over. Whichever way she had looked at it, she knew she had been badly let down. Worse still, Maggie had been denied a father all her life. Her only regret now was that she had not had the chance to see her husband on his return, before he had left for the Canary Islands. She felt cheated. Robbed of the chance to confront him and give him a good dressing down. To smack his face good and hard and perhaps kick him where it hurt.

Quietly approaching her mother, Maggie hesitated and then sat down on the settee, looking at Edie's profile as reflections from the burning coals danced across her face. She was trying to be mature and brave about this. It was clear that her mother knew she was there but she did not look up. In a soft and tender voice, Maggie finally said, 'Mum . . . there's someone outside who wants to see you.'

'Is there?' said Edie, still wrapped in her solitary thoughts.

'Yeah. It's someone very special.'

'Special to who?'

'You and me, but you in particular.'

Slowly turning to look at Maggie, a frightened expression on her face, Edie spoke without thinking. 'Your father?'

'No . . .' said Maggie, her voice tinged with caution. 'How could it be? He's dead.'

'Is he, though? Who can say? And what if he weren't?'

Drawing closer to her mother, Maggie put an arm around her shoulders. 'Come on . . . this is not like you. Is it because of me that you're feeling low? Me and the baby?'

'Maybe,' said Edie, taking a deep breath and pulling herself together. 'But I don't think so. We all need to sit down quietly at times and reflect. There's no real harm in it. In fact it probably does us the world of good in the long run. So who wants to see me, then?'

Lifting Edie's hand, Maggie placed it against her cheek and looked her mother in the eyes as her own filled with tears. 'Mum . . . it's your dad over from Canada. He's waiting on the stairs. With your half-brother.'

Edie could do no more than stare into Maggie's face. Eventually she said, 'Say that again.'

'Your dad and your half-brother Ken are waiting outside to see if you'll see them.'

'My dad,' whispered Edie, 'and the brother I've never met are here?'

'He saw Aunt Naomi's ad in *The Times* just after you got engaged to Dennis. He thinks you might not want to see 'im. If you don't, Mum, he'll go away quietly and he won't blame you for it.'

'My dad is outside?' said Edie, her eyes filling with tears. 'My dad? Outside our flat? Maggie, are you sure? Are you absolutely sure it's him?'

'Of course I am. I wouldn't do that to you. Tell you without knowing properly. It's him, Mum – and your half-brother.'

'Oh my God,' murmured Edie. 'He's come home.'

Before Maggie had a chance to say anything else, Edie was up from her seat and running out of the room, calling for her father. Calling out over and over, 'Daddy! Daddy! Daddy!'

Ten minutes later, while Maggie shared a pot of tea with her mother's half-brother around the small table in the kitchen, Edie was with her dad in the living room. After an awkward silence the tension seemed to melt away, and once a few tears had been shed they talked as if they had not been parted at all. Now, more settled, they were beginning to touch on the past. Edie's father asked about her recent move away from Cotton Street and whether she missed living there.

'The street suffered a lot during the war, Dad,' she said. 'It never quite seemed the same after that. Especially since some of our neighbours had been hit.'

'And killed?' asked her father, a sad expression on his face.

'Afraid so. Death seemed to be everywhere. If ever there was a time when me and Jimmy needed a father figure it was then. But there. You had your own life to lead all those miles away, and your own family. Ken was a lot luckier than me and Jimmy. He had you all the time, whereas we only had you in our childhood.'

'Sweetheart . . . do you think I don't know that? I missed you too. All three of you – your mother included. If it's any consolation I deeply regret what I did. If I could turn back the clock I would. I was a very confused and foolish young man at the time.'

'You were an adult, Dad. And a father of two. Don't start making excuses and apologies now. It's too late.' Reverting to the subject of Cotton Street, she said, 'You remember Mrs Wheat?'

'Sure I do,' he said, clearing his throat. 'She was the overweight woman with the bandaged legs, if I'm not mistaken. A more kind-hearted person you couldn't hope to meet.'

'That's right. Well, she was in Old Man Lipski's house, feeding him some of her famous farmhouse soup. They both copped it. Neither of 'em would 'ave had the time or the inclination to go down the workhouse shelter. And they weren't the only ones, but there you go. Plenty of us did survive.'

'That brings back memories. The Victorian workhouse. Is that still there?'

'It is, and I s'pose of all the places that should 'ave been turned to rubble that was one of them. Still, no doubt the bulldozer will soon take care of that. There are plans for the street to be cleared and new council houses built.'

'The workhouse,' he said, sadly shaking his head. 'It certainly had a macabre history.' Then, as he remembered times gone by, he smiled at Edie, saying, 'You loved it, though, from what I recall. You liked to pretend it was haunted. And it could have been, for all we knew. By those poor devils who were literally worked to death.'

'It was a weird place, it's true, but I still thought of it as my secret world that I could creep into and explore.'

'That's right. You were always sneaking in there. It was your mythical world, I guess. What about the Coopers? What happened to them?'

'They left in a truck with a huge van following up behind. They were really happy to go. Off to Harlow . . . to begin a new life in the country. Snapped up a brand-new council 'ouse.' Relieved that the conversation had turned away from the time when they had been a loving family, Edie continued, 'Ben left and then went back again and Joey stayed put. A few others did as well, but they finally gave in and moved on. Joey and Ben are still there, though. But they'll have to face facts soon, put the past where it belongs and move on.'

'Yeah, but . . . it's not that easy, sweetheart.'

'If you want us to talk about Mum . . . I will, but not too deeply. I take it you know that she took 'er own life?'

'Of course, Edie. That almost destroyed me. I hadn't guessed or anything but I made enquiries and so on,' said Alex sadly. 'It must have been a terrible time for you and your brother Jimmy. I wanted to come back but it just didn't feel right. And I felt for sure that the door would be slammed in my face. If not by you then by my son. And I knew your Aunt Naomi would have been there for you.'

'It doesn't matter now. We got through it and, yes, Naomi was wonderful and still is, and both me and Maggie love her very much.' Turning her face away, she went on, 'You know, Jimmy always said he didn't want any children in case their marriage didn't work out and their children might feel the hurt and loneliness that we went through – when you left and after Mum died. I'm sorry to be so blunt but I thought it best to get that out of the way.'

'I can understand that. But I had to go, Edie. I can't explain it and I wish to God I hadn't been so obsessed with my own needs, but there it is. I did and I have to live with the guilt. I can understand perfectly that Jimmy wouldn't want to see me.'

'He might. I don't know. It would be nice if we could just pick up and forget that you ran off with another woman who you'd been seeing for years and who had had a son by you . . . but that's a bit much to ask of us. It was a terrible shock when Mum first told us what you'd done and why. Are you planning to live back in England, then?'

'I would love to,' said her father. 'I've been here for almost five months now, going around the art studios, but it's very quiet. Advertising in Britain is somewhat behind Canada and the States.'

'And that's what you're involved in now, is it? Advertising.'

'Yeah. I paint a little too but I no longer work as a draughtsman. Thankfully. There's nothing I would like more than to live back in England but I don't think I can afford to. In Canada I have more work than I need – over here it's scarce and nowhere near as well paid. So no . . . I don't think I could afford to come back home on a permanent basis.'

'That's a shame. What about your second wife?'

'We separated, Edie. Ten years ago. She fell in love with a younger man. A writer.' He shrugged and smiled weakly. 'I couldn't compete.'

'So there's no woman in your life now?'

'None that I would want to marry. I have my work and my friends . . . and that's fine. I get by well enough. Besides . . . I'm a grandfather now. Ken's kids keep me busy.'

'You've been a grandfather for nearly sixteen years, Dad.'

'Maggie. I know, I know. Don't think I haven't wondered if you had children. Of course I did. Your brother Jimmy too. He hasn't, from what you've told me, of course. That's pretty hard to take, I will admit that, but there's not much I can do to make amends, is there?'

'Well . . . he *says* he doesn't want any kids but Helen, his wife, can't have children, I don't think. I know they were trying for a while – she told me. But it hasn't happened. Jimmy says he's not bothered to save her feelings from being bruised. I think they might adopt.' Changing the subject, Edie said, 'So now that you've found us – what next? When will you be going back?'

'In a month or so. I thought we might go for a meal and take in a show . . . or something. Would Maggie like that, do you think? And Harry, of course . . . and dear old Naomi.'

'Harry?' said Edie, going cold. Could he possibly know that Harry was still alive? She decided to feign innocence, saying, 'Harry never made it back from the war, Dad. Missing, presumed dead. Killed on the shores of Turkey. An accident. A boat that smashed into the rocks.'

'I'm sorry, Edie I wasn't thinking . . .' He pushed a hand through his hair. 'What can I say?'

'It doesn't matter. You weren't to know.'

'Oh dear.' He sighed. 'It seems you've had a tough time of it, sweetheart. I'm really sorry.' He attempted a smile. 'But you're to be married soon. The ad in *The Times* said you were engaged . . .'

'That's right. Fifteen years on. That's how long I kept a torch burning in case the authorities were wrong.'

'And now you're ready for a new beginning. That's good. I'd like to meet your fiancé.'

'Dennis. His name's Dennis.' Leaning forward, she placed a hand on his arm. 'Look, Dad . . . I don't want you to think I'm bitter or anything like that, but this is all a bit sudden and to be honest I'd rather not . . . well, you know. I mean, I can't just turn the clock back like that and pick up from when you left us. Too much 'as happened. Mum and everything. But I'm pleased you came.'

'I can understand that,' said Alex. 'I wasn't expecting a hero's welcome, sweetheart.'

'Why *did* you come, then, Dad? After all this time.'

'It felt like fate . . . when I saw the advert I just felt as if you were calling me. Up until now I imagined you must have borne some kind of resentment. If you never forgave me for leaving I wouldn't blame you. No one would.'

'You saw the ad in *The Times* over here, but why did you come in the first place? Was it to find me? And Jimmy?'

'I came back to see if I could settle here again, Edie. I knew I would find my children again. I wouldn't have given up until I found you. The ad was a bonus I never expected. I thought you would all hate me. I thought I was going to have to make amends for a very long time before you took me back – if ever you did take me back.'

'I never hated you for going, Dad. I cried a lot and I missed you . . . but I got over it. I had Jimmy and Aunt Naomi. We clung together after Mum killed herself. We're very close. Even now.'

'That's good, sweetheart. I'm glad. Do you see your brother often?'

'No, not really. We don't live in each other's pockets, we lead different sorts of lives, but we still feel the same. I'm there for Jimmy and he's there for me. We always spend Christmas together. And we see each other about once a month. Sometimes more than that, sometimes less. It just depends.'

'And do you think he would see me?'

'I can't answer that. You'll have to write and ask him what he wants to do. He's younger than me, don't forget, and to be honest, I don't think he remembers that much about our life together before it all happened.'

'Well, no, I guess he wouldn't.'

'Would you like me to come with you . . . when you go to visit?'

His expression was one of relief. He smiled at her. 'Oh, Edie . . . I'll say I would.'

'All right, Dad. How long will you be here for?'

'Three more weeks, then we take the long haul back to Canada.'

'I'll see what I can arrange. Where are you staying? I'll need to get in touch with you.'

'In a rented apartment in Golders Green.' He pulled a pen and a small notepad from his inside pocket, wrote down his telephone number, tore the page out and handed it to his daughter. 'Edie . . . I really would appreciate it if we could meet up. Very much so.'

'I can't promise anything but I'll talk to Jimmy. And then it's up to him.'

In his hired car on the way back to Park Drive Edie's father was quiet and his son Ken knew him well enough to realise that conversation was not something he wanted right then. He was a deeply emotional man who had been carrying the burden of guilt for having deserted his family since the day he had left England for Canada. And it was the shadow of that guilt which had in the end been partly to blame for Ken's own mother leaving him for another man. 'What goes around comes around' was the proverb that Alex had repeated over and over after she had left.

Fortunately his work in downtown Toronto had

kept him busy, not only with a heavy workload but also with a social life with other illustrators who, like himself, frequented the many local taverns. Essentially these were bars with a stage, small nightclubs where many famous jazz musicians from the United States came to play. He and Ken were also fans of the Toronto Maple Leafs ice hockey team. Occasionally they attended home games at Maple Leaf Gardens and they would nearly always watch the game on television on a Saturday night.

Once he had arrived in Toronto, two decades earlier, Alex had secured work at a large firm of engravers that specialised in producing mail order catalogues. He had had to start at the bottom as a junior illustrator, but even then the pay had been better than in England, where he had been manager of a small printing company. He worked his way up to become a fashion artist and eventually head of the fashion illustration department in a studio that employed over forty specialist artists. Now, with photography improving rapidly, it was only a matter of time before many of the artists, himself included, would become redundant. It was mainly for this reason that he had come to London. His house having risen sharply in value within the past few years, he had been considering his options – one was to sell up, pay off his mortgage and with the cash left over return to England and live in a furnished apartment until he found a position in a studio in the country of his birth. So far he had found that Britain lagged behind Canada as far as the advertising art studios were concerned, and illustrators were thick on the ground. With his wide experience, however, he still hoped he would find a position in the advertising world. He had found his beloved daughter again and now he badly wanted to see Jimmy – the lad he had also walked out on all those years ago. As he mulled all this over the car continued silently towards Park Drive.

# 5

Nonnatus House, a convent for midwifery training
and practice, situated in the heart of London's dock-
lands, covered eight hamlets, including Stepney,
Bethnal Green, Whitechapel and the Isle of Dogs.
From here an order of nuns devoted to bringing safer
childbirth to the poor had opened houses not only
in the East End of London but in many of the slum
areas of the cities of Great Britain. Raymund
Nonnatus, the patron saint of midwives, obstetricians,
pregnant women, childbirth and newborn babies, had
been delivered by Caesarean section in Catalonia,
Spain, in 1204. His mother, astonishing no one, died
after giving birth. Raymund later became a priest and
died in 1240. Nonnatus House, to which Edie was
making her way this afternoon, was in an area heavily
populated by poorer families, and yet it was in the
heart of old London town, the Tower being within
walking distance.

Historically this part of the East End had always
been overpopulated, and given that it was so close to
the City this was unlikely to change. Ironically it was
living cheek by jowl that kept the people in good
neighbourly spirits for most of the time. They were

poor, they were overcrowded and they were often hungry by the time Friday came round – before Father's pay packet had reached the kitchen table – but there was a sense of belonging and of pride at being at the heart of things, with little or no pressure on people to feel they must rise above their station.

Be that as it may, many working-class offspring, in this buoyant second half of the twentieth century, were determined to better their lifestyles and raise their standard of living. It was not difficult to see that, with hard work, long hours and the backing of the working man's strength of character and acumen, the prosperity gap could be narrowed between the wealthy and the poor. It was becoming clear to the British people that if progress continued at the present rate the country of their birth would, before the end of the century, become a classless society. With improvements in education for ordinary people and the on-going building programme for new homes, stores and factories, opportunities for work within the labouring sector for both men and women were plentiful. Lads leaving school were being encouraged to learn a trade, and the prospect of future wealth was beginning to be more a reality than a dream.

Today, on this lovely late September afternoon, Edie took heart from the carefree atmosphere as groups of children played here, there and everywhere. Their laughter, shouts and chanting echoed throughout the narrow streets and alleys. Women who were not working at this time of day, young and old, were enjoying the sunshine as they sat on their doorsteps or stood by open doorways, nattering about nothing of great importance. As she walked past the locals, Edie was reminded of her past, when she was a child living in Cotton Street. Here things were no different, and the warm, colourful scene brought memories flooding back. She remembered her own mother, her arms folded, wearing a faded paisley-patterned apron, enjoying a harmless gossip outside her own front door or on the step of one of her neighbours. Passing a bombsite, clearly the most adventurous of all play-grounds, Edie recalled the time when she and her friends had played in those bombed houses which still had parts standing, sorry that she had lost touch with those chums who had moved out of the area, or were still there but too busy to contact old friends. She made a promise to herself there and then that she would one day try to trace one or two of them.

Arriving at Leyland Street, Edie looked up at St Nonnatus House and wondered whether she had perhaps got her facts wrong. She was expecting the place to look more like a convent, having imagined it to be an elegant building, tall and clean and a touch holy. Instead she gazed up at dark red-brick Victorian arches and turrets covered in layers of grime. The rusty iron gate gave a sinister look to the place, and there were no lights shining from within. Cautiously pulling the bell handle, she shuddered at the resounding echo from within the hall.

As the door slowly creaked open she came face to face with Sister Kathleen, a tall woman with a lovely smile, who, if appearances were anything to go by, was aged somewhere between fifty and sixty. She had an open honest face and pale ivory skin. At a loss as to what to say to this gracious lady, Edie felt her usual confidence drain away. She opened her mouth to say that she had come to the wrong place but found herself asking a question instead. 'This is Nonnatus House, isn't it?'

'Yes it is,' said the woman, an understanding expression on her face. 'Can I help you?'

'I'm not really sure. I suppose what I'm looking for really is advice,' said Edie, feeling ashamed now for coming here behind Maggie's back. 'It's my daughter ... but she doesn't know about this. Maybe you'd rather I came back with her?' Once again the sickly feeling of something being wrong swept through her.

'Well, why not come in for a little chat,' said the woman, standing aside. 'I was just about to make some tea. The kettle's on the stove, in fact.'

'Well, if you're sure I won't be wasting your time. And if you promise to stop me from pouring out my worries if you think it's wrong – my daughter not being here with me . . .'

'Oh, I'm sure it'll be all right. I can see you mean no harm. Do come in.'

Edie followed the nun through the hall into a spacious room with a high ceiling and little to enhance it. This was the kitchen and dining room. The floor was tiled with worn grey polished flagstones, and apart from the various store cupboards of all descriptions taking up all the available wall space, there was little else other than a long, wide pine table surrounded by motley wooden chairs. 'Please, do take a seat,' said Sister Kathleen, adding, 'Would you like a slice of Madeira cake? Sister Helen baked it fresh this morning.'

'No, I won't, thank you. My stomach feels as if there's a knot in it at the moment. But a cup of tea would be lovely.' Edie could hardly believe that she was here inside this sacred place which had no real sense of holiness about it other than the echoing sound which resembled that of a church.

'So your daughter doesn't know of this visit. I shouldn't worry too much over that. You're not the first, my dear. I should think that I alone must have embraced over fifty worried mothers in my time here.' Once she had turned up the gas under a large black kettle, the nun turned around to face Edie, a tender expression in her eyes. 'It's why we are here, my dear. At least, partly why we are here. But it is an important side to our work. Very special, in fact.'

Feeling less out of place in this kitchen, Edie began to relax a little. 'No, I didn't tell Maggie that I was coming. I didn't tell anyone. In fact, I wasn't that certain that I would come to the door. But I did and I'm glad of it.'

'I suppose it must be a little daunting for those not used to the building.' Sister Kathleen sat down at the table opposite Edie. 'But really it's quite homely when there are more of us about. Especially when we're all in from our rounds. It's not usually this quiet, I assure you. Now then . . . I am Sister Kathleen and your name is?'

'Edith. Well, Edie mostly.'

'And how old is your daughter, Edie?'

'Fifteen. I did mention Nonnatus House to her. I've not kept it a secret. I explained as best I could all that you stood for, from what I had heard, but I don't think she was really taking it in.' Raising her eyes, Edie looked into the sister's face. 'She won't be sixteen until next spring . . . and she's missed two periods.'

'Oh dear.' The woman's face broke into a sympathetic smile. 'I'm not sure that we nuns can help your daughter. But if it helps to talk about it, I'm all ears. And of course you may rest assured that anything you tell me will go no farther – unless you request it. We do have a weekly meeting when we discuss existing cases and new ones.'

'I think that just talking to you about it would help. One of the women where I work was talking about this place once and so I thought I'd come and see for myself.' With a touch of sorrow in her voice, Edie went on, 'I was under the impression that you had places where young unmarried mothers could go until their baby came and before it was put up for adoption.'

'Well, we do know of such places. A few in London and others spread around the country. Is that why you came? To see if we could find a place for your daughter?'

Edie pulled her handkerchief from inside the sleeve of her cardigan and dabbed at the beads of sweat that had broken out on her forehead. She suppressed a sudden urge to run. She felt as if she had made a mistake in coming here, and the sense of guilt for having gone behind Maggie's back was worsening. 'I will admit, Sister Kathleen, that I was half hoping you might know of a refuge where my daughter could go. And that you might be able to find a good home for the baby. A couple who can't 'ave children perhaps but want them badly.'

'Before I answer that I will just say that when I have been asked this before I have questioned the mother, or the aunt or the grandmother for that matter, as to whether they might themselves know of such a couple. A couple who for one reason or another, and it is usually medical, cannot have children. And you would be surprised, my dear, as to how many, when they think about it, do know already of a married woman who is longing to nurse a baby and bring it up as if it were her very own child.'

Edie was taken aback by this. Of course she knew of someone. A couple. Her very own brother and his wife. Shuddering at the thought of seeing Maggie's baby in the arms of Helen, her sister-in-law, she slowly shook her head. 'I do know of a couple but it would be too painful for my daughter, and me for that matter, to see someone else nursing her baby.'

Sister Kathleen smiled knowingly. 'That is the most usual reply. But you know, you'd be surprised by how such an arrangement can work beautifully. It means that the natural mother doesn't spend her life wondering what her child looks like or where he or she might be at certain stages of their development. It also makes the chosen relatives or friends very happy.

Altogether a life-changing experience, in fact. It might be something worth thinking about.'

'I don't think so. It's my brother and his wife who are having difficulty. Well, I'm fairly certain that it's Helen. She's never had a period. I think she's been told she's infertile but hasn't admitted it to herself, let alone my brother. I'm only surmising from things she's said.'

'Well, of course, you know the situation best my dear. If you think it wouldn't work out then of course you mustn't take too much of what I've suggested to heart. One does have to be sure of something so very important.'

Steering the talk away from her brother and sister-in-law, Edie said, 'The father is from a good Catholic family. I'm sure Maggie wouldn't mind the baby being brought up as a practising Catholic.'

Pulling her chair closer to the table, Sister Kathleen reached out and gently took Edie's hands in hers. 'My dear . . . the chimes do sometimes ring a sad tune and it is at such times that we must do all we can to soothe those souls who are suffering. But with the best will in the world you are not doing your daughter justice by coming here. She must walk this path herself. She must make her own decision as to what is best for her and her baby.'

'I can see what you're saying and I do understand, but Maggie's only fifteen and not particularly grown up for her age. Well, at least, I don't think so. At heart she's still a child.'

Sister Kathleen leaned back in her chair, reflecting.

'Yes, I can see that that is how you see her, but you would be surprised by how she would be viewed when in other people's company. In adult company. Children are always children to mothers until the mother must turn to *them* for advice.'

'I'd never thought about it like that before but I think you have a point. In fact, I'm sure you're right,' said Edie, choked at the thought of Maggie being seen by anyone as a woman – a mature woman. 'But I don't think she's mature enough or capable of making the right decision. She wants to have her baby and be its mother. But I think that if I can find a comfortable alternative . . .'

'The decision must be hers, my dear. You wouldn't want a rift to grow between Maggie and yourself, would you?'

'But she's too *young* to make a decision like this. She's only just out of ankle socks. She's got a whole lifetime in front of 'er. She's—'

Sister Kathleen raised a hand. 'If your daughter is old enough to be with child she is certainly old enough to make her own decisions. Of course you feel as if you know her better than she knows herself, but I have heard many mothers in my lifetime say the self-same thing. It simply isn't true, my dear. Try to remember what you were like at her age.'

Edie raised an eyebrow. 'To be perfectly honest with you I'd rather not. It was around that time when my father left home and my mother, soon afterwards, committed suicide. I had to cope the best way I could and look after my younger brother.'

'Oh, my dear child. I am sorry. But then surely you must see what I mean? You've coped with far more responsibility and grief than lies ahead of your daughter. And what of your husband? How does he feel about all this?'

'I'm a war widow,' said Edie, her tone resolute. She did not want to have to lie more than necessary. 'I haven't told Maggie's stepfather-to-be yet. In fact I've only told my aunt – who's been like a mother to me. And I did break it to my close friend, Jessie. I probably shouldn't have but I did.'

'But you haven't told your fiancé.'

'Not yet. But I will presently. We're getting married in December.'

Sister Kathleen gazed silently over Edie's shoulder, as if looking into another world, and then quietly said, 'God will be good to you. He sees everything. I believe that you shouldn't put off telling your fiancé. In fact my advice would be that you should speak to him about it as soon as possible.' She then looked directly at Edie. 'Men are softies at heart, you know. I've probably seen more men cry when a baby is delivered than women. You may be surprised by his response.'

'Maybe you're right,' said Edie, as she visualised herself breaking the news. 'We'll just have to wait and see. To be honest with you, I've been dreading the day when I do mention it. He may well decide to walk away from it all. And who could blame him? A future stepdaughter expecting a child at fifteen. It's hardly something to celebrate.' Edie smiled. 'Anyway . . . I've taken up far too much of your time already and you've given me plenty to think about. I'm glad I came even if I didn't get the answer I was hoping for. A place for Maggie where she'd be with other girls in the same predicament.'

'Well, let's not get too down about it yet. I shall make enquiries. And please don't leave feeling as if you've wasted my time or yours. You needed a little comforting and I'm flattered that you came to us when in need. And what better place than this building, where God's love is in every corner. Going to your vicar might have proved a little too awkward for you at this early stage. I'm certain he will be kind, but sometimes it's easier to talk to a woman about such things. Especially when one is face to face.'

Edie knew this was the time to leave. She thanked Sister Kathleen again before adding, 'Maggie is mulling over the idea of living with her boyfriend until she's sixteen and they can be married. In Scotland. I can't say I'm happy about that either but choices are few and far between.'

'Does she have a place in mind? Where they might live?'

'One's been offered to them. Her boyfriend's uncle has a flat above a small Italian café and another above a fish-and-chip shop. Between them they would 'ave to run one of them. Whichever they choose. Neither are in my area so our neighbours wouldn't see Maggie's stomach growing. I'm sure you must have come up against gossips and know what they can be like. How they can hurt people's feelings.'

'Well, yes, but the blame is not always theirs.

Troubled minds are more often the case. We must
always keep a place in our prayers for them. But I
do see what you mean. You have a great deal on your
plate. Indeed you do.' She leaned back in her chair
and studied Edie's face before saying, 'If you could
come back and see me in, say, a week's time, I will
have made some enquiries by then. There is a refuge
for young women in your daughter's condition in
Scotland. I can't promise anything, of course, but it's
worth a letter – which I shall pen today.'

'Thank you,' said Edie, humbly. 'I would miss her
badly but that may have to be the road that we go
down . . . if we're lucky enough to secure a place
for her.'

'It is a possibility, but please try not to let your
hopes rise too high. Sadly, there are hundreds of girls
in your daughter's predicament across the country.
Would that we could do more for them. Would that
we could. You see, the funds are simply not available.
And the board does tend to give preference to those
who are the victims of rape or who have been abused
within the family. Even so, finding a place for them
is not always easy. On the other hand, I can tell you
that with the wider availability of the sheath the
number of girls getting pregnant does seem to be
going down. To some this is not a good sign, but to
us who know personally of the suffering it is something that we have been praying for. Whether we like
it or not, we simply have to move with the times.
Awful though they may appear to us now.'

'Yes, I see what you mean,' said Edie, wishing to

hear no more. 'And now I must leave you to get on. You've been really kind. I can't thank you enough for putting me in the picture.'

'Not at all, my dear. You're not the first to have knocked on our door and you'll not be the last. You've suffered greatly during your life. I shall pray for you, and I believe that God will be good to you. The answer will come when you're least expecting it. "Seek and ye shall find" is not always appropriate. We don't necessarily have to search to find the answer to our prayers.'

'There is one other thing,' said Edie. 'The others who've come to you for help in the past . . . what happened to them? Those you couldn't place in a refuge for unmarried mothers-to-be?'

'Oh, my dear, it varies so very much. We sometimes end up delivering their babies in a relative's home and the newborn remains with the family, being looked after by a grandmother, aunt or even a cousin of a mature enough age. More often than not, however, it is the grandmother of the child who takes care of it. Have you thought about that as a possibility?'

Edie spoke in a quiet voice. 'My Aunt Naomi suggested that. She thought I should tie a cushion around my stomach.'

'It wouldn't be the first time that's happened.' Sister Kathleen smiled. 'On that you may trust me.'

'I don't doubt it,' said Edie, feeling no desire to go down that particular road again. 'So you think that no matter who brings up the child my daughter should have her baby regardless.'

'It would be a sin not to. If our Lord has blessed her with a child then He has blessed her. Speak to your fiancé . . . and your husband too, if you are still lighting a candle for him, that is.'

'I don't light candles but I will have a word when I say my prayers tonight.' Edie never said her prayers either but she couldn't think of anything else to say to this lady, who seemed to be living in a totally different world to the one Edie knew – the tough world of the street where prayers came after the tragedy. 'As for Dennis, my fiancé, who I'm to marry in a few months' time, I thought I would mention it once I've arrived at the best solution. I'm not sure how he'll take it.'

Rising from her chair to attend to the boiling kettle, Sister Kathleen said, 'Well, my dear, when all else around you fails, remember that God is there for you. Always.'

Before Edie had a chance to answer, two nuns arrived talking about a fragile mother who had just given birth to a nine-pound baby boy. Rising from her own chair, Edie said goodbye to Sister Kathleen, nodded politely at the arriving nuns, and left Nonnatus House believing that this would be the last she saw of it – or of Sister Kathleen for that matter.

On her walk back home she recalled everything the cleaner at work had told her. The St Raymund's midwives had worked in the slums of the East End since 1850, and had continued working tirelessly through the various epidemics: cholera, typhoid, polio, tuberculosis. They had also nursed people through two world wars and had stayed in London throughout the Blitz and its concentrated bombing of the docks. They had delivered babies in air-raid shelters and Underground stations. And they were still here, passively working through long nights and tedious days.

She approached a somewhat forbidding Victorian tenement block and cut through the grim inner courtyard, snaking her way between washing lines, thanking providence that this was not where she lived. By comparison to these red-brick flats, which had been built in the 1850s, Scott House, on the Barcroft Estate, was unbelievably modern. And compared to these families who had little choice other than to live in cramped conditions with overflowing communal rubbish bins which encouraged rats and cockroaches, she and Maggie had little to complain about.

The entire journey had been an eye-opener. Not that Edie had been unaware of the poverty in some of the backstreets. She appreciated what her family and others like it had been given by way of housing, even though she was aware that there was still a long way to go before all those who deserved better received it. It would be fair to say that most homes did now have running hot and cold water and a flushing lavatory, and that bathrooms were becoming more widespread. Not in the tenements, however. Here hot, steamy public wash houses were still very much a part of everyday life for hundreds of families. The steam and Turkish baths also continued to attract regular visits on a Saturday afternoon.

Contrary to much outside opinion, to the working

classes living in the slums of London cleanliness, when it could be attained, was high on their list of priorities, as was a hot meal, with or without a cut of meat. To an outsider the cheap traditional pie and mash was something to be tried once, but to the local inhabitants it was a mainstay of life. In most homes the wireless was now commonplace, and television, mostly on rental, was beginning to make its way into the poorer people's culture. Community halls for dances were still popular, and among the young clubs where teenagers could dance to hit records were gaining ground in working-class London. Slum clearance was well and truly under way and the birth pill, a light at the end of a dark tunnel, was on the horizon. Too late for Maggie, though.

When Edie turned the key in her front door the last person on her mind was her brother Jimmy and his wife Helen, who were in her kitchen drinking tea with Naomi. She recognised their voices from the hall, especially that of her sister-in-law, who, from the sound of things, was in high spirits.

Believing that Naomi had let Jimmy know that their father was back, and that this was the reason they were here, she entered the kitchen a little apprehensively. She hadn't been sure whether to tell him or not, but knew that Naomi would make the right decision for her once she had been told earlier on.

'Hello, sis!' Jimmy beamed as Edie appeared in the kitchen doorway. 'We was just about to give you up. Where you bin?'

'Jimmy?' said Helen, 'Why are you slipping back into cockney just because your sister's arrived?' She then turned to Edie, rolled her eyes, slowly shook her head and finished with a sweet smile as she stood up to greet her sister-in-law. 'What am I going to do with him?' she mused, placing a hand on Edie's shoulder and brushing a kiss lightly across her face.

'Hello, Helen,' responded Edie, giving her a gentle hug. 'Hello, Aunt Naomi. Let yourself in with your key again, did you? Or is Maggie hiding somewhere?'

'Well, with you *both* being out, my darling I really had no choice other than to let myself in – or go away,' said Naomi, standing up and holding out her arms to Edie. 'I chose the former. And as I am sure you will agree, it is as well that I did. Poor Helene and Jimmy would have had to stand on the doorstep, waiting for you to come home.' Kissing her niece's cheek, she whispered that she had not yet mentioned her father's return.

His focus still on his wife, and how best to keep her in an easy mood, Jimmy spoke in a deliberately comical cockney voice. 'And as for you, my good woman, you're not gonna do nuffin' wiv me! If I wanna talk in my native tongue, I will.' He then held out his arms to his sister. 'Come 'ere, you.'

Falling into his arms, Edie could smell the faint scent of his Brylcreem. 'Sorry, I wasn't in, darling,' she said, patting his back as if he were still her little brother. 'Maggie should 'ave been back home from the library by now.'

'I *was* going to suggest that we take you out for a

meal as a treat,' said Helen, her singsong voice grating just a little. 'I thought we could all go for a nice little drive out to Forest Gate and to the Italian place. But there, your brother wants fish and chips because he's back in the East End.' Then, giving Jimmy a wink, Helen, who was simply glowing now, added, 'Well, go on, then. Give your sister the good news.'

Pulling back, Edie looked into Jimmy's warm brown eyes. 'What good news?'

'He's started up his own little business,' said Helen, answering for her husband with pride in her eyes. 'We were hoping that Dennis might call round. Jimmy could put some work his way, couldn't you, dear. There's always room for a good electrician.'

Raising an eyebrow at her brother, Edie smiled. 'Is that right, love? Well, congratulations on starting up on your own, but as for Dennis . . .'

'I know. Take no notice of 'er. He's got plenty of work, thank you very much.' He turned to Helen. 'He was running 'is own business long before Edie met 'im, silly cow. It was Dennis who talked me into startin' up.'

'Is that right?' crooned his wife, gently scratching her neck with the tips of her fingers. 'I thought it was the other way round. That we told him he should work for himself.'

'No, Helen. *You* told him. We didn't like to remind you that he was already doing just that.'

'Oh well, Jimmy,' she said, not one to be put down easily, 'if that's the way you remember it, then so be it. Who am I to argue? We women know nothing about these things, do we, girls.' The gloating tone in her voice, intended to amuse both Edie and Naomi, went down like a dud firework and silence filled the kitchen.

Used to Helen, Jimmy was quick to fill it. 'Dennis is doing all right. I could take a leaf out of 'is book and will. Is he coming round after work, Ed? I would like to 'ave a chat with him. Good electricians are like gold dust.'

'Oh . . .' crooned Helen. 'So you do listen to me *sometimes*, Jimmy.' She put a hand on her husband's arm and gave it a squeeze.

'You know I do,' he said, winking at her, giving his wife what she needed most now – to be the centre of his attention. 'Edie and Aunt Naomi know that you're the brains behind the scene, Helen.'

'Of course we do. We've always known it,' said Edie, who really did not want to hear all this hogwash. The news about her dad returning was being squeezed out by whatever was on her brother's mind. 'We just didn't want her to get too big headed, that's all.' She looked across at the gas stove. 'Any tea in that pot?'

'I've just made it,' said Helen, getting up from her chair. 'You sit down, Edie, and I'll be mum. I've brought you one of my special fruit cakes. It's wrapped in greaseproof in the cupboard. It'll be best kept a day, but if you fancy a slice now . . .'

'No, I won't, thanks, Helen,' replied Edie, trying to be friendly when really all she wanted was her flat to herself. The expression on her aunt's face had not gone unnoticed. Knowing full well that Naomi had never taken to Helen, she didn't need her to show her true feelings now. Naomi was too quiet for comfort, and Edie could see that she was irritated by her sister-in-law.

'What about you, Naomi?' Helen's shrill voice cut through Edie's thoughts. 'Would you like some cake with your tea?'

'Thank you, but no.' Naomi smiled, wanting to remain in the background. 'I shall have to be going shortly. Things to do and so on.'

'Always the busy lady, eh?' said Helen, taking another cup and saucer from the cupboard. 'You should slow down a bit. You're not getting any younger, after all's said and done.'

Edie ignored this, and her aunt's disparaging look. 'Did you put the cake at the back of the larder, Helen?' she said as she flopped down into a chair. 'It'll keep longer in there.'

'Larder!' Helen chuckled, pouring a little sterilised milk in each cup. 'That's not a larder, it's a wall cupboard.'

'Actually,' said Naomi, 'it *is* a larder. It is in the coolest part of the kitchen away from the gas stove and it has a small window with mesh instead of glass.'

'It's a cupboard, Naomi. Don't be silly. Larders are tall and you can practically walk into them. Silly thing.' She smiled and poured the tea.

'No, I'm awfully sorry, but you're wrong. The type you're speaking of is terribly old fashioned. Nowadays a space is left below for when people purchase refrigerators.'

'Girls, girls!' Jimmy grinned, splaying his hands.

'Does it really matter? And haven't we got more important and wonderful things to talk about? Our Maggie, for instance?'

'What about Maggie?' said Edie, alarm bells ringing in her head.

'Oh, come on, sis, you know. The *news*.'

'The very *good* news.' Helen beamed.

'You tell *me*, Jimmy. What have you heard?' Without thinking Edie shot Naomi a venomous look, believing for a split second that she might have accidentally spilt the beans.

'Your lovely daughter wrote us a letter, Edie. But you must know that, *surely*? She wouldn't have written to us behind your back, would she?'

'I didn't know she'd written to you but there's nothing mysterious about that. She's a working girl now. A grown-up.' Edie's frown gave her away, and Helen had not missed it.

'Oh dear. I've a feeling that we might know a secret that we mustn't tell,' she carolled smugly.

'Jimmy,' said Edie, turning to her brother, 'what has Maggie told you?'

'Well, first off, that's she's gonna have a baby . . . and second, which I hope she's discussed with you, Ed, that she would like me and Helen to foster it.'

'*Adopt*, if you please, Jimmy,' said Helen. 'All or nothing. You know that's what I said. Don't back-pedal now, if you don't mind. I've set my heart on this.'

Staring in disbelief at her brother, Edie was only just aware of Helen's voice floating over her head as she droned on about getting things straight right from the beginning. She paid no attention to it, simply murmured, 'No, Jimmy.'

'You mean . . . no she never told you about us having the baby?'

'No, Jimmy. I mean, no. She didn't mention it and you are not to even consider applying for adoption.'

'Applying?' said Helen, her smug voice grating. 'What are you talking about, Edie? Apply to who, may I ask? If our Maggie wants us to bring up her child I can't see why we have to *apply* to anyone.'

'The courts, if necessary, because that's where I would fight you. If Maggie has, in a moment of weakness, written to you offering up her baby once it's here, forget it.' She turned to face Naomi. 'Do you agree?' The expression on her face defied her aunt to go against her.

Leaning back in her chair, Naomi gazed up at the ceiling, a calm and well-rehearsed smile on her face. 'The young these days are so impetuous and quite confused. It's a time of change and it's all happening so fast. It doesn't surprise me one bit that she wrote you a letter on the spur of the moment, Helene. I don't think you should set too much store by it just yet.'

'There. Even Naomi thinks it the best possible solution,' said Helen, her face becoming redder by the moment. 'We would—'

'As I was *saying*,' said Naomi, stopping Helen in her tracks, 'it doesn't surprise me one iota that my great-niece should have written more than one letter. The emotional state of her mind at the moment, and so on. I, of course, did *not* take it seriously, and unlike you, Jimmy, my darling, I will not jump in before giving your sensitive young niece time to see that she has acted out of panic. Or worse still, desperation. Once she has had time to sit down and think about it, of *course* she will see that it is the worst option put forward thus far. To have either myself *or* Helene as the adopted mother would be *disastrous*. A constant reminder of her own inadequacies. It is a recipe for disaster, if ever there was one.'

'Well,' said Helen, tight lipped, 'I can see that *you* would hardly make an ideal mother, Naomi, with all due respect, but I would have thought that Jimmy and I would be an ideal choice. We've got a beautiful home, with three bedrooms, and as a matter of fact we're having a refrigerator delivered next week. So there'll be no question of milk going off, if that's what you're thinking.'

'Darling, of course you have a lovely home – and you have every *reason* to be proud of it – but bricks, mortar and a refrigerator were not on my mind when I inferred that it was out of the question. You are *family*. And if my much treasured Maggie does decide to have her baby adopted it would be *far* better that she never sees it again. Surely, even *you* can see that?'

'No, I can't actually. I disagree wholeheartedly. Maggie can come over to us and babysit whenever we go out and bond with the baby as an aunt. Now what's better than that, tell me?'

'Well, I think that covers everything you came here for, Jimmy,' said Edie, desperate to be by herself. 'Except to say that it might be better if you all leave before Maggie gets back. I'll talk to her about it tonight and I'll get her to pop another letter in the post. I didn't know she'd written to you and I think the fact she did at this stage shows her state of mind. Confused and unstable.'

'You want us to leave?' said Helen, her usual tactless self, not having fully absorbed what Edie had just said. 'After we've come all this way from Ed*mon*ton! I don't think so, Edie. No. We'll wait for Maggie and see what she's got to say.'

'We won't, Helen,' said Jimmy, his face serious. 'Edie's right . . . and so is Aunt Naomi. We 'ave jumped the gun a bit. Maggie needs time.' He gave his wife a look that spoke volumes, clearly signalling that they should leave and leave now.

'No, we have not jumped the gun, thank you! Maggie turned to us in her time of trouble and when something like that happens you don't wave it off as if it's nothing!' Turning to Naomi, she continued, 'Besides which, Naomi, that baby, when it comes, will be my Jimmy's blood relative. His great-nephew or niece. So he's got a right to a say in how it's brought up. Or what's done to it!'

'What do you mean, Helen?' said Edie, sombrely. 'What do you think *we* would do to my daughter's baby? My grandchild? What could we possibly do that would meet with your or anyone's disapproval?'

Folding her arms, Helen adopted an expression that would have made some people long to slap her face – Edie being one such person. 'I wouldn't put the idea of abortion past either of you two. I dare say

Naomi knows all about that, the kind of life she's led, with free-loving actors and the like. And there are always plenty of backstreet rippers on the lookout for a few pound notes.'

Slowly raising her hand, Edie pointed a finger at her sister-in-law. 'Now you just take that back, Helen. You take it back and you apologise.'

'Oh? So you're saying that the thought never crossed your mind, are you? That you didn't suggest it to your only child?'

'Did Maggie say I suggested it?'

'No . . . but then she wouldn't, would she? She's a lovely girl and I would be only too pleased to look after her baby as if it were my own. I wouldn't take any old baby in. I would want to know who the mother was, I can tell you.' Helen tipped up her chin proudly. 'We would love that baby. Love and look after it as if it was our very own flesh and blood – but we'd always let it know that Maggie was its real mother. *If* that's what Maggie wanted. Anyone else interfering I would ignore. We would do everything properly and in the best interests of Maggie and that baby. You should know that, Edie. You should know that without me having to say it.'

'Darling, of course Edie knows that,' said Naomi, quite moved by Helen's sorry confession. For clearly this was what it was – a confession that she was desperate to mother a child. 'All Edie is saying is that you allow a little more time before approaching her daughter.'

'I mean to say,' continued Helen, as if Naomi hadn't

spoken, 'it's not as if I don't want to have children of my own, is it? It's not my fault that it hasn't happened. Or Jimmy's. Some couples can't have babies and maybe we're one of them. So why shouldn't we want to adopt, and adopt one from our own family?' She turned to Naomi, hoping that she had found an ally. 'You'd want the baby to stay in the family, Naomi, wouldn't you?'

'Well, yes, actually I would, Helene. As a matter of fact I would like Maggie to keep her baby. What I am more interested in is finding a place to which she might retreat until her time has come. Then we shall go from there. Day by day. All pulling together and helping as much as we possibly can.'

'At fifteen?'

'Sixteen, actually. She'll be sixteen by the time it is born.'

'Fifteen, sixteen, what difference does it make? She's a child herself. She couldn't possibly take on the responsibility—'

'Hardly a child any more,' said Naomi, smiling serenely. 'And it will be *her* breasts filling with milk and not yours *or* mine. Which,' she added, raising a hand to prevent Helen from interrupting her, 'is how it *should* be. I will admit that at first I thought it might be better for Edith to have it look as if it were *her* baby. I was wrong, however, and with my hand on my heart I will admit my error in making the suggestion in the first place.'

'And you don't think that her own aunt and uncle would be better parents for the child?'

'I do not. I am now one hundred per cent sure that my great-niece is capable of looking after her own child . . . with the devotion of any mother, naturally.'

'Well, I don't agree with you. And what's more—'

'Come on, Helen,' said Jimmy, his face taut as he gripped his wife's arm. 'I'll do a little detour on the way home and take you to the Dick Turpin for a bite to eat and a couple of gin and tonics.' In truth he felt like strangling this woman he had been saddled with.

'Before you go, Jimmy,' said Edie, a telltale quiver in her voice, 'I've got something to tell you, but I don't want a debate over it. Not now. Not after all this.'

'That's all right, sis. You don't 'ave to look so worried. Go on, then. Get it off your chest. I won't bite you. Helen might, but I won't.'

Taking a deep breath, Edie spoke in a quiet voice. 'Dad's back in England. He came to visit me with our half-brother. He wants to see you.'

Stunned, Jimmy could do no more than stare at his sister open mouthed. Grabbing the opportunity to respond for him, Helen said, 'After what he did! I don't think so. No. Over my dead body will we entertain that monster!'

Giving his wife a vicious look, Jimmy took Helen firmly by the arm, picked up her handbag and all but marched her out of the room. Talking over his shoulder as he went, and still reeling from the news about his father, he spoke quietly, saying, 'I'll drop in one night next week after work, Edie. And I won't mention a word about the letter from Maggie if she's here.'

'It would help if you were to have a telephone connected!' yelled Helen from the door. 'Your new bloke is s'posed to 'ave money! Get 'im to put 'is 'and in 'is bloody pocket!' The slamming of the front door brought sighs of relief from both Edie and her aunt.

'So much for Ed*mon*ton grace, wit and charm.' Naomi smiled.

'You can be so clever when you put your mind to it,' said Edie. 'You handled that really well, but I can't help feeling sorry for Helen. She's so desperate to have a baby.'

'Precisely. Too eager. Which may be the problem. I'm afraid that your brother's wife, now that they are quite well off, is of the mind that she may have everything she wants. And I'm sure that is almost true where material things are concerned. But when it comes to bearing her own child it is a different matter altogether. If she really does want to adopt there are children's homes teeming with moppets who are longing for new parents to come along and take them home.'

'That's true,' said Edie, thoughtfully. Smiling, she added, 'Maggie never did write you a letter, did she?'

'Well, actually . . . no, she didn't. And I am of the opinion that to have come up with such a tale, and within seconds, was nothing less than pure genius.'

'It was. Please God I'll be as wise as you when I'm in my seventies.'

'Only just in them, Edith. Only just.'

Feeling more like herself once she and Naomi were settled in the living room with their second pot of tea, and having talked non-stop about the visit from her dad and half-brother, Edie told her aunt where she had been and why. As ever, Naomi took her by surprise, saying, 'Oh, darling, I do wish you had asked me to come with you. It would be wonderful to see the inside of that place again.'

'You mean to tell me that you've been in there? When? Why?'

'It was a very long time ago. When midwifery and nursing were in a shameful state. And when it was not deemed a *respectable* occupation for any woman of breeding. Filthy, gin-swilling women were funny to read about in novels, but not if you had had dealings with some of them. My lovely friend Harriet could tell you a tale, had she the mind to. But there. You don't want to hear things from the past, dead and buried.'

Leaning back and closing her eyes, Edie let out a contented sigh. 'What is it about you that makes me want to lie back and forget all my cares and woes?'

'I have absolutely no idea. I *presume* by your posture and the expression on your face that you would like me to resume? Nonnatus House?'

'You know very well I would. You've roused my interest – as always. Go on, then. Take my mind off Helen behaving like a vulture.'

'Oh, darling, let's not be *too* hard. She is desperate to be a mother, after all's said and done.'

'I know,' responded Edie, in a softer tone. 'But that's what it felt like. I'm only being honest.'

'And of course she does have a point. Jimmy would make a wonderful father, and he is of the same blood.'

'You're not saying it'd work, are you?'

'No. No, I'm *not* saying that. I am merely suggesting that we treat them *both* with kid gloves. Let them feel special perhaps. They are your future grandchild's only living aunt and uncle – that we know of – in this country. Harry had cousins, I'm sure he must have done. But no brothers, no sisters and parents who went their own separate ways years since. Leaving him to fend for himself at the age of fourteen. And with no word from either of them from that day to this.'

Edie didn't want to think about Harry's sad childhood and his lonely life before she had met him so she steered the conversation back to her brother. 'God knows what our Jimmy must have felt like today. I never really got the chance to say anything to him about all this. You and Helen did all the talking. I could tell by his face that all he wanted was to have me to himself. I saw that old familiar little-boy-lost look. Never mind Maggie's letter – he had just heard that his dad was back home.'

'Indeed,' said Naomi, 'which is why I didn't want there to be a rift between you and Jimmy. Let them blame me for any bad feeling Helen may harbour. Jimmy's *silly* old aunt who's losing her marbles.'

'You don't miss a bloody trick, do you. Oh, let's forget Helen for now. Tell me about Nonnatus House and your connection with it.'

'Well, there's not really that much to tell. I was hardly connected. But I will say that the nuns had their hearts in the right place. People like Florence Nightingale did actually change the face of nursing for ever. She and other dedicated souls devoted their entire lives to raising the standard of nursing. The midwives of St Raymund Nonnatus followed in her footsteps and followed exceptionally well. Up until Miss Nightingale's arrival on the scene, I would say that midwifery was in a shameful state. The nuns devoted their lives to bringing safer childbirth to the poor and opened houses in the East End and in many *other* slum areas. In those days most people could not afford to pay the fee that doctors charged to deliver a baby. Hence the untrained, self-taught midwives. As a child I remember neighbours who had been abandoned to an agonising death when any serious problem developed during labour.'

'Nao . . . you're meant to be cheering me up. Leave out the grisly stuff . . . if that's possible for someone as theatrical as you.'

'Of course, my darling – I will admit that I *was* getting rather carried away. The nuns saw that the answer lay in the proper training of midwives and, *much* to the local hacks' fury, they brought about control of the disgraceful practice by way of legislation.' Naomi paused, glancing at her niece to check she was still listening. She was.

'Go on, then,' said Edie. 'I'm all ears.'

'Good. So I may continue.' Naomi was secretly pleased that she had Edie's undivided attention.

'You will in any case, so get on with it.'

'You have *such* a way with words. Now then, where was I . . . ah yes. Their struggle for legislation, in which the feisty nuns met fierce opposition. It's not too difficult to imagine the resistance. Many back-street abortionists who also delivered full-term babies stood to lose a reliable ongoing income. Fortunately the Nonnatus nuns would not be badgered into sub-mission. And it is for that reason that I am sitting here now.'

Taken aback, Edie said, 'Are you trying to tell me that the nuns delivered you as a baby?'

'Yes . . . after a certain Mrs Cunningham had made a bit of a hash of things. There but for the grace of God . . . My mother, your *grandmother*, would have bled to death and I would not be here to tell the tale. At that time we were living, if living is the word, in the bottom half of a poky house in Aldgate. A neighbour heard my mother's screams, by all accounts, and ran all the way to Nonnatus House and fetched two nuns who were by then prac-tising midwives.'

'But why haven't you ever told me this before? I can't believe you'd keep something like that to your-self.'

'It's a little too close to the heart, Edie. I am hardly made of stone.'

'I know that, you daft thing. You're as soft as sponge. But the point is that you might not have made it, Nao. And nor would my grandmother, by the sound of things. And you were born before Mum so . . . I wouldn't be here either if it wasn't for those women, and neither would Maggie.'

'Which is why I have not bothered to tell you. You are here and so is Maggie and, very shortly, so too will be your grandchild.' Silence filled the kitchen, aunt and niece both lost in their thoughts.

'For thirty years the battle continued for those strong-willed nuns,' Naomi continued eventually. 'And in 1902 the first Midwives Act was passed and the Royal College of Midwives was born. We have much to thank them for, my darling. Much.'

'I'm sure we do,' said Edie. 'You only just scraped through the door of life.'

'Yes, I am lucky to be here.'

Steering the conversation away from herself, Naomi asked whether anyone at Nonnatus House had been able to help Edie in deciding the right thing to do. Edie then gave her a brief résumé of what Sister Kathleen had said – that if there was a place available where Maggie could go for the duration of her pregnancy she would put her name forward – adding that she had been more or less of the same opinion as Naomi, believing that they should hold on to one of their own if at all possible.

Relieved that someone else had suggested this too, Naomi smiled. 'Well, that doesn't surprise me, my darling. Having heard all that I feel rather guilty for not having given something back by way of my time. I'm sure they could do with as much help as they can get.'

The sound of the front door opening and shutting

again brought silence to the room. Maggie had returned.

'Don't say anything about Jimmy and Helen coming round!' instructed Edie. 'Not even a hint of it!'

'Oh, please, darling. Do you really take me for a fool? Of course I shan't say a word.'

Bounding into the room, a radiant smile on her face, Maggie looked lovelier than ever. Her light green eyes were shining. 'You'll never guess what I've got, Aunt Naomi! Not in a million years will you guess.'

'Well, I'm sure you will tell me, poppet . . . in the fullness of time.'

Pulling a folded sheet of paper from her pocket, Maggie waved it in the air. 'Thirty-two names! And that doesn't include their partners. And they're still signing up!'

'They?' said Naomi, intrigued.

'And they're not all wrinkly with walking sticks neither! Miss Lightfoot said that those showing interest are anywhere from forty years old to eighty!'

'Well, it all sounds fun, my darling, but what on earth are you talking about?'

'The tea dances, of course!' She waved the list again. 'This is only the beginning! We put a notice on the board in the library, and now look! Thirty-two have signed it to say they want to go. And if you take into account their partners . . .'

'Maggie . . . that *was* clever! Now why didn't I think of that. Of course, libraries.'

'And the art gallery in Whitechapel. Miss Lightfoot is always in there looking at the paintings. She's got to know the people who run it and so they're bound to agree to put the notices up for us.'

'One of my leaflets, you mean?'

'No. They'll be on the side for people to take. We worked out a notice putting the idea across and saying where you was gonna hold the dances and then another sheet of paper that people could sign if they would like to go! It was Miss Lightfoot's idea! She's brilliant. Quiet as a mouse, meek as a lamb, and then all of a sudden she comes up trumps!'

Naomi smiled. 'And I thought you would find it all rather dull.'

'No. 'Course not. I'll tell you more in a minute. I'm starving.'

'Oh ... I've not even peeled the potatoes yet, Mags,' said Edie, equally touched by her daughter's enthusiasm for this new enterprise.

'Good. Can we afford fish and chips? I'll go and get 'em if we can. I've bin thinking about fish and cod in crispy batter with salt and vinegar all day. I'm so hungry I could eat a horse.'

'Well, how strange,' said Naomi, 'so have I.' She dug into her red shopping bag and withdrew her purse. 'Tea is on me,' she said. 'And don't forget the pickled onions.' She thrust her hand forward, proffering a ten-shilling note.

'You're a Hollywood star,' said Maggie. Then, bending over, she kissed first her aunt and then her mother on the cheek. 'Love you both.'

Glancing at each other, Edie and Naomi knew instinctively that something had happened.

At the door Maggie said, 'We've got everything worked out, by the way.'

'Have you, babe?' said Edie, all ears.

'I'm gonna serve in Tony's uncle's fish shop in Roman Road and Tony's gonna do the frying and his two uncles are gonna help him convert the flat above and decorate it while he lives there.'

'And you?' said Edie, cautiously. 'I thought you wanted to run the Italian café in Islington?'

'I do one day. We've changed our minds for now though. No harm in that, is there? Once I've got experience with frying fish and chips to perfection — we'll move on. We think we could really make a go of a café-cum-restaurant. Tony's mum 'as got some old family cookery books.'

'You can't read Italian.'

'No, Mum . . . but Tony can. And the recipes are for simple easy to cook meals.'

'To suit a cafe?'

'Definitely. Anyway, I'll stop here till Baby comes. Until I'm sixteen. Then we'll all go to Gretna Green and stop overnight in a bed-and-breakfast place. Tony's dad and 'is uncles are gonna foot the bill. All that we'll 'ave to fork out for is my outfit and the train fares. Not bad, eh?'

'And do we have a say in all these arrangement, perchance?' said Naomi, calm and collected. 'Where you will live and work and get married?'

'Only if you fink there's something wrong with it. Is there?' Maggie's expression had changed from exuberant to concerned within seconds. 'You don't think there's anything wrong in my working in the fish and chip shop for now do you? Until I'm ready to run a café?'

'I thought it was a restaurant,' said Edie, amused.

'It's a café now but we'll turn it *into* a restaurant! A small one but—'

'And the library?' Edie cut in. 'Do those who employ you know what's going on to date?'

'I've told Miss Lightfoot everything! She's gonna arrange it so I'll be there until I become a bit too obvious. Then I can take leave without pay and go back *if* I want to once I'm ready to leave my child with you two to look after during the day. *If* I don't take to cooking for the public that is. I'll get Aunt Helen to child mind if you don't want to do it.'

'Ah,' said Naomi, believing that this was the right time to mention that her uncle and his wife had paid a visit. She could only hope that Edie would be of the same mind. 'As a matter of fact Helene and your Uncle Jimmy were here earlier.'

'Oh. Right. I s'pose they told you about my letter, then. Oh well. I'll go round the phone box on the way to the chip shop and say I've changed my mind.' She looked from Naomi to Edie, who was clearly puzzled by the way her daughter had suddenly become so confident and was very much in control of her own life.

'You won't mind, Mum, will you? If Helen looks after your grandchild for two days a week?'

Edie shrugged. What could she say?

'No, I didn't think you would. I'm gonna check up

on the buses and trains and find the best route for 'er. What d'yer want, then? Cod or haddock?'

'Cod . . . please,' Edie murmured.

'Haddock,' said Naomi.

'Righto. Won't be long.' With that Maggie was away, leaving both Edie and Naomi feeling as if they were slow and old.

'Well,' said Edie, 'my trip to see the midwives of St Raymund was obviously a waste of time. She's got it all worked out for herself.'

The door suddenly flew open again and Maggie's face appeared around it. 'You don't 'ave to worry either . . . about me and Tony. He won't stay one night in the flat. We're not gonna do anything like that again till we're married. It's all to do with self-control . . . according to my fiancé. Oh, and that's another thing. He's gonna buy me a little dress ring. Then, later on, once he's saved up, he's gonna buy me a diamond one.' She flashed a quick smile and departed again.

Edie slowly shook her head. 'Talk about scatter-brain. It must be her hormones. What do you make of all this, Nao?'

'For this, my darling, we must look to Shakespeare. "Love laughs at locksmiths."' She smiled serenely. '"Were beauty under *twenty* locks kept fast, Yet love breaks through and picks them all at last."'

'I wasn't thinking about love and romance, Nao. I was thinking about the neighbours and what they'll say when madam's walking around with her belly up front.'

'*Gossip*,' said Naomi, 'is like the yellow smoke that

comes from the dirty tobacco pipe. It proves *nothing* other than the bad taste of the smoker.'

'And I'm supposed to take heart from that, am I?'

'You may take whatever you wish, Edith, my darling. But when I was singing on stage in a packed music hall and dying from the yellow smoke, it was the *only* thought that kept me going. T.S. Eliot has much to be thanked for. Not the original quotation, true, but Eliot was a little too long-winded for my liking.'

'Let it stick in their throats and not ours.'

'Precisely. We will christen that baby when it comes . . . with the very *best* of wine. We shall celebrate the arrival . . . not commiserate the birth. We are, after all, speaking of *my* great-great-niece . . . and *your* grandchild.'

'Well, put like that, there really is no other way of looking at it,' said Edie.

'Precisely. Now . . . would you like me to speak to the Baroncinis?'

'I think so. If anyone can break the ice, if it needs to be broken, you can.' Edie's face showed concern again. 'Everything will be all right, won't it?'

'Edith . . .' Naomi reached across and took both her niece's hands in her own. 'Have we not *always* made the best of the worst? And have you not had every worst thing in life thrown at you and still come up bucking the curse of bad fortune?'

'Have I?'

'Yes, you have. And with my hand on my heart I can *honestly* say that you are the bravest, most enduring person on this planet. Being blessed with a grandchild, albeit out of wedlock, will be no worse to you than an angel brushing its wings against a cloud on a summer's day.'

'I hope you're right, Nao. I hope to God you're right.'

# 6

During Naomi's canvassing for new members for the dancing club which she, Ben and Joey were organising, she had also managed to persuade Becky and Nathan, the old Jewish couple who lived on the estate, to have the first meeting in their house – the house next door to the Turkish family with whom Naomi had become friendly. After their very first meeting in the spring, when the problem of Harry and his common-law wife in Turkey had been discussed at length, Shereen and Murat had wiped their hands of the whole sordid affair and a pact had been made between themselves and Naomi never to mention either of the couple again. Naomi was only too happy to oblige. The less she heard about Harry the better, especially now that she had told Edie that he was alive. Even in his absence he had managed to cause a rift with his secret comings and goings.

Sitting in the living room of his and Becky's terraced council house, enjoying a cup of Camp coffee, Nathan was as happy as a lark to be telling the story of when he used to enter ballroom dancing competitions. He simply glowed while reliving the old days, when he had danced beneath revolving mirrored balls and worn full black tie hired from Mannie Cohen's shop in Whitechapel. Telling of the competitions he had won at the Forest Gate roller skating rink, he let slip that it had been there that he had met Becky. Having heard this many times before, his wife simply sat there, looking at him through half-closed eyes. Noticing her bored expression, Nathan diverted his attention to her, saying how beautiful she once was.

'Once I had brought Becky out of her drab old self,' he said, trailing a hand through the air, 'she stood out like a single large star in a navy blue sky, surrounded by millions of tiny stars.' Seeing the tortured smiles on the faces of the others he was unable to resist winding his wife up a little more. Leaning back in his chair, he sighed forlornly – all part of his act. 'Now, of course, it's a different story altogether.' He shrugged. 'Once she started to lose her mind, that was it. I'll have to lay out a dress and her dancing shoes for the do – because as sure as I'm a genius she'll forget and put on an old pinafore frock from the war days.'

'Like I have to run your bath, shove the soap in your hand and warm a towel by the fire, eh, Nathan? Is that what you mean?' Becky turned to the others and tapped the side of her head. 'Touched. You can't trust anything he says.' She then nodded towards his neighbour, Shereen. 'She knows. She knows he's a bit wrong in the head. Not altogether bonkers but touched. Shereen has to listen to him yelling and screaming when he can't find a sock. These walls are solid brick but still she can hear him.'

Shereen chuckled. 'You're both wicked. One day they take you both away.'

'When I first saw her across the dance floor, to be perfectly honest with you, I started to laugh. She looked like candy floss on two sticks.'

'Ha! There! You see? When we first met it was 1926! You couldn't get hold of pink net then. Not for love nor money. At that time I wore long and slinky satin and a row of beads around my head.'

'Who said anything about pink net? I said you looked like candy floss.'

Becky wiggled her forefinger at him. 'I know what you said. And that's what you used to say when I did wear my beautiful pink gown . . . in 1947! Just after the war. Your bloody memory stinks!'

Longing to join in now that the conversation was of fashion through the ages, Naomi bit her tongue. They were here, after all, to finalise details for the hiring of the church hall and everything else that came with organising events. But mention of the 1920s gave her an idea. The opening evening should have a theme, and what better than to dress in the fashion of the period? Fancy dress would get around the problem of some people not being able to pull something appropriate from their wardrobe the way she could. This idea she would keep to herself until Becky and Nathan had finished their banter, which, from the expression on their faces, they clearly had not yet. Now it was Nathan who was jabbing the air with a crooked finger.

'Don't tell me what I saw with my own two eyes,

woman. You wore a bloody pink frock when I first saw you. And you had something or the other stuck on your head.' He brought his hand to his chin and rubbed it thoughtfully. 'I think it was a plastic flower.'

'Don't talk so daft. Plastic flower.' Becky shook her head mournfully. 'They drag other poor sods off in a straitjacket but him they can't even be bothered with. And who can blame them? Who would want to be cooped up all day with that?'

'Only a halfwit.' Nathan laughed. 'See what I mean? She ties herself up in knots every time. Still . . . I don't mind. I have to show her what to do most mornings. She's worse then. Walks about in a daydream till she knows what's what. I give her advice on what to wear . . . that kind of thing.'

'You bloody liar. You're the one that has to be mothered. He couldn't care less if he's got odd socks on. And if I let him he'd wear his long johns for a week. Memory like a sieve.'

'Makes you wonder,' murmured Nathan, scratching his ear. 'Makes you bloody wonder. Still, she's not a bad cook. Not brilliant but not bad. And she keeps the place clean. Too clean but you can't have everything. Can't iron, though. Not for love nor money. At least she's harmless. Mad and manic? No. I wouldn't put up with that. She'll be out the back door and on the back of a barrow the minute she gets like that. I'll dump 'er outside the Jewish home for the aged. No labels, no identification. They'll take 'er in. Have to.'

'You see . . .' Becky grinned. 'I leave him to talk

and he shows who is not right in the head. Have you finished? Can we discuss the club now?'

'I've been good to her, though,' said Nathan, looking around the room at the others. 'All right, she never was all there.' He swirled a finger at his temple. 'But is that her fault?'

'Change the record, Nathan. They've heard it all before and more than once.'

'When I first saw her across that dance floor looking like candy floss I said to myself, "The poor cow looks as if she's come straight out of a camp."'

'That's not funny. You think that's comical? Some poor devils on this estate were in one of those places. Being beaten and starved to death.' Becky turned to Naomi, hoping to get her on her side. 'He's always putting his bloody foot in it. No matter where we go. In Vinestein's delicatessen, in Bloomberg the baker's, outside the eel stall in Aldgate. He sees anyone who doesn't look short and round like him and he says they must have been in a Nazi camp. The bloody war's been over for how many years?'

'It's a turn of phrase, woman,' said Nathan, shrugging. 'You think people take any notice of that rubbish? You're sick in the head if you think that. But then you're sick in the head in any case. Still . . . whose fault's that? Your mother's, that's who.'

'You see?' Becky smiled. 'He slips out of one corner and pokes around in another. If he's in the wrong he has to bring up my mother. He uses her like a weapon. Self-defence.'

'Still,' said Nathan, staring down sadly at the floor,

'I've never known a woman who was the full walnut. So she's not the only one.' He looked up slyly at Naomi and then at Shereen to see that both were suppressing laughter. He gave each a crafty wink and then said, 'Men *pretend* to be daft – that's the difference.'

'I blame the wireless,' said Becky, a glazed look in her eyes. 'Nobody reads as much as they used to – not after the wireless. Reading improves the brain. The wireless makes it lazy. He's always listening to the bloody thing.'

'Warm milk and honey and a good old-fashioned Victorian novel,' said Naomi, attempting to bring this conversation back to something to do with everyone. 'There's nothing quite like it – except an evening out at a dance. I remember my doctor once saying, "To read a book is mind-enhancing – to dance in the night is soul-enhancing."'

Ben, even though he had enjoyed the comic interplay between man and wife, seized his opportunity. He too realised that it was time to get down to business. 'Whose idea was it to start tea dances in the afternoon? I can't remember now. Was it yours, Joey?'

'It might have been. Who knows? Maybe I sowed the first seed. What difference does it make in any case? It's a cracking idea. And since that's why we're here, why don't we discuss the next step?'

'Yes, I do think we should,' said Naomi, leaning forward, 'but please promise to let me know should I happen to stray off the track. If you're not careful we shall have ourselves in the thick of my most favourite period of all times. The Roaring Twenties. And the men might fall asleep on us.'

Shereen nodded furiously, saying, 'Yes, yes. We must discuss tickets and everything.'

Ben held up his hand, as if this were a proper meeting. A procedure of sorts was beginning to take shape. The rest of them fell quiet and waited for him to speak. And he lost no time.

'From what I can make out, there are a lot of people out there who want this to happen. Now whether it's because it's tea dances or simply a chance to join a community club, I don't know. And I don't think it matters. The important thing is that it is something that people want. If you like there's a big gap in our lives to be filled.

'It's all right for the young. They've got their rock and roll, their coffee bars and below-floor nightclubs. But there's nothing for the likes of us – only the local pubs. And do you know what really moved me?' He placed a hand on his heart. 'It wasn't one of us pensioners who got the ball rolling but young Maggie. A fifteen-year-old saw the benefit of us having a bit of a social life and put herself out to do something about it.' He pulled a folded piece of paper from his inside pocket. 'Fifty-three names,' he said, gently waving the list. 'I think that tells us something. It tells us that even the young think it's a good idea.'

'Sixteen in the spring,' said Naomi, instinctively seeking to protect her niece's good name even though none of them in the room had any idea whatsoever that she was carrying a baby.

'Fifteen, sixteen, what's the difference?' said Ben. 'The point that Joey's making is that she was happy enough with our idea to put a notice in the library, and no doubt she's given it a bit of word of mouth too. I don't think we should look too lightly on that.'

'I absolutely agree,' said Joey, brushing a speck of dust off his perfectly pressed suit trousers. 'It's a wonderful thing when the young meet with the old and share the same thought – that this country needs to bring back a few of its old traditions. Dancing in the afternoon? Wonderful.'

'Well, we'd best work out a plan, and quick,' said Nathan. 'I can hear her mother walking about up there. She comes down and deigns to join us and we'll have to say everything three times over. The woman's going on ninety and won't stand still for more than an hour, up and down, up and bloody well down them stairs.'

To the relief of the others, the sound of the doorbell shut him up momentarily. His passing remark to Naomi as he went to open the street door made them all smile. 'Can't you take her in for a bit of company? She can still cook a decent meal. You could tack a blanket up across the corner of your living room and stick a camp bed behind it for 'er.'

'Open the bloody door,' said Becky, adding to the others when he was out of the room, 'One of these days she's gonna come up right behind him and hear every word. Then he'll be sorry. She's bloody strong for her age. And she keeps a heavy old policeman's truncheon under her bed. I don't know where she got it from.'

'So . . .' Naomi smiled. 'I think we agreed that we should book St Peter's hall on the second Wednesday of each month. Did we not? And am I to understand that the vicar has very kindly agreed not to charge anything for the hire of the hall but come around with his collecting box for the church funds? Which I think is perfectly reasonable.'

'Daft, more like,' said Ben. 'All he'll get is farthings and old foreign coins found in the gutter. Still, if he doesn't want to charge rent he doesn't have to.'

'You think we should insist he take our money, Ben? Is this what you're saying?'

Ben clasped a hand against his chest and adopted the expression of a man who was flabbergasted. 'God forbid. A church hall should be free to people like us who're forming a social club. God would have a fit if we had to pay to go into his church hall. Charge members to cover costs but that's all.'

'That's a point,' said Joey. 'What should we charge people to come? If it's free they'll think it's not gonna be any good or that there's a catch, and if it's too dear they won't come.'

'A shilling,' said Becky. 'Sixpence for entry and we'll give them a cup of tea and a biscuit. And if it all goes well and they want a day out on a charabanc in the summer then we'll put it up to half a crown a fortnight – they can pay the extra when the time comes round, when we know what we can get free and what we can't get free. We'll say we're a charity and get what we can.'

'Charge a shilling and give them a cup of tea and

a biscuit? We *would* be a bloody charity if we did that. Charge them one and sixpence.'

'Pensioners can't afford one and six, Ben.'

'Well, charge them who've not bin pensioned off yet one and sixpence.'

'I think that's a perfect solution. Those who can afford will pay full price and those who are pensioned or simply out of work a shilling.'

Coming back into the room, Nathan had a different demeanour, that of a gentleman – a gallant gentleman. 'We have a very special visitor,' he said, reaching out and graciously taking Miss Lightfoot's hand. 'A distinguished visitor, as a matter of fact. The librarian from the Bethnal Green Library.'

To the sound of gentle clapping, Miss Lightfoot held up a hand. 'Oh, please . . . I came because I wanted to and Margaret said it would be all right if I simply turned up and that it was a sort of general meeting, so to speak. I do hope I haven't interrupted anything?'

Becky was up from her seat in no time – the perfect hostess. 'Oh, don't apologise. We're honoured to have you as our guest. Now then, you come and sit on this chair over here in the corner next to me, and don't mind my husband.' She threw Nathan a warning look. 'He sometimes rambles on a bit but we try to ignore it until he stops. Then I let him have it. It's the only way when you're living with . . . well, what can I say that you haven't already guessed?'

'Shut up for five minutes, woman, and let the poor soul relax. Take no notice of 'er, Librarian – she's not all she should be upstairs. And to answer your question, you haven't interrupted a thing. We're pleased to have your support. Any help you can give will be welcome.'

'Well, I'm not sure that I've much to offer but I would certainly like to be involved if there is anything at all that I can do. I think this is such a worthwhile cause. I really do.'

'You know,' said Nathan, shuffling in his seat to stop himself breaking wind, 'we have a lot to thank you for. It was very decent of you to put up that notice and allow people to sign the list. Not many in your position would do that.'

'Hear hear,' said Naomi, clapping her hands again.

'Hear hear,' echoed the others.

Once seated, the clapping over, Miss Lightfoot had no choice other than to take the chair since they were all looking at her expectantly. Clearing her throat, she began with an apology for being late and then quickly went on to say that the chief librarian was terribly impressed with the response and enthusiasm of both the elderly and the not so elderly, all of whom were terribly keen to join the club and were especially thrilled at the idea of the tea dances in the afternoons. She then offered to do any typing or clerical work that might need attending to once they were up and running.

Naomi was deeply touched when the librarian mentioned Maggie more than once, telling them how helpful she was and how she had already said that in time she too would quite enjoy being involved in the

running of events. Following her short talk, Miss Lightfoot asked whether there were any other ideas to be
added to the list, such as visits to a pantomime at
Christmas or a charabanc ride to the seaside in the
summer. Various ideas were proposed and the conversation became quite animated. It had taken a reserved
and shy spinster to bring this little group meeting alive.

An hour soon slipped by, and apart from the strange
smell that was now wafting through the room everything seemed to have gone very well. Everyone seemed
to have taken to Miss Lightfoot, whose sense of smell,
fortunately, did not seem to be as sharp as the others'.
'I've been meaning to join the library, as a matter of
fact,' said Becky, ushering the woman out before she
had time to catch a whiff of one of Nathan's specials.
'I used to go all the time when we lived in Whitechapel.
Before we moved on to the estate. Maybe we'll see
each other again tomorrow – when I come in.'

'I shall look out for you.' Miss Lightfoot turned to
the others and bade them goodnight.

Quick to join her, Naomi left at the same time,
wishing them all a very good night. Once outside she
offered her hand and Miss Lightfoot shook it with
gusto – she had enjoyed herself and felt as if she had
made friends.

'I shall look forward to seeing you again, and thank
you once more for coming,' said Naomi.

'Oh, it's been a treat, as a matter of fact. They're
so sweet and so keen to get this club off the ground.
I think it's wonderful.'

'So long as we do get it off the ground. As you no

doubt realise, an awful lot of nattering goes on in between the business.'

'Oh, but they're terribly funny. All of them. The silent ones made me want to laugh just by their expressions.'

After a brief silence, Naomi said, 'You won't mind if I ask you something personal, will you?' She looked into Miss Lightfoot's face and smiled demurely.

'No, of course not. Well . . . I don't think so. I'm sure it can't be anything too personal. You hardly know me.'

'Which is exactly the point. May I ask your first name?'

'Oh, of course! How silly of me. It's Daphne.'

'Well, Daphne, welcome to our funny little world. If you should find us a touch on the old and dull side, please don't think we shall be offended if you don't come to the meetings.'

'Oh, I didn't find it dull at all. On the contrary. I don't usually do very much after I've finished at the library, except go home, of course. Occasionally I might go to see a film if there's one out that I particularly want to see. Other than that . . .' She shrugged, embarrassed. 'I don't really go out in the evenings.'

'And neither do I. I live alone too, you see, and it sometimes takes someone else to give us a little nudge. If you would like, I wouldn't mind making a regular thing of going to the cinema, say once every four or five weeks, depending, of course, on whether there is a film I would like to see.'

'Oh, well, then why don't we go together? I would

like that very much.' A lovely smile spreading across her face, Miss Lightfoot added, 'I'm so pleased I came this evening. I'm usually quite shy, but I didn't feel in the least bit intimidated in there.'

'And neither did they in your company. You were rather a guest of honour, Daphne. Your unexpected arrival changed the course of the discussion and brought it to a point. You're obviously used to public speaking.'

'Goodness, no. I did attend drama classes when I first left school. In the evening. That sort of thing. And that helped enormously. I was terribly shy as a child. To the point of hiding in a cupboard when I was very small, apparently. If a visitor came.'

'Well then, we have much in common. Not the shyness, I hasten to add. If anything I am too out-spoken and always have been. But the drama classes are a different kettle of fish altogether. I'm an actress. Well . . . retired now, of course, but I was professional and played in many of our theatres.'

'I didn't know that. Your great-niece didn't say. How absolutely marvellous!' Daphne was overjoyed. Without thinking she slipped her arm into Naomi's, and as they walked slowly away from Becky and Nathan's house they talked non-stop until they arrived at the one-bedroom ground-floor apartments for the elderly where Naomi lived.

'You're very welcome to come in for a drink, if you would like,' she offered.

'Oh, well, that's very kind of you, Naomi, but I do have a train to catch.'

'Another time perhaps?'

'Yes . . . I shall look forward to it.'

Having said farewell, Naomi went inside and looked slowly around, content. It was not even a year old, the paint was still fresh, and with her collection of old and interesting furniture she had carted around with her for decades – the paintings, drapes and fringed silk shawls – it was homely. Her little castle, her little nest on a council estate.

Enjoying a little time to herself in the late September sunshine as she sat on an easy chair on her back balcony, Edie closed her eyes and tried to imagine the following spring, when she would be wheeling her grandchild in a pram with a white broderie anglaise cover and shade. More resigned now to the fact that there really was no alternative other than to let Maggie freely choose her own future, still the knot in her stomach would not go away. The sense of there always being something wrong was there before she went to sleep at night and seemed much worse when she woke, until she had had that first cup of tea.

Thinking about the brief conversation she had had with Tony's parents after they had been told the circumstances, she found it difficult to believe that they had been so understanding about the whole thing. Given that they were Catholics, she had expected that they would spurn Maggie first and then lay the blame at Edie's feet for not being more watchful over her only daughter. They hadn't been thrilled to bits with the news when told by Maggie and Tony, but they had accepted it by the time Edie had gone up to see them.

Guilt did drift in and out of her consciousness from time to time, but it went as quickly as it came. She knew she wasn't to blame for what had happened, although she did sometimes wonder whether she had been too wrapped up in her own personal life to take enough notice of Maggie.

As well as spending more of her time with Dennis, she had also been preoccupied with the idea of having a new baby to cuddle – *before* her daughter had broken the news that she was pregnant. In fact she had been experiencing maternal urges herself since the spring of that year, and didn't believe that in her mid-thirties she was too old to carry another child.

Pushing these thoughts from her mind, she told herself that she would have to be patient and wait until she and Dennis had been married for at least six months before she broached the subject. She had no idea whether her fiancé had any paternal feelings, and was sure it would be a mistake to talk about such things at this early stage of their courtship. Too soon and too ambitious. A man of few words, Dennis had nevertheless told her earlier in their relationship that he had previously been engaged three times, and he had flatly refused in the nicest way possible to go into the reasons why he had not married any of the girl-friends he had promised himself to.

To Dennis, yesterday was gone and tomorrow would take care of itself; today was there to be treasured. Although this was not how Edie thought, she admired him for having the courage to live according to his beliefs. The only thing that did sometimes cause her concern was the fact that, although they had arranged to be married in December, he avoided any discussion to do with the wedding. As far as he was concerned it was up to Edie to make the arrangements. All he really wanted was as little fuss as possible, envisaging them simply strolling into a register office and signing the necessary documents. He hated the fuss of weddings, the upset sometimes caused by relatives, and the cost of flowers – especially in the winter-time.

All this had been aired, albeit briefly, in her living room one evening when they had been enjoying a drink together. He had been quite matter-of-fact about it, expressing no resentment whatsoever at the idea that she might wish to do things her own way. He had said he would go along with it if she wanted to make an occasion of the day. He would foot the bill and agree to the ceremonies and celebrations, but he was not prepared to be involved in the arrangements. Edie thought this honest and to the point, albeit lacking in joy and enthusiasm.

To Naomi, however, this was the best news she could have wished for. She and Edie had carte blanche to invite who they wanted, shop for what they wanted, and all with no interference from a man. Wonderful!

With Maggie out with Tony, and this not being one of the evenings when Dennis came round, Edie was more than content to relax with only her own thoughts for company. She had treated herself to hot saveloys and pease pudding, and her ironing and housework were up to date. Now, having enjoyed her ready-made meal, she could look forward to simply passing the time, either reading her library book or watching the television. When the doorbell rang she was in two minds as to whether to answer it or not, but curiosity got the better of her.

On the doorstep, a guilty smile on her face, Jessie looked as if she wished she hadn't rung. 'If you're in the middle of anything, Edie,' she said, 'say so and I'll go away.'

'I am,' said Edie, opening the door wide. 'I'm in the middle of having a cup of tea on the balcony. Come on in.'

'Are you sure?'

'Jessie, do I look as if I don't want your company?'

'No, but you look as if you might have been enjoying the quiet. You look half asleep. I don't wanna spoil anything.'

'You won't, don't worry. Now come in or go away.'

Ten minutes later the two friends were curled up in armchairs with the afternoon sun coming in through the open window. The cottages in the Norfolk village were still in the forefront of Jessie's mind. Max had offered to take her up to see Alice and Jack in Elmshill, and she clearly wanted to talk about it. Having broached the subject, and seeing that Edie was happy to listen, she made a small confession. 'The thing is . . . I know I would be going behind Tom and Stanley's back and in one sense I don't care, but on the other hand it feels wrong. I can't really explain it.'

'No . . . you don't have to. I think I would be the same. It does seem a bit underhand even though I know that neither you nor Max are like that. Why don't you just tell Tom that that's what you want to do?'

'I don't know.'

'You're sure about that, are you?'

'Of course I'm sure. What are you getting at?'

'Well,' said Edie, as she curled her legs under her and sank farther into her cushions, 'the way I look at it is that you either want to get in before Tom and buy one of them yourselves or you would rather be going with Tom and not Max to look at them.'

'Neither. Me and Max couldn't afford to buy one. Unless he borrows the money from his sister, Moira, who's filthy rich. Her husband's hard-earned money, not hers, I might add. Not that you would know it. And as for me going up there with Tom, no, I wouldn't dream of doing that to Max.'

'I didn't say you *would* go with Tom, I said you would *rather* be going with Tom. There's a difference.'

'True. And what if it was you in my place? If Dennis offered to take you and Harry was still around and was gonna take Maggie to look at them, what would *you* rather do? Go with Dennis or Harry?'

'How can I answer that when Harry's dead?'

'He's not dead, though, is he?'

'He is to me now, and he is as far as the authorities and Maggie are concerned. That'll do, won't it?'

'But we're only talking about what we'd *prefer*. Aren't we?'

'All right. I would *prefer* it if Harry had come home during the war and it was us going to look at a cottage in the country. But mine is an impossible dream. Whereas yours isn't. Tom's still your husband and he wants you back. All you have to do is choose between Max and Tom.'

'And you reckon that's easier than you having no choice?'

'No. I think it's a hundred times worse. But that's life.' Edie narrowed her eyes and studied Jessie's face. 'There's no gettin' away from it. You're facing making the biggest decision of your life. And the trouble is – you love both of them in different ways.'

'And if I *was* thinking along those lines, which I'm *not*,' said Jessie, almost as if she hadn't heard what Edie had just said, 'what would you do in my place?'

'I've no idea. And I'm not going to sway you one way or the other. I'll listen. I'll reason. I'll make suggestions. But I won't make the decision for you. It's too big and it's too important. I don't know Tom. I do know Max – and I think he's a good man. That's all I'm prepared to say.'

'I wonder if it would be any different if Tom had the option of taking another woman with him?' said Jessie. 'I wonder how I would feel then?'

'My thoughts entirely. The balance would be even. While he doesn't have anyone, you've got more chips than he has. It's not *such* a gamble, is it? You're not about to lose him to someone else. Whereas you could divorce him and marry Max. How do you think he must feel?'

'Edie, he left *me*, don't forget. Lived the life of luxury as a millionaire while me and Max was struggling to keep afloat . . . *and* keep his two children.'

'But he wasn't to know that, was he? When he walked out, Max was doing all right and you still had your little house. What did he have? Nothing except doubt and suspicion eating away at him. And he'd just come back from the war.'

'They kept him back for desertion.'

'All right. And when he deserted, where did he head for each time?'

'Yeah, all right, Edie. You've made your point.'

'Well, answer me, then. Where did he head for?'

'Home. Me and the kids.'

'There you are, then. You've found your answer. And will you go to the cottage with Max? To Elmshill to see Alice and Jack?'

'No. I can't do that. That would cut right through Tom.'

'Well, we took a long route to get there but we did it in the end. You won't be going. End of story. Now stop feeling sorry for yourself. What say we go to the Carpenter's Arms this evening for a couple of drinks? The sound of old Sid the sailor plonking out his tunes on the piano with Maud singing along will do us the world of good.'

'How do you make that out? Sounds bloody awful at the best of times.'

'It won't be romantic is the point. Just down-to-earth, everyday life . . . in a pub.'

Jessie looked at her wristwatch. 'I've left Emma watching television by herself. Maybe once Billy gets back home. He went with his mate, Johnny, over the river to Bexleyheath to watch speedway racing. Johnny's brother's in the race apparently. I don't know why the kids got a day off school. Something to do with the war. It might have been the day it started. I can't remember. It was in September – I think. September '39. Who cares anyway? Bloody war.'

A sudden urgent banging on the door broke into their thoughts. 'Bloody hell,' said Jessie. 'Where's the fire?'

'Oh, don't say that.' Edie rushed from the room.

Jessie imagined it could be only one thing – kids playing knock down ginger but when she saw her son being guided into the room by Edie, his face drawn and white, she was up from her chair in a flash. 'Billy, what's happened?' she asked. 'Where's Emma?'

The fourteen-year-old stood there, looking at his mother as she pushed his sweaty hair off his forehead and wrapped her arms around him, kissing the top of his head. 'It's all right, babe. Whatever happened it's over now and you're here with me.'

'Shall I get him a glass of water, Jess, or a cup of sweet weak tea?'

'Water.' Pinching her lips together, Jessie closed her eyes and hoped to God that nothing horrible had happened to him over the river. He and his friend had chosen to take the route through the Rotherhithe tunnel rather than Blackwall. And there had been talk between the boys earlier of walking through the tunnel to save on the bus fares. She had a vision of a vehicle stopping to give them a lift and things going horribly wrong.

Recently there had been headlines about a young lad found dead in scrub land. The details of what he had been through had been too painful to read. Getting grip on herself, she gently led Billy to the settee and eased him down into it, her eyes not leaving his face. His own innocent blue eyes stared back at her, and she could tell by his heartbeat as she held him close that he had been running – and running fast.

Jessie's hands were trembling as she took the drink Edie brought. She put the glass to Billy's lips. 'Sip it, sweetheart. Just keep sipping it. You'll be all right in a minute or so.'

Nodding obediently, Billy did as she said until the glass was empty. Then, after drawing breath, he whispered, 'I'll be all right now.'

'I'm sure you will, darling, but just take your time. There's no rush. No one's gonna hurt you. You're safe here at Edie's, you know you are.'

'We're not safe,' he said, his eyes still glassy as he stared at her. 'We're not safe.'

'Of course we are, silly.' She smiled. 'The door's shut and no one can come in.'

'They wouldn't bother to come in. No need. They can do what they want. They're not ordinary like us.'

'Who, Billy? Who're not like us?'

'Whoever they are. No one saw 'em. They never came out.'

'Out? Out from where?'

'The spaceship. At Bexley. All the kids saw it, and some parents. On the heath. It landed on the roadway and took up the whole road and the pavement. It wasn't on the ground and it 'ad massive suckers. The cockpit in the middle wasn't moving. The rim was spinning so fast you would hardly know it was moving. It had white lights flashing. Brilliant white lights. We was all too shit scared to move an inch.'

On this occasion Jessie let his swearing pass. Her priority right then was the state of her son's mind. 'Billy? Did you go to the pictures? Is that it? You bunked in to see an X-certificate film and got pulled up for it afterwards?'

'No. I went to Bexleyheath. It was all arranged.'

'OK. So you went to the speedway. Did you see your friend's brother racing?

'Yeah. Before we saw it. We weren't the only ones. We all saw it. It sped off into space again and we ran. We ran all the way back through the tunnel and only stopped once to catch our breath. We thought it was gonna come in the tunnel. We could hear it humming.'

'That would have been the traffic, Billy.' Jessie chuckled. 'Those tunnels are strange places. You should have taken the bus.'

'We'd spent our fare. Where's Emma?'

'Indoors. Watching television.'

'She's not. I knocked, and loud, but she never came to the door. It could 'ave come over this way. They take people to experiment wiv. You shouldn't 'ave left 'er on 'er own.'

'Billy, stop it. You're being silly. And you're scaring me.'

'She's not indoors. I knocked twice, three bangs. You should 'ave bin looking after 'er. What's Dad gonna say? A copper at Bexley said they take people to experiment with.'

'He was pulling your leg, you daft thing.'

'No he wasn't. She's babyish for 'er age. And ten's not that old anyhow. She'd go off with anyone.'

'Stop it, Billy. Emma's all right. If she's not fast asleep she'll be playing jacks on the doorstep of Jackie Simon's house.'

'What did it look like, then, Billy?' asked Edie cheerfully, trying to lighten the atmosphere. 'Was it scary?'

'It 'ad windows but not like ours. They was hollow and moulded and you couldn't see in. Two kids went close to touch it but a bloke got 'em by the scruff of the neck and dragged them away.'

'What colour was it? Or wasn't it a colour?'

'Black and silver with a shiny surface like polished steel. And there wasn't any noise. None. It was eerie. Loads of white lights brighter than stars. Brighter than anyfing I've ever seen. And then it shot off before you could click yer teeth.'

'Well . . . I don't think you could make something like that up, Billy. And why would you want to?' Edie sank into an armchair.

'It must 'ave been a prank,' said Jessie, ruffling her

son's hair. 'Big companies will do anything to get attention. Spend a fortune on advertising.'

'Everyone there said it couldn't be a prank. It was right up close to us and no one 'ad ever seen anyfing like it in their lives.'

'Well, if it did 'appen, I s'pose it'll be in the papers.'

'It did happen! And there'll be more coming! The sky'll be filled wiv 'em and we won't stand a chance. Not a bloody chance! One of their airships could 'ave come over our flats and you wouldn't know 'cos you've bin in 'ere gossiping.'

'That's enough now, Billy,' Jessie warned. 'We'll see what the papers say tomorrow. Come on – upstairs with you.'

'No. You fetch Emma down if she's in. If not, I'll go down and see if she's playing jacks wiv 'er mate.' He turned to Edie. 'Is Dennis coming over?'

'No, sweetheart. But Max shouldn't be too late home. You can talk to him about it.' She glanced at Jessie, whose expression told her that Max would be working late again.

'What about Maggie? What time do yer reckon she'll be back?'

'Not till later on, I shouldn't think. But you never know with her.' She grinned.

Feeling for her son, who was obviously very scared, Jessie said, 'Wait here with Edie while I find Emma. Then we'll go for a walk round to see Nanny and Granddad. That sound all right?'

'I don't care,' he said, clamping a hand to his face. 'I feel sick.'

Losing no time, Edie grabbed her new black-and-white metal wastepaper bin from beside the fireplace and thrust it under the lad's chin, just in time. 'You hold on to this, Jess, while I go and get him another glass of water. Keep his head down in case he gets giddy. And don't worry about my bin. You just let it come out, love. Better out than in.'

Alone with his mother, and having emptied his stomach, Billy murmured, 'I wasn't making it up, Mum. The others saw it as well as me. Most of 'em run off straight away. But I couldn't. My legs wouldn't move. I don't know if they paralysed me or not.'

''Course they didn't, silly. If they had of done it would have been so they could take you off with them, and they never did that, did they? And that's because there wouldn't 'ave been anyone on board. It was the Americans, Billy. And one of their advertising campaigns. Probably for a new set of toys coming out. You wait and see. I bet the toy shops'll be full of flying saucers which look like the one you saw. And too expensive for ordinary families to buy.'

'It couldn't 'ave been a prank,' said Billy, looking at her with red-rimmed eyes which stood out against his white face.

'Of course it was.'

'But it moved faster than lightning. No one 'ad a camera and it wasn't there long enough for anyone to run off and get one.' With that he heaved again and made the most of Edie's shiny bin.

Returning with the water, Edie knelt down and put

it to Billy's lips. 'Here we are, sweetheart. Sip this and you'll feel better.' She placed a hand on his forehead and smiled gently at him. 'At least you haven't got a temperature. Shame you feel so rough, though, eh? Otherwise you could wrap one of my sheets round you and go down and frighten that old cow whose bin driving me to distraction over the dripping pipe.'

Billy spoke with a slight tremble in his voice. 'She blamed Mrs Bonatovitch the other day because the rain from the overflow on the roof made a mark on the inside of 'er bedroom wall.'

'Poor woman – fancy having to live next door to an old crab, eh?'

'She never goes out, that's the trouble. Keeps polishing and dusting and then looking at what she's done. Spends ages on 'er winder cleaning and then keeps coming out and looking at 'em. She's nuts.'

'Nor does the lady who sits in the sink go out. But at least she's got a nice nature. Naomi's bringing 'er out of herself, though. I don't think the woman can settle to living in a flat. It's not everyone's cup of tea – even though me and your mum love it.'

'I think it's good,' said Billy, stretching and placing a hand on his stomach. 'I think I'm all right now.'

'The colour's coming back into your cheeks. That's a good sign.'

'I was all right all the time. Just felt sick, that's all.'

Edie wiped beads of sweat from his forehead with both thumbs. 'All that running made you sweat but you haven't got a temperature. So I don't think you're going down with anything.' She looked up at Jessie, who was watching her son being mothered. 'An early night for this one, I think.'

'No. I'm all right. We're going to Gran and Granddad's. Once we've found Emma.' Pulling himself to his feet, Billy swayed a little. 'So Max won't be 'ome till late, then, Mum?'

'Not till about eight, darling. He's up to his eyeballs in the company tax returns. Why?'

'I just wondered, that's all. Can we go round Nan and Granddad's now, then? You, me and Emma?'

'If you like. If that's what you want.'

'It is. I wanna tell Granddad what 'appened. It'll be in the papers tomorrer. One of the people watching said it wouldn't but another said they couldn't cover this up. Too many of us saw it.'

'Empty talk, darling . . . that's all that was. Trust me. It would 'ave been a stunt to get publicity for a new toy that's coming out. You see if I'm wrong.'

'It wasn't a prank! It was real. Uncle Stanley'll believe me. He thinks there are plenty more planets like ours in the universe. Some millions of years in front of us and some still in the dark ages and some only just coming to life with insects and that. That's what he says, anyway, and I believe 'im. Especially now. He'll wanna know about this straight away. Can we go round Aunt Dolly's house and tell them as well?'

'No. But if you like, once we get to Granddad's you can 'ave fourpence and call Uncle Stanley from the phone box and tell 'im all about it. If he thinks there's more to it he'll be round Granddad's like a shot, firing questions at you.'

'All right. Let's do that, then.' He turned to Edie and offered a faint smile. 'Fanks for looking after me. I feel much better now. Tell Maggie what happened and tell 'er I'll knock later on and give 'er all the details. Tell 'er to go round Naomi's 'cos she'll wanna know if somefing's going on. These things are bound to 'appen sooner or later. We're a sitting target. That's what Uncle Stanley reckons, anyway. We could be put out just like that by an alien planet.' He clicked his fingers and then sauntered out of the room.

'Right,' said Jessie. 'Looks like I'll be seeing Tom today, then.'

'Maybe it wasn't an alien planet but God showing you the way.' Edie grinned before covering her mouth to stifle her laughter.

'Stop it, Edie!' hissed Jessie. 'If Billy comes back in and sees you laughing . . .'

'I know, I know. Go on. Get going. And shut the street door behind you in case I can have a good belly laugh over this. Spacemen and spaceships? Whatever next?'

'It's all right for some,' said Jessie, leaving.

Going out on to her back balcony, Edie leaned on the rail and looked over at the arches, remembering Maggie's dream of her father calling her to him. All the talk about who Jessie truly loved, Tom or Max, had left its mark. With Harry on her mind now, the good times, when they were deeply in love, returned. Memories of the summer days when they used to enjoy walking along by the canal and stopping for a cool glass of shandy in the Old Tavern, picnics by the pond in Victoria Park Gardens and the boat rides on a lazy Sunday afternoon. If the war hadn't happened she had no doubt that they would be together now, not living on this estate but in a three- or four-bedroom cottage perhaps with front and back garden. Harry had always said that he wanted three children – two sons and a daughter.

Watching some boys below on their go-karts and bikes, she tried to imagine what her and Harry's son would have looked like. Maggie was the image of her father and a constant reminder. Maybe a son would have looked like her? Plucking a dead marigold from her window box, she caught the attention of one of the lads. With one hand shielding his eyes from the late afternoon sun, he peered up at her and called out, 'Is Maggie in, Mrs Birch?'

'No, she's not. Why, did you want her for something?'

'Yeah! We wanna book from the library on spaceships that 'ave bin seen in the past. We've just seen Johnnie Collins and he reckons that him an' Billy Smith saw a UFO over the river in Bexley! Fantastic it was! He's telling everyone there's gonna be an invasion!'

'Is that right?' Edie smiled. 'Well, I'll have a word with Maggie about the book. But I shouldn't lose too much sleep over it! Spaceships 'ave bin reported before and they've all been a hoax!'

'Nar they ain't! That's wot the government puts out so as not to cause panic. My old man knows all about it. His mate works in the print. They stop stories

from being told. But not this time! Johnnie Collins
ain't gonna keep 'is mouth shut! It'll be all over the
front pages tomorrer. He reckons we should all board
up our winders tonight.'

'Well, I should ask your mothers first before you
do!' With that Edie turned away and went back into
the living room, smiling. The lad's echoing voice
drifted in from the open doorway. 'And the BBC are
just as bad! They won't report it! Load of wankers!'

'Charming,' mused Edie. 'Very nice.'

Another voice pierced the air – another lad with
another opinion. 'Take no notice, missus! It's all
bollocks! Load of cobblers!'

Returning to her armchair, Edie lapsed back into
her earlier lazy mood. She glanced at the calendar
before turning the page from September to October,
something she had forgotten to do. The lovely early
autumn scene of a thatched cottage with the blazing
red leaves of a Virginia creeper covering the walls and
growing around the front door reminded her of
Harry's dream. Of living in the country in a cottage.
She envied Jessie now for possibly being on the brink
of having what she could only hope for.

On her way to her in-laws, Jessie half listened to Billy,
who, in a more buoyant mood, was telling his story
of the flying saucer to Emma, who had actually fallen
asleep on the sofa when he had knocked on the door
earlier. He repeated the words 'world war' over and
over and she was reminded of the Blitz on London
in August 1940 when Tom, like other British soldiers,

was away fighting the enemy. The Royal Air Force at that time were having great difficulty competing with the German Luftwaffe on home ground. As powerful as the British armed fighter planes, the Hurricanes and Spitfires, had been, they could not rival the enemy's numbers.

The air raids on London, and especially the East End, had caused more and more families to escape to country villages throughout England. Jessie and Tom's family, however, like many others at the beginning of the war, had held firm to their belief that it was safer to be at home, where there were adequate air-raid shelters and they could keep a keen eye on each other's welfare.

Throughout it all, some young women, such as Jessie's girlfriends, had made the best of bad times and managed to enjoy life to the full under the circumstances. Taking turns at each other's houses, they had played the gramophone, sung noisily, danced and drank brandy, given to them by sailors on leave. Their way of handling the nightmare had been to get too tipsy to worry about the bombs dropping around them. The morning after a good session the girls often returned to work in the offices and on factory floors to find empty chairs and benches where workmates had sat before the previous night's bombing.

During an air raid while out shopping with her mother in Whitechapel, pushing Billy in his pram, Jessie had found Max in his mother's delicatessen after not having seen him for a while. He had sauntered in while she had been waiting for some cold salt beef to be sliced. They had had little choice other than to go together down into one of the public shelters while his mother took care of Billy in the small cellar beneath the shop.

In a quiet corner of a nearby underground shelter, Jessie and Max had sat huddled together in a corner, hoping that the warden would shortly sound the all clear, but it had been an unrelenting attack which had gone on for most of the night.

Squeezing her arm and drawing her close to comfort her, Max had been wonderful, reassuring her that Billy would be fine in his mother's cellar and doing his best to allay all her fears. But around them, cramped together, women, old folk and young alike were quietly crying or praying, silently terrified of what was happening above and wondering whether or not they would be buried alive.

The words she had whispered at the time came floating back. 'I'll doze if you will, Max.' And his reply: 'I intend to, Jess. After all – this is the only chance I'll ever get of sleeping close to you.'

After five hours of dozing on and off, the welcoming call of a warden could be heard from above as he shouted the all clear and told them that fresh tea would be served. Jessie and Max, easing their way through the jostling crowd, had slowly made their way up towards the light. As they emerged from the shelter they had witnessed a pitiful scene – swarms of petrified people who had emerged from various safe places and who were making their way home, shocked into silence by it all. The Luftwaffe had been busy. Shops, houses and factories along the White-chapel Road were alight and heartbreaking cries could be heard amid the chaos as survivors called out for their loved ones from whom they had been separated in the panic.

Others, also in a state of shock, were reporting which buildings had been hit. One poor wretched soul in particular came to mind and brought a lump to Jessie's throat. She recalled the expression on the old Jewish woman's face as she cried out in a trembling voice, 'Jubilee Buildings have gone. They bombed Jubilee Buildings! Where am I to go? What am I to do?' Under less traumatic circumstances, someone would have comforted the old lady, but that day her cry had simply mingled with those of others who had heard from the wardens which streets had been hit.

With Billy and Emma walking ahead chatting, and everything around them peaceful, it was difficult to believe that the war had ever happened. And it was hard to imagine it ever happening again: East Londoners, reputed to be as tough as old boots, had been reduced to quivering wrecks as they ran to their homes after a sudden air raid, praying aloud and begging God to let their families be among the luckier ones whose homes had escaped destruction. It was hard to believe that Billy had been a baby in a pushchair when she had taken refuge in a crowded, dark and stuffy underground shelter with Max. Kind and lovable Max, who had helped her through those dark days of the Blitz – something Tom had never appreciated or simply didn't want to accept, his jealousy being stronger than his sense of gratitude. He had always feared that she might have run to Max – even after they were first married. They had once been engaged to be married, after all was said and done.

'Silly old fool,' whispered Jessie to herself, 'I loved you more than I could love anyone.' She was, of course, referring to Tom.

Turning the corner into Grant Street, Billy and Emma-Rose ahead of her, Jessie counted her blessings. She recalled that awful day when she had walked this very route to find devastation in the street where she lived and piles of smoking rubble where houses once stood. A neighbour, whose windows and doors had been blown out by the impact of a falling bomb, had approached Jessie in a state of shock and given her the grave news that her and Tom's little two-up, two-down had received a direct hit. By the time she had arrived at her front door the fire brigade had put out the flames but the roof had caved in and part of the front of the house was a pile of rubble. Jessie had been able to see into the shambles of her front room.

Passing that house, which she no longer owned, and which was looking as smart as the day she had sold it, she felt as if she would burst if she did not release the grief caused by the loss of so much that she had once cherished. But this was no time for tears. She had to put on a brave face, had to keep her emotions in check. She knew that in reality she hadn't moved on and put the past behind her. She still loved Tom, and as deeply as ever.

Billy knocked loudly on Tom's parents' door and Charlie opened it. 'Gawd love a duck,' he said, grinning from ear to ear. 'Look what the wind's blown in! Well, you can bugger off and go back 'ome 'cos we're just goin' out!'

'Granddad! Stop telling lies!' said Billy. 'I've got important news and we've come especially to tell yer!'

'Go on?' teased Charlie. '*Im*portant news? And you've come *all* this way!'

'He . . . he . . . he's not telling lies today, Granddad. He saw a . . . a—'

'Shut up, Emma! It's my news, all right? You'll only get your facts wrong.'

'Oh, get inside,' said Jessie, giving them both a gentle shove and rolling her eyes at Charlie. 'You're as bad as they are. Tormenting sod. Is Emmie in?'

'Nope,' said Charlie, closing the door behind them. 'She's run off with the greengrocer.'

'You said that last week,' said Emma. 'Only . . . it . . . it was the milkman.'

'Well . . . you know your gran's eyesight ain't all it should be. She mixed 'em up.'

'Take no notice,' said Jessie, and then gave Charlie a kiss on the cheek. 'You're looking well.'

'There you go. You will let looks fool yer. I should be on that couch, with my feet up and being waited on. Go on through, the lot of yer. Emmie's in the back yard pegging up the clothes. And not one bloomin' blackbird in sight.'

'If you don't wanna hear my news, Granddad, I'm not bothered,' said Billy, sauntering through into the living room.

'Wouldn't be any point in you telling me anyfing, son. I've gone deaf.'

No sooner had Charlie closed the street door than there was the sound of a van pulling up outside. Recognising its noisy exhaust he opened the door again and saw that it was indeed his youngest son's van. He left the door ajar for him and went to join his grandchildren, hardly able to contain his own excitement because of the little treat he had for them in the top drawer of the sideboard. The previous Sunday morning he had been to Petticoat Lane and got himself a very good deal on the cheap jack stall – twelve boxed games for five shillings. Predictably, Billy and Emma were already out in the back yard by the time he was in the living room. Standing in the back doorway, he called out to them, 'Don't you go upsetting them chickens or they won't lay no more eggs for yer breakfast!'

'You 'aven't bin keepin' a check, Granddad!' Billy called back. 'Florrie's still sitting in the back of the run. I told you she was and you wouldn't 'ave it!'

Laughing, Charlie strolled outside, pulled his cap off and scratched his head. 'Is that right? What, and you reckon she might be a bit off colour, do yer?'

'No! You know what I mean. Stop tormenting!' Billy turned to his gran, Emmie, his face flushed. 'She's gonna hatch some chicks out, Nan. And if we don't put a dish of food right up close to 'er she'll starve!'

'Is she, Nan?' said Emma, quiet and serious. 'Is Florrie gonna give us some chicks?'

'She is, love, yeah. And your granddad knows full well. He's tormenting Billy. Tomorrow, I should reckon. Tomorrow they'll be pecking their way out of them shells.'

'See!' said Billy, to his granddad. 'I told yer! You never listen to me, though, do yer? And I don't s'pose you'll take any notice of what I saw today either. You'll say I made it up, I know you will.'

'It's gonna be in the papers, Granddad,' said Emma, all knowing. 'Spread across the front pages.'

'Go on. A daylight robbery, was it?'

'No, actually,' said Billy, 'it was a flying saucer. It landed at Bexley and *I* saw it. I was this bloomin' close. I was gonna touch but a bloke pulled me away. Said it was dangerous. That's why we've come round. To tell you about it.' He glanced at his mother in the doorway. 'Tell 'im, Mum – he'll believe you.'

Standing in the living-room doorway, Tom's brother, their Uncle Stanley, cut in: 'It landed in the roadway and took up the width of it. Even overlapped the pavement, but it wasn't quite on the ground. It 'ad eight massive suckers and white lights were flashing. The windows were glass but concave and moulded together so you couldn't see in. It lifted slowly off the ground, hovered above people's heads, then tilted slightly and sped up into the sky like lightning and disappeared.'

'Did Mum tell you all that?' Billy was mystified.

'Never 'ad to. My mate's doing some building work

near by – at the school. He used their blower when the secretary wasn't looking and phoned me at home. More excited than you, he was. But then he believes in all that stuff. It was a clever stunt, by the sounds of it.'

'It wasn't a stunt! I bloody well saw it! It was massive. Its surface was polished shinier than Nan's ever got her brass up! You would 'ave loved to 'ave seen it, Uncle Stanley! My life, you would 'ave! That's why Mum fetched me round so I could tell Granddad and Dad if he was in. But he's not, and anyway it don't matter 'cos you can back my story now.'

'Yeah,' said Stanley, quietly amused. 'I'll back your story, but not so much of the "bloody". And what was you doin' over the river anyway?'

'Went with my mate. Speedway racing. That was good an' all.'

'What, you took a bus, did yer?'

'Yeah. We went through Rotherive instead of Blackwall. The bus conductors are all right. We don't usually pay on the way back. Say we've lost our money or summink. And anyway, you can walk through Rotherive.'

'And your dad knows you get up to all that, does he?'

'I'm fourteen, Stanley!'

'Uncle Stanley to you.'

'So . . . what d'yer reckon of it, then? D'yer fink they was just coming down to 'ave a look at us? D'yer reckon they'll be back? To invade full on?'

'I reckon America 'ad somefing to do with it. You

get commercials coming on the television now and I wouldn't be surprised if it's something to do with that. You see if I'm wrong. You'll be seeing that same spaceship advertising somefing or the other on the television. I bet you a dollar.'

'That's what Mum says. Half a dollar and you're on.'

'Half a dollar it is.' Stanley showed the flat of his hand and Billy slapped it, saying, 'Easy money.'

'So why didn't you go for a dollar, then? Five shillings is twice as much as half a crown.'

''Cos I take after Granddad, that's why. He's cautious when he has a bet on the dogs. You said so yourself.'

'Fair enough. Right, come and 'elp me unload the van. I'm gonna wallpaper Nan's bedroom and paint the kitchen for 'er. Leave your mum and dad to themselves in the front room.'

'I didn't know Dad was in,' said Billy, a hint of worry in his eyes. 'What they talking about this time, then? Not the cottages, I 'ope.'

'That's for them to know and us to guess. Come on. Move yerself before Granddad insists on helping. He's a pain in the arse at times. "Do it this way, don't do it like that, waste of time if you ask me . . ." Stanley mimicked. 'One of these days I'll lock 'im in that shed with 'is flippin' chickens.'

Following his Uncle Stanley out into the street, Billy glanced at the front window, wondering why it was quiet and why his mum and dad weren't yelling at each other. But then, as he knew from recent experience, they always started off nice and calm and ending up slamming doors. 'I wanted to tell Dad about the men from Mars. I 'ope Mum's not gonna drag me off in a rage.'

'What're you talking about, Billy. What rage? They're talking, that's all.'

'Yeah . . . but is it the calm before the storm?'

'You've been listening to your gran for too long, sonny boy. That's your trouble.' Stanley opened the back of his van and pulled out a stack of wallpaper rolls. 'Here. Hold our yer arms and carry these upstairs into the boxroom. And don't listen at the front-room door. They might be kissing.'

'No they won't be!' snapped Billy, taking the load from his uncle. 'I told yer. They'll be 'aving a go at each other about summink or the other. Like a pair a kids.'

'Well, you're not far wrong there.' Stanley chuckled. Privately he was thinking just how sad it was that his brother and Jessie weren't still together. To his mind they had been torn apart over a silly misunderstanding. And some of the blame lay at his own feet for misconstruing an innocent meeting between Max and Jessie just after the war as something more devious. He hadn't intended mentioning it to Tom, and it had only been a passing remark after too many drinks at their family Christmas get-together. As far as Stanley was concerned, they should still be living together as man and wife. He knew that their marriage had been volatile at times, but that was all part of the game they liked to play, to his way of thinking.

They had always fuelled each other's fire one way or another. He knew that Tom idolised Jessie, always had done. He had never forgotten the way his brother had behaved the night Billy was born.

When Jessie's waters had broken and she was very close to delivering her baby Tom had shown himself in a new light. He had been beside himself because their first baby was coming before he was due and he feared for Jessie. Panicking, Tom had run straight past his parents' house from his own after Jessie had yelled for him to get his mother. He had been able to think of nothing else other than fetching the midwife, who at that time lived four turnings away. By the time he had returned home, perspiring and breathless, Jessie's birth pains were coming every five minutes. Almost out of his mind, he had paced the pavement outside, waiting for the midwife and the doctor to come. Seeing the woman he loved so deeply in so much pain had been too much for him. Not that he would have admitted it. Not Tom – he was above all that!

When the midwife finally arrived he followed her upstairs. She managed to soothe his nerves a little before she ordered him downstairs and out of her way. All had gone quite well from then on until Jessie gave the final push and the house lights suddenly went out. While Tom below, with a struck match in one of his trembling hands, foraged in his trouser pocket for a sixpenny bit for the meter, the midwife had been yelling at the top of her voice. It hadn't been just the dark which had caused her panic – something else had been wrong. And there, but for the grace of God,

Billy could so easily have been strangled at birth. The umbilical cord had been around his neck.

Fortunately, Emmie had heard the yelling and run out of her house into theirs. She put a much needed coin into the electric meter, giving the midwife light to work by. At first there had been no sound from above and even Emmie had been too scared to venture up the narrow staircase. It was the awesome silence which spurred her on. And while Tom was on his knees, praying for his wife and baby, she had rushed up the stairs and into the bedroom. Below, still on his knees, no longer praying but shedding a tear, Tom was stopped short by the sound of a sudden piercing scream which sent a cold chill down his spine. But then Emmie had yelled out, 'You've got a son, Tom! A cracking baby boy!'

And now that baby was fourteen years old and helping his Uncle Stanley to unload his van, wishing that his dad and mum would love each other again. So far he hadn't hear any raised voices and a calm mood did seem to be prevailing in his grandparents' house, as if everyone was silently wishing the same as himself. Outside in the back yard, Charlie snipped dead roses off his favourite bush and Emmie was on her knees gently lifting the belly of her mother hen to see whether any of the eggs had hatched out. Emma-Rose was close to her gran and staring at Florrie, desperate to see a tiny face peep out from beneath her.

'Another day and I reckon they'll all hatch at the same time. She's sitting on five, Emma, so it's all worth the wait, eh?'

'I'll come back in the morning, early . . . shall . . . shall . . . shall I?'

'Say that again, sweetheart, with only one "shall" and I'll let you stop the night.'

'I'll come back in the morning, early, shall I?'

'See! You *can* do it. It's a habit you've got to break, Emma, and you will. One morning you'll wake up and you'll say everyfing once only.'

'Will I, Nan?'

'Yes, darling, you will. Now then . . . how about picking some of the ripe tomatoes for me. It's Spam fritters, new-boiled potatoes and a bit of salad for tea. How does that sound?'

'Lovely. Billy'll want to stay, though, I'm warning yer.'

'There's plenty for all of us. And I'll tell you something else as well. Nanny's made a Bakewell tart.'

'With icing?'

'With icing, darlin', and a red cherry on top.'

'And Uncle Stanley's stopping as well, is he?'

'I expect so. Why?'

''Cos Billy'll need 'im to tell Dad that he did see . . . you know . . .'

'People from outer space?'

'Well, no, he never saw any spacemen. He did . . . did . . . did see their spaceship, though. He's gonna draw it later on.' She narrowed her eyes. 'What are Mum and Dad talking about, Nan?'

'I 'aven't got a clue, love, but best leave 'em alone in there, eh?'

'Do you fink they might get married again? And

if they do, what about Uncle Max? Will he still live wiv all of us?'

'We'll let them sort that out, Emma. Ask no questions, hear no lies. Tomatoes?'

'All right. And you won't 'ave to gimme a three-penny bit 'cos I love doing it. And I won't ask Mum about . . . you know.' She gave Emmie a wink and grinned, showing the gap where a milk tooth had come out.

Five minutes later, Emmie was by the butler sink in her kitchen, looking out of the window at her lovely granddaughter, while her grandson Billy was in the room above helping Stanley to shift furniture out of her and Charlie's bedroom into the boxroom. Emma's words had struck through her heart and now, alone, she could give free rein to her thoughts. Of course she wanted her son Tom and Jessie to get back together, but there was an awful lot of burying the past if they were ever to forgive and forget. To her mind Tom had made the biggest mistake in his life when he had dragged Jessie back from the safe haven in Norfolk and secreted her away in rooms in Stepney, in Matlock Street. The landlady had proved to be far too house proud, happy to take in lodgers provided she never saw them on the stairs or in the back garden. In short she had wanted both Jessie and Billy, a baby at the time, to be invisible and silent. Once Tom had left his little family in her care, having gone back to fight for his country after his sick leave, she had changed from friendly and obliging to formidable.

At the time both Emmie's and Jessie's houses had

been war damaged. Emmie and Charlie had slept on a bed in the front room until repairs had been made. She recalled the day when Jessie had taken her one and only grandson away to Norfolk. Of course she had been sad to see them go and had missed them badly, but worse things were happening at sea. By then she had already lost her eldest son Johhnie at Dunkirk, and her youngest, Stanley, had been listed as missing, presumed dead.

When Jessie had returned to Stepney and taken those rooms in Matlock Street, Emmie had been over the moon. After visiting the terraced house, and receiving a lecture from the landlady as to the rules concerning visitors, Emmie had not been too disappointed. The house had been in meticulous condition, the front door freshly painted and everything as clean as a whistle. There had been the scent of lavender polish in the air which, even though it had been tainted with the background smell of bleach, was lovely.

At first, Mrs Catling had welcomed Jessie and given baby Billy a big smile. It was only later, once Tom had left, that things changed. The house rules were made very clear to Jessie. She had to stop storing Billy's pushchair in the spacious cupboard under the stairs and fold it and carry it to the top of the house where she was lodging. Here everything had been clean and in its place but there had been a clinical feel to it. In Jessie's two rooms there had been a small double bed but no cot for the baby, as promised. On the landing there had been a cooker, a sink and a

larder cupboard in a very confined space. This was
her kitchen.

A few days after moving into the house, while Billy
was asleep, Jessie had received her first visit from her
neighbour – someone who, at first sight, did not look
the sort of person who would live in rooms in Mrs
Catling's house. Edna, a bleached blonde with a
ginger rinse, had a sunny appearance. Her eyebrows
had been completely shaved off and a black arch had
been pencilled in above her bright blue eyes, which
stood out beneath heavily black-mascared lashes. This
wonderful character, a transvestite in show business,
had been the saving of Jessie. He had made her laugh,
listened to her troubles, advised and comforted and
been a wonderful friend. They had been close, and
this had made Emmie feel a lot better about her son
dragging poor Jess from the Norfolk countryside to
lodge her in a cold, unfriendly house.

Chuckling, Emmie made a mental note to ask Jessie
whether she had recently been in touch with her old
friend. A ladies' night out in a pub with a stage was
on her mind, especially if Edna was up there singing
and entertaining the customers with her side-split-
ting, off-the-cuff jokes. But that could go on the back
burner for now. Her daughter-in-law still on her mind,
Emmie could not help wondering why they were
taking so long together in the front room. She knew
better than to disturb them, even though there was a
part of her longing to take them both in a cup of tea.
Her granddaughter arriving with a bowl of tomatoes
soon distracted her.

'Some are still green, Gran. And some are really, really small. Granddad said you would make chutney wiv the green ones so it doesn't matter.' She looked up questioningly. 'Does it?'

'What, sweetheart?' said Emmie, preoccupied. 'What are you talking about now?'

'Chutney: Will you make some and if you do can I help?'

'I will, and yes you can. But that'll be later on in the month.'

'Good.' With that Emma-Rose placed the bowl proudly on the kitchen table, marched out of the kitchen and went boldly into the front room.

'Saints preserve us,' murmured Emmie, hoping that the pair of them were not in there having a cuddle for old times' sake.

She needn't have worried – they had been talking, going over past events and in their different ways making their apologies while defending their reasons for everything they had done. As many times before, Tom had quizzed Jessie as to whether she had still loved Max, the man she had once been promised to, when they themselves had first been married – and especially when Tom had walked out on her and their children. Tired of the question, Jessie had refused to answer him. As luck would have it, their daughter had, in her own innocent way, intervened at just the right time.

Coming into the kitchen, a little sheepish, Tom kept his eyes down. Emmie was under no illusions as to why. He loved Jessie as much as he had always loved her, and he was hurting inside. And when one of her sons was hurting the pain for her was doubly worse.

'You all right, son?' she said quietly, avoiding his eyes.

'Yeah, I'm all right,' was his short, sad reply. 'Where's Billy?'

'Upstairs with your dad. They're clearing our bedroom ready for when you and Stanley've got time. The wallpaper's lovely but don't tell your dad I said so.'

'He knows you like it, Mum. Why else didn't you kick up a fuss?'

'Got to get the balance right and keep things tickety-boo.'

Filling the kettle, Tom quietly chuckled. 'Anyone'd think you were a pair of clocks the way you talk. And behave. Always winding each other up.'

'Do we?' Emmie stopped checking the tomatoes that Emma-Rose had picked. 'Don't you think you've got that a bit lopsided, son? I would 'ave said that it's you and our Jessie who always wind each other up. Not me and your dad.'

Setting out cups and saucers for the fresh pot of tea he was brewing, Tom said, 'Well, it all depends on who's watching who, don't it. What's all this about Billy seeing a spaceship, then? He's a bit old to be making up kids' stories, I would 'ave thought.'

'Have you spoken to Stanley about it?'

'No. Jessie mentioned it, that's all. Why?'

'Because I think you'll find he'll back the story. One of 'is mates phoned 'im. He's working on a school over at Bexley and he's all excited over it as well. Personally, I think we should all be worried. Anything could 'appen. We're sitting ducks to what might be up there.'

'Don't be daft. Put all the weapons and armies on this planet together and we'd blast anyfing out of the sky before it could set little green men down. It's all a load of hogwash.'

'You think so? Well, I don't agree, son. We might be considered to be living in the dark ages by other planets. And let's face it, there are a lot of bloody stars up there – as far as the eye can see, never mind what's beyond.

'No . . . if you ask me there's more to this sighting than a joke over a pint on a Saturday night. We're being studied, Tom. And not so much us and all the other animals and suchlike but our planet. Our earth. One day there'll be different kinds of wars, but it'll all come down to the same thing . . . territory. Never mind that Hitler wanted to rule Britain. That'll be peanuts compared to when the time's ripe for a war of the worlds.'

'Well, ain't you a bundle of joy today,' said Tom, pouring a little milk into each cup.

'I'm not down over it, Tom. It just stands to reason, that's all. No point in worrying 'cos there's not much we can do about it.'

Tom knew his mother well enough to realise that she was leading up to something. In a more relaxed mood, now having aired a few matters with Jessie to do with the cottages and life in general, he was able to give her a free rein. Going quiet was always the best way as far as he was concerned – keeping his mouth shut and simply waiting. He wasn't wrong. Checking that Emma-Rose was still engrossed with Florrie outside, she finally asked the question. 'You and Jessie had a little heart-to-heart, then, did you?'

'Yeah, as it 'appens, we did. And before you ask, I told her that once we've done the cottages up she and Max can spend a week up there with the kids. I thought that'd please you.'

'Good. That's good.' After another short silence she continued, 'Be nice if she and Max could go up to have a look at them before you start work on 'em. I bet Jessie can't wait to have an excuse to go back to that little village.'

'No reason why she can't do. Max might put his hand in his pocket and chuck a bit of money in. You never know. Not all of the Jews are tight.'

'That's not funny, Tom, and you know it.'

'Wasn't meant to be. Between the three of us – me, Stanley and lover boy – we could make something of the cottages. Sell our Johnnie's house and we could build an extension on as well.'

'Oh, no,' said Emmie. 'You leave that house out of it. That's been willed to all the grandchildren now. When me and your dad 'ave gone they'll have that house and this one between them to sell. I'm not going to my grave worrying whether they'll have somewhere to live in the future. The rate that the immigrants are flooding in there won't be enough council places to go round one day. You see if I'm wrong.'

'Fair enough. Just thought I'd mention it, that's all.'

They fell silent as Jessie came into the kitchen. 'Been talking about me again?' she said, before smiling and giving Tom a knowing look.

'No,' said Emmie, 'we were talking about the cottages.'

'And you,' said Tom, getting in quick. 'You and lover boy.'

'Don't start, Tom,' said Emmie, rinsing her hands at the sink. 'I'm sick of hearing it.'

'Take no notice, Em. We had a lovely chat in there and cleared the air once and for all. He might go on about Max as if he's jealous but he's not. Your darling son is in love again, if you ask me. I reckon there's a woman in the wings.'

'Well, you reckon wrong, then, don't yer,' said Tom as he left the room to go upstairs. 'Pour out the tea, Jess, and make yourself useful for a change!'

Jessie *was* wrong but as far as Tom was concerned it was good to keep her wondering. He knew her well enough by now. There was no other woman in his life – he still loved Jessie and wanted her back.

Once she was sure he was out of earshot Emmie spoke in a quiet voice. 'He seems to be in a good mood, Jess, I grant you. Maybe he has met someone.'

''Course he has. Your son's back on top of things, Em. He's got his old confidence back and he's wearing Old Spice again.' She grinned.

'Wouldn't that be something. You, Max and the kids all settled down together and Tom partnered up with someone who loves him. That's a mother's dream if ever there was one. I expect it's what you want as well.'

''Course it is. All of us all right. Happy even. That'll do me.' And on that note both women lapsed into silence, each getting on with their chores in the kitchen, Emmie thinking that Tom and Jessie should be together and Jessie filled with dread at the thought of an attractive woman living in the cottage with Tom and becoming a stepmother to their Billy and Emma-Rose.

'I'll give him a good hiding if he fetches an old tart home,' Emmie said, playfully.

'You do that, Em – you do that. But let me know first so I can watch.'

As strong as Emmie was, she knew that even she could not alter the course of people's lives. The most important thing at that moment was that Tom and Jessie had had a good heart-to-heart and they were on proper speaking terms again – and all in the name of their children. If it was for Billy and Emma-Rose that they had each agreed to bury the hatchet and put the past behind them, then so be it. What she wanted now was peace all round and to be able to spend time in their company without the awful tension that had been evident between them for too long. But they still loved each other – of that she had no doubt.

'You'll never guess who drifted into my mind earlier on, Jess.'

'My mother? You've not seen 'er for a while and she does ask about you, now and then.'

'No, not Rose. Edna.'

'God, yeah . . .' murmured Jessie. 'I wonder if he's still living over Bethnal Green? Last time I heard he and his partner were doing up a flat above a pub. Making it really nice. I think it was the Rising Sun, but I can't be sure.'

'Must be a good few years since you've seen Edna. Could be dead for all you know.'

'No, he won't be dead. I would 'ave felt it if he'd gone. I don't think he'd still be around this way, though. Don't know why. I'm glad you've reminded me. I'll see what I can find out and let you know. You liked him a lot, didn't you?'

'I liked *her* a lot. Sorry, Jess, but I just can't think of Edna as a man. Even if she is wearing a suit and tie by now. She wore some beautiful clothes and to me she was a woman. 'Course, I wouldn't say that in front of the men . . .'

'God, no. But I will say this. I would defend him with my last breath. I was really down when he walked into my life, and if it hadn't of been for 'im, I'm not sure I wouldn't have gone down the pan. Bloody war. I went from pillar to post looking for somewhere to live.'

'Don't remind me, Jess, there's a good girl. We're all on track now so let's be thankful for that.'

Startling them both, Billy crashed into the room, a look of fury on his face. 'Sometimes Granddad torments me but this time I think he means it! Me and Emma's room's gonna be wallpapered white with stupid little pink and yellow flowers all over it! He said she chose it when he took 'er down Whitechapel to the wallpaper shop! How come he never asked if I wanted to go and choose?'.

Emmie smiled. She had forgotten about the wallpaper, although she had been expecting this reaction from her grandson. Keeping her back to him, she said nothing as he went on at Jessie about favouritism and life not being fair. To her mind, as long as it was only a bit of wallpaper that was the biggest problem he had right now, that was fine. Having been reminded of the war and all the scars it had caused her, this was bliss by comparison.

Blocking out the two of them, mother and son, as they tried to work out a compromise on how the room could be fashioned in a way to suit both boy and girl, Emmie looked out of her kitchen window into the back yard. One section of the garden had been turned into a vegetable patch and looked healthy and fruitful, with runner beans trailing up against the old brick wall while potatoes, Brussels and cabbages filled the rest of the patch, except for where the tomatoes grew. Along the edges on both sides marigolds grew like a thick carpet.

Coming quietly into the room, Tom slipped his arms around his mother's waist and gave her a squeeze. 'I like your perm, Mum. It suits you.'

'Just as well, because I was gonna ask you and Charlie to treat me to it. It cost seven and six. Well, seven shillings, but I gave sixpence as a tip.'

'Course we'll treat yer. And you know why? 'Cos you're the best mum in the world, that's why.'

Turning slowly to face Tom, she looked into his eyes, wondering what he was after. But the sparkle she saw told her that he was happy and the expression on his face confirmed it. Maybe Jessie's right, she thought. Maybe Tom has found someone else to love. Part of her was happy for him . . . and part of her was sad. Sad that it wouldn't be 'To Tom and Jessie' that she would be writing on the Christmas card this year, or the next.

# 7

It was now five weeks since Maggie had confessed her condition to her mother, yet to Edie it felt as if only a week had gone by. So much had happened in that short period of time that she was beginning to wonder what might happen next. Her daughter had been thrown into adulthood before she had had time to establish herself in a profession or been farther afield than Margate. She had learned that her husband, who she believed to be long since dead, had returned to England, caused trouble and gone away again without a hello or goodbye, and her father, who she had adored, had come home from Canada after almost twenty years with a half-brother in tow who she had not set eyes on before. And having been living effectively as a widow for years with no thoughts of finding romance, she had suddenly met Dennis and was engaged to be married.

Things seemed to be going along the right track where Maggie was concerned, however, and to Edie her treasured daughter remained the most important person in the world. After all that had happened she could hardly believe that she was now relaxing on her settee, idly looking through a *Woman's Own* magazine with nothing coming at her in the way of bad news. Nor did she any longer have that dreadful heavy feeling in her chest caused by recent worries and the sense of failure and hurt once she had discovered that Harry had betrayed her and had been living with and loving another woman.

Edie had no doubt as to who had helped her attain this sense of calm – her Aunt Naomi, of course, but more importantly her new neighbours and soulmates, Jessie and Laura. Maggie, suddenly becoming a friend she could talk to as well as her loving daughter, had also gone a long way to bringing back her old self-confidence. Dennis, kind and considerate, who came and went without creating a ripple of trouble, would, she knew, make a good husband. Not the type to socialise, he seemed content with Edie's company and enjoyed spending three evenings a week with her when Maggie was out and when she would otherwise have been alone. Neither of them needed anything more than each other's company, watching the tele-vision and savouring a healthy home-cooked meal with the lights down low. To show his appreciation of her hospitality, Dennis always brought a box of her favourite Black Magic chocolates. Not that she expected anything in return for cooking for two instead of one, but that was the way her fiancé liked to do things. He was a gentleman through and through, and Edie could not fault him. Nothing much had changed since the night they had met at the New Year's Eve dance. His behaviour remained flawless. Always agreeable and as reliable as clockwork, Dennis could do no wrong, and yet something didn't feel right, all was not as it should be. And Edie knew it. The worst of it was she didn't know *what* it was that wasn't right about their relationship.

When it came to Naomi it was a different story. Even though she was now voicing her sentiments in Dennis's favour, Edie felt that, for whatever reason, her aunt still did not fully trust him. It was one of Naomi's back-handed compliments which had sowed this seed in her mind – 'He is almost *too* good to be true, darling.' This had been said more than once during the ten months that she had known Dennis. At least her aunt hadn't criticised him outright – and if Naomi had felt there was good reason for doing so, Edie felt sure she would have done. Her best friends, Jessie and Laura, had taken to Dennis from the beginning and had been happy for her when the engagement had been announced. So what was wrong?

Now, on this Friday evening during the first week in October, Edie was waiting for Laura to return from the hop fields of Kent and was looking forward to hearing how the season had gone. She and Jessie had planned a little welcome-home party for the three of them, to be held in Edie's living room that evening. They had clubbed together to buy a bottle of vodka and some lime cordial. And as a special treat Edie was roasting a small chicken, and Jessie had bought freshly baked crusty bread from the Jewish baker's and a portion of cheesecake on her way home from work.

The girls had missed Laura during her break in

Kent, but they had made up for her absence by having a weekly evening drink together at Edie's and trying to guess whether or not their pal had taken the plunge this year and enjoyed more than just a flirtation with the handsome owner of the hop farm. Equally, they couldn't wait to fill Laura in on all that had happened in their lives during the past month. Having experienced a torrid time of late, Edie now felt that at last the wrath of the gods had run its course and they had seen fit to leave her alone.

As for her daughter, there had been further developments in Maggie's life. The flat above the fish-and-chip shop was being decorated and there had been changes at the home of her best friend, Rita. Her mother, Eileen, was now working full time at the library, keeping the building clean and polished and in tip-top condition. She had also seen the back of her no-good husband, who had moved in with his other woman. This sudden transformation in her life had affected Rita considerably. Her visits to Maggie in Scott House had become more frequent and she seemed much happier, always ready to give Edie an update on the way things were going.

Rita's mother was patiently waiting to move out of the old house and into a self-contained two-bedroom flat, next door to her sister and brother-in-law. The new arrangements, whereby Rita would now share with Maggie on a temporary basis, had reluctantly been accepted by Tony. With everyone else however, it had been greeted with relief. It seemed the ideal solution. Tony's mother, Ida, had also welcomed the new plan. It meant she could have her son under her roof where she could keep an eye on him and at the same time keep their priest happy.

Tony and his brother had been working on the flat during any spare time they had and it was beginning to look quite striking. The ceilings and walls had been painted white and the original fitted cupboards with their old brass fittings pale green. Mrs Baroncini had run up some thick red-and-white cotton curtains which looked fresh and perfect for young people. Items of furniture had been donated by both Tony's and Maggie's families. All that was needed now was a rug for the living room, to which Naomi had said she would treat her niece.

Concerned for her daughter, Rita's mother, Eileen, had called in to see Edie for a chat once it had been confirmed that the girls would be sharing. The two women had got on fine and of course had something in common – both their husbands had deserted them. During the two hours that Eileen had been at Edie's the women had talked non-stop – or rather Eileen had. She was excited about her own imminent move away from the house that had almost become her ball and chain, and doubly pleased that she now had a proper daily full-time job at the library. The previous cleaner, who thought that bleach was the answer to everything, had taken umbrage at having to work alongside someone else and so had left in a huff, taking a few old leather-bound books with her as a leaving present to herself. The note she left for Mathew Browning had been short and sweet:

*Goodbye, you miserable old bastard. I'm off to serve teas in a factory among proper men.*

During their talk Edie learned more about Maggie's friend, Rita. And the more she had heard the more she liked her. Rita was Eileen's youngest child, and there had been a long gap between the elder sister and her. So in a sense both Rita and Maggie had been treated as only children, with one parent taking full responsibility – the mother. Rita hadn't been wrapped in cotton wool as Maggie had, but then not everyone had an Aunt Naomi. As a baby Maggie had been watched over almost every hour; as a child she had been protected from all outside influences, taken to and from school and fed by Naomi at lunchtimes instead of staying for school dinners like most of her classmates.

Living at that time at the top of a three-storeyed house in Cleveland Way in self-contained lodging rooms, Naomi had been only a stone's throw away from Maggie's school, so it had all worked perfectly. Once she reached the age of ten, however, and when her great-aunt had to be elsewhere, she had her own key on a long chain around her neck, hidden beneath her vest. This meant she could let herself into her Naomi's flat to eat the cold lunch that had been left for her. It wasn't until Maggie was fifteen and working at the library that she realised just how wide and exciting the outside world was. Her best friend Rita, by contrast, had had to fend for herself as a child and young teenager. Her mother had always worked a full day and more. Her father, of course, had been preoccupied with his own private world and had used their house as somewhere to lodge rather than as a home. But now all that had changed. He had gone at last.

The sudden ring of the doorbell reminded Edie of the alarm clock piercing her dreams at dawn when all she wanted was to turn over in bed and go back to sleep. She knew this was going to be Laura, or perhaps Jessie, come to tell her that the lorry had arrived. Having anticipated this moment all afternoon Edie now felt it was an anticlimax. She wanted to hold on to the privacy of her own world – over the years she had become very used to her own company.

Opening the door, expecting to find one of her friends on the doorstep, she was taken aback to see Sister Kathleen, the nun from Nonnatus House, standing there looking demurely at her. Breaking into a smile, and without thinking about it, Edie held out her arms and embraced the woman as if she were an angel sent down from heaven. Holding on to her emotions, she spoke in a quiet voice. 'Thank you so much for coming.'

Gently pulling back, Sister Kathleen placed a finger under Edie's chin and looked into her watery eyes. 'My dear, did you think I had forgotten you? And why wouldn't I come? Especially after you sent such a touching letter after your visit to thank me, when really I had done hardly anything to help.'

'Being honest and simple helped a lot,' said Edie, and then, standing aside, she invited the woman in, deeply moved that she should be visited by this kind person whom she hardly knew. In the living room Edie asked the nun whether she would like something to drink. Sister Kathleen gracefully declined. 'I'm afraid I have only a few minutes to spare but I would love to share a pot of tea with you some other time.'

'You'll always be welcome in this house,' said Edie, 'always. You may not have realised it, but your hospitality when I came to see you, without making an appointment first, helped clear my mind more than you can imagine. I was feeling very low and didn't know quite which way to turn or who to turn to.'

'And now?'

'Now? Well . . . as much as I wish Maggie wasn't in the predicament she's in, I've accepted it. And you've helped me to do that. She's going to stay in a nice clean flat above a shop in the Roman Road and share with her best friend, Rita, until the baby's due.'

'And then?'

'Then she and Tony will be married in Scotland. Her friend will move in with her mother and the young couple will live in the flat. I'm not sure what the plan is after that. I don't think any of us have thought that far ahead.'

'Well, that's no bad thing, my dear. One day at a time. One day at a time.' Allowing a few seconds of silence to pass, Sister Kathleen then said, 'You'll be pleased to know that I've spoken to Mother Superior and she's quite agreeable to my suggestion that one of our midwives visit your daughter before the birth and then delivers your grandchild into the world. If that's what you would like.'

'Oh,' said Edie, relieved. 'That would be the best thing that anyone could do for us. I won't pretend that I wasn't terrified at the thought of Maggie having to go into hospital to have her baby. I wouldn't be able to be there for her night and day. I still see her as my little girl, I'm afraid.'

'And why not? Even as mature adults we are still God's children. And after all, my dear, Maggie is your only child. Your precious child, and no doubt a reminder of the husband you loved and lost. We must never forget our soldiers who were killed in the line of duty.'

Suddenly aware that if she did not correct Sister Kathleen she would in a sense be lying to her, Edie wasn't quite sure what to say. But how could she even begin to explain what had happened? It was all far too complicated. Obeying her sixth sense she kept quiet and let the silence be her answer. The nun would have to take it whichever way she was inclined to.

'But there . . . we mustn't remind you of your grief but celebrate your daughter. Will she be coming back home to this lovely apartment to have her baby?'

'Yes,' said Edie. 'Most definitely. She'll spend the last week of her term with me, here.'

'Good. And you will write to me with the address where our midwife may visit her in the meantime?'

'I will, of course I will.' Running a hand through her hair, Edie added quietly, 'I can't tell you what this has done for me. You've lifted a weight that's been keeping me awake at night. I can't thank you enough. And if there's anything by way of help that I can do for your cause you will let me know, won't you? I want to repay the kindness and all I've got to give is myself and my time. I work during the week but I can always give up a weekend every so often, or an evening during weekdays.'

'I'll bear that in mind,' replied Sister Kathleen. She placed a hand on Edie's shoulder. 'But I think you are going to have enough on your plate for a while.'

'Well, later on, then. Once Maggie's married and settled.'

'Yes. Later on. I shall look forward to it.' With that the woman bade Edie farewell and left, passing Jessie on the doorstep. Edie's friend had come to announce that the lorry carrying Laura back from the hop fields had arrived below.

Her eyes bright, Jessie had a mischievous smile on her face as she eased her friend back into the flat and privacy. 'I've seen 'er!' she said. 'I was just back from the corner shop and there it was, drawing to a halt. She's as brown as a berry and the cheeky cow gave me a wink that said it all! She's 'ad a good time, all right. I wish Nao was 'ere.'

'What about Jack?' Edie said. 'Has he got a long face?'

'Nope. Grinning from ear to ear with the same old sexy twinkle in them blue eyes of 'is. I don't reckon he's got a clue. Bloody good luck to 'er an' all, is what I say. He's terrible. A right flirt.'

'And how would you know that, I wonder?' teased Edie, picking up the bottle of vodka and giving it a shake. 'Ready for one now or is it too early?'

'No. Sod it. What the eye don't see the men can't knock. Pour three and I'll nab Laura at the top of the stairs.' She cocked her ear and listened. 'That's 'er now. Hark at 'er yelling at Jack to get a move on! Lover boy must be something special if he's brought out the mettle in 'er.' She turned to go and then stopped in her tracks. 'What was the nun doing here, Ed?'

'Another time, Jess, another time.'

'Fair enough.' She ran out of the flat to catch Laura before she reached her own street door. Her friend was glowing with good health and looked lovely.

'Well, look at you.' Jessie grinned. 'If that little holiday's not done you the world of good I don't know what would. You jammy cow. You've 'ad a very good time, 'aven't you.'

'Shows that much, does it?' said Laura.

'I'll say it does. Put that suitcase down for a minute and listen.'

'Jess . . . I've only just got off the lorry. I need something to drink.'

''Course you do. Put the bloody suitcase down. No one's gonna nick it. Edie's got three vodkas and lime poured for us.'

'You're kidding me? You've not been sitting in that kitchen waiting for the lorry? Surely not?'

'Shut up and get to Edie's before the men come up. You can chuck the drink down. We've got more planned for later on. A little party for three women. Four if Nao turns up.'

Laura listened at the top of the stairs but there was no sound of Jack coming up. 'He's probably flirting with Milly. It's the last he'll see of 'er till this time next year. Go on, then. But one drink and I'm out of there. He's not daft, you know. He'll wanna know what this is all about. He'll either think we're a bunch of ladies in trousers or that you can't wait to hear what I've bin up to in the hop fields.'

At Edie's, on seeing her friend standing in the kitchen with a sly smile on her face, Laura looked from her to Jessie and then burst into tears – to the sound of their laughter. She had bottled up her feelings in the lorry on the journey home, putting on her public face to keep up appearances.

She had had a wonderful holiday – not just because she had been constantly in the place where her lover lived and worked, but also because she had had little to worry about other than looking after her own and her daughter Kay's welfare. To Laura picking hops was a pleasure and the social scene a bonus. Sitting on the edge of a picking bin, with the dappled sunshine filtering through the thick bines which hung high above her on criss-crossed wires, was far more relaxing than lying on a crowded beach by the seaside. Natural shelter from the midday sun, while enjoying a picnic lunch washed down with a small flask of tea, had been her idea of heaven and could not be measured against anything else.

Living for ever in England's garden, Kent, was something she would now enjoy dreaming about, both in her sleep and in her waking hours. She was going to miss the hop pickers singing their ballads, the sound carrying across acres and acres of fields. She was going to miss sitting around the campfires at night talking about everything and nothing. Especially now and for the next few weeks, until reality forced its way back into her busy world. She knew that this year it was going to take longer for her to settle back down to London life again now that she and Richard had become lovers.

She was going to spend the mornings drinking tea in her kitchen instead of in her cosy little hut, where only a floral curtain separated the tiny living space from where she and Kay slept on straw mattresses on a raised timber platform, with only the low glow of their brass oil lamp in its pink glass shade to see them through the night. Cocoa before bedtime was not the same at home as it was in that magical place. And neither was a breakfast of steaming hot porridge oats covered in melting brown sugar.

This particular year the yield had been good and the hops plump and plentiful. With the help of her daughter Laura had managed to pick on average thirty bushels a day at a return of tenpence a bushel. So not only had she come home glowing with the memory of her romance, but with her purse lined ready for Christmas.

Drying her eyes, Laura laughed softly. 'I never missed you two. Not one bit.'

'Good,' said Edie, checking the drink into her hand. 'Now get the rest of that down you and tell us in a word – did you or didn't you?'

'Don't rush me,' said Laura, raising her hand. After a few sips of her vodka and lime she spoke in a quiet voice. 'It's not easy coming back to brick buildings all round you when you've been used to relaxing outside a cosy little hut after picking in the fields all day. And then enjoying a pot roast cooked on the open fire.'

'Did you or didn't you?' Jessie demanded. But her friend was not going to be rushed into a confession judging by the expression on her face – one of well-deserved self-satisfaction.

'The best bit of all was the views,' said Laura, dreamily. 'Landscape on all four sides and the setting sun spreading warm pink light in the sky.'

'Listen to it,' said Edie, poking fun. 'We 'ad our sunsets as well, you know. And we sat on our balconies sipping tea from china cups while listening to Ruby Murray singing "Softly Softly", Eartha Kitt with "C'est si bon" and "Under the Bridges", the Inkspots and "The Gypsy", Johnnie Ray and—'

'Don't tell her about the two blokes who shared it with us. She'll be gutted to have missed out on the visiting Italian men from above.'

'As if,' said Laura, and then, gazing out at nothing, a look of love in her eyes, she murmured, 'It was awkward at first. When I first saw 'im. Everyone everywhere. All we could do was smile and nod at each other. But then on the Monday, once we were on the fields picking, he made it easy for me to approach him if I wanted to. So I did.'

'What do you mean – *you* approached *him*?'

'Why not? He was making himself available if I wanted to pick up on it. Perfect set-up, if you ask me. I wish all men were like that.'

'But what did you say?' Edie wanted to know – this was all very new to her.

'Hello . . . it's good to see you again.'

'And that was it? That started it off?'

'Of course – it depends on *how* you say it and how you look at your lover to be. Not that I make a habit of it. It just came naturally.'

'Sounds a bit cut and dried to me.' Jessie shrugged.

'No, it wasn't that. Imagine being in the hop gardens by moonlight . . . or snug in his little cottage that he uses as an office in front of a small open fire. Or an ancient church with the moonlight coming in through the stained-glass windows. With the man of your dreams, tall, broad, rugged and tanned, with the sexiest warm brown eyes, warm enough to melt ice . . . holding you close and slowly drawing up the material of your skirt until you feel the cool night air on your thighs . . . and then leaning against an old oak tree, perhaps, with only the sound of owls in the distance . . .'

She slowly turned her head to look at them, only to find that they were somewhere else, in their own private little worlds of fantasy. 'I know what you mean,' Jessie murmured. 'There was one of those in Elmshill. Rupert. There's something about a man bred around farmland. A ruggedness. A clean, earthy smell of freshly cut hay and soap. Do they do it on purpose just to get us in the sack?'

'Who cares?' said Edie. 'So long as they do what they did to you two. Why am I the one missing out here? Where have I been all these years? I mean,

Dennis is all right but ours is more of a quick slam and thank you, ma'am. All over in ten minutes.'

'Like most men.' Jessie laughed. 'Well, all I can say is that as soon as Tom's got those cottages finished . . . it's us women up to Norfolk. What d'yer reckon, Ed? A rugged country squire or three. You up for it?'

'I should say I am. A week amidst men like you've just described would be better than a month by the sea.'

'She'll start singing "Somewhere over the Rainbow" in a minute,' said Laura, quietly laughing at her friend, usually strait-laced when it came to sex talk and men.

'I'll talk to Tom about it, if you like. We might even be able to go before they're done up. I think that Stanley's got hold of a couple of old caravans from the early thirties that he's gonna tow up there. We could stop in them.'

'I don't care,' said Edie. 'Just get me up there. Flying high as a kite.'

'We will, don't you worry.'

'And was Richard Wright in your heart all of the time?' Edie continued. 'Or only when the full moon was out?' She turned to Jessie. 'If this is what love's done for her, maybe *we* should go next year to see what it is these gentlemen of Kent have to offer.'

'As it happens, I think you should come with me next time. You'd love it. I know you would. It's good for the *soul*,' Laura said theatrically.

'Ah, but will you share your lover with us?' Jessie looked across at Edie and winked.

'Oh, that goes without saying, surely,' said Edie, answering for her friend. 'Because really and truly, the way it sounds to me, the romantic setting can only really be appreciated when there's a bit of forbidden fruit around ... a handsome, rugged landowner.'

'Think what you want. Say what you want. Do what you want.' Laura finished her drink and waved a hand in the air. 'It was magic, girls. Pure magic. And I ain't sharing him with no one. Not even my two best friends.'

'And what about Romeo's wife?' said Edie.

'Her name's Julia ... and she's not much of a wife. Not the way we lot are. We cook, wash and iron for our men while she gets people like us to do it for 'er ... and treats them like dirt in the process. A worse snob you wouldn't *want* to find. Theirs is a marriage of convenience. She packed her kids off to boarding school so she could maintain a "social life" – while Richard worked long hours running the farm and doing all the bookkeeping himself. She doesn't go in for illicit relationships but she does like to have one lover on the go, from what Richard told me.'

'And that,' said Jessie, 'sounds like a well-rehearsed speech to justify your actions, Mrs Jackson.'

'No, it's not. It's true. That's Julia Wright in a nutshell. She hates having us low-class lot around – but there's nothing she can do about it. That farm needs us. She wouldn't pick a bloody apple off the tree, never mind twenty bushels of hops a day. So don't start feeling sorry for that one.'

'Why don't he give 'er the shove, then?' said Jessie.
'If she's that bad?'

'The children. As simple as that. *And* . . . his uppity
family. It wouldn't go down well if there was a blemish
on the family name. So . . . he keeps up a front and
she does the same. She keeps up the charade because
she loves the lifestyle and especially being the lady of
the manor. She wears something different and expensive every day. Country style.'

'So that's the way the other half live, then,' said
Edie. 'Good luck to you for sliding in and sliding out
again is all I can say.'

Jessie, however, was unable to resist one more quip.
'If I come hop picking next year for a day out . . .
can I 'ave a look at him? Up close? I promise I won't
touch.'

'No. Stop here and look at my Jack instead. Watch
the little knowing winks he gives the women he's
having on the sly.'

Jessie's face broke into a warm smile. 'Well then
. . . you've every right to 'ave had a lovely time. And
you did, by the sound of it. And I think I would do
the same in your place. I mean, it's not harming
anyone, is it – and look what it's done for you. You're
lovely and brown and blooming and I'm green with
envy and grey from them steam trains going by every
half an hour.'

'Is his wife really that bad, Laura?' said Edie. 'Or
are you just saying it because you feel guilty now
you're back in dirty old London?'

'No, I'm not. She is a cow, Ed. Do you know what

she started doin' this year? Coming on the hop fields in her truck with an ice-cream refrigerator in tow. Just like the one outside Cooper's, the sweet and tobacconist shop. Great for the kids except that she charges more than the little kiosk that used to sell lollies, ice-cream cornets and drinks just ten minutes' walk away. She stopped an old country lady earning a few shillings. A Kentish woman who lives in a tiny tied cottage.'

Won over by this testimonial, they turned their conversation to what had been going on in their own neck of the woods, Maggie and her predicament being the main topic. Edie gave her a run-down on all the options but in the main she wanted to know whether Laura agreed that Maggie should brazen it out and live above a fish-and-chip shop out of the area so no one would recognise her. After a short debate Laura said she thought that was the best option, and to change the subject, Jessie briefly related the sighting of the flying saucer by Billy and others.

'Poor little devil was terrified,' said Edie, chuckling at the memory. 'Billy still won't have it, will he, Jess? Swears he saw what he saw.'

'And he's not the only one apparently. But as you might expect it was only reported in the local paper for Bexley. The rest of England pooh-poohed it. Others tried to make their voices heard but were laughed at. One was a lad of fifteen, a labourer – swore on his mother's life that it was real. His elder brother said he saw it as well.'

'I'm glad we weren't here,' said Laura. 'Kay would

still be 'aving nightmares, I should think. She's asked for a comic book about aliens taking over the earth for Christmas. It's all the kids in her class at school talk about, by the sound of things. Trouble is – they believe all that stuff. Whoever planned the hoax should be taken to task. It's not funny.'

'You don't have to tell me that.' Jessie sighed. Billy was in a state of shock when he got home after seeing it. Whatever it was he saw. Trouble is there's no evidence to prove anything. And so far . . . no confirmation that it was a stunt. So we'll never know the truth will we?'

'What can you expect?' Edie shrugged. 'Comics and American B-movies are overflowing with horror stories of alien visitors planning a takeover of Earth.'

'You should 'ave phoned the television people, Jess,' said Laura. 'They would 'ave been interested.'

'Apparently not. According to Tom's brother, Stanley. His friend and others were ready to hold up their hands and say what they saw. One even phoned the wireless news service and was told that they received at least a dozen calls a week about sightings. Even Stanley's beginning to believe that such things are quashed by those on high – so as not to cause panic.'

Interested though she was, Laura's mind was still on her lover. 'Never mind,' she murmured, 'it'll come out in the the wash.' Richard's warm smile, light brown eyes and broad shoulders were the only apparition she could see right then. She could almost smell the aftershave he had worn the previous night, when they had made love on a comfortable old sofa in front of the fire.

'So, Laura, now that you're home, and you've given your opinion as to what you think is best for Maggie,' said Edie, picking up on her own account of what had been happening in her world, 'I can relax about her living above a chip shop?'

Laura thought about the question and then said, 'I do think so, Ed. But more important – what about once the baby comes?'

'They'll get married in Scotland.'

'And live where?'

'Above the shop, of course. It'll be respectable enough for Tony to move in by then.'

'And what about her friend, Rita?' said Jessie.

'She'll probably go and live with her mother'.

'And if she doesn't want to move out of the flat?'

'Oh, she will,' said Edie. 'I know Rita. She'll be ready to fend for herself and more than likely will be planning to find her own bedsit by then. You can bet your life on it.'

'And will you and Dennis live here or in his house?' Laura was curious to know.

'Exactly what I asked,' said Jessie, pleased that Laura had broached the subject.

'Don't know yet.'

By the tone of her voice and the expression on her face, both women knew that this was not something Edie wanted to discuss. As to why, they had little idea, but Edie's private life was her own affair. 'And what about your wedding?'

'What about it, Laura?'

'Well . . . Mags'll be five to six months showing by then. Or don't that bother you?'

'That's true,' murmured Edie, looking from one friend to the other. 'Why didn't I think of that?'

'Because you've 'ad your daughter's welfare at heart and as usual not really thought about yourself. About your wedding, which is just as important as anything else.'

Edie fell quiet as the obvious dawned on her, and then shrugged. 'I'll have to postpone it till June next year. Maggie'll be back to her normal shape by then.'

'Just like that?' said Laura.

'I think so. And as a matter of fact I don't think I could handle all the arrangements now. Not now. Everything's changed since we first decided on Christmas. I can't believe Naomi's not pointed that problem out. I know I've been walking about as if I'm in a trance over this baby thing, but she always brings me up short with the next thing we have to sort out.'

'Well, she's not getting any younger, Ed,' said Laura. 'My dad's the same. He used to be the one we could rely on to keep us on our toes, but not any more.'

A sudden banging on the front door stopped them in their tracks. Laura knew it was Jack, there to drag her back to her duties and more importantly to give him the key to their front door so that he could take in all he had unloaded from his brother-in-law's lorry.

'That'll be your old man, Laura. I'll go and soften

him up a bit for you. Offer him a cup of tea.' She went to open the door. 'Hello, Jack, where's the fire?' she said, giving him a flirtatious smile which she knew he would appreciate. This man could not resist a bit of encouragement normally. But not today. Today he just wanted to unload the lorry and get life back to normal.

'I take it she's in there, gossiping?' He spoke without a hint of a smile.

'Who? Laura?'

'Who else, darlin'? The Queen of Sheba? Tell 'er to get a move on.' With that he turned and strode along the balcony to his flat.

Coming back into the kitchen, Edie was quietly giggling. 'Them blue eyes of his are glowing, Laura. You'd best go and give him the door key.'

'Let 'im stew. In too much of a hurry to get away again, that's 'is trouble. No doubt he's found a new bit of skirt to lift while I've been away.'

'Laura . . . what's good for the goose is good for the gander,' teased Jessie.

'Yeah, but I've got to wait another bloody year before I can see my Richard again. Fair or what?' she said, making to leave.

'Well, you know what they say,' Edie chimed in, 'it's not quantity but quality that counts.'

'And you think I don't know that?' Laura gave her a wink and left.

'I know this will sound daft,' said Jessie, once she was alone with Edie again, 'but I'm really looking forward to hearing more about it. Not what they did under the covers but the romance of it all. It's like a

Hollywood movie. My sister Dolly could write a romantic story about them two on the hop fields.'

'Well, we'll 'ave to invite her round when we have our next ladies' night in, then, won't we?'

'Yep.' Jessie laughed. 'We certainly will.'

Edie leaned back in her chair, thoughtful. 'It must be lovely to be able to write novels. Do you think your sister will ever get her work into print?'

'Dolly? 'Course she will. She was writing stories before she was thinking about boys. One of her teachers at school, the music teacher as it happens, used to say that Dolly had ink in her blood.'

'I wonder what it is that makes people want to write?'

'Same thing as makes some people want to act or bake cakes or do needlework all the time or go for bloody long walks into nowhere in the middle of winter. I don't know, Edie. But one thing I can say – Dolly's got an incredible imagination. It's as if she sees things going on in another world . . . and then writes it down. It's probably why she walks about as if she only just woke up.'

'She enjoys it, though?'

'Living in a trance or writing?'

'Both.'

'I don't know. She just . . . does it. Every day now, by all accounts. Clacking away on that old black type-writer. Stanley offered to buy 'er a modern machine but she won't let go of the old one. She bought it in a second-hand shop years ago. That'll tell you how old it is.'

'I thought Dolly was gonna visit Laura in Kent this year so she could see what it's really like. Sleeping in a hut on a straw bed for the experience.'

'Take no notice of that. She likes her home comforts too much . . . and she always says things and doesn't do them, Edie. I don't think she needs to go there anyway. She asks all the ins and out and before you know it she's got it in her head. Smells are the thing. She has to know what something smells like before she can write about it. I'm sure she's a bit loopy. She did ask Laura to fetch her some hops back. I hope she's remembered.'

'People who go hop picking always bring back bundles of hops, Jess. I've seen them in the back-streets strewn across the windows like paper chains at Christmas. I used to envy those families. They were really happy when they left and just as happy when they got back. And always looking forward to the next September – the picking season. I don't think I could do it, though. Washing in cold water every morning.' Edie shivered and hugged herself. 'Oh no. I don't think I'm tough enough for that.'

'Never mind the cold water – what about sleeping on a mattress filled with straw? And a straw-and-hop pillow? Bending down and cooking over a campfire – for over a month. I can just see Max coping with that. One night and he'd be back behind that steering wheel heading for our flat and a hot bath.'

'And to be honest, so would I.'

'I wouldn't mind giving it a go,' said Jessie. 'Our Dolly might have ink in her blood but I think I've got the countryside in mine now. Anyway . . . enough of that. Back to what's really important. You and your wedding. You're not really going to put if off till spring, are you?'

'I am, Jess, yeah. It seems so obvious now. And to tell you the truth it's taken another little worry away. It was a bit too soon really. I'm so used to my own company. I don't know what it would be like not to feel lonely in the evenings – or in bed at night. I think I'd miss it. Does that sound mental?'

'Yes and no. But I know what you mean. In fact . . . I know exactly what you mean. Always having a man next to you in bed is as bad as never 'aving one. I was by myself for years during the war. You get used to it. It's like . . . having your own private place. *Your* pillow, *your* blankets, *your* space to spread out and think and dream whatever comes into your head.

'The only time I didn't appreciate it was when Emma-Rose went into the children's home. That was worse than anything. God . . . I missed 'er coming into my bed in the middle of the night or first thing. Billy still did but my baby was gone.' Jessie shuddered. 'Best leave that where it was. Right back there in the bloody forties during that sodding war!'

Edie was stunned by this admission, which had come out of the blue. Jessie had put her baby in a children's home? She could hardly believe it of Jessie, the doting mother who idolised her children. Wishing to change the subject for her friend's sake, she tried to think of something cheerful to say – as if she hadn't heard what had been said. But she couldn't. Words failed her. The silence that now hung in that room was going to have to be broken by Jessie. Edie waited as the seconds ticked by.

'So there we are,' said Jessie brightly, putting on a front. 'It's come out at last. Now you might think differently of me. I'm not gonna make excuses for what I did – except to say that at the time it seemed the right thing to do for Emma. It was a lovely place she went to. In Essex. All the houses where the children and their foster parents lived were set around a huge tree-lined oval. She never suffered, Edie. Honest to God she never.'

'Jess, stop it. Don't say any more just now. I'll make us a cup of tea while you go in the living room and watch a bit of television or just sit quiet . . . and then, if you want, you can tell me. Pour it all out. If you don't want to, then don't. What time is Tom fetching the kids back?'

'He's not. They're stopping over and going with 'im to Norfolk in the morning.' Jessie raised a hand. 'Least said the better, Edie.' She turned and went into the living room, choosing to sit in the easy chair by the open balcony door. She recalled the first time she had seen the children's home when she had taken Emma-Rose to have a look and decide for herself whether the place was somewhere she could leave her treasured little daughter during the latter part of the war. And after the very first sighting, Jessie *had* felt happy about leaving her there. With its villagey feel it was a palace compared to being cramped in an overcrowded terraced house with only bombed houses as a view and with rats in the back yard. She knew now, as she had known then, that it had been the best thing for Emma-Rose at the time, but that didn't stop the sickening waves of guilt from sweeping through her every so often.

Each time they'd gone to visit Emma, when Jessie had asked Billy, then a five-year-old, why he had been so quiet on the journey, he had simply replied, 'I'm sad.' And that would be followed by him asking if they were going to take his baby sister home with them, especially once the war was over. She had had to explain time and again that Emma had to stay in care until their house in Stepney was repaired. Never satisfied with that, he would go on to ask each time whether he could stay with her overnight, saying that he had clean pants and socks in his pocket. It had been a heartbreaking time for all of them, but particularly hard for Jessie – always having to tell her small son no and having to explain why he could not keep his sister company.

The train journeys to Ongar had been quite relaxed because Emma-Rose was the prize at the end of it. Since those dark times Billy had had a passion for steam trains and railway stations. They had been his saviour, allowing him to see his baby sister. Into the bargain, he had loved the small Essex town, which really was no more than a village with a single main street. He had loved the bustling railway station with the London and North Eastern trains running in and out of it.

In fact, both Jessie and Billy became so used to

Ongar and the country village atmosphere that it had felt like home after a while. The old-fashioned shops were something of a novelty, especially the butcher's, where there would always be a display of poultry and game – chicken, rabbit – hanging in rows on large metal hooks. All reared locally or caught within the surrounding forests of Essex.

Apart from all this, Ongar was steeped in history, and Jessie had made it her business to read a book on Essex country villages, so she could relate bits of it to Billy during their train rides there, which he had loved. Especially the chapter that covered the Norman Conquest, when the small town had been in the hands of Count Eustace of Boulogne, who was very close to William the Conqueror. When the town became Chipping Ongar it had already turned into a market town fit for a king to visit, and this is exactly what Henry II did – in 1157.

Thinking of the wrought-iron gates into the children's home, Jessie felt her stomach lurch, the way it had every time she had gone to visit Emma-Rose. Her own acting ability had stretched only so far – beneath the smiling face she had been a grieving mother, and after each visit left broken hearted. Her dreams of a happy family life together had been blown apart by the war. But the place had been a haven compared to the bombed backstreets of London. From every chimney at Stony Park children's home smoke had curled upwards, and from every house a light shone, and in the autumn and winter, when dusk fell early, the gas lamps circling the grassy oval had been lit.

She recalled the day when she, Tom, Billy and her mother and father-in-law had gone in hope of being allowed to bring Emma-Rose home. This was the day after Tom had been demobbed and the war was behind them. Among other children playing outside on the green, their three-year-old had been standing by a tall fir tree, wrapped up warm and clutching her much loved toy bear. Her eyes had been fixed on the entrance gate, and once she had spotted Jessie and Billy she had come running across the oval. The sight of her little girl in a pair of Billy's long grey socks and her old blue coat, with her long, curly blonde hair blowing in the breeze as she ran towards them with her arms outstretched, had almost been too much to bear. Falling to her knees, Jessie had opened her arms and waited for Emma-Rose to fall into them, and as she did so the child had wet herself. This had been a frequent occurrence when the three-year-old was nervous or overexcited.

With Emma-Rose snuggling into her breast as if she were trying to burrow back inside her mother, where she would be safe, Jessie had felt as if they were the only two people in that small world. She remembered it all so vividly, especially when she had looked into her daughter's soft, pale face and brushed her fingers across her long fringe to see her wide blue eyes and had said, 'Guess who's come to see you, sweetheart. It's your daddy, Emma. Daddy's come back from the army.'

Squinting up at Tom, Emma-Rose had inched closer to him and then sniffed the sleeve of his overcoat and pulled a face, repelled by the smell of mothballs. Tom had been speechless. His emotions getting the better of him, he had been able only to look at her. Look at his beautiful little girl with snow-white hair. Falling to his knees, he had finally managed to say, 'I brought you some sweets and a present . . .'

The soft voice of Emma-Rose's temporary foster mother suggesting that they go inside had gutted him. He hadn't seen her coming. 'We'll go into my flat,' she had said, 'and have some tea and biscuits.' She had spoken and behaved as if she were Emma's guardian, which of course was how it should have been – but still it cut to the bone. Tom had felt as if he had lost the daughter he had come home to see for the first time.

Wiping her runny nose on her coat sleeve, Emma-Rose had asked Billy when he was going to live there with her. His mournful silence had been the only answer. Billy knew deep down even then, when only five, that he would never be able to share the place with his baby sister and look after her. False prom-ises made at the beginning of Emma's stay had never been forgotten.

With one eye closed against the sun, and looking up at the father she had never seen before then, Emma had innocently said, 'You . . . you . . . you got an art and fisher leg?' Bursting with laughter, Tom had shaken his head, telling her that he didn't think so. She had gone on to say that her friend Richard's dad had one from the war. Lifting his daughter into his arms, Tom had beckoned for the foster mother to lead the way. It had all proved too moving for him. Striding along, he hadn't been able to stop kissing his baby girl on the cheek, telling her that she was the image of her mother.

Once the visit was over and it had been time for them to go home, Tom had slipped away and had a quiet word with the matron, the headmaster's wife. Using every bit of his charm he had tried to persuade the woman to let them take his daughter home that day, but it had been futile. The authorities would have come down on the woman like a ton of bricks had she have given in. As far as the matron was concerned a soldier returning from war *should* have his family around him, and a small child of three and a half should certainly have been with her parents. Sadly, officialdom would not allow this. During the war, when Jessie had been all but homeless, Emma-Rose had been listed as a child in need of fostering. To remove her Jessie and Tom were told that they would have to approach the board of governors in Hackney, and that formalities would have to be seen to before Emma could be allowed home.

Waving goodbye to the sad little figure as she had stood at the gate clasping her foster mother's hand and holding firmly on to her toy bear had been bitterly painful for all of them. Once Emma-Rose's carer had disappeared behind the trees on her way to the hair inspection room, Tom had, without shame, broken down and cried.

It had been his dad Charlie who had comforted him. Placing an arm around his son's shoulders and gesturing for the others to go on ahead, he had given Tom a squeeze and told him that he would get used to the visits after a while. That the pain would wear off. To Charlie's way of thinking, his granddaughter had been in a far better place while London was being bombed. A broken man, tears rolling down his cheeks, all Tom had been able to say at the time was, 'I want to take my daughter home, Dad.' Collecting himself, he had gone on to tell Charlie that he had come here with the idea that he would be able to persuade them to give Emma-Rose back to her family.

Charlie had had to be strong for the two of them. Strong and firm. He had all but lectured his grown son to get his message across, telling him that it would have been a far worse thing if his granddaughter had had to stay in a lousy run-down home with strict rules and uncaring, overworked people to look after her. He had scolded him for not being more stout hearted, if for nothing else then at least for his son, Billy, only five years old then, who had been missing his baby sister far more than he had ever let on. Tom had bravely pulled himself together and they had caught up with his mother, Emmie, and Jessie, who was carrying Billy in her arms.

Removing Emma-Rose had in fact been easier than Jessie had imagined. Once the authorities had been satisfied that there was a safe home for the child the necessary paperwork had taken only a few days to complete and the family had been together for the build-up to Christmas, which had turned out to be one of the best and one of the worst ever. Everyone had enjoyed being together on Christmas Day with Emma-Rose the centre of attention. Billy had hardly left his little sister's side, and when he had it was to ask Jessie or his trusted granddad, Charlie, whether they were going to take her back to the home after Boxing Day. Try as they might, they hadn't been able to quite convince him. It had been Tom who had taken Billy aside and talked quietly and firmly to him. Man to boy. Father to son. And it had worked. He did finally get the message across – that they were a family, that the war was over and that nothing and no one would separate them again.

Tom couldn't have known then that most of what he had said had been empty promises. He had not been quite as strong in character as he had imagined – and his emotions immediately after his return from the army were all over the place. That Christmas week had led up to the fateful night when he had stormed off in a fierce temper, ravaged with jealousy after a flaming row with Jessie. No matter how innocent she was, and how desperate to make Tom see sense, he had refused to listen. The innocent kiss on the cheek given to Max Cohen outside the Blind Beggars at Mile End Gate before she went inside for a drink with him had been their downfall. This had been witnessed by Tom's brother Stanley and innocently reported back in jest to Tom on Christmas Eve after one drink too many. This titbit of information about something so small had had huge consequences. That night Tom walked away from his family and was not seen again until several years later.

'Feel better now you've had ten minutes to your-self, Jess?' said Edie, coming in with the tea tray.

'I always feel better once I've sat in this room. I don't know what it is about your flat but it's just so homely. And Edie . . . I will tell you about the time I had to put Emma in a home, but another day . . . if that's all right with you?'

'Of course it is. And I couldn't wish for a better compliment about my flat, Jess. But so is yours homely. It's lovely, in fact.'

'Yeah . . . but it's not as cosy as this place. And speaking of which, I'd best drink this tea and get back. If we're gonna have this ladies' night in, my casser-ole needs to go in the oven on low. Max has a good appetite no matter what time he gets in. He'll be ready for a good meal.'

'Plenty of time,' said Edie. 'Ten minutes won't make much difference.'

'True. But we'll have a couple of hours to our-selves later . . . if Jack lets Laura out. I mean, after all, they have been apart for a while, except for him going down to Kent at weekends.'

'She'll be here, don't you worry. She can't wait to tell us more about her lover. And why not?' Edie sat down and passed Jessie her cup of tea. 'Put your own sugar and milk in.'

'She'll be missing 'im like mad. Do you think they're in love or just . . .'

'Just,' said Edie. 'And long may it last. Romance, Jess. That's what this is all about. And if you can get it – why not?'

'True. At least Tom was romantic even if he was a bastard with it.'

'He wasn't a bastard, Jessie. Don't exaggerate.'

'He was. He left me, Edie, with two children to look after. Lived the life of Riley with a lot of money which didn't belong to him but to a dead man. Had as many women as he wanted and lived in an Elizabethan house in its own grounds for a few years . . . and drove around the country lanes in a very nice car, thank you.'

'You're joking. Tell me you're joking?'

'No. Because I'm not. He was on a train coming home after demob and helped another old soldier who was shell-shocked, to say the least. The bloke was as rich as you like but never looked it. He was stark raving bonkers. So much so that he gave Tom his kitbag, which had everything in it anyone could need to live a life of luxury. Keys to two fantastic houses – one in the West End of London and one in Suffolk.

'When the train pulled in at the station the bloke jumped off in front of another one coming in on the next track. Hey presto – Tom's a rich man. He took on the chap's identity. The money he spent during those years on a flash car and beautiful women, until the brother of the dead man turned up and claimed everything, could 'ave paid for my little house that I sold. And no, before you ask, he wasn't angry about it. The brother was already rich and eccentric and took to Tom, impressed by his cheek. So my ex-husband walked away with his back pocket lined, which kept him going for a few years, I s'pose. When he finally turned up at his mother's place he was down at heel.'

Edie could hardly take this in. 'The things that men get up to is completely beyond me, Jess. Do you know what? I think that you, me and Laura should go for a bloody good night out. Go to a little nightclub where the lights are low, red and blue, and the music is live and seductive. Where men from all walks of life sit around listening to the blues or slow jazz. We should 'ave a little table in a corner and watch the predatory bastards at work. See if we can learn from them.'

'But would we learn from it? That's the point. I bet you would take Harry back if he came cap in hand with love and promises, chocolates and flowers. And so would I too – if I wasn't with Max.'

'Not now I wouldn't. Not after all this time.'

Glancing at Edie, and seeing the faraway look in her eyes, Jessie felt it was time to go. Her friend was clearly thinking of her first husband and privacy seemed the order of the day. She had, after all, almost without blinking, put her wedding back to the spring, and Jessie was wondering whether she was having second thoughts.

'What time do you want me to come down, then, Ed?' she said, looking at her wristwatch. 'Seven? Eight?'

'Eight. That'll give Laura plenty of time to unpack and that.'

'Suits me fine.' Jessie smiled. 'Why am I looking forward so much to hearing all about this love affair?'

'Because it's real and because it'll be a better story than most of the mushy films we see or books we read. This is earthy, Jess. And we know the heroine personally.'

'Maybe that's what it is. If it can 'appen to Laura it can 'appen to us.'

'It already is where you're concerned. Never mind all you've just said about him. Tom's simmering with passion on the back burner – and you know it.'

'I told you before, Ed . . . that's all behind me. Me and Tom are over and done with.'

'If you say so.' Edie grinned. 'If you say so.'

# 8

By the second week of November the nights were drawing in, fog was beginning to fall at dusk and before early evening lights were glowing in windows and fires crackling in grates. People coming home after a hard day's work were wrapped up in their winter clothes with thick scarves across their mouths serving as a shield against the smog. No different to any other November, except that here on this new complex, Barcroft Estate, there was a sense of a thriving community. People had settled down and were very much at home with their way of life. Change was taking place throughout the East End of London as more and more of the old terraced houses were being bulldozed to the ground. Historic buildings in need of repair were also being razed to the ground. There was a strong sense of 'down with the old and up with the new', with no real thought for preserving the old East End of London. Corner shops, old factories, historic grand houses, Victorian baths, music halls and small local pubs – anything seen as antiquated was disappearing in a thick cloud of dust.

Barcroft Estate showed evidence of a good time having been had by the children and adults who had celebrated a communal Guy Fawkes night. Scattered about were the remains of burned-out fireworks which had been left to rot after the local lads had gathered those in the best condition to add to their collections, as they did every year after 5 November. And while embers from the huge community bonfire smouldered on a piece of wasteland on the estate, which was destined to be a tarmac football pitch, smoke from the tiny fires in flats swirled up into the foggy sky. Winter had arrived.

Inside Bethnal Green library, where Maggie was due to work for just one more week before taking her leave, it was warm and welcoming, in deep contrast to outside, the spines of the books on polished wooden shelves decorating the walls as no wallpaper could. In an upstairs room, Maggie was finishing her tedious filing while below, come to collect another list of names and addresses of those interested in the tea dances to be held in St Peter's church hall, was Naomi, with those she had already coaxed to join the library – Becky and Nathan, Shereen and Murat.

Ben, also in the party, was seriously thinking about becoming a member too. To his mind, now that his wonderful old London was being replaced by a faster-paced, more uncaring one, it was good to see that the free library at least was continuing and was under no threat of being replaced by a cut-price bookshop. Joey, an avid reader, having been coming to the library since he was seven years old, was here to exchange his books.

Strolling up to the counter where members had

their books stamped before they were issued, Naomi felt proud of her niece for having secured a position here. It was her fondest wish that Maggie should return to further her career once the baby had been weaned. She wanted to have a private little chat with the chief librarian, if not today, then soon – to make certain that she had got her facts right, that her great-niece's position here in the library would be open for her if and when she was ready to return. However, the small group of friends she had arrived with were fully aware of her main reason for wishing to see Mathew Browning today. Since he had been gracious enough to allow Maggie to place a notice on the board, and put up with his members filling the small space in the lobby while signing it, she wished to honour him. She glanced at Daphne Lightfoot, who was preoccupied and unaware that she and the others had arrived. Sending her friends off to select their books, she caught Daphne's attention and beckoned her over in silence – respecting the library rules.

A little timid with Naomi, whom she held in high esteem, Daphne came across the room and whispered, 'How lovely to see you again.'

'Oh, my dear – how sweet of you to say so,' responded Naomi. 'I wonder . . . could we possibly find somewhere more private?'

'Of course.' An earnest expression on her face, Daphne looked around. 'The only problem I can think of is that Mathew is expecting the rep quite soon with a delivery of new books. At the moment he's having a private word with Eileen, Rita's mother, on the first floor. I'm sure he wouldn't mind if you went up and gave a tap on the door. They shouldn't be long in there.'

'Oh well, let's wait until he appears, shall we,' said Naomi, her face lighting up at the mention of new books. 'And how terribly exciting for you – to have a delivery. Are we talking brand-new books recently published?'

'Oh yes. It's that time of the year. Not all of them have just come out but none will be older than a few months or so. And you are so right, Naomi. It *is* very exciting, actually; for me, that is. I adore the smell of the fresh covers and . . . oh, well, everything about them really.'

'I'm sure you must. The virgin print, as it were. To read a book before anyone has turned a page of it is rather a luxury, I always think.'

'Oh, absolutely.'

'Maybe if we just slipped out on to the front steps?' suggested Naomi. 'I've only one tiny question to ask. But I would rather Mr Browning didn't hear. I want to get your views about something we would very much like to do. I wouldn't want to embarrass him into agreeing to something when he might prefer not to. And I've just seen him over your shoulder, with Eileen, but he isn't looking this way. In fact they have eyes only for each other. Which is rather sweet, don't you think?'

Daphne's face suddenly lit up and she leaned closer to Naomi. 'Actually, they are getting on terribly well. I can hardly believe that Mattie is the same man. He's still very professional while in the library, obviously. But they've been out together three or four times. To museums and that sort of thing during the daytime. At weekends. Isn't it good? I'm terribly pleased for him. That he should have a close friend, I mean.'

'Darling, we all need our friends. More than anything else, actually. Ah . . .' Naomi smiled. 'He's looking this way.'

'Is he? Well, I shouldn't take too much notice of that. He can be a little hawkish when it comes to his beloved library. He keeps us all on our toes, actually.'

'And for that we must admire and respect him.'

'Well . . . it can be a touch irritating at times. What is it you wanted to ask? My brother can't lip-read. And you know, I don't mind you referring to the fact – to me, that is – that he's my brother. It's just other people, really . . .'

'Thank you. I take that as a compliment. The thing is, Daphne, since Mathew has been so tolerant of us using his library as an advertising board—'

'Oh, he doesn't think of it like that at all. He's rather chuffed about the whole thing.'

'Really? That is terribly charitable, you know. Especially since he takes the efficient running of this place so personally. I hope I didn't offend you by saying that.'

'No, of course you didn't.'

'It's just that we thought it would be rather nice if he were to officially open the new club in St Peter's church hall and cut the ribbon which will be pinned across the doorway. Do you think he might agree to that?'

'Oh, my goodness me. He would be absolutely thrilled!' said Daphne, her own enthusiasm apparent.

'Would he?'

'Yes, indeed. Why don't we go into the office and I'll call him in? I can always chat with the rep until he's ready.'

'Actually, my dear . . . I *do* think the others would like to be present when I ask. This is *rather* a special occasion for them too.'

'Oh well, yes, of course they must. And in that case . . . I don't see why you can't use the small board-room instead. It's just over here.' Daphne pointed. 'I'll ask Mr Browning to go in, if you would like to round up your little party?'

'Oh, thank you, Daphne. If *only* others were as charitable as you. I do appreciate all you've done for Maggie and for our little enterprise, too.'

'Oh, it's nothing, really. And actually it's you who we should all thank. You seem to be full of lovely ideas . . . and the determination to see them through.'

'Well, that is *one* way of putting it. I was always told, when in the theatre, that I had a directorial streak. I suppose I *am* a bit of an organiser.'

Mathew Browning agreed to the meeting straight away. It was obvious to anyone that he too was enjoying this injection of excitement into his otherwise dull life.

Once inside the small room, and with her self-esteem at its peak, Naomi settled herself down with the others, whom she had managed to round up, and coughed to draw their attention. Lack of conversation between these friends was never a problem – they were never lost for words, especially Becky and Nathan. Once silence prevailed, Naomi glanced at Mathew Browning and smiled benignly. 'First and foremost I would like to thank Mr Browning on behalf of *all* of us present here today, and also those absent friends who have joined our club. Without his help we would never have come this far in such a short space of time. Secondly, and I come to the point purely because we *do* realise how precious your time is, Mr Browning . . .' She paused for a few seconds and then continued: 'Mr Browning – would you consider doing us the great honour of cutting the ribbon and *officially* opening the new club to be held in St Peter's church hall? Of course, we expect the press to be there and so fully understand if, since you appear to be a very *private* man, you would rather *not* be in the limelight, as it were.'

'Well . . .' Browning smiled, completely taken aback by this. 'I don't know what to say. I mean, are you sure? I'm not exactly a celebrity.'

'That's the whole point,' said Joey, his face earnest. 'This is very much a local affair, which admittedly could take off in other areas. But since it is local and since you've to take a good deal of credit for the response we've already had, we want you and nobody else to cut the white ribbon.'

'Well, put like that, how can I possibly refuse? Not that I would have, of course. Indeed, no. I am deeply moved and very honoured that you've asked me.'

'So the answer is yes, then?' asked Nathan.

'The gentleman just said so . . . You want it written down on a piece of paper now?' Becky rolled her eyes and then smiled at Browning. 'I'm very pleased, you know that. Very pleased. You're such a gentleman. And there aren't many of those in these parts. My father . . . now he was a lovely man. You would have got on very well with him. He put me in mind of Little Nell's grandfather. Such a lovely old gentleman. I'm taking the book out again, you know. It'll be my third read of it, but I don't care.'

'She reads *everything* three times. Has to. So it sinks in.'

Becky turned to her husband. 'A well-written and meaningful book should be read more than once. You should try reading some proper literature, Nathan. *The Old Curiosity Shop*. You might learn something. And *A Christmas Carol*. Yes.' She nodded. 'You should read *A Christmas Carol*. You might find you have a great deal of affinity with Mr Scrooge.'

'I must apologise for my wife, Mr Browning. She's not right in the head. Not brain damaged exactly, but not right. You know what I mean.'

'And Joey . . . you should also join today,' Becky continued. 'Take out *The Merry Men and Other Tales*. If only to read "Thrawn Janet". But only on a dark foggy winter's night by the fireside with a couple of candles alight and shadows dancing in the corners. Wonderful writer. The man makes you feel as if you're there. It'd scare the pants off Nathan but it would be worth it.'

'I joined the library decades ago, Becky. That's three times now that I've told you.'

'I don't think so, if you'll excuse me for challenging you. I know men don't like to be opposed but I know I'm right. If you had said so I would remember.'

'Becky . . .' said Naomi, cutting in. 'I think we ought to move on. Mr Browning is a very busy man.'

'No, please,' said Browning, clearly enjoying himself. 'Miss Lightfoot will tap on the door if I'm needed. I must say it's quite rewarding to hear one of our readers speak in such praise of one of our authors.'

'Wonderful author,' said Becky. 'And his characters. I'm telling you – you wouldn't want to meet the Reverend Murdock Soulis at dusk. It would do Nathan the world of good, but not you, Mr Browning. No. You're a gentleman.' She shrugged in true Jewish style. 'You wanna hear the best quote of the century, then hear this.' She pulled a strange face, lowered her voice and spoke with what she believed to be a blood-curdling inflection. '"*His eyes could pierce through the storms of time to the terrors of eternity.*"'

'I don't think any of us will ever forget that line,' said Nathan, his eyes half closed. He looked around the table. 'You think any of you can sleep tonight without having nightmares now? I don't think so. I keep telling her to go on stage. A travelling circus, that kind of thing.'

'Of course, Nathan only reads cheap detective

stories but you have to take certain things into account. You think he could manage to read *anything* that Robert Louis Stevenson wrote? I doubt it. He is good at figures, though – I'll give him that. He knows exactly how much my weekly shopping should come to.'

'Have you read much else by RLS?' asked the chief librarian, longing to keep this going for as long as he could. 'He is a very fine writer.'

'Fine? The man's a bloody genius!'

'He's not a patch on Dickens.' Ben sniffed. 'Doesn't come anywhere near.'

'Well, of course, that's a matter of opinion,' said Becky, releasing a little trapped wind from her chest. She turned to Naomi, hoping to get her on board. 'You're a woman of the world. Who do you read . . . if not RLS?'

'RLS.' Nathan chuckled. 'She only has to hear something once, I'll give her that. RLS. She might be up a tree most of the time but she *can* be funny. Makes me laugh anyway.'

'Actually,' said Naomi, used to this pair, 'I only read published plays, I'm afraid.' She glanced knowingly at Browning. 'But then I suppose that's only natural. Having spent most of my life in the theatre. I prefer Oscar Wilde to Shakespeare, however – controversial though that may be.' She waited for a response but there was none. They simply gazed at her with blank expressions until Ben finally spoke to fill the silence.

'I like wearing boots but I hate wearing shoes,' he said. 'So what? It's a free country. You read what you want, Naomi.' He then peered at his wristwatch, quite deliberately, and Browning picked up on it.

'Well . . . time runs on. And to answer your request – I would be honoured to officially open the tea dancing club.'

'Good job,' said Joey, rising from his seat. 'Good on you, sir. Time I was getting back as well.'

'We can't go yet,' said Nathan. 'I haven't picked out the books I want. We've only been here five minutes.'

'You see?' said Becky, smiling. 'An hour or so goes by and he thinks it's five minutes. I pop out for a chat over the garden wall for ten minutes and he says I've been gone three hours.' She shook her head and curled her bottom lip. 'It's hard. Very hard. But what can I do? It breaks my heart to see him like this. It's a sad thing when it happens but at least it didn't come as a shock. Premature senility has its plus points. It's given me time to adjust. Thirty years or so, as a matter of fact.'

'She's not a bad cleaner, Chief Librarian. You couldn't find five or six hours a day for her, could you? Always polishing. Sit still for five minutes and she'll give you a wash and shave as well.'

'No, I, er . . . I'm afraid we are fully staffed at the moment,' said Browning, desperate to keep a straight face. 'But I will bear it in mind, sir.'

'Speaking of which,' said Naomi, 'would Eileen the cleaner be in the building?'

His face suddenly lighting up, Browning nodded and clasped his hands together. 'Yes, indeed. Indeed, yes. You'll find her on the second floor. Rearranging a few bookshelves and dusting and polishing as she goes. Wonderful woman. Excellent worker. Indeed.'

'Ah well, if she's busy . . . I shall leave it to another time. Do give her my good wishes, Mr Browning, and thank you so much for your hospitality.' Naomi gracefully offered her hand. The chief librarian was momentarily perplexed. Should he shake it or kiss it?

Stretching his aching back, Ben, with a hand on the door handle, said, 'The date for the official opening has changed again. It's now the fifteenth of December.'

'Well, that sounds like an excellent idea. A Christmas opening. Season of goodwill and so on. Indeed.'

'Of course, we shall hand in to Miss Lightfoot a new poster giving the time, date and the fact that it will be a dance with live musicians—'

'Oh?' said Browning. 'That's interesting. Very interesting. Any room for a saxophonist?'

'I should say there is! You don't play, sir, do you?' Joey looked hopeful.

'As a matter of fact I do. The occasional wedding, that sort of thing.'

'Well I never.' Joey grinned, scratching his head. 'We came to get ourselves an eminent person to open the show and we find we've got a musician too.' He laid one hand on his chest and held up the other. 'Here's my heart and here's my hand. May we never quarrel.'

Browning responded with a firm handshake and a look of joy in his eyes. 'I shall have to get some practice in. Haven't given a public performance since late spring. A double wedding in Stratford East. Black and white, as a matter of fact. And it all worked so remarkably well.'

'Listen, darling,' said Becky, 'this is only the beginning. With so many of the coloureds coming over we'll be a mixed race in years to come. There'll be no true blue British people left. We'll all be fudge coloured.'

'Listen to her,' said Nathan. 'Where does she think our forefathers came from? Silly cow. True blue British?' He shook his head solemnly. 'It's very sad when it happens. Anyway, she still goes to the synagogue so she must know she's a Jew.'

In a world of his own, Mathew Browning was letting the banter go over his head, thinking of what he might wear for the occasion. 'Yes . . .' he said thoughtfully, a hand rubbing his chin, 'I shall have to dust up my performance for this special occasion. Indeed I shall.'

'Well, that all seems to be settled,' said Joey. 'Can we go now, Nao?'

'Of course. We mustn't take up any more of Mr Browning's precious time.'

'Mathew. It's Mathew, Naomi.' Another small step had been taken. Mattie Browning was beginning to feel like his old self again. The old self that was once a young man. His thoughts still on the dance, he could see himself on stage and then on the dance floor, steering Rita's mother around the room. He in black tie and she in a long, flowing pale blue frock.

Once he had shaken the hand of each and every one of them, and the door was closed behind them, Mathew Browning sat on the edge of his table, arms folded, and stared out of the window. Why things seemed to have taken a turn for the better he had no idea, but clearly they had. His sister Daphne had told him that she had confided in Maggie that they were brother and sister and now, having accepted her suggestion that he employ Rita's mother, he felt sure that his life was truly looking up. A person similar to himself, quiet and unassuming, Eileen had stirred something deep inside him – and he wasn't quite sure what that was. But he had found a soulmate and that was enough. From the moment they had first spoken to each other they had been at ease and he had not felt in the least bit awkward in her company. He had been expecting a wiry woman full of energy and a touch impertinent. Rita, of course, was the reason for this assumption and he would, if asked, openly admit that he had been quite wrong.

His sister seemed to have blossomed too since Rita and Maggie had joined them. Her friendship with Naomi was growing and she had not stopped talking about the meeting that she had attended at the home of Nathan and Becky and how funny the couple were. Now he knew for himself. The strange array of people who had just left his room had brought so much with them and taken so little away.

He knew that from then on he and his spinster sister were going to be part of a close-knit bunch of convivial people they could call friends. At last loneliness would no longer be something he felt when he slipped into his empty bed at night. He now had dreams to fulfil, and being part of a community again was one of them.

Strolling back home through the Bethnal Green gardens, Naomi, arm in arm with both Ben and Joey, was waiting for the two men to stop talking so that she could get a word in edgeways. They were, characteristically, going on and on about recent changes, and in particular the loss of Louis Collett's, the ladies' and gents' tailor in Mile End Road.

'I'm telling you,' said Ben, 'it was me who wrote the bloody thing.'

'It wasn't. Louis wrote it down on the back of an old beer mat when we was in the Golden Eagle. I made it up – he wrote it down.'

'You're wrong.' Ben was adamant. 'I made it up and you gimme the odd word, here and there. If anyone should get the rights to it, it should be me.' He stopped and looked into his best friend's face. 'Can you remember – word for word?'

''Course I can bloody well remember it. "If a dress suit or lady's frock you wish to don, visit a craftsman who you can rely on"—'

'"Customers come from near and far—"'

'"By foot, by plane, train or car"—'

'Not plane. Plane was never in it. Who'd fly halfway across the world for a suit?'

'Plane was in it. I should know. I wrote that line.'

'"In all sorts of weather, rain, snow or sunny"—'

'"We're good value for money."'

'"Our fabric, tailoring and cut are a boon"—'

'"And because of this – hope to see you soon"—'

'No. No, that's wrong.'

'It's not wrong. I should know.'

'"And because of the above, hope to be seeing you soon,"' they chorused together.

'Oh, well done,' said Naomi, her mind on other things. 'You really should become an act, you know. The amateur dramatic clubs are desperate for talent.'

'They don't pay enough,' said Joey.

'They don't pay anything,' said Ben.

'Well, no . . . but in some circumstances even you boys are prepared to give your time for little reward, I would have thought.'

'Wait for it.' Ben laughed. 'She's after something for nothing.'

'Take no notice, Naomi. What d'yer want?'

'Information, actually. Which you will only come by should you be prepared to do a little snooping. All in a good cause, naturally.'

'Well . . . it can only be to do with young Maggie or Edie,' said Joey. 'And I'd stake my shirt on it being Edie. You want us to find out a little bit about that chap of hers. Correct?'

'As a matter of fact, yes. Am I really that transparent?'

'No. I've been expecting it. Why have you left it this long? I was beginning to think he was a hundred per cent.'

'No decent bloke is a hundred per cent,' said Ben. 'If he were I would be very suspicious.'

'I'll put the feelers out. But don't expect much. He's a bit of a mystery that one. The man from nowhere.'

'Really?' said Naomi, hoping for more.

'You wouldn't be getting us to ask questions if not.'

'True,' said Naomi, 'very true.'

Maggie was not disappointed once she had seen the finished flat above the fish-and-chip shop. It was all she could have hoped for. With the rays of the afternoon sun coming in through the sash windows it looked wonderful. On the newly painted white walls, Tony had hung two old, richly coloured woven wall rugs which his grandmother had given him, and on a small carved table in the corner of the room was a highly polished old brass lamp with a white glass shade.

With one hand cupping her mouth, Maggie turned to the future father of her child with tears in her eyes. She was moved by the trouble he had gone to. He had taken care of every little detail – right down to the small glass vase in which he had placed a single red rose. She could manage only a few words – 'It's lovely, Tony. I love it. I just love it.'

Holding out his arms, he stepped forward and drew her close to him, brushing a kiss across her cheek. 'And just I love you, Maggie Birch.'

'And I love you, Tony Baroncini,' she whispered, before they kissed as they had not kissed before. Not with hot passion but with a deep, warm love.

'Ah-ha!' Tony's cousin, who had been helping him get the room ready, appeared in the open doorway holding a small tray on which stood a carafe of red wine and two glasses. 'The lovers are ready for their wine – no?' He placed the tray on a small table.

'No,' said Tony, friendly but firm. 'If we start to celebrate we'll be too drunk to walk home in a straight line.'

'Home? You are not going home, my friend,' his cousin said, continuing to speak in an exaggerated Italian accent. 'The boys are coming soon . . . so that you may show your appreciation.' He waved a hand in the air. 'For *all* that they have done for you – myself included.' He looked from Tony to Maggie. 'You like?'

'I love it,' she said. 'I really, really love it.'

'Thank you,' he said, bowing courteously. 'I always try-a my best for a beautiful lady.'

'You only painted one wall,' said Tony, raising an eyebrow.

'Two bloody walls, actually!'

'Yeah, but I had to give one of them a second coat.'

'Well, that's because you're a perfectionist.'

'Bye-bye, boys,' said Maggie as she swanned across the room towards the door. 'Don't drink too much! See you back at the flats, Tony, after I've been round Rita's. I should be home around eight!' She descended the narrow staircase, noting that these walls were still marked with time and stained with nicotine from pipe tobacco. Pushing open the old door that led into the shop, she winked at Tony's Uncle Michael and then gave his busy Aunt Maria a little squeeze as she eased her way past her, whispering, 'Don't let the bad boys work you too hard.'

'They should try,' she said, shaking boiling oil from a fresh load of crisp chips in a large square mesh drainer before tipping them into the chrome warming cabinet. 'Be careful, darling, eh?'

'You bet,' Maggie called back over her shoulder. As she sidled past the long queue of customers, hungry for their fish and chips, she came face to face with Sarah James, the nosiest person in the block of flats where she lived, and another woman. She smiled cautiously, in two minds as to whether to stop or rush past. She had little choice, as it turned out, because the women manoeuvred themselves so as to block her path. By the smug look on both their faces she knew they were going to be horrible.

Normally she could shrug off the comments of the offensive women in Scott House, but not here, not in this secret little bit of the East End where she had believed she was far enough away from the council estate not to find one of her mother's neighbours. And not these two women, of all people. Giving Maggie the once-over, Sarah, who was short and wiry with her arms folded under her bosom and her shopping bag hanging from her arm, nodded knowingly. Glancing at her bosom buddy, the troublemaker who lived in the flat below Edie, she raised an eyebrow and spoke loudly enough for everyone in the shop to hear.

'Strange 'ow some people just love to be in wiv the foreigners!'

'What would you expect?' responded her friend, enjoying this. 'The Jews are always in and out of 'er mother's flat. I know some women like old men, but old Jewish men?' She began to cackle – showing the gap in her front teeth.

'If you're alluding to Joey and Ben,' snarled Maggie, rising to their bait, 'they *happen* to be friends of my Aunt Naomi and we'd rather have *them* in our kitchen than the likes of you.'

'Oh, you don't 'ave to tell *us* that. We've seen all the comings and goings. Fancies herself as an actress, don't she? Your old aunt. Ha. Mutton dressed as lamb.'

'Well, I'd sooner spend time with mutton that a mad cow who never takes the curlers out of her hair or the turban off her head.'

'If I want to take my curlers out, I will,' was the smug reply. 'And if I choose to wear my turban all the time, I will. Not all of us women dress up to the nines just to get the men. And foreign men at that.' She lowered her voice a fraction. 'One of this lot, ain't he? Your young man? An Italian. One of Hitler's mates. Nazis in a different suit.'

'Talk a bit louder so Maria can hear. She'll have you thrown out in a flash, you old bitch.'

Sarah James laughed in her face. 'Fat chance of 'er throwing us out! Money . . .' she said, holding out a hand and rubbing her thumb against her finger. 'That's all the Eyeties care about. Taking our money.'

'And you can't bear to pass it over to them . . . but you *have* to if you want what they've got on offer. The *best* fish and chips in the East End!'

'Let 'em slave for hours – it's what they was born for. I don't care. They can 'ave my shilling. They know they're the underdogs. Use 'em all, is what I say!' Sarah waved her arm in the air. 'Use all the bleedin' foreigners who come over 'ere taking the work away from our men! But there we are, no point in talking to the likes of you over it. You like a bit of foreign blood. Next fing we know you'll 'ave a black man on your arm.' She cackled. 'One of them bleedin' Jamaicans that's coming over by the boatload.'

'When's yer muvver gonna move out?' Now it was the turn of the woman from the flat below. 'I'll be glad when she's gone. Flooded my 'ome, she did. Ruined the paintwork. If it 'appens again I'll sue 'er. Take 'er to court.'

'She never flooded anywhere, you silly cow. The drainpipe was cracked and had been since they built the block of flats. And it never ruined your paint-work! The caretaker told Mum it never! You're just out for *anything* you can get. Everyone on the block knows that and they can't stand you. Did you know that?'

To the sound of their mocking laughter, Maggie turned away, leaving the shop. But Sarah James was not finished. She called out for everyone to hear, 'I see you've put a bit of weight on! Carry on like that and you'll soon look like a big fat Italian mama!'

Annoyed with herself for rising to the gossips' bait, Maggie pushed her way through the Saturday market shoppers as they crowded around the various stalls. The worst of it was that she had let them get to her while in earshot of Tony's Uncle Michael and Aunt Maria. Two harder-working people you could not hope to meet. Proud people whose forefathers had first come to Britain almost a century earlier, and still, here in the East End, they had to bite their tongues at the insults from certain types of customer. Insults from the likes of Maggie's worst neighbours. She had no doubt whatsoever that behind the counter, and above the sound of fish and chips frying and other people talking, they would have heard everything the witches had said.

Knowing now that she was not going to be able to hide away here in the Roman Road market, Maggie felt as if she were back at square one. She realised now that it had been stupid to think that, just because the Roman Road market was some thirty minutes away by foot, people from the estate and her old turning and the school she had attended would not go there to shop. To Maggie it had felt like new territory because the Bethnal Green market, the Whitechapel market and the Jews' market were closer to home, and these were where her aunt and her mother had always taken her to shop.

So caught up in her thoughts was she, she hadn't realised how close to home she was. Turning off the main road into Barcroft Estate, she made her way to her Aunt Naomi's apartment, hoping she would be in. She didn't want to face her mother or her mother's friends, who might have dropped round for a cup of tea and a chat, this being Saturday and their day off work. When she saw the small skylight window in the living room open, the let out a sigh of relief. She desperately needed her aunt right then.

'Maggie . . .' said Naomi delightedly as she stood in her doorway, looking at her great-niece. 'I simply cannot believe you've turned up like this. And at this precise moment.'

'If you've got company, Aunt Naomi, ask them to go away. I need you more than they do right now.'

'Darling, of course I would do that, but I don't have company.' She stood aside and waved Maggie in. 'God works in such *mysterious* ways.'

'Why? What's happened?'

'You, my sweet child,' said Naomi, closing the door, 'is what has happened. I have been sitting in my arm-chair for the past five minutes or so with nothing else on my mind but you and I had absolutely no idea why.'

Maggie slumped down in a chair and placed her handbag on the small table. 'We both know you're an old witch.'

'Not old, if we are to believe I am a witch. Witches live for hundreds of years. To them I would be regarded as being in the prime of my life. I take it you would like a cup of tea?'

'No. Strong coffee, please.'

'Strong coffee it is,' said Naomi, knowing that something was wrong with her much loved niece but keeping it to herself for the time being. 'For the middle of November it is a gloriously warm day – don't you think?'

'I'm hungry, Aunt, but I don't want you to start fussing. Is there anything in your cupboard that's ready made? A leftover bit of meat for a sandwich or some stew or soup? A lump of cheese would do.'

'Actually, no, I don't have any leftovers but, as luck would have it, Benjamin should be back any minute with pies and mash.' Spooning ground coffee into her percolator, Naomi wondered just how to handle Maggie, who was obviously downhearted. 'No doubt he will bring back two each for the both of us – his eyes now being bigger than his belly. As one gets older the stomach does tend to shrink a little, so—'

'Aunt Nao . . . please,' said Maggie, interrupting her flow. 'You can eat two pies no trouble and so could Ben. But I won't feel guilty if you share them with me. All right?'

'Of course, darling. I was only—'

'I know. But don't. Just be my Aunt Naomi because I need you to be.'

Tipping her head to one side, a sorry expression on her face, Naomi said, 'What is it, my darling? What's happened?'

'I've just been to see the flat and it looks lovely. Much better than I thought it would be and bigger now all the old stuff they were storing in there has gone. And it's plenty big enough for when Baby comes. And definitely clean enough to satisfy a welfare officer.'

'But?' said Naomi, one eyebrow raised, expecting to hear that at the very least Maggie had seen mice or a rat.

'I bumped into the horrible neighbours in our block. The ones who've got nothing else to do but sit inside their flats wondering who's doing what and who they can victimise. They were in the chip shop. And they saw me coming from upstairs and said insulting things about foreigners, and especially Italians.'

'And Tony's family heard all this?'

'Of course they did. They were meant to. It was aimed at them. They pretended not to for my sake but they heard all right. They had a go at me too.'

'Oh, Maggie . . . those types of people will stick pins into anyone they believe will take it to heart. You must learn not to let them bring you down. It simply serves to fuel their ego.'

'They said I was putting on weight and looked like a fat Italian mama.'

'Ah,' said Naomi, leaning back in her chair. 'I see what you mean. That was cruel. But of course it doesn't *necessarily* mean that they had detected the reason for your having put on a little weight.'

'They looked me up and down with a smirk on their faces. Of course they could tell.'

'Well then, my darling, did they not show themselves as malicious and petty? Which is the reason why they have only each other for company.'

'That's not the point, though, is it? The point is that they were *in* there and it's probably where they *always* go after they've shopped in the market. It's what *everyone* does when they go shopping. Whether it's Bethnal Green or Brick Lane. You go to the pie shop or the fish shop in between or after shopping.'

'Ah. Yes. If *they* shop there, how many others from this estate might also go to that particular fish-and-chip shop?'

'Exactly. I'll have to keep right out of everyone's way. We'll have to take the flat in Islington instead. Where no one knows me.'

'Well, I suppose that does make sense, my darling. In Islington you'll be seen as a young married woman expecting a baby and no more than that. You could easily be taken for eighteen now that your hair has settled into a nice grown-up style. And the extra weight does tend to make you appear more womanly.'

'So you think that's what I should do as well?'

'If it's what *you* want, then yes I do. It will hardly be for a lifetime. And who knows . . . you might enjoy living in a different part of London.'

'I know.'

'My advice, should it be asked for, would be for you to make a final decision and stick to it no matter what. If you would rather go to the Roman Road flat then be bold and do so. If not – go to North London.' Naomi poured coffee into light blue mugs. 'Furthermore I think it is time you wrote to Helene and your Uncle Jimmy to apologise for the letter you sent them.'

'I've already done that. And stop calling her Helene. It's not funny. And I've been over to see them since. I'm sure I told you that already.'

'Did you, my darling? I don't remember. But then my memory is not what it was.' Naomi felt sure she hadn't told her. 'I take it you've not had a change of mind there? On the subject of adoption.'

'Oh. So now you think I *should* let them have my baby?'

'Indeed I do *not*. If you remember, when we last spoke about it I said that you might like to think about letting your baby go to a lovely couple who could not have children of their own. I said *nothing* about your Uncle Jimmy. I don't think they *should*—'

'Good,' said Maggie, cutting in again. 'Because I'm gonna keep my baby no matter what.'

'And that, my darling, is exactly what I wish to hear. I thought that perhaps those dreadful women in the fish-and-chip shop had made you think differently. That's all.' Naomi smiled serenely at her niece.

Maggie sipped her coffee and then said, 'So what do you think of my living over the Italian café?'

'It's all rather *confusing* for an old great-aunt, darling. What with all the changes of heart and so on.'

'North London makes more sense.'

'Whatever you think, my darling,' said Naomi, forcing a smile. 'Whatever you feel is best. So long as you keep to it.'

'At least no one there would know me.'

'Well, yes . . . and that is important. But you must check this with your mother and with Tony and his family. Don't go jumping the gun as is your wont.'

'I think she'll be fine about North London.'

'And that is what *you* would most like?'

'It makes sense, Aunt Naomi. Let's face it.'

'Well, I suppose so. And if you return to have your baby at home, what is the plan from then onwards? Shall you have the neighbours believe that it is your mother who has given birth?'

'She won't go for that, Aunt Naomi. And it was a bit much to ask.'

'*Did* you ask?'

'Kind of.'

'Well, she might not mind *now*. Now that she's had time to mull it over. And mull it over she will have been doing. On this you may trust me. I know her as well as I know myself.'

'I must admit I did think it was a bizarre idea myself at first, but then thinking about it . . .'

'Exactly my point. I threw it at both of you in the beginning because, unlike your worldly great-aunt, you and your mother are terribly old-fashioned at times. I happen to think it was a brilliant idea – as a matter of fact.'

More relaxed now, Maggie talked more about the predicament she was in and how wonderful Tony and his family had been about it. She admitted that she had behaved irresponsibly, and for the first time properly apologised for going off the rails. She finished her confession by telling her great-aunt that she now believed her to have been right to be concerned the previous Christmas when she and Tony had met and fallen in love at first sight. Going together in the dark to the old house to collect the box she had left behind *had* been tempting fate – even though nothing had happened. The thrill of being alone together like that, and in a private, dark place, had excited her, and from that something else had emerged – the first real longing to have a young man make love to her.

'Darling, there is no shame in the desire and

longing that come with adolescence – especially when there is a handsome young Italian madly in love with you. To love and be loved is a gift from the gods to make up for everything else we have to endure.'

'So we didn't do wrong, then – me and Tony . . .'

'Indeed you did. You went *too* far. Romance is one thing – sex for the sake of it is something else. You could have enjoyed a wonderful long courtship, dancing close together in small, romantically lit nightclubs and walking hand in hand on a summer's day in the parks. Instead of which you must serve behind a cooked-food counter and live in rooms above the premises. A lesson learned young is a painful one.'

Ben's timing was perfect. Her great-aunt was building up to an oration about her own juvenile experiences of love and romance when he knocked on the front door, having returned with the pies and mash. All thoughts of romance, however, were quashed once the delicious aroma of Naomi's favourite parsley sauce, kept hot in a flask, reached her nostrils.

Over their meal the conversation returned to the idea of Edie feigning pregnancy, gradually adding more and more padding to her midriff. This time, however, instead of being conducted in a serious tone, it induced peals of laughter all round. But by the end of their meal the seed was firmly sown in Maggie's mind. Naomi, in her own clever way, had persuaded her that to have her child reared as if it was her brother, or sister, would be a brilliant idea. She had managed to come full circle, for this was what she had suggested at the very beginning, when she and Edie knew that a baby was on the way.

With this in mind, Maggie made her way home to Edie believing that things could work out ... *if* her mother agreed to her part in the plan. Of course, Dennis had to be taken into consideration. His reaction might be one of shock and he might refuse to play any part in the subterfuge, and who could blame him? So far he had been so easy-going about everything that it hadn't even entered Maggie's mind that he might reject the idea. He always chose to take a back seat when she was around, offering no more than a smile and a nod and asking whether she was all right. And that suited her fine. She hadn't been looking for a father figure, and if she had been Dennis would not have been her number-one choice. To Maggie he was a bit of a mystery. Now, for whatever reason, she was asking herself why she had never sat down and talked to him about his life beyond their flat.

All any of them really knew about him was what they had gradually picked up along the way. That he was in his late thirties, still a bachelor, and had no family or close friends whom he deemed fit to introduce into their world. From the offset this had disturbed Naomi, who had, nevertheless, apart from dropping a little hint now and again, kept her thoughts to herself. Maggie had always been under the impression that Dennis was a private person who kept his cards close to his chest. But now, given that her aunt's idea would involve him, she was beginning to wonder why he had no family – no previous wife, no children.

Alone, deep in thought, resting her elbows on the window boxes on her back balcony, Edie was enjoying a cup of sweet tea, hoping that it would fuel her energy. She had woken early that morning soon after dawn had broken, and had not been able to get properly back to sleep as a result of a vivid dream. In the dream, she, her mother, father and younger brother Jimmy, in their old house in Cotton Street, had been playing Lotto at the dining table in their small living room in front of the gentle hissing of a coal fire. Just like now, it had been a Saturday afternoon in November – too early for the excitement of the coming Christmas to have taken proper hold, but not too soon for all the children to start thinking about snow, sledges, Santa Claus and carol-singing in schools and outside neighbours' front doors.

With all this floating through her mind as she stood on the balcony watching the sun go down, she could not help but think of her half-brother Ken, whom she had recently met for the first time. She recalled the bashful expression on his face when he had stood watching as his father greeted Edie after so many years of separation. His nervous habit of pushing up the frame of his spectacles where they rested on the bridge of his nose was endearing. She wished now that she had spent a little time getting to know him the way Maggie had when they were in the kitchen together.

She recalled her brother Jimmy's expression when she had told him of the visit out of the blue. At the time he had gone quiet and cast his eyes down to hide his feelings. The intrusion of Helen's voice had steamrollered any possibility of easy conversation about the gentle man they had lost so many years ago and who had now returned. Her attitude then and now was 'How dare he show his face after all he did to you and Jimmy. Not to mention your mother.'

Sighing, Edie closed her eyes and wiped them all from her mind. No matter how she weighed things up, life *had* dealt her and her brother Jimmy a rough hand. But that was all behind them now, buried in the past, and she had good things to look forward to. She didn't want reminders of her old life, even though she did want to see her father again – not now the pain of her mother's premature death had at last faded.

When her mother had committed suicide she had felt as if there were a hand clenching her heart and slowly ripping it out. She had been sixteen going on seventeen at the time, and it been the worst time of her life. The shock of suddenly being an orphan had almost destroyed her – Jimmy too. They had once been part of a loving family, and suddenly their mother and father had gone from their lives. It had been awful. And for her father to turn up out of the blue all these years later, which should have been wonderful, as she had always hoped it would, had in fact been a let-down. With his arrival he had brought heartbreaking memories to the surface.

Now that some time had elapsed since his impromptu visit, Edie was more able to take it all in and enjoy the warmth that he had shown, the warmth of a father's love. She realised that most families had their share of grief and probably, just like her and Jimmy, chose not to broadcast it. There was only one way of healing heartache, to Edie's mind, and that was to let time take its natural course. Personal grief could not be halved by sharing it.

The possibility of her father and half-brother having returned to Canada without having said goodbye to her and Maggie was now beginning to look a strong one. Previously, when this had crossed her mind, she had pushed it away, telling herself that she didn't care one way or the other. But she did care, and now she longed to see her father and half-brother again. She wanted to write to them at their rented house in Golders Green and tell them to come and visit again. Not to go away without saying goodbye. Not to go away at all.

The sound of the front door opening and closing brought her out of her reverie. She knew this would be her daughter – Naomi, even though she had her own key and often used it, would always knock or ring the doorbell beforehand. Taking a deep breath, Edie went into the kitchen, where she could pretend to be busy. She didn't want anyone, not even Maggie, to guess her present mood – nostalgic and longing to have her family back.

Breezing into the room with a lovely smile on her face, Maggie held out her arms. Before Edie could respond her daughter was hugging her tight and saying, 'You're the best mum in the world and I love you.'

'Am I, now?' said Edie, having just been given the best tonic a mother could wish for when feeling low. 'And why's that?'

'Because you're gonna have my baby,' Maggie said, a hopeful look on her face.

Edie was thrown by this. 'That's a strange thing to say, sweetheart. What exactly do you mean by it?'

'You know . . . Aunt Naomi's suggestion. Remember? We laughed at it at the time, once she'd gone home and you told me . . . but really, it's not so daft, Mum. And it would make it so much easier for me.' Maggie squeezed Edie's hands and held them tight, a pleading look on her face. 'Will you? Will you do this really very special thing for me? I'll make it up to you. I'll do anything you want me to. Please, please just say that you'll do it. Please?'

'You want me to let people think I'm expecting a baby? Maggie . . . I know we laughed about it when I told you what Naomi had suggested, but really, even though it was a silly idea, it wasn't *that* funny.'

'No, I know it wasn't. And I know I'm an embarrassment—'

'No one said that, Mags. Don't start—'

'But I am, Mum! I know I am! Everyone around here will say it's a disgrace once I start to show. And I was stupid enough to think that if I tucked myself away in a chip shop in Roman Road until Baby was born everything would be tickety-boo. Well, it won't be. Because it's only a short bus ride away and neighbours from this estate use the market.'

'So you want me to pretend that I'm having a baby – even though I'm a widow – and walk about with padding under my clothes. While you . . . what? Live here and hide inside for months on end?'

'No. Me and Tony could run the Islington café and live above it. No one knows me there.'

'But Tony wasn't going to "live" with you above the chip shop. He was going to come and go and not stay overnight. Until you're old enough to be married in Scotland. *After* the baby's born. I thought that Rita was going to share the flat with you.'

'She was. But sometimes things don't work out the way we plan them, do they?'

'And what about the Baroncinis? They've had the flat in Roman Road done up for you. Now you want them to alter all their plans and let you run the café in Islington. And for why?'

'What?'

'For why, Maggie! Why suddenly change your mind again? You were set on running the fish-and-chip shop when you left here this morning! This is not a game!'

'I know that. Of course I do. But I've thought it all through and if you pretended you were pregnant and then when the baby's born brought it up as your own child and not your grandchild . . . I could still love it like you loved Uncle Jimmy when he was your baby brother. Couldn't I? And you know how much you loved him. What difference would it make if people think the baby's yours? We'd know and we wouldn't care, would we? Aunt Naomi always said we're a close-knit family, even though there's not many of us. Well, there'd be one more, wouldn't there?'

'Aunt Naomi. I'll kill her for this. She's planted this idea in your head.'

'Please, Mum . . . please say you'll do it. It would make my life so much easier. Please?'

'Just . . . slow down a bit, all right?' said Edie, pulling away from her daughter. 'Just calm down and tell me what's happened to make you suddenly want this. Something must have happened, Mags. I wasn't born yesterday.'

'Malicious gossips. Rat-face from downstairs that keeps 'aving a go at you and her from upstairs who keeps 'aving a go at the kids. Both of them were in the queue in the chip shop and they had a go at me.'

'Ah. I might have known it was something like that. And what did they say?'

'It doesn't matter now. They did me a favour without realising it. They made me see that it's not gonna be easy. Living in the East End while I'm carrying. We don't know a soul in Islington. I'll be able to work in the café out the back and serve now and then. The customers won't take any notice.'

'I can see what you're saying but . . . it's a very strange thing to be asked to do. I think I need a lot of time to think this one over.'

'We won't be the first family to do it, Mum. Nao said it's been going on for years, and on this very estate there're probably people who think that their mothers are their sisters or their aunts or cousins. Older people as well. I'm not just talking about now. Even in Victorian times—'

'I know, Maggie. I know all of that. But when it comes to our own doorstep it's a bit different. Very different. Let it rest for now and I'll think it over. It'll mean that I'll have to bring my wedding forward again. I don't think Dennis'll go along with it. In fact I'm sure he won't. What man would?'

''Course Dennis will. He's so easygoing, Mum. He'll go along with anything so long as he doesn't 'ave to arrange things. Easygoing or lazy, I'm not sure which, but who cares? And really, you don't actually have to get married – do you? Not yet. You could pretend to have tied the knot at a small private ceremony at the town hall. Who's to know?'

Edie pushed a hand through her hair, bemused. 'Well . . . Dennis will approve that bit. The less fuss and cost the better. And it's not illegal whereas bigamy is.'

'Bigamy? Den's already married? He's got a wife hidden away?'

'No, of course not. I was talking about your father,' said Edie, blushing. 'He could turn up out of the blue. Missing, presumed dead?' She shrugged, trying to cover her tracks. 'That's what the letter said.'

Maggie chuckled. 'I'm sorry, I shouldn't laugh but . . . the thought of you and Dennis and bigamy? As if you would go for that. Don't know about Den, mind you. He's a bit of a dark horse.'

'What do you mean?' Edie was quick to ask.

'Nothing much. Just that he is, that's all. Keeps his past life close to his chest.' She grinned and went to the sink and filled the kettle for tea. 'So what do you think, then? Think we could pull it off?'

'I don't know. I'll give it some thought. It's a serious thing you're asking me to do.'

'I just thought it would protect our family name and it would be lovely seeing my baby in your arms and being cared for by you for the first few weeks. That's the bit that terrifies me. When they're so fragile. I'd take over as soon as I could and we could bring it up together. Mum and grandma. Taking turns in looking after it.'

'Put like that, it sounds a bit like a fairy story,' said Edie, warming to the idea.

'It can be whatever we want it to be, Mum. You've said yourself that a problem shared is a problem halved. And this little baby growing in here is a bit of a problem. Poor little thing. Good job he can't hear us, eh?'

'You won't be much good to your baby if you're in Islington and he's here with me.'

'That'll only be temporary. Until I've had the baby. Then, once I'm slim and back to normal, I can come home and look after him, feed him the bottle and that. Then me and Tony'll get married in Scotland and run the shop in Roman Road market. And Baby can live with us because we'll be married by then. Everyone round here will think that it's too much for you to look after it so I've taken over. You could pretend to be ill at first. Something like that. You are old to have a baby, after all.'

'I am not. Late thirties is not too old, thank you.'

'And really,' Maggie went on, 'it's either that or let Uncle Jimmy and Helen adopt it. That's my second plan now. I've thought it through properly. On the way home from Nao's.'

'I was thinking about my brother Jimmy just before you came in, as a matter of fact. About him and my half-brother, Ken, and your grandfather. I've only seen them once in all the months they've been in England. Maybe they weren't too impressed with us. I should think they've gone back to Canada by now.'

'No. They wouldn't do that. They wouldn't go without coming to say goodbye. Your brother's really nice. And he was just as sorry as you are that you're like strangers.'

'Well, you seem to know a lot more about him than I do. I suppose that's because you were in the kitchen talking to him. He hardly said a word to me.'

'That's because he's shy.'

'I don't even know what my brother does for a living. Or if he's married even.'

'Your dad must have filled you in on all that, surely. You never asked me anything about him so I thought that's what you talked about. Him. Me. And the rest of the family.'

'Yes and no. Mostly my mum and your dad and old times. It was all a bit sudden, wasn't it? I think I was too shocked with his sudden arrival to think straight. Dad's other son hardly said a word to me.

I don't think he felt the brother–sister bond either.'

'He wanted you to have time with your dad. He said so. He's nice. Genuine sort of a bloke.' Maggie took the boiling kettle off the stove and filled the teapot.

'Well, since you got to know him you might have thought to tell me before now what he's like. I mean . . . is he married? Does he have children? It would be something to know just that. But you never said a word, Maggie. And you've not mentioned him since. I presumed you felt a bit like I did. They came and they went and so what of it.'

'Not really, no. And I don't think you felt that either, Mum – not deep down. You won't ever change, though. But then I wouldn't want you to.' Maggie poured a little milk into each of their teacups.

'Two heaped sugars for me when you're spooning,' said Edie.

'Two? And heaped? You usually have one and flat.'

'Never mind that. Put the sugar in. All the worry of you 'as made my face drawn. I need fleshing out a bit.'

'Well, there you are, then. My idea'll be a good excuse for you to have cream doughnuts whenever you fancy.'

'We'll see. Let it rest for now and tell me about my half-brother.'

'OK. Your brother, my Uncle Ken . . . he lives, with his wife Joyce, in the new suburb of Scarborough, north-east of the centre of Toronto. In a new bungalow. His two children, boys, are called . . . Mike and Donald, I think. They go to the local school and they're both mad on sports. Your brother is a salesman for a large agricultural firm called . . .' She closed her eyes, made a circle with her forefinger and thumb and concentrated. 'Massey Harris.'

'Why are you doing that?' said Edie. 'The thumb and finger?'

'This?' said Maggie, holding up her hand, perfecting the circle to the best of her ability. 'This is an old Italian custom. You close your eyes and say to yourself. "I am remembering." One of Tony's aunts showed me. It works as well.'

'Fair enough. Go on, then.'

'Ken's a travelling salesman, going round by car, selling farm machines and stuff. His wife doesn't go to work and they have two cars. Not big American cars and not brand new. Your dad and brother came over third class, which is quite luxurious compared to our second class even.

'The journey on the liner took about six days from Montreal to Southampton. Your dad works in downtown Toronto on mail order catalogues. He lives in his own house, an old semi-detached in an older part of Toronto, St Clair, that's becoming trendy and pushing up the prices. And that's it.'

'Well . . . there's nothing wrong with your memory, is there. That was good, Mags. I'm glad that came out at last. I should 'ave—' The sound of the doorbell cut her short. 'That sounds like Den's ring. I wasn't expecting him yet. Go and open the door for me, Mags, there's a good girl. If it's anyone other than him or Nao, tell them I'm having a nap.'

'When did your last servant die?' said Maggie, and then asked, 'Why don't you want to see Laura or Jessie?'

'I'm a bit tired, love. That's all. And I've got a headache coming on. I'll be in the front room.'

'But it's all right if it's Dennis?'

'Of course. I can't turn him away, can I? He's not gonna take this messing around with the date of our marriage as well as you think. I'd rather get it sorted out now if poss.'

'You are gonna do it for me, then?'

'If Dennis goes along with it, then yes,' she said, going out of the kitchen and into the living room.

'Nao didn't think he'd care one way or the other,' Maggie called after her. 'Thanks, Mum. I'll never forget this. Never!'

During the few seconds she had to herself, Edie repeated Maggie's last words. 'Nao didn't think he'd care . . . one way or the other?'

'Hello, sweetheart,' said Dennis, coming into the room, his tall, broad frame making the place feel smaller. 'Any dramas today?' He tossed his early evening copy of the *Standard* on to the coffee table and slumped down into the armchair opposite Edie.

'Not exactly . . .' said Edie, giving him a look she knew he loved to see – one of vulnerability. 'I didn't think you'd be round.'

'Nor did I. Spur of the moment. Not a problem, is it?'

''Course not. Maggie's just come back from the flat in Roman Road. There's another change of plan.'

'Right,' Maggie chipped in, 'this is where I duck out.' She picked up her handbag and said to Dennis on her way out, 'Only do what you think is best for you and Mum.' She too was playing the vulnerable female.

'Where are you going now?' said Edie, not too bothered óne way or the other.

'Round Rita's. *Ciao*!' With that Maggie left the room and the flat.

'Do what for the best?' said Dennis. 'What's going on, Edie?'

'Maggie wants us to bring our wedding forward.'

'We've only just put it back to spring, for Christ's sake.' There was an expression on his face that she recognised. A mixture of frustration and boredom.

'Let me finish. I was going to say that we don't actually need to bring it forward. We could pretend that we've crept off and got married in secret. All we need is a gold band on each of our marriage fingers.' Taken aback by this, Dennis went quiet and chewed the inside of his cheek, a habit that Edie had noticed before. She could tell he was thinking about it. 'It's just an idea, that's all.'

'It don't bother me one way or the other, babe, but why? Gimme a reason. I need a reason.'

'Can't you say yes first and then listen to the reason?' she purred, sidling up close, trying to get him in a nicer mood. She knew he was irritated and she hadn't even told him the half of it yet.

'All right. Yes. Now tell me why.'

So much for her attempt at acting the seductress.

'All right, then. Since we are gonna get married in any case I didn't think it would matter if we lived a little white lie for a few months. And maybe stretch one white lie into two white lies.'

'At least I'm intrigued. Go on.'

'It's just an idea so far but, to save face all round, I thought it would look better if I was the one who was pregnant. And when the baby's due, we smuggle Maggie up here for the delivery. I then get rid of my pregnant look and everyone thinks I've had a baby.'

'Right. And so . . . why won't we be getting married as planned? I don't want to sound thick, babe, but what difference would it make?'

'A lot. I want a nice wedding and I want to look lovely for you. I can hardly do that with cushions stuffed up my dress, can I?'

'I know where this 'as come from. Tony's family. The Italians want everyone to think that it's your baby and nothing to do with one of them. They're a crafty lot. And you've fallen for it hook, line and sinker.'

'No, darling. You've got it wrong.'

'No, Edie, *you've* got it wrong.'

'No. *You* have. We're talking about Tony's baby. Ida won't let it out of her family for all the tea in China. Maggie can stop here with us after the baby's born, right? Then, off she goes to get married and live with her husband and the baby. I tell people that I couldn't cope so Maggie's fostering it for a while and leave it at that. Simple, really. We should 'ave thought of it in the beginning. Well, one of us did as it happens. Nao. Always one step ahead of us.'

'Once that baby's born, Edie, Maggie won't leave this flat. Why should she? She and Tony will be in her room and before you know it we'll be ousted. That's what this is about. Maggie wants to live 'ere with Tony. She's trying to ease you out of here and into my place.'

'No, of course she isn't. She and Tony want to run a restaurant together one day. A proper one. So Islington with rooms above is a good starting place for them. Tony's family don't mind which one they take. The entire family'll end up in North London eventually. Ida and her husband will be looking for an exchange in a year or so. Most of Tony's cousins are over that way.'

'And that's what she's *told* you or what you're *assuming*?'

'A bit of both. Why?'

'Because you can't trust youngsters these days as far as you can throw 'em!'

'Dennis, we're talking about Maggie, sweetheart.'

'I'm telling you. The next thing she'll come up with is us moving into my place once the baby's born. And hey presto, they've got a lovely two-bedroom council flat to themselves. The youngsters can be very crafty.'

Seeing a very different side to her fiancé, Edie lapsed into silence for a moment. Eventually she said, 'And that way she can bring the baby up here on this safe estate and it'll look as if she's doing it for me . . . and everyone'll think it's her little baby brother. And admire her for it. It's not a bad idea, Den.'

'You've got it in one. It's clever. I'll give 'er that. Very clever.'

'So you think Islington's just a stopgap? That all she really wants is to be here – in her own home, with her little family?'

'Of course Islington'll just be a stopgap. She's using it and good luck to 'er for that. But don't let her use you, Edie – or me. Because I won't stand for that.'

Edie's mind was on a different track now. Without realising it Dennis had just mapped out the plan for her and simplified it. Why she was warming to this idea of Maggie's she didn't know. But she did know that Dennis was wrong about her daughter's motiv-ation. Quite wrong. She felt as if he didn't know Maggie at all. Cutting through her thoughts, Dennis spoke in a slightly bored tone. 'They won't know how old she is over in Islington, will they? She can wear a wedding ring and let people assume that she's eighteen. She could pass for it. Pregnant, married, eighteen . . .' He shrugged. 'No problem. Who gives a toss when it's not one of their own? Let her have her baby and be proud of it. In Islington. She needn't even run off to Gretna Green. If everyone thinks she's married, why bother? Any tea in the pot? I'm gasping.'

'Do you know what I'd like to do? Come and see your house in Bow in case I fancy living there. I don't need to wait until all the decorating's finished. Take me there this evening.'

'Don't talk silly, Edie! I've only just got 'ere and I've been up to my eyes in paintbrushes all day. Finished the bedroom at last.'

'But why are you bothering to decorate it right through if you're coming to live with me here once we're married?'

'Precaution, my darling. That's why. Don't forget that the other three women I was engaged to froze out in the end. And only because they couldn't break through my barrier the way you've done. And that's because at last I've found the right woman. You. I want to spend the rest of my life with you – simple as that.'

'But not in your two-bedroom house in Bow?'

'No. I'll keep it on, though. In case I can't get on with living in a flat – we'll move into the house. But I want that to be my choice. Our choice. Not forced on us by Maggie and 'er Italian boyfriend.'

'Tony.'

'Yeah, all right – Tony.'

'But if you love the place, and I would rather live in a house than a flat given the choice, and given the house is nicely decorated as well . . . why *don't* we live there and let Maggie and Tony have this flat? The house is practically ready. You've laid quality lino right through.'

'Nearly finished is what I said, darlin'. Good couple of months to go yet before you'd want to set foot in it. Building materials all over the place. It's a mess. And I *think* I said that I'd picked out and ordered the lino.'

'All right. But if you moved in here wouldn't you miss your private little garden? You love sitting out there on a Sunday morning reading the paper. You've said so more than once.'

'What is this – the third degree? If you don't want me to move in, say so! It was you who brought it up, sweet'eart. And if you don't mind my saying so – to pretend that you're pregnant is bloody stupid.'

'Well, all right – let's forget that bit for a minute. But if I said I wanted to live in your house with its lovely back garden, would you agree to it? Maggie aside.'

'No, because you wouldn't like it there.'

'Why wouldn't I?'

'It's mostly the older generation living in that street. You're best in this flat with the new friends you've got coming and going. And it's lovely – look at it! And as for a garden . . . we'll 'ave a garden bigger than the one I've got now one day when we do move off the estate. Chigwell in Essex is where we'll go, Ed. Lovely houses there.'

'Sounds idyllic, Den. Lovely. But what if I really like your house and want to move in straight away?' Without having planned it, Edie was now testing him.

'And let Maggie and the Italian live in this flat? Once she's 'ad the baby?'

'No! She won't want to live here! I'd let the flat go to some other family desperate for something like this.'

'You'd be prepared to let go of a lovely new two-bedroom flat? With a balcony out back and front? You're not thinking straight, Edie. I wish I'd never come round now. I don't need all this. A fifteen-year-old is changing everyone's lives just because she couldn't say no.'

Suppressing her anger, Edie managed a smile. 'I

know . . . she is still a baby. My baby. Come on. Let's get out of here and show me what you've done to that little house of yours.'

'No can do.' He glanced at his wristwatch. 'I'll have to be going soon. I only popped in for a cup of tea and a kiss. Seeing a bloke about a little bit of business in a pub off Globe Road. Anyway . . . as far as my house is concerned, forget it. I can't see us living there. I've told you before, babe. I've bin unlucky there where love's concerned. I'm not taking that risk with you. We'll be all right in this flat for a couple of years – especially once Maggie's gone and we'll 'ave it to ourselves. I mean . . . we don't get much time on our own, do we?'

'I thought we did. We always sit in and have a nice time when you come round.'

'I know but . . . it would 'ave bin nice to stop the night now and then.'

'But we agreed on that in the beginning. It would be too embarrassing for me knowing that Maggie's in the next bedroom. You didn't seem to mind.'

'And I still don't mind. But if she's not gonna be here – end of story. I think it's a good idea that I move in earlier.' He shook his head, as if in wonder. 'I never in a million years would have thought that you'd 'ave come up with the idea of us pretending to have got married. You're a dark horse, Edie, darling, a dark horse. Do you want to choose your wedding ring or let me surprise you?'

'So you'd go along with that but not with me pretending to be pregnant?'

'Of course. Not a problem, is it, babe?'

'But the only reason for cancelling the wedding would be because of that plan. I wouldn't want to look six months' pregnant in my wedding outfit. If I'm *not* gonna help Maggie out in that way, we can get married as planned. Can't we?'

'If you like. Whatever you say, sweetheart. Just let me know the date and time,' Dennis said, looking again at his watch.

'And if I don't agree to have it appear that I'm the one who's having a baby, to protect Maggie's name, and once Maggie's moved to Islington . . . you'll fetch your suitcases and move in with me?'

'Just give me the nod, sweetheart. Just give me the nod and I'll be in like a shot.'

'And if I want you to wait before moving in until we're married, you'd be just as happy with that?'

'I'm easy any which way, babe,' he said, anxious to be away. Beads of sweat were breaking out on his brow.

'And if you do move in, which of course you will one day in any case . . . you won't mind Nao popping in now and then?'

'No. So long as it don't get too much of a habit.'

'Well, during the day won't matter, will it? Once I'm back from work and before you come in. Late afternoon. She only comes round three nights a week.'

'Three? That's pushing it a bit, babe. Still, not to worry. I could make them the nights I go out with the boys for a drink. Now – I really must fly.'

'She comes sometimes of a Saturday as well, and

usually on Sunday mornings she pops in for a bit. She lets herself in during the week if she's been to the market and bought a job lot of sausages or chops at a bargain price. She leaves little gifts for me to come home to.'

Dennis was chewing the inside of his cheek again. 'She's got her own key, then. Fair enough. The thing is, though, babe . . . with my kind of work I don't always 'ave to go out every day and I do like a lie-in now and then. If she came in the mornings on week-days, she might find me in bed. I don't want 'er to think I'm a layabout. And if she does have a go, she'll soon find I'm not as easy as you are. I've never bin a pushover, darling, and I don't intend to start now.'

'OK, Den. Best we get everything clear from the beginning. And having said that – I don't think you'll find that Naomi's meek and mild when it comes to a debate. It should be fun watching the pair of you.'

'We'll see,' he said, 'we'll see. Listen, I really am gonna 'ave to fly, babe. Don't wanna miss this meeting.' He gave her a peck on the cheek then looked into her eyes. 'You're the best thing that ever happened to me, babe. I'll see myself out.'

Left by herself in the quiet room, Edie felt an icy wave sweep through her. She shuddered when she heard the street door slam shut after Dennis and stared at the open living-room door, wondering whether he would ever swagger through it again. Gripped by an urge to chase after him, she forced herself not to. Going into the kitchen, with only the silence of the flat for company, she turned on the cold-water tap and filled a glass. Her throat was dry. Talking to herself, which was nothing unusual when she was alone, she scolded herself. 'Edie . . . you've got to learn to trust a man not to walk out of your life. Just because Dad was there one day and gone the next doesn't mean that everyone does things like that. And Harry would never have left you high and dry but for that bloody war.'

Having put the kettle on the gas ring, she went back into the living room and sat on the edge of the settee, staring at the floor, dark thoughts continuing to run through her mind. She wondered whether there really was a house in Bow and, worse still, whether Dennis was leading a double life, just as her father had, without leaving any obvious clues. She had, after all, been courting this man for nine months and he had never taken her to the house. She had mentioned it before, more than once, but there had always been a sound reason why they couldn't go at the time. And she had not met any of his family. Perhaps he really did have none to speak of.

Furthermore, as an electrician with his own little business, why hadn't Dennis regaled her with any stories about the people he worked for? Characters and places, the homes he went into in and around London. An image of the inside of his small blue van filled her mind. Always neat and tidy and with no sign of tools or equipment. Could a man be that tidy and organised? She recalled the time when she had praised him for it, when Dennis was taking her to see a film at the Empire picture palace in Hackney.

'There's a place for everything, darling,' he had said, 'and I've got a little shed in the garden for tools. All under padlock.' All very sensible, and she had had no reason to doubt him at the time, had even been impressed by his explanation. But now, as other questions crept into her mind, Edie was feeling more and more uncomfortable. Why, for instance, did he never smell of grease and sawdust – only soap and after-shave? He was a full-time labourer, after all said and done. Even electricians got their fingernails dirty.

Shaking herself out of this doubting mood, she went back into the kitchen to make a pot of tea and berated herself for letting her imagination run wild. Of course Dennis loved her. And of course he was bound to make an effort to always look clean and smart during their courtship. She wouldn't really have wished it to be any other way. And as for the family and close friends she had never met – she would bring this up and maybe insist that she become more involved in his private life. After all, she didn't even have a proper address should she want, or feel the need, to make a surprise call on him. A little house in Bow was all she had to go on.

Naomi had asked her more than once about his family and background, and even she had shrugged it off when Edie had told her that Dennis was a very private man. But now her intuition was screaming at her that something was wrong. 'It's time to take stock, Edie,' she told herself. 'To look at this relationship and be honest.' She knew she found it hard to accept the truth when the truth looked as if it might cause her pain, or worse still break her heart yet again. She had no reason to believe that Dennis had gone from her life and yet she felt very strongly as if he had. As if he had found her questioning and planning too much to cope with. As if she had driven him away.

# 9

Turning the corner that led to her best friend's street, Maggie felt sad at the thought of Rita's mother giving up the house and moving away. She had always loved the cosy small living room with its two armchairs either side of a Victorian fireplace in which a small coal fire always seemed to be glowing, except during the midsummer months. The door leading into the kitchen, wedged open, allowed the lovely smell of homemade cakes, shortbread or fruit pies to waft through the house on baking day – Saturday. Today would be no exception. Now that Rita's father had finally done the right thing and left home, the strained atmosphere seemed to have vanished with him. Believing that Rita's mother would be feeling sad, she had popped into the sweet shop on her way over and bought her a small gift – a box of Cadbury's chocolates to cheer her up.

Eileen, now also involved in the arrangements for the forthcoming opening night of the tea dance club, had gradually got to know Mathew Browning, who was coming to visit her this very afternoon. They were to go over details for the sale of entrance and raffle tickets, a project she had suggested and offered to take care of. Their brief chats in the library at tea breaks about the new venture had led to them telling each other about their own lives, their aspirations when young and their interests. They had discovered a common passion for early films, and especially silent pictures. To anyone watching these two people, both in their early forties, it would be obvious that a relationship of sorts was steadily forming.

Having knocked on the door, Maggie stood back and admired the house that she might be visiting for the last time. She would badly miss coming here. It reminded her of the house in Cotton Street. Suddenly she felt as if yet another part of her life was disappearing. She and Rita had been friends since they had first started school at the age of five, and Maggie had sometimes slept overnight here, playing board games or cards before bedtime with Eileen joining in. Pillow fights and climbing out of Rita's bedroom window were among the things they had got up to. They had even dabbled in spiritualism. Having sneaked into Eileen's bedroom and taken her circular ouija board from under the bed where it was hidden, they would then conceal it in Rita's room until the midnight hour. Once they had set the atmospheric scene, with only two candles alight in the darkened room, they had scared themselves silly until they could take no more.

'God almighty,' said Rita, opening the door, 'you look older by the day. I like the haircut hair and style, though. Where'd you get that done?'

'Aunt Naomi gave me a trim last night and used

her curling tongs. Are you gonna invite me in or leave me on the doorstep?' said Maggie, flattered by the compliment, rare from her friend. 'I've got some bad news which is no fault of mine.'

'Go on through.' Rita closed the door behind them. As she followed Maggie through the narrow passage she chuckled. 'Looks like most of the weight you've put on 'as slipped down to your arse.'

'Don't be coarse, Rita. It lets you down.'

'Oh, pardon me for being honest.'

'The truth can hurt, you know.' Not in the least bit upset by the leg-pulling, Maggie went into the sitting room, where the table had been laid with cheese-and-watercress sandwiches and freshly baked butterfly cakes decorated with lemon butter icing and slithers of red glacé cherries.

'Hello, Maggie, love,' came the usual warm greeting from Rita's mother. 'We were about to have our tea. You're just in time.'

'Lovely,' said Maggie. 'I love your cakes. And here's a present to show how much I appreciate the way you look after me when I come round.'

'Oh, you shouldn't 've done that, love. Shouldn't waste your money on giving me luxuries. No, you keep them for yourself.'

'Well, if I'm wasting my money on you, you're wasting it on me when you feed me every time I come round.'

'Oh, that's different. I just make things go round, that's all.'

'Then you can open them later on and share them

with madam. I want you to have them, Eileen. It's a little thank-you present, that's all. Not much but it's something.'

'That's really nice of you, love. I'll enjoy eating them all to myself. It's not often I get presents. And I love Dairy Milk. Thank you very much.' Eileen was genuinely touched by the gesture.

'I've told Mum by the way,' said Rita, 'so you don't 'ave to 'ide your belly under that coat. And I told 'er to make extra cakes. I said you eat like a horse now.'

'Take no notice of her, love. She can be a tormenting moo at times. She never said that. And you look lovely. That's a very pretty scarf.'

'Thanks. Nao gave me it. It's pure chiffon.'

'From out of 'er trunk filled with stuff from the twenties and thirties by the look of it,' said Rita.

'That right. You'd wear it if you 'ad the chance – even if it wasn't free and you had to buy it.'

'No I bloody well wouldn't. It makes you look older than you are.'

'Good. That's exactly what I want.'

'You could pass for eighteen in that. Twenty, even. Is that what you want?'

'Might be.'

'And as for the cakes, Maggie,' said Eileen, giving her daughter a scathing look, 'I love baking, you know that. Especially now the pig's gone. When I made a Victoria sponge he'd all but scoff the lot before we got a look in. Greedy devil. No thought for me nor Rita.'

Easing herself into a fireside chair, Maggie stared

into the flames. She wasn't sure whether she ought to pick up on the fact that Rita had broken the news to her mother or stay silent. She chose to wait and see whether it was brought up again. 'I don't know what I'm gonna do once you've moved out, Eileen. I love coming round here. It's seems a lot cosier now as well. Why d'yer think that might be?' She knew exactly why, but this was one way to divert attention from herself.

''Course it feels more homely. Take your coat off, love. It's a pity he never left years ago, eh? I should have gone down his pockets sooner. There was enough in the letter I found there to tell me where she lived. It was the best thing I'd ever done, knocking on that door. Her face was a picture. Especially when I threw a sack filled with his clothes into her passage. Dirty clothes, mind – not laundered. I'm just about to boil some milk for cocoa. I expect you'd like a cup too, Maggie?'

'I'd love one,' said Maggie, amazed by the change in Rita's placid mother. 'We never 'ave cocoa except in real winter,' she added, 'and only just before going to bed. Daft, really. I think we should 'ave it when we wake up on frosty mornings, not when we're about to get into a warm bed.'

'Warm?' said Eileen, a wry smile on her face. 'In the winter?'

'Oh, yeah. I always 'ave two hot-water bottles in for ten minutes beforehand. I might 'ave three this year.'

'You might *need* three given the size of your bum,'

said Rita, helping herself to a sandwich. 'Put on weight, Mum, ain't she.'

'Never mind that. She's blooming and that's what counts. Have you put on much weight, love?'

'No. My breasts are just filling out, that's all.' Maggie was still a touch shocked by Eileen's open and frank account of her husband's womanising. 'I think Rita's jealous, though,' she added, trying to maintain a normal conversation, 'She's jealous 'cos she's still only got fried eggs and I've got what they call a film-star figure.'

Rita gave her friend a mischievous look and then subjected her to more torment. 'Not for long, though. Mum knows, so you can talk about it.'

'All right, Rita. Leave it be. If Maggie wants to tell me she will, when she's ready, thank you. Take no notice of her, love. She's a torment. Always was.' Eileen went into the kitchen, shaking her head.

'I'm not being a torment. I'm just trying to get Fanny Adams here to bring it out into the open and stop looking like she's just pinched things out of a shop. The way she walks about with 'er shoulders hunched you'd fink the boys in blue were on every corner waiting to nab 'er.'

'I don't walk about like that, Reet! Don't be so bloody insulting. It's not funny. Nor is it kind. You're supposed to be my friend.'

'It is kind. Innit, Mum? That's what you always say. "Truth will out when you're up the spout!"'

In the kitchen, spooning cocoa into large cups and talking to them through the open doorway, Eileen said, 'I never did say that and you know it!'

'As it 'appens,' said Rita, beaming, 'she never. I just made that up. Good, innit, Mags? Clever old cow, ain't I?'

'Pity you don't do something more worthwhile with your brain, then. Instead of winding me up. Not that I'm taking a blind bit of notice.'

'She eats twice as much as you do, Maggie,' said Eileen. 'I don't know where she puts it. Too much energy, that's the trouble. Burns it off.'

'So, what's the bad news that's not your fault, then? We can't move into the flat or Tony's gonna move in here with me and Mum instead of you. We'd keep 'im warm in bed at night, Mum, wouldn't we?'

'Don't be disgusting, Rita,' said her mother. 'You'd get a slap round the back of your legs if you was a couple of years younger. And I wouldn't like to think what Maggie's mother would say if she heard you talking like that.'

'Well then, Mag, you old slag,' said Rita, who loved to tease her mother. 'Out with it.'

To the sound of Eileen tut-tutting loudly, Maggie said in a quiet voice, 'I'll explain when we're by ourselves.'

'No you won't. Tell me now. I've got my life to sort out thanks. You're not the only one who'll need somewhere to live. I'm not gonna live in a flat with Mum and right next door to 'er blooming sister as well. I'll end up like the pair of 'em. Fruit cakes.'

'You *can* stay in a flat with me, but I think it should be the Islington one. Above the restaurant.'

'So you lost your nerve, then? After all your brave

talk you're gonna run to Islington so you can 'ide away. So what's brought this on, then?'

'Common sense. People who know me will see me in Roman Road. I was daft enough to think that Mum's neighbours and that wouldn't get on a bus to go to a market—'

Eileen interrupted, 'Oh, that was daft, Maggie, love. I'd sooner get on a bus and go to Roman Road than shop in Green Street market, and that's just round the corner.'

'But do you, though?'

'Every other Saturday, love. I meet up with my neighbours there as well. Don't see much of them in the turning, mind. So that'll tell you. More stalls up there, I expect that's why everyone loves it so much. And a pie-and-mash shop. Cafés, even.'

'So,' said Rita, cutting her mother off, 'you're gonna go to Islington instead. Fair enough. I'll come wiv yer and we can make a success of that. Tony can run the fish-and-chip shop with one of 'is bruvvers.' She raised an eyebrow and smiled. 'Suits me.'

'I think it *would* be better if Rita was to lodge with you instead of that young man of yours,' said Eileen, coming in with their cocoa. 'I don't think you can trust a man not to want to get his leg over.'

Both Maggie and Rita were stunned by Eileen's passing remark, coming as it did from someone who was usually very proper and went to church one Sunday in every month. Barely aware of their reaction, Eileen continued without blinking an eye. 'Most men think with their candy stick. You keep to your original plans, love, and don't let 'im bulldoze you into anything. They're like that. Give them the steering wheel and you'll be in a dead-end road fighting for your self-respect within seconds. Dirty bastards.'

Chuckling, Rita was enjoying this sudden change in her mother. She had never heard Eileen swear or use rude words before.

'He made a big mistake when He modelled a man. He should have put their dicks where we could see them. Hiding them away under their trousers like that . . .' Cool as you like, she turned to Maggie and said, 'Help yourself to a sandwich, love, or a butterfly cake.'

Watching Eileen at the small dining table, delicately nibbling a sandwich, the girls looked at each other in disbelief. Having the floor to herself, without her morose husband sneering at her, Rita's mother continued, her voice very matter-of-fact, 'God knows why He formed men the way He did – it's a mystery to me. You'd have thought He would have made them more appealing. They fart, they burp, they pee in the corner of the garden when they can't be bothered to come inside and climb the stairs. And they have pubic hair growing on their face and call it a beard, as if it was something to be proud of. I ask you. Who wouldn't be relieved to have got rid of one of them? I shall padlock the front and back door. I'm not having that slimy devil creeping back in when I'm out.'

'All right, Mum,' said Rita, 'that's enough. You're embarrassing Maggie.'

'No she's not! I'm enjoying this.'

'And as for company,' Eileen continued, 'well! I'd

rather see a hippo sitting in that chair than the man I married. Moan, moan, moan. Mention something just because you're bored to death and want a little bit of conversation and he'd find something to criticise in it. Never had a good word to say about anyone. Thank God he's gone.' A smile crept on to her face. 'Freedom is the best gift of all.'

The room fell quiet, the girls not looking at each other for fear of laughing. Looking radiantly happy, Eileen was obviously enjoying herself. She was positively glowing as she said, 'You wait till that woman sees the colour of 'is long johns when he takes 'em off. He always put clean on when he went round there and yet here he leaves them lying on 'is bedroom floor, skid marks up.'

'Sounds like you're better off without him, then, Eileen.' Maggie chuckled. 'What made him go in the end, then?'

'A few strips of Elastoplast. I could hear the snoring through the walls of my little bedroom. Rita never, of course. Out like a light once her head hits the pillow. I went in to give him a shaking and that's when it happened. There he was, lying on his back, the smell of beer in the room, his mouth wide open and out for the count. So I went and got the reel of plaster and a pair of scissors and taped up his dick. He never felt a thing. Then I went back to bed. Ten minutes later he was screaming. Silly git woke up and tried to pull the plaster off.'

The room filled with laughter. Eileen relished the image of her husband coiled in pain at the top of the stairs. 'Thank God I won't have to look at his bleary eyes no more. Rita thought he'd kicked a toe in the dark at the time, so I let her believe it. If I hadn't of thrown the little bolt on my bedroom door I swear he would have come in and bashed me. Thank God he's gone and I'm free. Free to do what I like. I'll keep my little job on once I've moved out.'

'It's not a little job, Eileen. It's full time,' said Maggie. 'I don't know where you get the energy from to bake and keep this house so clean and tidy on your day off.'

'Half-day off. I went in this morning.'

Rita leaned forward and peered into her mother's face. 'You're wearing make-up. And you've 'ad your curlers in.'

'See what I mean, Maggie? I went out this morning looking like this. And she hasn't noticed till now. Even she started to see me as invisible. I could have been a model once upon a time. I was asked to sit for a photographer who took pictures for an advertising company. I was too shy to do it. Not now, though. I'd do it now, except I'm too old.'

'You're only forty-three, Mum. That's not old.'

'I know it's not. You don't have to tell me that. It's too old to be a model but it's not too old to go out dancing again. And that's what I shall be doing. Anyway . . . enough about me. It's you I'm worried about, Maggie.'

'Well, you needn't. If Rita really means what she said it could all work out.'

'I did mean it. I'd love to live in Islington for a

while. I'll help you run the café and we'll share the flat till you've had the baby and got married.'

'It takes more than two people to run a restaurant,' said Eileen. 'And what with Maggie's condition . . .'

'Café,' said Rita. 'It's a cafe that serves some hot food at lunchtimes.'

'But what about the commercial course you're taking at evening classes, Reet?'

'There'll be evening classes in North London. It's a big world out there, you know. I'm fed up with working in that library in any case. Stuffy place.'

'Well . . .' said Eileen, cupping her face thoughtfully. 'If you did leave, Rita, I could do your work in the library, no trouble. I'm sick of polishing and cleaning.'

'Good idea. You've got a brain – you should use it. I've told you enough times.'

'I intend to, Rita, I intend to. Especially now that I've had such a good result. I thought that plaster idea was very clever of me. And it was. Saw that mean old bugger off.'

'You should 'ave done it sooner,' said Rita, sipping her cocoa.

'I know. Ne'er mind. He's gone now.'

'So it could all work out all right,' said Maggie, pensively. 'It really could.'

'Anything can be worked out, love,' said Eileen. 'If anyone's realised that, I have. Look at me. At my age. They say life begins at forty and I do believe it does.'

Touched by Eileen's hope for the future and with her own situation in mind, Maggie chose her next words carefully. 'Do you ever look back, Eileen, to when you first met your 'usband . . . and see 'im as he was then? When you were in love?'

'Not any more. I used to but it made me cry, so I tried my best to push it out of my mind. Then, over the years, I didn't even want it in my mind. The man I fell in love with and married died a long time ago.'

'Oh, don't talk wet. 'Course he didn't die.'

'Yes he did, Rita, love. To me anyway. He changed bit by bit until I used to look at him and say to myself, Where are you, John? Where's that lovely man I once loved so much?'

'Did something particular happen to cause the change?' asked Maggie, moved by the confession.

'No. Not that I can think of. Perhaps he was in love with another woman – not the tart, but someone else in the early days of our marriage – and felt trapped with me. I don't know. I think he just changed, though, looking back. They say some people do.'

'That's right, Mum,' murmured Rita, 'and so will you now. Now that you're free. You don't have to be lonely or unhappy any more. He's gone and you can live a bit.'

'And if you don't mind my throwing in my penn'orth, Eileen, I think you deserve a better life than you've had,' said Maggie.

'Oh, I know that, love. It's a bit late in the day, but I know that now.' She sighed and then said, 'So if you and Rita live above the café and run it, what will your young man do?'

'It's obvious, Mum,' said Rita. 'He'll run the one in Roman Road with his brother or cousin or whoever.'

'And the customers will see Tony coming and going when he visits and so no one will wonder where your husband is. You wear a wedding ring and they'll all presume you're a young married woman. You look old enough these days to be married, so that should be all right.'

'So you think it could work, Eileen?'

'I think so. Yes. If you keep it simple it could work.'

'Thank God I came round. My mind feels a lot clearer now.' Maggie sat back in her chair and smiled. 'Mum's gonna stuff a cushion inside her clothes and pretend she's the one who's pregnant. The wedding's gonna be brought forward especially. If Dennis agrees, that is.'

'What?' said Rita. 'You are joking? That is a joke?'

'Why?' Eileen could see no fault in it. 'Locally, the baby'll be thought to be Edie's. Brought up by her own daughter instead of herself. I've known that to be the case, and more than once. Who thought of that?'

'Aunt Naomi.'

'Well, good for her. The older you get the wiser you are. What about that lad's family? Will they agree to all this?'

'They'll have to. And anyway, it'll only be temporary,' said Maggie. 'Once me and Tony get married we'll bring the baby up ourselves. I'll go back to have the baby at Mum's and stop there for a month or so.

Then Mum can pretend she's ill and that I've taken the baby to look after until she feels better. Mum and Dennis'll probably get married then.'

'I think it's a brilliant idea,' said Rita.

'I don't know what Tony's gonna make of it. We were looking forward to spending a bit of time together in that flat. It looks lovely now they've decorated and furnished it.'

'We're only talking about six months at the most,' said Rita. 'By the time you're married your flat in Islington will 'ave been done up, the way Tony and 'is brothers get on with things. They don't let the grass grow, do they? This time next year you'll be used to wearing a pinny and cooking a Sunday dinner. And doing all the washing up.'

'That's true.' The stars were back in Maggie's eyes. 'But would you really be prepared to give up your job and work in a café, Reet?'

'I said so, didn't I? There's nothing around here for me. Mum won't even be living in this neck of the woods soon, will she? And once you and Tony are living in Islington I'll be off somewhere else. In a bedsit all of my own in Soho.' She grinned. 'They say the business is good there. Better than in Aldgate. Better class of men. Richer.'

Rita had never been out of the East End of London except for window-shopping expeditions or visits to Holborn to see her sister and brother-in-law. This new adventure was a big step for her, and only the beginning to her mind. Like Maggie, she had been brought up in different circumstances to most of their schoolmates – without a father to lay down the ground rules and look after their welfare, or simply to be a loving, caring dad. Of course, Rita's father had been there in the flesh, but not in spirit. And whether either of the girls knew it or not, this gap in their lives did tend to make a difference to their relationships with their peers.

Years of wearing a brace on her teeth and National Health glasses had all but crushed Maggie's self-confidence. In contrast Rita, with her feisty spirit, had always been seen in the classroom as someone to be respected, but not necessarily someone to play with. And later, once she was in senior school, the boys had found her to be an intimidating character and not someone to mess with. This also affected the way the girls behaved towards her, because all they wanted to do once they had arrived in their teens was impress the boys, not frighten them off.

The doorbell intruded into all their thoughts. Without saying a word Eileen strolled out of the room to answer it, leaving Maggie and Rita to speak more freely. Maggie was not slow off the mark. In a low voice she said, 'Reet, what about if people ask where my husband is? I'll be showing more and more as time goes on.'

'You're showing now, Mags. Anyway, why should you care? You put a couple of big photographs of Tony on the wall and point at them. Don't forget he'll be coming and going while we're there and anyway, not everyone works in the area where they live. It's what buses and trains are for.'

'But he won't be living above in the flat with me if you are. Don't you reckon that would look a bit odd?'

'No one'll know! How many people do you think will give a soddin' toss anyway? All that people go into a café or restaurant for is to eat, drink and have a chat with their friends or family who they've come in wiv. All they'll want from us is to get their meals on the table as soon as we can. And what do you think anyone's gonna do? Sneak up to the rooms above the café once we've closed to see if there's a husband there or not? Silly arse. They've got other things to think about.'

'All right, you've made your point. Now shut up.' Maggie smiled. 'Do you really mean it, though, Reet? Would you give up your job and everything? Because if you would, this has got to be the answer.'

''Course I will. I don't know why you never thought of it before. I'd love it. Me and you in Islington, sharing a flat, no parents around, and running a café between us. Lovely. I'll phone Islington Council on Monday from the library and find out about evening classes. And then I'll book in for the spring term. That way you won't be able to change your mind again for fear of ruining my career – will yer?'

'I wouldn't change my mind, Reet, 'cos there's really not a better choice than this one.'

'Well, there you are, then. That's you and my mother sorted out. What a difference in her, eh? I've been telling 'er for years to get rid of 'im. He made her feel as if she wasn't cut out for anything other than scrubbing floors. She wasn't always a cleaner, you know. Before she got married she worked in Moorgate doing clerical work in an office for a print firm. Bit of a Girl Friday, but from what she told me she loved it. Then she met him, got pregnant, got married, and that was it. Everyfing changed. There's a message for all of us.'

'That's not gonna happen to me, if that's what you're hinting at. Tony's a good person. I know we're too young for all this but we're both strong-willed. We'll make it work if nuffing else but to prove to everyone how much we love each other.'

'Good. 'Cos that's what you're gonna need. Bringing up a baby's not gonna be easy – even if your mum does help you take care of it at first.'

'I know.'

'So long as you don't forget.' Then, cocking an ear, Rita listened for voices out in the passage. 'Mum's in the front room with Mr Browning. I think a little romance might be blooming.'

'You're joking,' whispered Maggie. 'Him and your mum? Never.'

'He's all right. Just needed a friend, that's all. And he's found more than one now he's involved in the tea dances.' Rita pulled a packet of five Woodbines from her skirt pocket. 'I'll tell you what, though – she'll be putting the changes to 'im now. I bet you she's telling 'im that I need to leave and that she could do my job. And she'll get it as well.'

'I can't believe the way she's changed, Reet. You sure she's all right? I mean . . . this new mood of hers might be a cover-up. She might be unhappy under-neath 'cos your dad's left 'er.'

Laughing, Rita called her a silly cow and told her that her mother had not become a new person – it was simply that her old self had come up for air and her confidence was back. 'I'll tell you when her life took a turn,' she said, putting a match to the cigar-ette between her lips. 'When you put 'er name forward for the cleaning job. She won't ever forget that, Maggie.'

'Oh. I can't be that much of a drip, then, can I?'

'Well . . . that's a matter of opinion.' Rita drew on her cigarette and then held it in front of her. 'She don't even mind that I smoke in front of 'er now. It's as if a monster that was weighing 'er down 'as gone from her shoulder. I s'pose you want one of these.'

'No. I'd best stop smoking until this baby of mine is born. Did I tell you I felt it kicking?'

'Silly cow. It's probably not even formed yet.' Rita rolled her eyes and puffed at her cigarette. 'You worry me at times.'

'Reet – I'm five months. The baby's due towards the end of March. Right?'

'Bloody 'ell. *That* soon?'

'Yes.'

'So it could be moving, then?' She stared at Maggie's stomach. 'Or it could be wind. You're not fat enough to be that far gone. You sure that's not one great big bubble of air in there?'

'Reet, that's horrible. You say things like that and I won't let you be a godmother.'

'Oh . . . I never knew I was gonna be one.' Rita's face lit up at the thought of it. 'You never asked me.'

'I took it as read. And you'd better make a good job of it as well.'

Rita leaned back in her chair, just a faint smile on her face now. 'If you say so. A godmother, eh? I'm a bit on the young side, but yeah . . . I think I'd make sure you look after that baby properly and take her to Sunday school and that.'

'Her?' said Maggie.

'Yeah. You don't think you're carrying a boy, do yer? No. That's a little girl in there who can't wait to come out and see what we look like. She can hear us talking. My aunt knows about these things. She worked on the maternity ward at the London for years. Yep. I'd put a bet on that being a little girl with hazel eyes and red curly hair . . . and freckles . . . and wearing glasses and a brace on her teeth.'

'You're bonkers.' Maggie laughed, beginning to look forward to the new life ahead of her. It no longer seemed like a huge problem to be pregnant but rather something to be enjoyed – a problem still, but not huge, and certainly not unbearable. As far as she could tell, this new set-up, her and Rita sharing in Islington and herself wearing a wedding ring, with Tony coming and going, would work beautifully.

Eileen's talk of moving out of the area, being rid of her husband and new friendships, and her posi- tive attitude, somehow made Maggie's problems fade into pale insignificance. She was expecting a baby. It was not the end of the world but the beginning of a new chapter in her young life. And if Eileen, now in her middle age, could turn her life around, and with such gusto, so could Maggie.

All this was going through her mind on her way back to Scott House. When she arrived to find Edie and Dennis in the sitting room, quietly talking, she felt sure they had discussed things and he had agreed to the arrangements. In fact Dennis had returned to Edie to make amends. Edie, still troubled and wary, listened as he explained again why it was best they didn't live in his house.

Greeted by a warm smile from Edie and a fatherly wink from Dennis, Maggie asked whether either of them would like a cup of tea. They declined – each of them was nursing a glass of light ale. As Maggie turned away to leave the room, the smile on Dennis's face momentarily dissolved. Aware of this, and also feeling him tense up a little, Edie said, 'She looks well, don't you think?'

'Depends on how you look at it,' he said, shrugging. 'She still looks like a little girl from where I'm sitting. You should 'ave kept a closer eye on her, Edie.'

'Keep your voice down if you're gonna say things like that!' Edie whispered, annoyed.

'She can't hear me. These walls are thick.' He looked around the room, oblivious to her anxiety. 'You're lucky the plans for this estate were on the table before the war and that it was delayed till after it was over. You wait and see . . . new estates similar to these'll be popping up all over the place in the next ten years. They'll be built like egg boxes, though.

Speed and economy'll be the priority now. What with the cost of the bloody war and the thousands who've been made homeless.'

'Why did you say that, Dennis? About Maggie being a girl?' Still Edie's voice was no more than a whisper.

'Because she is. Face facts, Edie, and stop living in cloud-cuckoo-land. You've got a lot on your plate and it can only get worse once she's had the kid.'

'Kid? You're talking about my grandchild.'

'You know what I mean. Stop being touchy. This word, that word ... what difference does it make, babe? At the end of the day she's pregnant at fifteen. Good job there are no grandparents alive. They'd be disgusted.'

'There is a grandparent alive, Den. My dad.'

'Yeah,' he said, chuckling. 'And a million miles away from home. Don't forget, he's already got grand-children, from what you told me. Your stepbrother's. And all nice and respectable. Your dad won't come rushing back to play the old-fashioned grandfather, Edie. Face facts.'

Hurt by the way he was putting Maggie down, she withdrew her arm from his and then said, 'He won't know anyway.'

'Oh? You're not gonna write to him, then? I thought you was pleased that he came back and found you?'

'I'll write to 'im once the baby's here. But I won't say it's Maggie's baby – I'll say it's mine. Ours.'

'Whoa!' said Dennis, putting up a hand. 'Slow

down, darling.' He studied her face. 'Is this set in concrete, then?'

'It was an option from the start but I didn't want to do it then – now I do. You're right. She'll get nasty comments if I don't do this for her.'

'Did I say that?'

'Not in so many words, but yeah.'

Dennis became thoughtful. 'It's all a bit sudden for me, Edie, babe. I'm not saying I wouldn't go along with it but . . . it's a bit much to ask of me.'

'Not if you love us both. Me and Maggie. Because you do, don't you?'

Looking decidedly on edge, Dennis, shuffled in his seat and loosened his tie. 'I think the world of both of you, 'course I do. But for you to be walking around looking like you're pregnant – it takes a bit more thinking about. Take time to consider it properly is all I'm thinking.'

Seeing her fiancé in a new light, Edie felt herself go cold. There was no mistaking the fact that he was hot under the collar. 'It won't interfere with us, Den. We'll still be living here by ourselves, or in your little house, until the baby comes. And then we'll only be its foster parents for a couple of months while she's living with us and then she'll take it back with her to Islington. The gossips will have something to chew over but I don't care. I won't be the only one to be pregnant before I've got married.'

'But you won't be pregnant, Edie!' he snapped, 'Maggie will.'

'But they won't *know* that, will they? That's the

whole *point*. And who cares about gossips?'

'Not me, babe. I don't even waste my time thinking about that kind of thing,' he grinned, looking at his wrist watch. 'But I don't like the idea of living a sham. Walking about with padding and saying that we're expecting a baby? It's bloody madness.'

'Why?'

'Why? You ask me why?' he said, showing a frown. 'Because I prefer to live a normal existence that's why. I want us to be an ordinary couple that goes about their business. I don't wanna be in the limelight. It's barmy. Just like the one who came up with this idea in the first place. Your Aunt Naomi?'

'As it happens . . . yes. But I never listened at first, did I? I needed time to take it in, I s'pose. I think it's clever.'

'Well you should 'ave asked me first. It might be a different story now if you had of done.'

'I did. Earlier on. But if you don't want to go along with it now, say so.'

'I've got to get my head round it, that's all. Don't forget I'm used to being independent – living on my own. Now I'm surrounded by women. If it's not your Aunt Naomi it's your friends coming and going. And now this with Maggie.' He shook his head, as if he were trying to shake the whole problem away.

'You can stay in your house in Bow if you feel more comfortable with that. It won't be the first time I've had a baby without the father around. I could have been telling lies about Maggie's dad being missing during the war.'

'I don't want you to get too used to the idea, that's all,' said Dennis, full of his own thoughts. 'In case Maggie changes her mind and messes all of us up.' He sighed and added, 'I'd best be going. I'm expecting a bloke round the flat to give me a price on plastering a wall that's scruffy.' He rose from the sofa urgent to be away.

'Are you? Why? That's the landlord's responsibility, surely?'

'Landlords – they'd let you live in a pigsty rather than put their hand in their pocket. I'd rather pay out and get it done myself. Shouldn't cost much.' He leaned across, brushed a kiss across her cheek and stood up. 'Don't get up, babe. I'll see myself out.' His slamming of the street door gave Edie a deliberate message. This time he would not be back. She heard it and dismissed it.

Leaving Maggie in the kitchen having a fry-up Edie went upstairs to see her friend Jessie. She was upset and confused as to what Dennis was making of everything and unsure whether he was here to stay or would be gone tomorrow. The odd thing was that she was more irritated than emotional about it, and this puzzled her. As for his house in Bow and his profession, she still had nagging doubts. An inner voice was telling her to be careful, to put up her guard, not to let him make a fool of her the way Harry had. She was beginning to think that all men might be the same underneath – selfish when it came to their personal welfare.

And now, as she stood on Jessie's doorstep, she

asked herself why she was here, but didn't want to
face the truth – that she needed someone she could
trust to tell her what was right. She wanted a second
opinion on everything Dennis had said to her about
his rented house which she had never been invited
to. More than anything, right then Edie wanted to be
in somewhere where everything was even and normal.
Too much had happened too suddenly of late, and
now her stomach was churning as if something even
worse were on the horizon, waiting to swamp her.
She knocked on Jessie's door and realised that her
hands were trembling.

When Jessie came to the door, her face drawn and
with a look of desperation in her eyes, she peered at
Edie as if she hardly knew her. And then her expression changed to one of puzzlement, as if she were
waiting for Edie to tell her what to do. Something
was wrong.

'Jess? What's happened?' said Edie in a childlike,
frightened voice.

'Edie . . . how did you know?' There was no expression in Jessie's voice whatsoever. 'How could you
know? It's only just happened.'

'Know what, Jess? And what's only just happened?'

'I don't know how you could know. You're not on
the phone. And if you don't know . . . why have you
come up?'

'Jessie . . .' murmured Edie. 'What's wrong?'

Her voice deadpan, her eyes glazed over, Jessie continued as if she wasn't taking in anything that Edie was
saying. 'There's been a terrible accident, Ed. Really,

really bad. The fire brigade was there as well as an ambulance and the police. It's bad, Edie. Really bad.'

A chilling rush of fear shot through Edie. She could almost feel the blood drain from her face. 'Darling, who? Who's had an accident? One of your family? Is that it, Jess?'

Still Jessie did not move from the doorway. 'The firemen had to get him out of the car. They had to break the passenger door off to get him out.'

'Get who out, Jess? Who was in the car?'

'Max. They had to pull off the door to get him out because he was trapped by the steering wheel. The car went into the back of a lorry. It's bad, Jess. Really, really bad. They took him to the London Hospital. Unconscious. I don't know what to do, Edie. Should I go to the hospital? I didn't know who to phone so I phoned Emmie. She's coming over with Tom . . . I think.'

Gently pulling her friend's hand from the door latch, Edie eased her into the passage and then pushed the door shut with her foot. 'I think you need a cup of sweet tea, Jess.' With one arm around her friend, she guided Jessie into the kitchen and then eased her into a chair. 'Just sit there for a minute and don't try and talk.'

In a daze herself, Edie went to check on the children. Billy was lying flat on his back on his bed, his arms behind his head, staring up at the ceiling. She closed his door quietly and went into Emma-Rose's room to find her curled in a corner, clutching her old black-and-white panda.

'Are you all right, sweetheart?' she said.

Emma nodded slowly and then said, 'Mummy's crying.'

'I know, darling, but I'm here now. Everything'll be all right. You'll see. Your dad's coming with your gran.' She quietly closed the door and went back into the kitchen, trembling.

Jessie, staring down at the floor and in deep shock, was silent. Kneeling before her friend, Edie took her cold, trembling hands in hers. 'Darling, I don't know what to say to you. Are you sure that it's Max we're talking about?'

Slowly raising her eyes, Jessie looked blankly at Edie. She opened her mouth to say something but could not get the words out. She lowered her head again and simply repeated, 'It's bad, Jess. Really bad.'

'Do you want me to send for your sister Dolly?'

Jessie pinched her lips together. 'Poor Max. He never harmed a fly. It shouldn't be him, Edie. Not Max. Not my Max. He wasn't doing anything wrong. He's a careful driver. Why did it have to happen to him? He's the kindest, nicest person I've ever met.'

'I know that, Jess. Of course I do. But sometimes these things look much blacker than what they are. And he's in the best place. The London Hospital. The best specialists and surgeons in the world are there.'

'I think he's gone, Edie. I think he's gone. I don't think Max is alive any more.'

'Is that what they told you on the phone? Try to think, Jess. What did they say?'

'The police telephoned me. They said I should get

to the hospital straight away if I wanted to see him. I don't know what they meant by that but it sounded bad. Really bad.'

Edie, had to draw on all her reserves of will-power not to cry. She glanced at Jessie again and saw nothing in her face and there was clearly nothing she could say to make any of this any better. Tragedy had struck.

'He won't die, will he, Edie? If he is alive he won't die before I get there, will he?'

'No, darling, I'm sure not. It's bound to have sounded much worse hearing it over the telephone. He's probably being fussed over by a pretty nurse. You mustn't think—'

The shrill sound of the telephone made both women go cold. 'Shall I get it?' said Edie, frightened. 'Do you want me to answer it?'

'Yes please,' said Jessie, hugging herself, and then she repeated, over and over, 'Please God . . . let him be all right. Please let him be all right.'

When Edie came back into the room, her lips pinched together and tears in her eyes, she could hardly speak, but Jessie was looking at her, waiting. 'Jess . . . I'm so sorry . . . I am so sorry, darling, but Max . . . Max had a heart attack while he was driving. He wouldn't have known anything about it.'

'What do you mean, Edie? He wouldn't have known anything about it? Of course he would. It would hurt. He must be in pain. Surely?'

'Jessie . . .'

'They've made a mistake. The police told me on the phone that Max had been in a car crash – that's all. They never said anything about a heart attack. So it must be a mix-up.'

'No, Jess, it's not. That was someone from the hospital. They couldn't revive Max. He was already gone by the time he arrived there. It was a heart attack, Jess. The heart attack caused him to crash into the back of the parked lorry.'

'No it never. They've made a mistake. They've got it wrong. Max is a fighter. And he's strong. He wouldn't just keel over and die. He's too stubborn for that. Phone them back. Give 'em the sharp end of your tongue. Tell them that the nurse who gave you the message made a mistake. You said so yourself. He'll be all right. He's strong. And a fighter. He'll be all right.'

The sound of the doorbell was a great relief to Edie. Someone had come. Someone would help her with this. Someone would make sense of it all. Not minding the warm tears trickling down her own face, she went to answer the door to find Jessie's ex-husband Tom and her mother-in-law, Emmie, standing there. Taking one look at the expression on her face, they knew that the worst had happened. 'The hospital just phoned,' said Edie, 'Max has passed away.'

'Oh Christ . . .' said Tom, his eyes clenched tight.

Emmie, silent and serious, brushed passed Edie and went to Jessie. This was going to be a trying time for everyone. This had not been a long illness that had reached a sad end but a sudden bolt from the blue, a tragic and fatal heart attack.

★   ★   ★

Weeks later, with the funeral behind her, Jessie was alone in her flat, forcing herself to do what she had been putting off – the painful business of going through her and Max's wardrobe, cupboard and tallboy, removing his clothes and personal belongings to pack them into boxes for the Red Cross. She had chosen a weekday for this very difficult and emotional task so that both Billy and Emma-Rose would be at school.

In a calm and resolute mood, she was carefully folding everything as if she were packing the clothes ready for Max to embark on a long journey. To the sound of the wireless in the background, she worked without emotion, as if she were a robot. It wasn't until she pulled open the bottom drawer of the chest and saw his socks rolled up in neat balls that she felt as if a hand had suddenly grabbed her heart and was squeezing it tighter and tighter.

Already on her knees, she sank back and clutched a pair of odd socks, one brown and one black, which had been rolled up together until the matching two turned up under the bed or in the corner of a cupboard. Unrolling them, she held one in each hand and smiled as tears rolled gently down her face, remembering how he had often searched for the missing half of a pair. Max had been precise about everything other than his socks, which had always been the last item of clothing he removed at night, after his pyjamas were on. 'Cold feet, Jess,' he would say as he slipped in beside her, 'I've got cold feet all the time.'

'I don't know what to do . . .' Jessie murmured, as if he were there, in the empty room with her. 'If I throw them away and then find the matching socks, you wouldn't like that.' Then, gazing at them, she spoke for Max. 'Put them in with the rest, Jessie. Stop being sentimental. It won't get the job done.'

'I can't throw them away,' she said quietly after a moment, crying. 'I can't. You wore these, Max. These were on your feet. I can't throw them away. I can't . . .'

She rocked slowly to and fro on her knees, clutching a sock in each hand. 'It's not fair,' she whispered. 'It's not fair that you were taken before you'd achieved your dream. It was cruel of God to let that happen. Really cruel. And I'll never, never forgive Him. Never.'

The doorbell rang but she ignored it. She didn't care who was on her doorstep. She didn't want to see anyone. She didn't need to see anyone. She was getting things back to normal by herself. But whoever it was was determined and for no other reason than to stop the shrill ringing of the bell, still clutching Max's socks in her hands, she left the bedroom, went down the passage and opened the door to see Tom standing there, his arms folded, defiant.

'You can't hide away from the world for the rest of your life, Jessie, so nip it in the bud now,' he said, his foot positioned to serve as a stop should she try to close the door in his face. 'And I know Max was a Jew but he never scrimped on electricity. Turn the bloody lights on.'

'It's daytime,' murmured Jessie, gazing into Tom's taut face. 'I don't want the lights on.'

'It might be daytime but it's winter.' He flicked a switch and turned on the lights as he strolled past her into the flat. 'The sun might be shining in through the back windows but it's like the black hole of Calcutta in the passage.'

'What d'you expect if there's no windows?' said Jessie, following him into her kitchen.

'Electricity. One light bulb on in the daytime won't break the bank.' Tom dropped into a kitchen chair and looked from Jessie to the kettle on the stove. 'I don't s'pose there's a chance of a cup of tea?'

'Why 'ave you come round, Tom?'

'Mum told me to. Said you was 'iding away from reality.'

'Liar. She wouldn't say that.'

'She's worried about you, Jessie. Ain't that enough? She asked me to check if you was all right. I'll go once I've had a cup of tea. Kids all right, are they? About Max not being around any more?'

'No, as it happens, they're not. They miss him. He was good with them. Of course they miss 'im. It's understandable.'

'Which is exactly why you should pull yourself together. Skulking around in the dark hugging his socks. It'll be the straitjacket for you if you're not careful.' He glanced up at her face to check her reaction to his no-nonsense talking. She seemed OK. 'I think you should let both the kids help out with the opening of the club. Take their minds off gloomy things.'

'Such as?'

'You walking around holding Max's bits and pieces in your hands.'

'Actually, I was clearing his clothes into bags for the Red Cross, if you must know.'

'Oh,' murmured Tom, casting his eyes down. 'I didn't know that, did I.' He leaned back in his chair, his face tense. 'But it's good that you're doing that. It can't be easy.'

'It's not, Tom,' said Jessie, gazing into his face. 'It's not easy. So if you could manage it, I'd appreciate a little bit of charity myself. Be nice to me . . . please.'

'All right. Point taken. I came in like a bull in a china shop. I'm sorry.' He raised his eyes to meet hers and felt an old pain resurface. 'Do you want me to sort 'is clothes out for you?'

Jessie thought for a moment. 'Actually . . . I think I would. They're all going to the same place. The Red Cross. I don't want to keep any of it. I don't want to be reminded. I'm not being hard or anything like that. I just don't want mementoes all over the place. I want to forget how it was and get on with how it is now. Now that he's gone. It's too painful otherwise.'

'I know, I know,' said Tom, finding all of this hard to take. 'I'll 'ave everything cleared . . . once I've had a cup of tea and a smoke.'

'I'd really appreciate that,' said Jessie. 'He's gone now and nothing will bring him back, will it? I've got to face that. I've got to face that and get on with my life.'

'Well, don't expect it to be easy. It's not. I should know.'

'Should you?' said Jessie. 'You never lost someone you loved, did you?'

'Only my brother, that's all. Call me when the tea's poured out. I'll go and get on with packing Max's things. I wouldn't mind a sandwich, if that's not too much to ask.'

Once he'd gone from the kitchen, Jessie felt a touch guilty. She had forgotten about Tom's brother being killed in the war. Pulling a sliced loaf from the bread bin, she brought Johnnie's face to mind. His gentle, smiling face. All three of Emmie's sons were so different from each other. Tom's voice cut through her thoughts as he came back into the room. 'Am I allowed to keep one of his ties, Jessie?'

Turning slowly around, tearful again, she looked into her husband's face and then shrugged, avoiding his eyes. 'Do whatever you want, Tom. I really don't mind. And neither would Max – if he was here. Wear it for the tea dance. He'd see the humour in that . . . from wherever he is.'

'No, I won't go that far,' he said, before venturing a smile. 'He might come down and pull the knot too tight.'

'Max wasn't like that, Tom. How could you say such a thing—'

'Oh, for Christ's sake, Jessie! Lighten up a bit! It's over a month since the funeral. Pull yourself together. For the kids if nothing else.' Turning his back on her, he stared out of the kitchen window, and then said,

'Mum wants you to go round and go through the list of stuff she's baked for the dance—'

'I'm hoping to go round tomorrow—'

'She needs to know who's taking what. Pickles and all that sort of thing. She asked me to tell you to go round. She's not getting any younger. She could do with a bit of support—'

'I said I'd go round tomorrow, Tom. Don't start.'

'It was you who roped 'er into the club in the first place. And she needs to see you. Mum and Dad thought a lot of Max.'

'I know that.' She lifted her face and offered a faint smile. 'Maybe I'll go round before the kids get in from school,' she said, glancing at the clock. 'If there's time.'

'I'll stop till you get back. And I'll 'ave all Max's things packed up and loaded into the van. I'll drop 'em at the Red Cross tomorrer on the way to work. Mum's in all afternoon so you could go once you've drunk your tea.'

Jessie shrugged. She could see no harm in Tom being in her home by himself. It seemed strange but harmless . . . and she did like the idea of a nice walk all by herself. 'All right. I could do with a bit of fresh air. Thanks.'

'You don't 'ave to thank me, Jessie. Billy and Emma are my kids. Whether I look after 'em here in your flat or at Mum's or up in Norfolk shouldn't make any difference. The contract's gone through, by the way. One week and the cottages'll be mine and Stanley's. By the time spring comes round we'll 'ave one of 'em finished. You could spend a weekend up there with Dolly and the kids.'

'I don't want to think about the spring, Tom. Or Elmshill. I won't be going. You can take the kids, though. It's too soon to think about stuff like that.' She turned her back to him and covered her face with her hands. 'Go and see to Max's things for me, Tom.'

'Jess . . .'

'Please, Tom. Don't say any more. Just do what you said you'd do for me. That's more than enough.'

Placing a hand on her shoulder, he caught the familiar scent of the shampoo she used. 'I'm sorry, Jess. Really sorry. He was a good bloke. Pinched you from under my nose but that only proved one thing in the end. He had good taste as well as two left feet.' With that, Tom turned and walked back into the bedroom, leaving Jessie to gaze after him. So much had happened in such a short time it was too much to take in. Much too much.

By the time of the meticulously planned opening dance of the new club, Maggie had settled to the idea of living in Islington. Even though the flat had not been fully decorated in time for her to move in with Rita, between Edie, Naomi and Eileen they had it spick and span. All the paintwork, once the grime had been cleaned off, had been brought back to its original colour of pale green with the aid of sugar soap. The lined cotton curtains, once filthy and faded, had been washed and pressed and looked quite different compared to when Maggie first walked into the flat. Two single Victorian brass beds, which had belonged to an old Italian aunt, had been polished lovingly and almost brought back to their former glory. The small kitchen cum dining area sported a colourful new rag mat which stood out against the scrubbed black-and-white linoleum. On the living-room walls, Tony had rehung the two richly coloured woven wall rugs which his grandmother had given them. The small carved table, which had been placed in the centre of the small room, held the small vase in which Tony had placed yet another single red rose for Maggie. The highly polished old brass lamp with its white glass shade had also been brought over from the Roman Road flat and fitted nicely on a wide bookshelf.

Having shared the apartment for a week or so, Maggie and Rita were really enjoying their spell of independence and gradually learning the ropes in terms of how the café was run from one of Tony's aunts and a cousin, who, like the rest of his family, were relieved that he was not living above in sin with Maggie. Being responsible for getting a girl of fifteen pregnant was one thing, but living with her, especially since she was under age, would have been too much. This new arrangement had everyone sighing with relief.

During the busy hour or so before the office workers came in for their lunch, Maggie stood behind the serving counter, slicing cheese, tomatoes, cucumbers and other fillings for takeaway sandwiches. This part of Islington bustled with people going to and from work in the local factories, shops and office blocks.

Even though Maggie was clearly expecting a baby, there had been no question as far as she was concerned of her not helping out with arrangements for the opening night of the tea dance club. Tony, however, had had to be whipped into action by his parents, who had also become members.

And now, while Maggie and Rita reclined on top of their beds in the comfort of the flat, reading their chosen library books, Tony was rushed off his feet in the kitchen of the church hall, which had been used for several wedding receptions and Christmas dances over the years. Many functions and dances had taken place in the building, but never had it been so lively and joyful as it was this evening. White fairy lights and colourful paper chains decorated the hall and the worn oak floor had been polished until the surface was all but perfect for the gliding feet of guests and members as they waltzed to the sound of the band playing 'White Christmas'.

In the background, trestle tables covered in white damask cloths were being laid with piles of tasty sandwiches, created by Tony, among others, in the church hall kitchen. The smell of over-fresh sausage rolls and savoury flans hung in the air. Several trays of small round cases of puff pastry filled with savoury mixtures were being brought in, along with a variety of homemade pies. Dozens of fresh bread rolls from the local baker and platefuls of buttered sliced bread were piled high on a table next to a large round cheeseboard displaying whole Cheddar and Dutch cheeses, which had not yet been cut. Hundreds of mince pies were now baking in the antiquated oven, adding to the delicious aroma.

Emerging from the kitchen, carrying a large glass jug of freshly squeezed orange juice spiced with ginger, Naomi looked stunning in her ankle-length twenties black-and-pink beaded evening gown with matching headpiece. Slightly tipsy, and incredibly happy in this atmosphere, she was delighted when Alf the Overcoat, as gracefully as he could, took the jug from her, placed it on the buffet table and urged her on to the dance floor. Although she was much older than he was, Naomi proved to be an excellent match for this rotund cockney, who led her gracefully around the floor, weaving in and out of other partners, who were also clearly enjoying themselves.

'I do so admire your aunt,' said Daphne Lightfoot as she placed a tray of iced fairy cakes on the table. 'She is so full of life.'

'I know,' said Edie, 'and she never changes. She's always been like that and she will until she takes her last breath.' She glanced at the band, and added, 'Your brother's a dark horse too. Look at him playing that saxophone. He looks completely different in his black tie. No more the serious grey librarian.'

'Oh, the *librarian* isn't the real self. At least, I don't think so. It's his work and he loves it, but there's always been another side of Mattie which needs to be nourished every so often. I can't tell you how much this new club has done for him. Truly.'

'You don't have to. I can see. Maggie tells me that Eileen's put a sparkle in his eye too.'

'Well, yes, as a matter of fact they have been seeing each other, discreetly, of course. She is a work colleague, after all's said and done.' Daphne looked across at a small table for two where Eileen was seated, close to the stage and with a good view of the band. 'She looks a bit lonely over there but I've checked to see that she's all right and she is. Quite happy by herself. She's waiting for an interval, when Mattie will join her. I believe we're to hear some recorded songs?'

'That's right. A gramophone's been brought in specially. So your brother and Rita's mum will have a chance to dance.'

'Exactly. I'm sure they're both looking forward to it.'

As the tune being played came to an end, Alf steered his partner towards them and finished by gracefully twirling Naomi into a gentle spin, at which she laughed contagiously. With a delighted sigh she sank on to a chair, euphoric but in need of a rest.

'She's an inspiration for all of us!' said Alf, mopping his brow. 'Beautiful dancer. A true professional!'

'So are you, Alf.' Edie chuckled. 'Bit of a dark horse, eh? You can't tell me you've not entered competitions.'

'As a matter of fact, Edie, my darling, I have. But that was when I was seventeen, eighteen – who's counting? Now, of course, I'm a little bit too old and a little bit too stiff.'

'You're not old, Alf. Don't give me that.'

'Forty-one next birfday, babe,' he said, turning his attention to the lady in the lovely pale blue dress he had not yet been introduced to. 'Not that I feel old, you understand.'

'Well, you certainly don't dance as if you feel old,' responded Daphne.

'Thank you, fair lady,' said Alf, bowing majestically before lifting her hand and kissing it lightly. 'Now if I'm not mistaken, the band are about to take a break. When they get back up on that stage, would you do me the honour of a dance?'

'I most certainly would.' Daphne smiled, her cheeks flushed and her soft grey eyes shining. 'Thank you for the invitation,' she added, taking a sip from her glass of sherry.

'My pleasure.' He turned to Naomi. 'I shall question you later, my darling, as to where you have been hiding this little jewel.'

'Daphne is the lady's name and she is a very good friend of mine so don't break her heart.'

'I wouldn't dream of it, sweet'eart,' he said, turning back to Daphne and giving her a smile and a wink. 'Now if you will excuse me, my glass of beer is waiting at my table.'

Laughing quietly, Daphne sat down in the chair next to Naomi. 'He's quite a character, isn't he.'

'Indeed he is – and a perfect gentleman. I believe, here in the East End, he would be known as a rough diamond. For my part I would drop the word "rough". Had he not been born and bred in these parts that particular word would never have been applicable.'

'He's very nice,' said Daphne.

'And a perfect dancing partner. Not that I would ever dream of being a matchmaker.'

'Good,' said Daphne, thoroughly enjoying herself. 'Leave us to ourselves and we shall see, shan't we.' She raised her glass of sherry to her mouth and emptied it. 'Now then . . . would you like another drink too?'

'Not at the moment, thank you. I am quite happy to sit here and watch others enjoy themselves . . . for the time being.'

Once Daphne had slipped through the crowded dance floor towards the makeshift bar, Edie joined her aunt. 'You just can't help it, can you. Match-making again.'

'Darling, they are made for each other. Not that such a thought had entered my mind before this evening. But did you feel the flow of romantic energy between Alf and Daphne?'

'No.'

'Edith. Please remember that I do know when you are not fully telling the truth.'

'Well, all right, yes, there did seem to be an instant charisma, but leave them *alone.*'

'I wouldn't dream of anything but to leave them be. Alf is a professional bachelor and Daphne a resolute spinster. If there is to be a romance it will be long and slow.' Naomi studied Edie before continuing, 'You do look every bit the woman with child. Have people asked where the father has vanished to?'

'I haven't given them the chance. I get in first, saying that Dennis did a moonlight once he knew there was a baby on the way. So there we are, he did me two favours in one by going when things got awkward for 'im. I knew he wouldn't be back Nao. I saw it in his eyes before he left the room and walked out for good. And I don't hate him for it.'

'And you are truly not heartbroken, my darling? Honestly?'

'I'm too angry with myself to hate anyone now. I was a blind fool. If I see 'im I'll smack 'im in the face, though – in front of whoever happens to be there. Just to humiliate him – that's all. I'm finished with men, Naomi, finished.'

'Yes, dear . . . of course you are.'

Slowly shaking her head, Edie left Naomi to herself and went over to the table where Jessie was sitting with her sister Dolly and her in-laws. Pulling a chair up to their table, she said, 'Naomi's on top form tonight. I hope she doesn't get too carried away and ends up drinking too much.'

'Nar . . . leave 'er be. We can always wheel 'er back 'ome on a barrow,' said Jessie's father-in-law, Charlie.

'Yeah,' said Edie, 'and singing all the way. Sooner you than me.'

'So when's your baby due?' he asked, innocent to all that was going on.

'Early spring,' said Edie, hoping to end it there.

'And the father's not been in touch, *still?*'

'Shut up, Dad, for Christ's sake,' said Tom's brother, Stanley. 'Tact never was his middle name, Edie.'

'She's better off without him,' said Dolly, giving Edie a knowing wink. 'And I reckon that once that baby's arrived young Maggie'll be all over it. Be careful she don't steal it away from you, eh, Edie?'

'Well, that wouldn't be such a bad thing, Doll, would it?'

'I should say not,' Emmie chimed in, pleased to be party to the secret. 'From what I hear she and the Italian lad are madly in love. Wouldn't surprise me if they tied the knot. All they'd need then to make it complete would be a little baby to fuss over. Yours, Edie.'

'Don't be so bloody daft,' said Charlie. 'As if she'd give it to 'er daughter.'

'As if?' said Edie. 'Too bloody right I'd hand it over to Mags if she wanted it! I've got a life to live and I don't need to be soaking napkins and feeding bottles in the night. No, if she wants to be a mum I'll opt for grandma any day.'

'And I can't say I wouldn't do the same, Edie, love. It's lovely being the grandma. You can enjoy the little sods for a day and then hand them back. Exhausting at any age, they are. Wear you out.'

'So that's what you're gonna do, then, Edie, is it?'

'Possibly, Charlie. Who knows? Who cares?'

'Only the gossips,' said Jessie. 'And moaning old men.' She gave Charlie a grin.

'Not me! I'm not moaning over it! None of my business. Do what you like, all of you. The young nowadays don't know 'ow easy they've got it.'

'Right,' said Jessie, 'come on, Edie. We've got things to do in the kitchen. Don't want to serve raw sausages later on, do we now?'

'Well . . . it looks like they're gonna play some

records, Jess. Fancy a bit of rock and roll, do yer? The sausages will keep.'

'Rock and roll? In your condition!' Charlie shook his head. The way women behaved nowadays was a puzzle to him. He was relieved when he heard the introduction to the song on the turntable. It was hardly rock and roll. 'Ah . . . thank gawd for that . . .' The Four Aces and 'Heart and Soul' sang out. 'Lovely.' Looking up, he saw Tom come into the hall. 'Come on, then, Jess – there's still life in the old bones. Let's 'ave a little waltz.'

Jessie was pleased he had asked. The few drinks Charlie had plied her with had relaxed her enough to allow her to forget her misery. With no inkling that Tom was in the hall, she was happy to waltz around the floor with her father-in-law as if he were her very own prince charming. And as for Tom – he could not take his eyes off his wife, with whom he was still very much in love. On the day that Jessie had taken the children to Emmie and Charlie's house, when Billy had seen what he considered to be a flying saucer, Tom had spruced himself up and splashed on Old Spice – purely for Jessie. But she had not seen it that way. She had believed that there was a new love in his life. And still held to that belief. Watching her smiling and talking to his dad as they glided around a small area of the dance floor, Tom was filled yet again with passion for the woman he had lost. Even though she was now alone again, he did not believe for one minute that she would ever come to love or trust or rely on him again.

But as long as he could see her when she came to collect the children after a visit, he would be happy. If he could spend a little more time in her company once the cottages had been made habitable, so much the better. That was all he hoped for, and more than he had ever expected since he walked out of her life, motivated by sheer jealousy, which he still did not believe was unfounded. Hadn't Max got his feet under Tom's table before his departing footprints had melted in the snow?

Also on the floor were Mattie Browning and Eileen, talking and smiling at each other as the singer crooned, 'Three coins in a fountain – which one will the fountain bless.' They were in a world of their own, and this did not go unremarked by Laura, who was sitting on her husband's lap and singing along with Jack as he gazed into her hazel-speckled green eyes. The couple, whose relationship had become more loving since Laura's fleeting affair with her rich landowner, were seated around a trestle table they were sharing with Jack's sister Liz, her husband Bert and Laura's widowed father, Billy. As far as Laura could tell, romance was in the air this evening, and she too was now in the mood.

Propping up the makeshift bar with a few new friends and some old mates from the past were Ben and Joey, the two old gentlemen, who in their own quiet way, had played a significant role in everyone's lives – two old boys who, without realising it themselves, exemplified traditional London. Their 'pull together' values, which they refused to relinquish, had been one of the reasons why both of them, along with a few other neighbours, had refused to move from their rat-infested homes in Cotton Street. Now, however, having been shown by others, Naomi in particular, that life was easier with modern conveniences, both of them had accepted a place on the nearby Ocean Estate.

They were enjoying themselves, baiting and teasing Becky to the delight of her husband, and now they had got on to the subject of religion.

'Vicars, priests or rabbis,' said Joey, 'have you ever known one *not* to hold out his hand after a service? God should be free. He shouldn't be charging rent or admittance. Free to everyone, rich or poor, black or white. The Chinese I'm not so sure about. Maybe they should pay if they wanna stay the night. They don't seem to mind sleeping on the floor. I don't know. All I can say about them is that they have settled to our ways and they cook a very nice chow mein. With chicken.'

'I saw a Chinese man the other day down Commercial Road way – he was riding a bike with a sort of box on wheels behind,' said Becky. 'He wasn't selling ice creams. I don't think he was selling anything. I think he might have been delivering laundry. They're very good at washing clothes. You can't beat a Chinese laundry.'

'And when did you ever see or go in one?' said Nathan, a look of pity on his face as he turned to the others. 'How could she know what a Chinese laundry is like? It's very sad when you start to live in your dreams – or nightmares, depending on how you look at it.'

'In Chinatown. You see them all the time. You should get out a bit more, Nathan. Always listening to the bloody wireless as if the war's still on. He can't miss the news . . . even though they repeat the same thing four times a day, if not more.'

'If you are prepared to eat Chinese food I'll tell you where to go,' said Ben, with one eye on Naomi as she drifted around the hall, the perfect hostess, chatting to those who looked a little out of place. 'Ting Kee Refreshments in West India Dock Road. The best Chinese restaurant in Limehouse. I don't know if they're still in business, I've not been there for a decade or so. I think it might have gone once they closed the railway station.' He looked dolefully at Joey. 'Is it still there?'

'Who knows and who bloody well cares? I wouldn't go in one if you paid me. They skin and stew rats and tell you it's chicken. Not me. You wouldn't catch me in one of those places. A mate of mine used to live over West India Dock way. Maurie Barnett. Used to run a grocer's shop. One of his brothers, or cousins, was linked to the Jack the Ripper murders. They wouldn't talk about it, though. My mate reckons that most of the Chinese cooked and ate rats before the turn of the century. Whether they do now or not I don't know. It's all meat at the end of the day, I s'pose.'

'Where did your family come from, Joey?' asked Shereen, always eager to know more about the pair's background.

'Originally? Who knows? Poland, I think. Or Germany. Some bloody cold place or the other. I mean, if you're gonna run away, why not go where the sun shines? Why does everyone come to bloody Britain? Mad. They're all mad. Gimme a ticket and I'll be off to where it's nice and warm in the winter.'

'You should go to Turkey, my friend. Turkey is hot.'

'Maybe I will one of these days, Shereen. Maybe I will. But right now I'm gonna tell the conductor to liven things up a bit. "Three Coins in a Fountain"? I ask you. A bit of the Charleston is what we need. Where's Naomi?'

'Oh, don't start 'er off yet, Joey. She'll kill the lot of us off by ten and it doesn't finish until half past.'

'And?'

'We all paid for a full evening.'

Naomi, talking to the Baroncinis, was playing peacemaker – keeping things nice and smooth between all the future grandparents. If anyone could convince them that the plan that had been hatched was the right one, Naomi could. In truth the Baroncinis didn't mind which way Edie wished to play it, so long as they were not denied their rights as doting grandparents.

Making his way over to her, Joey was pleased with the choice of record that had just begun. It was hardly the Charleston but neither was it too sloppy. The Ames Brothers with 'Naughty Lady of Shady Lane' was fine by him. Nodding and giving Albino and Ida Baroncini a polite smile, he held out his hand to

Naomi, asking whether she would do him the honour of accompanying him to the dance floor.

'Darling, I would simply love to dance with you but this song isn't quite to my taste. May I take a raincheck? I would much prefer to glide across the floor with you to a more, shall we say, *romantic* record?'

'Has she got the gift of the gab or what?' said Joey, suppressing a smile.

Taking him aside and whispering in his ear, Naomi said, 'Please do be a good soldier and ask the lady in the pink-and-green dress to dance. She's sitting on her own at the small table near the kitchen door.'

'Why?' said Joey. 'What's the catch?'

'There isn't one, I promise. But she is a lonely soul whose husband returned from the war having been in a Japanese POW camp only to find life a different kind of hell. He finally took an overdose before going to bed as normal. The poor woman woke at dawn to find a corpse lying close beside her. Apart from all else the experience made her feel as if she had to bathe two or three times a day which she did.'

'Fair enough,' said Joey. 'What's her name?'

'Well, naughty children and cruel adults call her the Sink Lady. But her name is Gloria.'

'Why? Why the Sink Lady?'

'Because she used to bathe in the sink instead of in her bath so as not to waste so much water. She had all but lost her mind over the terrible shock. And to make herself feel better – she sang while she scrubbed herself. But not any more. I have befriended her and she is much the better for it. For her to be here this evening is quite an achievement.'

'Aren't we all an achievement?' Joey said, rolling his eyes. 'All right – I'll take my beer and sit with her.'

'And not dance?'

'If I feel like it I'll ask her. If that's all right with you?'

'Darling, of course. Of course you must do things your own way. Forgive me?'

'Listen. Do me a favour and get up on that bloody stage and give us a song. A right belter.'

'Of course I will, my darling. But not now. I'm entertaining our Italian friends. Oh, and speaking of which . . . Dennis?'

'Dennis? Well, yes, I suppose there is a connection.'

'Of course there is. The Italians are soon to become family. And should Dennis turn up again—'

'She's better off without him. Leave it be. Anyway . . . he won't be back.'

'And you are certain of that?'

'I said so, didn't I? Now go back to the Italians. I'll come back later on, and if you're good I might tell you a little bit more about Dennis.'

'No.' Naomi looked him directly in the eye. 'And I do mean no. Tell me now.'

'He's got a woman in every port. OK?'

'Thank you,' said Naomi, smiling graciously. 'I owe you a large beer.'

'Two large beers,' said Joey, and sauntered away towards Gloria. He stood before her with a hand held out, hoping that she didn't have two left feet when it came to dancing. Short, thin and pale, she hardly had the look of another Isadora Duncan. 'Would you like to dance?' he said. 'I'm not bothered if not. It's up to you.'

Taken aback by his approach, Gloria laughed, her face lighting up and her blue eyes shining. 'It's been a very long time since I've danced,' she said, up from her chair in a flash. Then, holding her arms out gracefully for him to take them, the mad woman who sat in the sink and sang took to the floor like a duck to water, in perfect harmony with the accomplished Joey!

Jealous and ready for some competition, Ben looked through the moving bodies on the dance floor for a partner and spotted Edie. Losing no time, he was by her side, smiling and offering a graceful hand, immediately. 'Would the lady like to dance?'

Pleased that Naomi was playing the hostess where the Baroncinis were concerned, and that Maggie's future in-laws looked relaxed in her company, Edie leant her head on Ben's shoulder and whispered in his ear, 'Thank you for everything. You were always a good neighbour in Cotton Street and you're still looking after me. Even now. After all these years.'

'I'm dancing with you because I want to dance. That's all.'

'No it's not. You've heard about Dennis doing a moonlight from Nao – and so you're being my partner. It's why we all love you, Ben. You're a special person. One in a million. And I respect what you did when Harry turned up. I know you got Joey to take 'im in the same way you helped him by hiding those other men during the war who were too frightened to fight.'

'And you've forgiven me for seeing him on his way to a far-off island?'

''Course I have. Maybe he'll sort himself out there, eh? He wasn't all bad, you know.'

'Misguided, Edie, that's all. Misguided and confused. That's what the government does to men when they send them to war with no experience. It's not right – but it's the way of the world and it always will be. While there are politicians there will be war. Harry was all right. He went off the rails and I'm not making excuses for that. He should have come back to you all those years ago. No question.'

'I don't really know why he didn't. I don't understand men, Ben, and that's a fact.'

'And men don't always think of the bed, Ed.' He chuckled. 'Harry's paying the price for it now, mind. Stuck out on some god-forsaken island. The sun is very nice, but when it's there all day and every day? No. An Englishman couldn't be happy with that for long. Not in my opinion.'

'You think he might come back again, then?'

''Course he'll be back. Maybe this time he will have learned a lesson from it. Who knows?'

As the song came to an end and the music faded, Edie stopped dancing and looked directly into Ben's face. 'Why do all the men in my life go away?'

Smiling, he said, 'Maybe you should also ask

yourself why two of them came back. First Harry and then your father.'

'But they both went away again so—'

'Did they?' he said, unable to stop his smile broadening. 'Wheels don't stop turning unless they're broken. I've been expecting someone this evening and he's just walked in the door. Go on,' he said, 'go and greet your father.'

Spinning around, Edie could hardly believe her eyes. 'Oh, Ben . . .' she murmured. 'He came all the way back again . . . from Canada?'

'No. He never left. He's been staying at the flat in Golders Green, looking for work in town. He also stayed with me for a few days until he found a place around here. Well?'

'But what's he gonna think of me looking like this. Looking as if I'm pregnant?'

'You think Naomi hasn't already filled him in on all that?'

'Nao? She's known all along?'

'You want me to risk my life by not telling her everything? Do me a favour – go to your father before *she* cavorts round the floor with him. Spare him that at least. He's your dad, Edie, and he's come home. For good.'

'And Harry?' she said, hoping he wasn't about to say that he too would be turning up. There was only so much a person could forgive in one go.

'He's still in the Canary Islands. I doubt he'll be back for a while yet. He hasn't had time to learn a very important lesson. You're a special person, Edie, and you deserve honest people round you. Harry's not up to the mark. Not yet anyway.'

'Good. Because I don't ever want to see him again. Ever.' With that she turned to her father and held out her arms, happy, really happy, that he had come home.

# 10

Christmas had been a quiet time for Edie and Maggie, even though Naomi had been there over the holiday period to jolly them along, and there had been a visit from Joey and Ben. Having completed all his arrangements with regard to somewhere to live permanently and a job, Edie's father had had to return to Canada in the third week of December to tie up loose ends. But now, in early springtime, with Maggie close to her time, Edie felt as if everything had settled down and the future looked brighter. That she had not heard one word from Dennis since she had demanded to see his house in Bow no longer upset her. Anger had taken over soon after the shock of his sudden departure and had by now faded into a resolve never to be quite so gullible again. She did hope, however, that one day she would cross his path again so that she could give vent to the tiny flame of fury that was smouldering on the back burner. She wanted to publicly expose him as the fake he clearly was.

Maggie had stuck resolutely to her decision to live in the flat in Islington with Rita. Between them they were running the busy café below, opening at 7 a.m. for breakfast and closing at 4 p.m. after the lunchtime session. With Tony and his brother Peter, who was keen on Rita, coming over to visit four evenings a week to play cards or take the girls out for a drink, there never seemed to be the time or the need for much beyond curling up with a book at bedtime. But in between it all Maggie and Rita had had time to chat about the café and how they might be able to give a better service and increase the takings at the same time.

People working in town, it seemed, wanted a hot meal during their one-hour lunch breaks, but food that could be served up as quickly as possible because of time limitations. So their reading time in the evenings had been diverted into researching cookery books. Spaghetti bolognaise, of course, was a must, and a dish easily prepared, but Rita, in her wisdom, had slowly been adding to the menu the occasional typically English, cost-effective meal. Beef stew with dumplings was the favourite 'meal of the day', with sausage toad a close second. The menu had always been discussed with Tony and Peter, who could also see the potential in turning a low-profit café into a lucrative small restaurant in the future.

So involved in this new way of life was she that Rita had swapped her one-evening-a-week class in commerce for one in domestic science, held in a nearby adult education centre, and was slowly falling for Tony's brother, who was plainly besotted by her. The girls' social life had changed for the better since the move to Islington, with Maggie's future extended Italian family dropping in for coffee in the café and inviting them into their convivial homes for lively get-togethers in the evenings. Looking radiant through her final months of pregnancy, with the telltale sparkling eyes and glowing complexion of a mother-to-be, Maggie was very happy.

Edie, of course, was aware of all of this, and it was the main reason why she had been able to get over the blow caused by Dennis disappearing into the night. Had it not been for the fact that her close friend Jessie had herself been through a dark period and was still mourning her partner, it might well have been Edie who lapsed into a state of shock over the way she had been fooled, deserted and, whether she admitted it or not, had her heart broken. Her broken heart did not take long to heal, however, especially after she had given her engagement ring to Naomi, who had said that she would keep it safe in case Dennis returned. She had other motives, however. She had immediately taken it to a jeweller she knew and trusted in Cutler Street to have it examined. He found it to be, not a diamond solitaire but white zircon, one of many examples that had been circulating in the East End over the past year. This Naomi had kept to herself at first, with the intention of challenging the man in private should he ever turn up again, but in the end she had decided that Edie was old enough and wise enough to know the truth, and so she had told her. And it was the best thing she could have done, because by giving her a fake diamond ring Dennis had clearly shown that from the start he had had no intention of supporting and caring for Edie, let alone her much treasured daughter.

As for Jessie, during and after the tragedy of Max's accident she had slipped into a world of her own where she believed nothing could hurt her. She had been there for her children, but as more of a robot mother than her usual warm self. 'I'm fine,' she would say when Edie, Laura or Naomi called in to give her some company. 'I'm on my invisible shelf away from the world.'

All those closest to Jessie had had to bear the hurt of not being able to comfort her for a few dark months. They too had lost a special person when Max had died, and they did not want to lose Jessie to a depression that might take a strong hold on her. But Jessie had not been and still was not depressed. She had simply been stripped of all feelings with the exception of grief and a hollow sense of loss that could not be filled by anyone, not even her own children. The irony of it all was that Billy and Emma-Rose, knowing their mother best, respected her wish for solitude and had settled for the alternative – attention from their gran, granddad and Tom.

Now, after four months, Jessie was just beginning to get back on track. The memory of the day when she had received the phone call, however, constantly drifted in and out of her mind. But she had confided in Naomi that the horror of it all was beginning to fade and the tight feeling in her chest beginning to ease. The worst of it all for her had been the agonising as to whether Max had suffered after the heart attack while trapped in the car. She had been told over and over that death had been instantaneous but nothing had been able to convince her. The specialist at the hospital had told her that, apart from a sudden intense pain, Max would have known little about it. And when she had asked why this had happened to such a young man the reasons given had been overwork, worry and anxiety and perhaps, forever chasing some unattainable dream. Even Jessie in her present mood could not argue with these reasons. The trouble with Max was that he had always, since boyhood, tried to live up to his elder sister's expectations of him. Moira and her successful husband had moved away from the East End some years back and were now living in a spacious smart house in Hampstead. It had been Max's everlasting dream to follow in her footsteps, and he had simply tried too hard, much to Jessie's frustration.

Laura and Edie had eventually managed to penetrate Jessie's barrier, and this evening, a week before Maggie's baby was due, the three young women were sitting in Edie's living room. After a couple of large vodkas they were managing to get a smile out of Jessie – especially when the cottages in Elmshill that Tom and Stanley had purchased were brought into the conversation. They then talked about Edie's situation and how she had managed to pull the wool over everyone's eyes by leading them to believe that she was the one who was pregnant, with no man around to support her. The scandalmongers had been quite aware that Dennis had been in Edie's flat for hours on end. When the first comment came, spoken loudly enough for Edie to hear – 'I wouldn't be in the least surprised if it's jet black! That family like foreigners!' – she had simply laughed at them, which had taken the wind from their sails.

'I passed that cow from below this morning,' said Edie, handing a plate of cheese-and-pickle sandwiches to Jessie. 'She was on 'er own for a change and not linking arms with Sarah James. And do you know what? She actually smiled at me. Not a nasty smirk this time but a nervous smile. I never said anything – just looked at her and carried on walking.'

'There you go, then, Ed,' said Laura, reaching out and taking a sandwich. 'You've beaten her at last. She knows she can't say anything to upset you so she'd rather be on your side. And if you noticed, at the tea dance opening she and her mate from below sat by themselves all evening at a table in the corner. So there we are. They get what they deserve – each other.'

'I know,' said Edie. 'Still . . . maybe they learned from it? Who knows? Who cares?'

'You're beginning to sound like Max, Edie. He was always saying that kind of thing. Live and let live was 'is stance. My brother Alfie used to call 'im Jew Boy instead of Max when he was younger. Just to see if he could get his back up. But Max let it all go above his head and Alfie soon dropped it.

'He was doing it on purpose because he didn't like the idea of me marrying into a Jewish family. 'Course, I'm going back a few years. But he needn't 'ave worried. They're no different to us once you get used to their idiosyncrasies. Max's bossy sister's the only one in 'is family who sticks rigidly to the Jewish rules. She was nice to me at Max's funeral. Which made a change. But then you'd expect 'er to be. I'm out of the picture now. Even though I did what they wanted and stood back when the arrangements were being made. I knew they'd want a proper Jewish funeral and respected it.'

As usual, Jessie had brought the conversation back to Max, but both Laura and Edie knew that to attempt to change the subject would be useless until she had had her say. It was still early days and she was still missing Max, and they realised that she needed to talk about him. Laura picked up on the mention of his sister Moira, hoping that this would lead to other things.

'Moira sounds like a bit of a dragon on the quiet. What did your family think of 'er?'

'They've never met 'er, Laura. Not that it was deliberate but their paths never crossed. Max used to visit her regularly. They were close – I'll give 'em that. It's just that Moira in her peculiar way made him feel as if he was a failure because of what happened after the war. Plenty of self-employed people lost their main customers to big companies. Max wasn't the only one.'

'It's different now, though, thank goodness,' said Laura, sensing an opportunity. 'I suppose that's why Tom's brother Stanley needed him to help out, eh, Jess? And why he keeps two casual labourers on. The days of the one-man band are over, I reckon. Give it fifty odd years and all you'll 'ave is a handful of giant building firms.'

'It was, as it happens. Mind you, they are close. Especially now that the past is behind us. It was Stanley who told Tom about me and Max in the first place after a few too many drinks at Christmas.'

'That's right,' said Laura. 'I remember you telling me that. It must 'ave affected you, Jess, 'cos you've told me three or four times.'

'Have I?'

'Yes,' said Edie, topping up their glasses. 'And me. Anyway, the main thing is that it wasn't Tom's fault. It wasn't anyone's fault. A silly misunderstanding – that's all.'

'That's what Max used to say. He was so easy-going it's untrue.'

'So, Edie . . .' said Laura, now changing the subject completely. 'How's the bump?'

'Mine or Maggie's?'

'Maggie's, of course. We know 'ow yours is getting on. Good job it's not summer or you'd be sweltering.' She turned to Jessie and gave her a wink. 'I can't wait for the summer, though. When we all trip to them cottages for a long weekend, eh, Jess? D'yer reckon your Tom'd let me and Edie go up there with you?'

''Course he would . . . so he could show off. We'd 'ave to go by train, though. From Liverpool Street to Diss station and get a bus from there. Max drove us when we went a couple of times just after the war, but of course his little car's gone to the garage in heaven – along with 'im.'

'I bet you can't wait to see how far the lads have got with them, Jess, can you?'

'I've not really thought about it lately, to tell the truth . . . but you're right. It would be interesting. They'll make a good job of it, I dare say. Max reckoned that Stanley's brilliant the way he does things with that artificial arm.'

'Artificial arm?' said Edie, pretending she didn't know in an attempt to keep Jessie off the subject of Max.

'Yeah – poor sod. He won't talk about it. But it was during the war. That much I do know.'

'Blimey – you'd never know it from looking at 'im. But then I s'pose you wouldn't do. It's covered for most of the time by shirtsleeves. Does it bother him? In summer when most men walk about showing off their arms?'

'No. He still wears long sleeves in summer. I think he feels as if it's part of his body now. Never takes any notice of it. Dolly painted a heart on it just to let other women know he was hers. Bit like a tattoo really.

'I told Max to have a little heart tattooed on his shoulder but—' The shrill ringing of the doorbell stopped her short. 'God, that sounds urgent!'

'No it don't. It sounds like a door-to-door salesman determined to get an answer.' Laura chuckled. The bell sounded again and this time Edie was out of the room in a flash.

'Oh my God! said Jessie, pushing a hand through her hair. 'Don't say something else has happened! I left the kids up there by themselves!'

'And not for the first time. They're hardly babies, Jessie!'

'I left the oven on low,' Jessie murmured. 'What if the gas light blew out? I put a casserole in there. I had to leave it on low. Oh my God, Laura. Oh please God, don't let anything have happened to one of my children. Please, dear God—'

'Jessie, stop it!' Laura screeched. 'Enough! Hasn't it crossed your mind that since this is *Edie's* house it might be an urgent call for *her*? That Maggie just might be in trouble? She's nearly due, don't forget! Or what if it's Naomi that's been taken bad? Show some respect in someone's else's house. And *stop* going on about Max. We loved 'im too, and yes, we're gutted about what's happened, but you never stop talking about him whenever I see you. I'm sorry, but you've *got* to pull yourself out of this and get on with *life*!'

'Get on with life? Only four months after Max's accident . . . and you can say a thing like that to me?'

'That's *right*, Jessie. I'm saying just what I would if Max *hadn't* had a heart attack and died. All right? And from now on I'm not gonna pussyfoot around you because all you talk about, think about and breathe is Max! You didn't before the accident, so why now and all the time? You've got to pull yourself out of this.

'People keep their distance, Jessie, when things make them feel too sad. And do you know why? Because none of us can take too much grief on a daily basis! For one thing it reminds us of what we've been through ourselves at one time or another, or what we *might* have to come in the future. Edie, for instance. Don't forget that *her* mother committed suicide.'

'Well, you certainly don't pull your punches when you've been put out, do you?'

'Only when I've been put out by people I couldn't give a toss about. Don't forget that Max didn't leave you of his own free will – whereas Dennis left Edie practically standing at the altar!'

So involved in their little dispute were they that they hadn't taken any notice of the shuffling in the passage as Edie helped Maggie into her old bedroom. She had come over from Islington by bus and then walked to Naomi's apartment where she had gone into labour – two weeks earlier than expected. Coming into the room, trying hard to hide her panic, Naomi smiled serenely and said, 'Jessie . . . would you be so kind as to use your telephone to ring this number for me?' She handed over a slip of paper on which was written Sister Kathleen's number at Nonnatus House. 'And if you would instruct her to send a midwife, the young woman who has already seen Maggie if possible? Otherwise whoever is free must come immediately by taxi. The fare for which will be paid at this end on arrival.'

'Oh my God,' said Jessie, up from her chair in a flash. 'Come up with me, Laura, in case I start trembling and can't dial.'

'Will you and Edie be all right, Nao?' said Laura hurriedly as she followed in Jessie's tracks.

'I'm sure we'll be fine! The pains are coming every thirty minutes or so. You'll need to tell Sister Kathleen that if she's there, and if not then whoever it may concern!'

The girls hurried out of the flat. As the street door closed behind them, Naomi slumped into an armchair. Behaving as if everything was going to be perfectly all right while accompanying Maggie here had been exhausting. The sound of her niece moaning with pain in the bedroom was good reason for her to go the cupboard where she kept her brandy. One for herself and one for Edie and Maggie was what was required as far as she was concerned.

As a child Naomi had seen many births, mostly through cracked and filthy windows, into which she and her friends would peer once word had got out that the midwife had arrived at one of the decrepit lodgings in Aldgate where her family lived. Not all the deliveries had taken place on the ground floor, of course, but there had been enough over the years for her to see exactly what went on inside. Should Maggie's baby decide to arrive before the midwife came, she herself would deliver her great-great-niece or nephew into this world.

One hour later, having received a message from Sister Kathleen, the midwife arrived. She was in the bedroom with Maggie and Edie for no longer than five minutes. She then came into the sitting room to give Laura, Jessie and Naomi the news that the baby would not be arriving for a couple of hours yet, that everything looked fine and she would be back later.

The fact that Maggie was so young, she added, meant that she was feeling the pains a little more than a mature woman might.

'Do you mean to tell me that you are going to leave her to attend to someone else? Or to take tea in Joe Lyons perhaps?' Naomi was flabbergasted. 'The child is in labour! She is about to give birth! Are you mad?'

Laughing, the young midwife tried to assure Naomi that she wasn't to worry. 'I promise you – everything will be fine.' She then fumbled in her trench-coat pocket and pulled out the ten-shilling note Naomi had given her. 'I used my bicycle to come here,' she said. 'And I shall use it to return. But thank you for the offer. It was very sweet. And I shall be at Nonnatus House.'

'And if you hear from our neighbour by way of the telephone that my niece is about to deliver?'

'I shall have to pedal faster, shan't I.' With that the young midwife bade them farewell and left.

'Well,' said Naomi, flopping back down into an armchair, 'if this is what it has come to I would have had Maggie registered with a proper nursing home! How dare she treat my great-niece and her baby with such casual indifference!'

'It'll be all right, Naomi,' said Jessie. 'She'll be fine. She's got hours to go yet. You should get some shut-eye. I remember when my pains were every five minutes and still it went on for an hour afterwards. The midwife knows what she's doing, Nao. Stop worrying and have another brandy. This time tomorrow you'll be holding Maggie's baby in your arms.'

'Oh, Jessie, if only I *could* think like that. But we have a long night to get through by the sound of it. Let's not forget that she is still a child. And not long since a virgin.'

'She'll be all right,' said Jessie again, and added, 'What about the Baroncinis? When shall we let them know?'

'Once it's here,' said Naomi. 'I really don't think we need the Italian melodrama right now.'

'Shouldn't we ask Maggie what *she* wants, Nao?'

'No, Jessie. This is one time when *we* must pull together with no outsiders present.'

'But they're not outsiders, are they? We are. Me and Laura. And what about the father-to-be? Tony. You haven't forgotten him, have you? He'll want to be here. She is a fortnight early, after all.'

'Whatever you think best,' said Naomi, 'but not just yet. In an hour's time. I am simply not up to having excited Italians around me at the moment.'

Just after the clock had struck midnight, two policemen, in the semi-lit street beneath Maggie's bedroom window, were chatting under a street lamp to the distant sound of a dog barking. Imprinted in a fine layer of frozen snow on the pavement and road was a complex of trampled, criss-cross footprints; wheel tracks and the fresh hoofprints of a carthorse belonging to the oil-and-paraffin man, who had recently led his faithful, hard-working mare homeward.

Before dusk the street had been teeming with

children, hoping for more late snow which did not come. Now, as most of the outside world settled down with curtains drawn and lights off, Maggie was about to deliver her much wanted baby into the world. With her mother to one side of her and her Aunt Naomi to the other, she listened obediently to the words of advice and instruction issued by the midwife, who was standing at the foot of her bed.

On top of a pine chest of drawers, which had become a working surface, was an array of utensils: forceps, scissors, stethoscope and cord clamps. In the corner of the bedroom a small electric fire radiated warmth. Close to the heater was a small wooden cot with colourful if faded paintings of flying birds around the base, which had been handed down through the Baroncini family. Having been in labour from late afternoon until now, Maggie was exhausted, but still trying her best to obey the midwife, who was softly but firmly telling her not to push once her present contraction had passed. Leaning against a wall by the closed door, Edie shed silent tears for her suffering daughter.

'Breathe deeply, Maggie,' the midwife gently repeated over and over. 'Just carry on breathing like that. Concentrate on breathing deeply.'

'She's close, Midwife,' said Edie, the strain showing on her face. 'Can't you give her something? Something to ease the pain? They're coming every three minutes. I've been timing them.'

'There really is no need.' The woman smiled. 'Maggie is one of the best patients I've had in a long while. She's worked hard and now she'll have her reward.' Giving her thigh a gentle pat, she moved her face close to Maggie's and whispered, 'Good girl. Keep panting like that and when the next contraction comes just concentrate on breathing deeply.' Then, listening to the foetal heart again, she said, 'One forty. Good. Quite normal.'

'It's coming!' said Maggie suddenly. 'It's coming, you silly cow! It's coming!'

'Maggie, don't panic!' screeched Edie.

'It's not panic. It's the transitional stage. She'll kick and swear and rip down my knickers if her hand happens to find them.' The midwife turned to Edie, her expression conveying an ultimatum. She could stay if she kept her cool, otherwise she must leave. She turned back to her ward. 'Breathe deeply, Maggie. Push a little but not too hard. We'll soon have Baby born.'

Crying out in pain again as the baby forced its way down the birth canal, Maggie pushed for all she was worth.

'Don't push any more, Maggie! Pant! Pant like I told you! Short breaths. Pant, pant, pant! Don't push!'

Maggie's eyes were open wide, as was her mouth, as she followed the instructions. With both hands over the crown of the baby's head, the midwife held it back until the contraction subsided and Maggie relaxed again into her deep breathing.

Speaking gently to her patient while stroking hair from her sweat-beaded forehead, the midwife said,

'You mustn't push with the next contraction, sweet-heart. Just let your stomach muscles do what they are there for. I want you to concentrate on panting and just let nature take its course.' She turned to Edie and smiled. 'Come and take her hand and let her squeeze it until it hurts. And maybe Aunt Naomi could take the other hand?'

Neither of the women had to be told twice. Without so much as a whisper they simply did as they were told, the strain on both of them beginning to show. The next contraction came within half a minute. The midwife guided the baby's emerging head to the sound of a determined effort from Maggie as she stopped panting and slowly pushed her baby out into the world. Once the presenting shoulder had emerged there was a brief pause and then a final contraction. '*Now*, Maggie!' ordered the midwife. 'Push and push hard! Push, Maggie, *push*!'

The second shoulder and an arm followed and then the whole body slid out effortlessly to cries of joy from Grandmother Edie and Great-great-aunt Naomi! 'It's a boy!' screamed Edie, overjoyed. 'A beautiful baby boy!'

'Is he all right?' cried Maggie. 'What colour's his hair? Tell Tony to come in! Show 'im to Tony, Mum!'

'Black hair.' Edie laughed, shedding a tear. 'He's got a mass of black hair, babe.'

'But he looks just like you, my darling,' said Naomi, kissing Maggie lightly on the cheek. 'Well done, sweet-heart. Well done.' Raising her eyes to meet Edie's, she flashed a message that it was time for them to leave.

Edie looked hopefully at the midwife. 'A few minutes more and then out you go. Both of you.' The midwife then clamped the baby's umbilical cord in two places and snipped it before gripping both ankles and turning him upside down to give him a gentle slap on the bottom. Maggie's baby took his first trembling breath and then another before he let rip with his first piercing cry, announcing his arrival into the world.

Wrapping him in a soft white towel, the midwife cradled and quietened the child before placing the little bundle into Maggie's arms. 'Here is your child, Maggie. Treasure him.'

Gazing into her baby's face, Maggie whispered, 'Hello, baby,' and then, 'He's perfect. He's just perfect.'

As if he had heard his mother, the now quiet newborn slowly opened his eyes and the bond between mother and child was sealed. 'He's got green eyes,' murmured Maggie as the tears rolled down her cheeks.

'Just like you, my darling,' whispered Naomi. 'His eyes are exactly like yours.'

'She's right, Mags.' Edie was stroking her daughter's face. 'But they're more blue than green. They'll gradually turn proper green, though. But they are just like yours. He's the image of you, darling. The image.'

'He's perfect. Look at his fingers. They're so tiny. We could never give him away, could we? I want Tony to see 'im. He never went back upstairs, did he?'

'Yes, my darling,' said Naomi 'To report to his

mother on how close you were and—' The sound of the doorbell stopped her short. 'That will be him letting us know that he's come back and with his family this time. I left the street door ajar for them,' she said, tidying Maggie's covers. 'Well done, darling. Well done.'

As exhaustion set in, all Maggie could manage to say was, 'Thank you, Mum and Aunt Nao. I love you.' And before Edie or Naomi could reply Tony came bursting into the room, crying, his mother close behind him, and following her the rest of the Italian family.

A firm expression on her face, the midwife held up her hand. 'I'm sorry, but only the father and only for a few seconds. My work is not yet finished.' She then ushered everyone out with the exception of Tony, who stood beside the bed gazing at his son, who was now sleeping. Too choked to say anything, the proud father leaned over and kissed his baby on the cheek, and then turned to leave the room as if he were in a trance. Maggie could not help smiling. Her voice soft, she said, 'What about me, Tony?'

Turning back, the tears rolling down his cheeks, he simply shrugged and splayed his hands. 'I love you. I love you both.' Then the proud young man closed the door between them and went into the living room, from where Maggie could hear sounds of cheering from the Italian contingent and then her baby's Italian grandmother shouting for joy. 'It is a boy! My beautiful son give me a grandson! He make me so proud! I have a grandson!'

Now Maggie had only the midwife for company. She looked at her and smiled weakly. 'Anyone'd think that he's just been through it instead of me.'

'I know . . . and that's all too normal. I've heard worse, mind. But it doesn't matter, does it, because you know who delivered this beautiful child into the world, and that's all that matters.' The midwife took the baby from his mother as again the sound of the doorbell pierced the flat. Placing it in the crib, she turned back, smiling. 'Congratulations, Maggie. Very well done.'

'Thank you. I wonder who that is.'

'Oh, take no notice of the doorbell today. Everyone loves to see a new baby. Or at least drink a toast to it.'

But it wasn't one of the neighbours from the block come to wish the baby and mother well. It was Edie's dad, whom she had telephoned from Jessie's soon after Maggie had first gone into labour. Naturally Edie was very pleased to see him, as was Naomi, who could not resist a little quip. 'Well, at least you managed to be here at the birth of your *great*-grandchild.'

An hour later, while the celebrations were continuing in Jessie's sitting room, with members of Tony's Italian family coming and going, Maggie and her baby, exhausted by it all, were slumbering. And below, having heard most of what was going on in the flat above, in her element now, a neighbour was sharing a cup of cocoa with her friend Sarah James in the wee hours. Between them they had kept watch over who came and went, and of course there had been no sign of the man they believed to be the father of the child, the man who had not been seen for months.

'I don't know how that woman can hold up her head,' said Sarah, pursing her lips. 'She hadn't known that man for five minutes before she let him bed 'er. And now that baby will have to go through life knowing it's a bastard. It's the daughter I feel sorry for. She was thrown out of that flat at fifteen. I s'pose she'll be let back in like a stray cat now that her mother's fancy man's run off. Her friends are no better. Laura Jackson's 'usband chases all the women and you 'ave to ask yourself why. And as for that Jessie Smith, well, her Jewish 'usband wasn't in 'is grave five minutes before that other bloke was on the doorstep. And she's even got the children to call him Dad! Disgraceful. She's a terrible mother is all I can say. That boy of hers spends most of 'is time on the roof with 'is mates looking out for flying saucers. The poor lad's not right in the head. And the little girl's got a stutter.

'I mean, you have to question it, don't you? Parents today – they've got no sense of responsibility. I'm glad I never had children. This world's not fit for children. Not mine anyway. Thank goodness we took up the offer to move into this block. I mean . . . someone's got to keep an eye out. Not that anyone appreciates it. Oh no. It's a thankless task, but there we are. We've bin put 'ere for a reason and if this is our mission then so be it. If there are men from space in flying saucers watching this planet it'll be for a reason. They'll be clocking it all. They'll know. They'll see what we see. Sin everywhere you look. Another cup of tea?'

# SALLY WORBOYES

## Jamaica Street

Errol Turner, a handsome and determined young man from Jamaica, has found the woman of his dreams in the East End of London.

Errol's only assets on arrival at Southampton in the summer of 1955 were his father's old sewing machine, a few pounds in his pocket and a touching faith in the greatness of Britain. Four years later, in love with the charismatic Rita, he is making his mark as a tailor – but in the aftermath of the race riots, racial hatred still simmers throughout London, endangering all their hopes.

Rita's best friend Maggie and her flamboyant great aunt Naomi try to ease the couple's fears. But far more sinister activities are going on under their own roof. When a woman is found murdered, vicious rumours and suspicions explode. It will take grit and cunning to bring the killer to light – and a true testing of friendship.

HODDER

# SALLY WORBOYES

## Down Stepney Way

In the turbulent East End of London in the thirties, Jessie Warner is growing up . . .

Emotions are running high in Stepney, with Blackshirts marching through the streets and the Jewish community under threat of violence. In the midst of this, Jessie discovers a family secret and turns to her mother for answers, but Rose is reluctant to reveal the past – for there is something that Jessie must never know.

In Bethnal Green, Hannah Blake is being forced by her cold-hearted mother to join the Blackshirts, despite deep misgivings. Next-door neighbour Emmie knows of the darkness surrounding Hannah's wretched past, but is bound by a vow of silence not to reveal it. And meanwhile, Emmie's son Tom, chipper and handsome, has just fallen for a blonde girl he wants to bring home to meet Emmie and Hannah. Her name is Jessie Warner . . .

'She brings the East End to life' Barbara Windsor

HODDER